THE REN]
TO THE GRA

CW01486642

(the book which nearly killed its author,
and near the end, turned her tongue black)

Eleanor Berry is of Welsh ancestry but was born and bred in London where she has lived all her life.

The works of Gorki, Dostoevsky, Gogol, Edgar Allan Poe and James Hadley Chase have strongly influenced her writings.

She holds a BA Hons degree in English. While at University, she completed an unpublished contextual thesis on the Marquis de Sade. In her spare time, she wrote a grossly indecent book entitled *The Story of Paddy* which she had the good sense to burn and inadvertently set a garage on fire.

Since leaving University, she first worked as a commercial translator, using French and Russian. Then she worked as a research assistant to the late Dr Victor Ratner, a Harley Street specialist. Since then, she has worked intermittently as a research assistant to other members of the medical profession.

For a short period of time, she did voluntary work and read Dostoevsky to the blind. She discontinued this abruptly when a 96-year-old woman mistook her voice for that of her 75-year-old son. She now spends most of her time as a writer.

Her interests, among others, include the cinema, amateur piano playing, sensational court cases, Russian literature, Russian folk songs and fair grounds.

Her book *Your Father Died on the Gallows* is now available in Russian; another is going to be made into a film.

Other books by Eleanor Berry

Tell us a Sick One Jakey
    (Formerly known as Eleanor Beckman)
Never Alone with Rex Malone
    (Formerly known as Eleanor Beckman)
The Ruin of Jessie Cavendish
Your Father Died on the Gallows
Robert Maxwell as I Knew Him
Seamus O'Rafferty and Dr Blenkinsop
Alandra Varinia Seed of Sarah
The House of the Mad Doctors
Jaxton the Silver Boy
Someone's Been Done up Harley
O, Hitman, my Hitman!
McArandy was hanged under Tyburn Tree
The Scourging of Poor Little Maggie
The Revenge of Miss Rhoda Buckleshott
The Most Singular Adventures of Eddy Vernon
Take it Away, it's Red!

Some comments.

Never Alone with Rex Malone
("A ribald, ambitious black comedy, a story powerfully told"). *The Daily Mail*
("I was absolutely flabbergasted when I read it!") *Robert Maxwell*

Your Father Died on the Gallows
("A unique display of black humour which somehow fails to depress the reader.") Craig McLittle. *The Rugby Gazette*

Robert Maxwell as I Knew Him
("One of the most amusing books I have read for a long time. Eleanor Berry is an original.") Elisa Seagrave. *The Literary Review*
("Undoubtedly the most amusing book I have read all year.") Julia Llewellyn Smith. *The Times*
("With respect, and I repeat, with very great respect, because I know you are a lady — all you ever do is just go on and on and on and on about this bleeding *bloke*!") *Reggie Kray*

The Scourging of Poor Little Maggie

("This harrowing, tragic and deeply ennobling book, caused me to weep for two days after reading it. I had not experienced this reaction since seeing the film *The Elephant Man*.") Moira McClusky. *The Cork Evening News*

Take it Away, it's Red!

("Despite the sometimes weighty portent of this book, a sense of subtle, dry and powerfully engaging humour reigns throughout its pages. The unexpected twist is stupendous.") Stephen Carson — the *Carolina Sun*

("Someone told me this book was dark, but dark was hardly the word. Well, knock me over with a feather, says I!") The actress, *Sarah Miles*

Pour mon ami, le bon Docteur Francis Dourdou

THE RENDON BOY
TO THE GRAVE IS GONE

(the book which nearly killed its author,
and near the end, turned her tongue black)

Eleanor Berry

ARTHUR H. STOCKWELL LTD.
Ilfracombe, Devon

All characters and situations portrayed in this book are imaginary. Any resemblance to persons living or dead is purely coincidental.

British Library Cataloguing in Publication Data.
A catalogue record for this book is available from the British Library.

ISBN 0 7223 3273-4

Printed in England by Arthur H. Stockwell Ltd., llfracombe, Devon.

Cover design by Eleanor Berry, Eddy Taylor and Harry Hobbs.

Cover printed in England by Arthur H. Stockwell Ltd., Ilfracombe, Devon.

CHAPTER 1

It was 6.00 o'clock on a crisp November morning in an affluent part of London.

Flames billowed from a high rise block of flats, overlooking the Thames. Two fire engines and three ambulances waited outside the building which swarmed with earnest-faced, yellow-hatted firemen, all of them nobly dedicated to their duties, despite their scandalously low pay.

Nearly all the occupants of the building had been alerted by the fire alarms and were waiting on the tarmac by the fire engines and ambulances. Three unconscious victims, a mother, father and eight-year-old son, were carried into one of the ambulances on stretchers.

A fireman, a well-built, grey-haired man in his late forties, was organizing the evacuation of the residents still in the building. The firemen taking instructions from him, let themselves in to the flats with skeleton keys.

"Check the whole of the rest of the building," commanded the senior fireman. "Check all the flats are empty."

Only one of the flats had remained occupied. It was a flat facing the Thames, on the eleventh floor. Black smoke was rising from the ninth floor, coming through the partly-opened window of its living room.

It was in this room that a woman in her thirties, was sitting at a computer, manically bashing its keys, like a trainee secretary trying to pass a typing test.

Her name was Juliet Silverman. She was a professional writer, who had already written sixteen published books. Her twelve-year-old son, Ephraim Rendon slept in one of the bedrooms, adjoining the living room. Like his mother, he was unaware that the building was on fire.

Twelve-year-old Ephraim Rendon was the illegitimate son of Juliet and William Rendon, a psychotic graced with god-like looks. He worked for most of his life as a pathologist at the Hammersmith Hospital, and though sweet and vulnerable, he was a multi-facetted, sex-crazed serial killer.

1

Juliet had a passion for writing. Apart from her son, it was her only interest in life. She wrote for four hours each day, and at night, she kept herself awake with amphetamines and rarely went to sleep until 7.00 o'clock in the morning. The more she wrote, the more unable she was to stop, and it was with sadness, rather than exhaustion, that she went to bed when satisfied with her labours.

Juliet was not a good writer. She was a brilliant writer. Indeed, many of her books had been translated into Russian. They were so popular among the Russian people, that the heads of many a *babooshka** were seen buried concentratedly into her translated books, as they sat huddled in doorways, on stools at street stalls and on wooden benches in kiosks, between selling tickets at the Bolshoi theatre.

These women also read Juliet's work, as they stood in freezing temperatures, queuing for food, fur gloves and milk, or for admittance to the tomb of the old pin-stripe-suited lag, Vladimir Ilyich Lenin.

Her gift for manipulating the English language was rare indeed. Her style was stark, witty and biting, her paragraphs refreshingly short and her narrative so gripping that her readers passionately yearned to turn the page.

Her books were macabre, black comedies. A reviewer had described her as being to Literature what Hieronymous Bosch is to Art. Another reviewer described her wit as "raw and haunting", and one of her books, about a gory aspect of the medical profession, was described as "putting even A. J. Cronin in the shade."

Although Juliet was addicted to her computer keys and liked writing one book after another, she was unaware that she was a talented writer. The thought did not occur to her. She saw her books as her children, and one literary pregnancy after another, kept her spirits alive.

Juliet may well have been a talented writer. Her abilities and skills did not stretch much further than her trade, however. She

*Old woman. Also means grandmother.

2

was not a practical person. She could not cook, and fed Ephraim on ready-made food. To keep him healthy, she made him eat plenty of fruit and dairy products.

She could not change a light bulb. Her balance was poor and she suffered from vertigo, even when standing on a chair one foot from the floor.

Though a genius at her trade, she had no understanding of its tools. She liked to print her night's work before going to bed at 7.00 o'clock in the morning. One night, her printer produced a wad of inkless sheets. All she could see was the imprint of her words, which she had been looking forward to seeing on paper and reading, before retiring.

The machine needed more toner which she did not know how to use. The thought that she wouldn't be able to see six hours' worth of her work on paper, threw her into obsessive desperation.

She dialled the Samaritans. Their line was engaged. This only increased her misery. She got through after fourteen attempts.

"Samaritans," said a gentle voice which gave her courage.

"I'm a writer," said Juliet. "I've been working for six hours. I want so badly to read my work before I go to bed. I've run out of toner. Could you send a man out to put more toner into my printer?"

"I beg your pardon?"

Juliet was almost in tears. "But you've simply *got* to send a man out to put more toner into my printer. I've got to write my books. How can I carry out my trade if I can't manage my tools?"

The Samaritan operator was furious.

"Look here, madam, this is a charity catering for highly distressed people, wishing to kill themselves. Your behaviour is outrageous. A person practising a trade should know how to use his tools. Do you imagine we would receive a call from a doctor who didn't know how to use his blood pressure monitor?"

"If you don't send a man out, immediately, I'll kill myself!" shouted Juliet.

The Samaritan operator hung up.

Juliet went to bed and had more toner put in her machine the next day. She started working again, for a few hours, the evening of the fire.

She continued to bang her computer keys, unaware that the building was on fire. She was a chain-smoker, and attributed the smokiness in the room to the excessive amount of cigarettes she had smoked during the night.

Her writing had been fast, fluent and succinct for the past six hours, as she had taken an extra dose of Dexedrine, the amphetamine.

She remained in absent-minded ignorance of the carbon monoxide in the smoke, coming through the partly opened window. The poisonous gas had added to the euphoria caused by the amphetamines. She was deliriously happy with the progress she had made with her book, which she had called "*Bring Forth Your Dead.*"

As she typed, she watched her words fill the screen. Her sentences and paragraphs were short and her prose satisfyingly devoid of subordinate clauses, split infinitives and lumbering gerundive clauses. She laughed in ecstasy and felt the joy of a creator, witnessing his pure and perfect creation.

She felt someone tapping her on the shoulder. She turned, still smiling, and saw three staggered-looking firemen and a female paramedic. The firemen wore oxygen masks. The paramedic did not. She was coughing and choking.

"If you're going to cough like that, would you mind going into another room," said Juliet. "Whatever it is you've got, I don't want to catch it."

"We've *got* to get you to hospital!" said the paramedic, in a tone which Juliet considered theatrical and hysterical.

"What on earth do you mean, you've got to get me to hospital? I'm not going to a hospital. I haven't got any symptoms of ill health. Is this some practical joke? Just who *are* all these people?"

"This place is saturated with poisonous gas. Your lungs are full of carbon monoxide," said one of the firemen. "Your lips are *blue*."

"Ha! Ha! Ha! And your hats are *yellow!*"

Juliet rocked backwards and forwards in her chair, with mirthless laughter. She broke into a spontaneous rendering of *The Farmer and the Cowman Should be Friends* from *Oklahoma*. Something had already begun to go wrong with her brain.

While Juliet sat singing, one of the firemen roused Ephraim from his sleep. He had hardly been affected by the smoke as he had been sleeping with his windows closed. The fireman helped him into his clothes, and took him down the fire escape, out of the building.

The same fireman returned to the flat and came into the room where Juliet was sitting, typing.

"Come on, luv. You've got to stop that, now. You're not making our job any easier. Come with us, there's a good girl. If you stay here, you'll die."

"Of what?" asked Juliet, angrily.

"Haven't you heard of carbon monoxide poisoning?"

"I'm not going anywhere. I'm trying to write a fucking book!"

The fireman spoke gently to Juliet and persuaded her to leave. She seemed undaunted by the thick, black smoke in the recess area between her flat and the fire escape.

"Where's Ephraim?" she asked.

"Is he your son?"

"Yes."

"We woke him up and took him outside, a few minutes ago."

"Was he afraid?"

"Not particularly. These things don't seem to bother him. Takes after his mother."

"He is all right, isn't he?"

"He's all right. There wasn't any smoke in his room. The windows were closed."

"Where is he, now?"

"He's outside. He's waiting by the ambulances."

"Has he asked where I am?"

"Yes. I told him you were OK and on your way down."

"Good."

The three firemen and the paramedic took Juliet down the fire escape into the hall. It was only then that it occurred to her that another manuscript she had completed, a hundred-thousand-words long, was in a drawer in her bedroom.

"My work!" she screamed, hysterically. "There's a hundred-thousand words of it up there. I've got to go back!"

"You're not going anywhere," said the fireman who had first spoken to her. "Out of the building, now, or you'll get burnt alive."

"I've told you, I'm going back!"

The fireman and one of his colleagues held her by the arms. The senior fireman, supervising the evacuation, fixed the struggling trio with a curious stare.

"All right," said Juliet. "All I ask is that you let go of my arms. I agree to do what you say and I give you my word that I won't resist you."

The two firemen relaxed their grip. For a moment, Juliet stood still and showed no intention of moving. Suddenly, she pointed to something outside the building.

"My God, look! There's someone out there, alight from head to foot!" she shouted.

Her captors relaxed their guard. She ran back to the fire escape and mounted the metal steps, two at a time.

The senior fireman turned to the two men.

"You've let her go, you couple of dozy gits. After her!"

Although she never took exercise and was physically unfit, her desire to retrieve her manuscript was so overpowering, that she miraculously mounted at least five flights of stairs, while the first fireman to speak to her, chased her, an oxygen mask rammed onto his face and a cylinder on his back.

She turned.

"What's the point of running after me? You'll never catch me. I'll come back when I've found my work."

She went on running, and disappeared into a heavy cloud of black smoke engulfing a section of the fire escape. The fireman was at a loss to understand how anyone could run through heavy smoke, without coughing or choking.

"For Christ's sake, woman, come back! If you don't, you're not going to live to see your bloody work. Are you something from outer space? Haven't you got lungs?"

He caught up with her and bundled her over his shoulder. She was in tears, because she knew she wasn't going to get that thing she so passionately wanted.

"You don't understand. My work's my baby. I made it with my own hands. Do you imagine I'm going to abandon it without a fight?"

The fireman took her out of the building where her son, Ephraim, was standing, waiting for her. The mother and son were told by two paramedics, a man and a woman, to get into an ambulance.

Ephraim got in first. He had not been harmed and was told to sit in a chair.

Juliet was lifted into the ambulance on a stretcher. The male paramedic suddenly became aware of her beautiful facial features. She had a soft, if soot-embedded skin, large eyes and a mane of the glossiest copper-coloured hair he had ever seen.

There was twice the amount of carbon monoxide in her lungs than there had been twenty minutes earlier, and the amphetamines she had swallowed were still surging through her system. Her mania had intensified.

An oxygen mask was placed over her face. In an instinctive gesture, she tilted it backwards, and took a packet of cigarettes and a lighter from her pocket. She put a cigarette in her mouth and was about to light it.

The male paramedic gaped at her as if she had urinated in his mother's tea.

"You ... you can't smoke in here! Are you insane? You'll blow us all up."

"I don't see any No Smoking signs," said Juliet.

"It doesn't matter. Just don't do it!"

Juliet had temporarily forgotten about her manuscript. Her spirits soared. She felt as if she had just had a heroin injection.

"Come over here and sit by your mother, Ephi," she said.

"Can I do that?" the boy asked the male paramedic. "Can I sit by my mother?"

The paramedic consented. The boy leant over to his mother and held her hand.

"What's it to be then, Ephi, *The Farmer and the Cowman*?"

"All right, Mother."

Juliet sang loudly. She could sing in tune but did not have an alluring singing voice. She sounded like a combination of an old bag-woman in labour and a dervish summoning Moslems to prayer.

Ephraim found the situation comical. Strangely, he was proud, rather than embarrassed, by his mother's phenomenal eccentricity.

The ambulance had turned off the Embankment, onto Lambeth Bridge, on the way to St. Anne's Hospital. It was a fine day and the dawn accentuated the majesty of the buildings on either side of the Thames.

Ephraim had joined his mother in song, and sang as loudly as she. Because his voice had not yet broken, he made an earsplitting, wailing noise, like a circus midget, trying to crack a table-load of glasses.

The pair made the effete, over-sensitive ambulance driver wince. He was sitting a few inches from Juliet's head. His whole body tensed and he felt as if a burning knitting needle were being pushed into his ear.

"The farmer and the cowman should be friends.
The farmer and the cowman should be friends.
One man likes to chase a cow, the other likes to
*   push a plough,*
But that's no reason why they cain't be friends."

"Could we be doing without the entire soundtrack of *Oklahoma*?" bleated the desperate ambulance driver.

Both woman and boy ignored him.

"I'd like to say a word for the farmer!" bellowed Juliet. This

was her favourite line in the song, and whenever she sang it, her voice increased in volume.

Ephraim continued with the next line. It was as if the performance had been rehearsed.

"*I'd like to say a word for the cowman,*" he piped. The pitch of his voice almost cracked the ambulance driver's glasses.

"Hey, driver!" called Juliet. "I've something to tell you."

They had left Lambeth Bridge and turned left into Lambeth Palace Road.

"What's that?" the driver asked, unwisely.

"I was the common-law wife of this beautiful-looking, hunky pathologist at the Hammersmith Hospital. He died of a heart-attack before Ephraim was born. He was adorable. He was diagnosed as being psychotic and his father was a Harley Street psychiatrist. My fella's name was William Rendon.

"He told me this story not long before he died. He went into his father's waiting room one morning, where he saw this man reading *Crime and Punishment*. Jesus, driver, do you know what he did?"

The driver wiped the sweat from his brow.

"No. Just tell me as calmly as you can, if you think I need to know."

"You won't believe it! He just went up to this man and sat astride him."

"Oh, did he?"

"Oh, God, driver, do you want to hear what he actually *said* to this man?"

"Well, all right. All I ask is that you stop shouting."

"OK, here it comes, pretty boy! Don't forget, he was in a crowded Harley Street waiting room, full of psychiatric patients. *Harley Street*, if you please! He shouted:

"'I say, when you read *Crime and Punishment*, do you ever get fantasies about being buggered by Raskolnikov on the floor of his garret?'"

Her words had nearly perforated the ambulance driver's eardrums. In an involuntary movement, caused by exhaustion and stress, his hand turned the steering wheel sharply to the right.

9

A bus carrying some old-aged pensioners to a community day centre, was travelling on the other side of the road. Its driver swerved off the road, onto the pavement and into some shrubbery.

The ambulance driver had broken out in a cold sweat and his heart was beating so fast that it hurt him. His words were unnaturally flowery and his tone of voice exaggeratedly pleading, even comic.

"Oh, please, I beg of you on trembling bended knee, please stop persecuting me. I'm only a poorly-paid ambulance driver. I just can't take the soundtrack of *Oklahoma*! I can't bear all this shouting and I don't want to *hear* about Russians buggering people in garrets. Besides, I don't think my mother would want me to be exposed to such utterly disgusting conversation."

The ambulance reached St. Anne's Hospital. The paramedics lifted the stretcher on which Juliet lay, and carried her towards a paved area outside the hospital. By this time, she was seriously ill but still in mania.

She saw her son run towards her with a look of urgency about him.

"Is something the matter?" she asked.

He was waving a plastic bag in the air.

"Have you got something to show me?"

"I have. I think it's something you want."

"Then give it to me. Don't mess about."

The boy continued to wave the bag in the air and transferred it from one hand to the other. He ran about, laughing.

"You'll want it far more if you wait for it, Mother," he said.

"Come on, give it to me!"

"I might. On the other hand, I might not."

He held it close to her and withdrew it and repeated his action. She snatched it from him, removed the rubber band securing it, and looked inside it.

CHAPTER 2

"This is the last manuscript, Ephi, the one I went back to get. How did you find it?"

"I found it as soon as the firemen came. When they told me to leave, I took it with me."

"Very well done, darling! Hold onto it." She spoke rapidly, her tone concerned, as if she foresaw the immediacy of unconsciousness, followed by death.

"Listen very carefully. Take this bag to my publisher, the nice man you've met so many times, Ian Rosen. His offices are in 151 Curzon Street."

"I know that, Mother," said Ephraim, impatiently. "You and I have met him there, many times."

"He'll tell you where my solicitor, Mr Eisenthal is. You remember him, don't you?"

"Of course I do, Mother, but not so well as Mr Rosen."

"Some time ago, I made out a will. God, this is a ghastly hospital! This has all got worse under that awful Blair. They've just left me here and there's no-one about. If the fumes kill me, your aunt, Miranda will look after you. You remember going to her house, don't you, 41 Lyndhurst Road?"

"Yes. She's always been nice to me. Besides, she's your sister. She used to play with me a lot when I was little, and take me to places."

"That's right. Her husband's name is Simon White. He's a dentist, but you hardly know him, do you?"

Ephraim looked gloomily at the ground.

"Not enough to like him, much. He's not very friendly. He's a bit strange. Why did you make the will?"

"Because it's an adult's responsibility, and your father is dead."

Ephraim had no idea of the changes taking place in his mother since she was able to speak, even if her speech was slurred. The likelihood of her dying did not enter his mind.

"I haven't seen aunt Miranda for some.time," he said.

"That doesn't matter. Her love for you hasn't changed. She's always wanted a child of her own. It's because she's such a loving person that she and I made a formal, legal agreement that she would look after you if anything happened to me."

"I don't understand why I can't go straight to her house, if you get ill. Why do I have to go to Mr Rosen's offices, instead?" asked the boy.

"Because Miranda's in Paris. Also, you've got to give this bag to Mr Rosen. He knows where she stays in Paris. I don't. He can get in touch with her."

Ephraim was irritated and bored, waiting outside the hospital. His resentment of the sight of his mother lying on a stretcher, with no-one around to take her into the building, escalated to anger. He kept shouting, "Will someone get their ass over here to help my sick mother?" but his words were unheard. Without intending to, he projected some of his rage onto his mother.

"What's aunt Miranda doing in Paris?" he demanded.

"There's a gentleman over there whom she visits from time to time, a business contact of Mr Rosen."

"Oh, she sleeps with him, does she?"

"There's no need to be so damned impertinent. That's no business of yours, and you know it!"

Juliet tried to raise her weight onto her elbows but fell back. Her physical state had suddenly weakened, but not the urgency behind her words.

"Apart from Miranda, you've got another aunt, Ephi. She's not good and kind, like Miranda. She's evil, and she will harm you."

"How? Why would I want to go near her?"

"You won't need to. It will be she who tries to come near you."

"Why will she harm me, Mother?"

Juliet sucked air into her filthy lungs.

"I'm afraid you never met your father. Kate Rendon is his younger sister, well half-sister. Your paternal grandfather left all his money to your father and his chosen lady. He left nothing to her. If I'm done for, Miranda will tell you why." She spoke in staccato blasts and her voice was becoming so frail that Ephraim had to lean over her with his ear an inch from her mouth.

He held his mother's hand, on seeing her lips go bluer and her face paler. This was the first time that he feared for her life, and despaired because there was no-one about.

"Did my father and Kate get on?" he asked.

"They never spoke." As Juliet answered, she coughed and forced more air into her lungs. "Kate will start looking for you if I don't pull through. All your father's money will go to you and she will do all she can to get it. She's a depraved, ruthless psychopath who'll stop at nothing."

"What can I do to stop it, Mother?"

"Lie low, boy. Speak to no-one. She has spies. She'll be all around you."

"What do you mean?"

"Just be warned. I told you that she and your father never spoke. That's not quite true. They spoke not long before he died."

"What did she say to him?"

"It's not a question of what she said. It's what he saw."

"What did he see, Mother?"

Juliet stared her son in the eye, as if desperate to tell him something. Her eyes suddenly turned to glass. The sun in them had gone out. Her mouth was partly open. She lay completely still on the stretcher. Her arms had fallen to her sides.

CHAPTER 3

After a long wait, several paramedics, including a white-coated doctor on his way into the hospital, swarmed to the scene, overlooked by the Houses of Parliament, lit by the pale November rising sun.

An abortive attempt was made to resuscitate Juliet on the concrete area outside the hospital. Ephraim watched in numbness, unaware of what was going on in his world.

He felt a wave of courage as his mother's stretcher was wheeled towards the hospital entrance. He ran after it and caught up with it. He put his arms round her neck, thinking he could still feel her presence from wherever she had gone. He followed the stretcher along the polished corridors to the Casualty Department. Medics, who would have been more useful to Juliet, had they been outside when she needed them, worked on her with belated but unwavering dedication. They tried to start her heart, first with the traditional manual method. When that failed, they slammed bulky machines, which looked like irons, onto her chest, causing her body to jolt. This gave Ephraim the misguided impression that she had come to life.

Juliet's death, followed by her apparent jerk back to life, and her state of lifelessness once more, was too much for Ephraim's psyche. He was unable to understand his own thoughts, and hid under a wheel-borne stretcher in a state of nausea and confusion.

The attempt to resuscitate Juliet started once more. The thudding noise made by the machines being slammed onto her chest, and the repeated jolting of her body, had a temporarily numbing effect on Ephraim. His mother had instilled a degree of toughness within him and there were occasions when he could block himself from reality, in adversity.

He listened to the unemotional exchange between the doctor and the paramedics.

"OK, wrap it up, lads! We could all be here till flipping Judgement Day, and we still won't shift a stubborn heart like that," said the doctor. "Have you got the exact time on you, mate?"

"08.07 hours," said one of the paramedics.

"Excellent! I'm recording 08.07 hours as the time of death," said the doctor. "I don't know about you, but I'm starving. I could do with some porridge and a plate of bacon and eggs. This is the first stiff we've had this morning. I'll find out who her GP is and let him know she's croaked, before we get her slung down the mortuary. I heard the bloody coolers have broken down again, but it's not really my problem, is it?"

"What would you say your problem was?" asked one of the paramedics, lightheartedly.

"Sleep deprivation, mate! Doctors of my rank work in conditions that would make Victorian workhouses enviable places to be in. If more doctors had been recruited, that poor bitch would still be alive.

No-one had seen Ephraim in Casualty, so keen were the medics to start Juliet's heart. No-one saw him running away in desperation from the Department, either.

He ran hopelessly along the corridors of the hospital, weeping. A nurse, on her way to the canteen for her tea-break, blocked his path. She was about twenty-five and her gaunt, prematurely-lined face bore a streak of kindness which encouraged the boy.

"You're lost, aren't you? I'm not surprised in a big place like this. Aren't you going to tell me your name? My name's Allison."

"I'm Ephraim William Victor Rendon," said the boy, in a deliberate tone. "My mother's just died after a fire started at home. It was the smoke which killed her. She made the mistake of going back into the building to collect the manuscript of a book she had written. I heard them say she was going to the dead house. Mother was a writer. She told me to go straight to her publisher, Mr Ian Rosen in 151 Curzon Street. Her publisher knows her solicitor. They were all friends."

Allison sat on her haunches, to put him at his ease.

"Where did you get your beautiful golden curls from?" she asked.

"Oh, Mother said my father had hair like that.

15

I never met my father. He died before I was born."

"I'll soon have you sorted," said Allison. "I'm on my way to the canteen. Come with me. I'll get you some tea. After that, I'm taking you to a lady who's known as an administrator. We can give her the address of your mother's publisher. We'll find the number and ring him up. The lady you'll be meeting will arrange transport for you."

Allison brought some tea to the table where Ephraim was sitting. He was fascinated by the men in white coats there, with stethoscopes round their necks.

"My father was a doctor," he said. "He must have gone round wearing clothes like that."

"Clothes like what?"

"I meant white coats."

"Ah, yes. Would you like me to get you some chocolate biscuits?"

"No thank you. I'm not hungry."

"Are you sure?"

"Yes, quite sure."

"You said your mother was a writer. What did she write?"

"Books."

"What, novels?"

"Yes."

"What name did she write under?"

"Her own name. Juliet Silverman."

"Juliet Silverman?" exclaimed the nurse. "*The* Juliet Silverman?"

"I don't think there are any others with that name."

"Did you know your mother was a very famous woman?"

"I know she wrote an awful lot. I didn't know she was famous."

"Well, she is. I've read nearly all her books. Very gripping, they are. I couldn't put any of them down. Have you read any of them?"

"No. Mother wouldn't let me. She said they'd upset me because they were so bloodthirsty, and unsuitable for children."

"They are a bit. You'll still be able to enjoy them when

16

you're older. Tell me about your father. Was he in private practice or in the National Health?"

"What do you mean?"

"I meant, did he work in a hospital or did he have private rooms?"

"Oh, he was at the Hammersmith Hospital. He worked there until he died," said Ephraim, adding with a secretive, conspiratorial smile. "But his father, my grandfather, that is, practised in Harley Street." He uttered the words "Harley Street", in a manner which Alison found snobbish.

"What was your father's name, Ephraim?"

"I never *met* my father."

"I know, but what was his name?"

"His name was William Victor James Rendon." Once more, there was a flaunting, theatrical note in the boy's voice. He had no idea how much his solemnly-uttered words terrified his companion.

Allison whitened. She felt a rapid drop in blood pressure. It suddenly became clear to her who he was. Just after William Rendon's death, the bodies of three women were found in the nursery of his father's Harley Street house. Rowland Rendon, a consultant psychiatrist, had died shortly before his son. He had committed suicide on learning that his son was a serial killer.

The News of the World had carried a double page splash, on the scandal. Half of one of these pages bore a close-up coloured photograph of William, accentuating his blonde, wavy hair, angel's face and huge, blue eyes, like those of his son. The words William Victor James Rendon — serial killer and Hammersmith Hospital doctor, were printed in bold letters beneath the photograph. The headline, covering the two pages, appeared in letters two inches high, "HARLEY SHRINK'S SON AND THE THREE NURSERY STIFFS".

The article outlined William's career as a pathologist. Some of his colleagues had been interviewed by the newspaper, and had told reporters about his fanatical fascination for death, his perpetual womanizing and his peculiar, but likeable personality.

The most unusual aspect of the case, apart from the three

murders, was the fact that William had been so mentally disturbed, that he had received a long course of psychiatric treatment from his own father, Rowland Rendon, who believed his son's case to be so severe that no other psychiatrist could handle it.

A notebook, which Rowland Rendon had kept, recorded the conversations, from each consultation. A workman, renovating the house after his suicide, had found the notebook and sold it to *The News of the World*. This enabled the newspaper to serialize the story over a three-week period.

Allison was fascinated by any unusual incidents taking place in Harley Street. It had been her ambition to work in one of its private clinics, or in a smart consultant's practice. She hated the National Health Service, its petty bureaucracy and its shambling management, causing tardy admission of seriously ill patients who died around her each day in droves. Like all her colleagues, she noticed the abrupt deterioration in hospital management and patient care, which had set in dramatically since the start of Tony Blair's Labour Government.

She had read the Rendon articles repeatedly, and the more she read them and absorbed their contents, the more fervently she yearned for a working environment of plush waiting rooms, pin-striped-suited doctors, high-ceilinged consulting rooms and shining, leather-studded couches.

It seemed as if only twenty-four hours had passed since she had curled herself up into a ball and licked the filth from the pages of *The News of the World*, like an underfed cat with its head in a saucer of cream.

She eventually summoned the courage to look the notorious serial-killer's son in the eye. She wondered whether the sweet-looking, innocent child, facing her would inherit his father's genes. The heat in the canteen was oppressive and uneconomical. She felt faint.

"What's the matter, Allison?" said Ephraim, in a sharp, arresting tone.

"Nothing. Why?"

"There *is* something troubling you. I can tell. We were

18

talking just now, and suddenly you looked as if you weren't feeling very well."

"I'm fine."

"No, you aren't. You're not feeling very well, as I said. When are you going to take me to see your friend, the one you said was an administrator?"

"Don't you want any more tea?"

"No. Tea's not what I want. I want to go to my mother's publisher."

Allison rose to her feet and felt even fainter. She bent over and supported herself on the table.

"You see? I said you weren't feeling well, didn't I?"

"Give me a minute. It's very hot in here and I'm feeling faint. It'll pass. Then I'll be able to help you."

Ephraim sat down and waited for Allison to recover. Hot tears rolled down his cheeks, unchecked. He was afraid that some of the younger doctors in the room would think him a sissy.

Allison straightened herself.

"Come along, Ephraim. We'll go and see her, now."

Allison took Ephraim on an interminable walk, up and down slippery corridors. They weaved through white-coated doctors, surgeons, beds bearing patients being fed on drips, injured and sick patients on stretchers, medical secretaries, hospital managers and a cacophony of lost visitors.

They eventually stopped walking. Allison knocked on a scratched, dented door which she heaved her weight against, on hearing a woman's voice saying "come in."

The office they entered was small, dismal and devoid of natural light. Its occupant, Elizabeth Hastings, was sitting behind a desk, cluttered with disordered papers and birthday cards. She was thirty-eight. She had poorly-conditioned, long mouse-coloured hair and wore a navy blue designer suit and a lapel bearing her name, followed by the words "Senior Hospital Administrator."

Elizabeth was unhappy and disgruntled. She had once occupied an airy, high-rise office in the hospital, overlooking the

19

Thames and the Houses of Parliament.

She was ordered to move into her present office without warning, and when she complained that an office without natural light was a deterrent to her health, she was threatened with dismissal.

Elizabeth had been a Senior Hospital Administrator for twelve years, and throughout that time, had been loyal and industrious. Her husband was a drunkard and could not work, and she had two children to support.

The sharp rise in unemployment under Blair's Government, had made it hard for her to find another situation, and her grim surroundings depressed her so much that she lacked the courage to contemplate change.

She was no longer interested in her work. She was playing *Solitaire* on her computer when Allison and Ephraim came into her office. Although she could see them, she failed to look up.

"Mrs Hastings," began Allison.

"It's Staff Nurse Allison Bennett, isn't it? Who's that boy?"

Allison was brief and succinct when accounting for Ephraim's loss of his famous mother, after a domestic fire, his reason for being in the hospital and his mother's dying wish that he visit her publisher.

"Staff Nurse Bennett hasn't identified you properly, yet. What is your name?"

"Ephraim William Victor Rendon," replied the boy, in an assertive chant, as if his name were the only thing he had to hold on to.

"With a name like that, you ought to be in a bloody uniform! Who's this publisher your mother told you to go to? What's his name?

"The name's Ian Rosen. My mother's name was Juliet Silverman. She said he could be found c/o Thomas Rosen and Son, at 151 Curzon Street, London, W1. She said he knew the 'phone number of her solicitor who took charge of her will," said Ephraim.

"This Mr Rosen, what's his telephone number, dear?"

Ephraim disliked being addressed as "dear", and felt even

more insulted by someone speaking to him in that way, just after his mother's death.

"Please don't call me 'dear'," he said.

"Never mind. Do you know his number?"

"Why don't you try ringing Directory Enquiries?"

"I'm going to. Do you know your mother's solicitor's number?"

"No."

"Would you mind if I had a word in private with Staff Nurse Bennett?"

"No."

"Good. There's a little room next door you can sit in, while I address this matter."

She opened the door to the other room and ushered Ephraim through it. She closed it, quietly. The door dividing the two rooms was thin, and the boy could hear every word spoken in the Administrator's office. He felt too restless to sit down and paced up and down, like one of Ted Hughes's leopards, while the two women spoke in the main office.

"Why did you have to pick this boy up and bring him to me?" asked Elizabeth.

"Through humanitarian responsibility."

"I understand that but you could have dumped him somewhere else?"

"He's just lost his mother!" shouted Allison.

"Kindly don't shout in here. I could report you to the person you're answerable to. I suppose I'll have to find out this bloody publisher's number."

"It would be a start," said Allison.

Elizabeth found Rosen's number from Directory Enquiries. Her discontent with her career caused her to shed her inhibitions. She didn't care what kind of language she would use, if she succeeded in speaking to Rosen. A secretary answered. She put Elizabeth through.

"Is your name Mr Rosen?" Her tone was angry and disinterested.

"Yes. Is your enquiry about a forthcoming publication?"

21

"No. Something else. I'm Elizabeth Hastings, Senior Administrator at St Anne's Hospital. You wouldn't want my job. My office has no natural light and my husband's a drunk."

"What makes you think that's any business of mine?" said Rosen.

"Perhaps it isn't. Unforeseen circumstances have prompted me to ring you. A nurse has just come to my office about a woman called Juliet Silverman. I'm told she was a famous writer."

"What the hell's going on?" said Rosen. "Why are you using the past tense, like that?"

"Because she's dead. She had smoke inhalation, following a fire at home. She was taken to a place of safety outside the building, but she stupidly went back in to find the manuscript of one of her books. Her body's in the hospital mortuary. If it's of any interest to you, the bloody cooling systems have broken down in there."

"Oh, Christ!" said Rosen.

"I've got this boy in here," Elizabeth continued.

Rosen was devastated, both by the news and the callous manner in which it had been broken to him. He shovelled potato crisps into his mouth with one hand, and chain-smoked with the other.

"What boy?" he asked.

Though from a Jewish family, he spoke with a husky, singsong, slightly Welsh accent, inherited from his maternal grandmother.

"Juliet Silverman's bloody son! What boy do you think I'm referring to? Says his name's Ephraim Rendon. Apparently, his parents never married. He says you know who his mother's solicitor is."

"I am astounded by your extraordinarily rude manner. Kindly identify yourself, other than by saying you're a Senior Administrator at bloody St Anne's Hospital," said Rosen.

"That is my rank," she said. "I've already given you my name."

"Who are you answerable to?"

"I don't have to provide that information. Isn't that boy the son of William Rendon, the serial killer?"

"How dare you!" shouted Rosen.

"I don't know how I dare. I just do," said Elizabeth, flippantly. She hated her office so much then, that she wanted to be reported and dismissed.

"The late Miss Silverman's solicitor is a personal friend of our firm's, and it will not be difficult to arrange a meeting with him and Ephraim in my office," said Rosen.

"What's his number?"

"Do you think I would be prepared to give it to you, and put him through the shattering experience of hearing you break the news of Miss Silverman's death?"

"That would save me from having to ring him up, wouldn't it?"

Rosen ignored the remark.

"I will ring him," he said. "He knows Ephraim well. And so do I. He frequently accompanied his mother on her visits to both our offices. Once I've spoken to him, I'll ring you through your switchboard."

"When's that likely to be? I'm meeting a friend in the pub in half an hour."

"You're meeting a *what*?" exclaimed Rosen.

"A friend."

"Women like you don't have friends. Keep Ephraim with you and wait for my call. You'd better be nice to him! Being rude to an adult is one thing, but if word gets through to me that you've been offhand with a bereaved child, I'll have you stripped of your rank and flung into the river! Do I make myself clear?"

"As clear as an unmudded lake, sir. As clear as an azure sky in deepest summer."

CHAPTER 4

Rosen poured himself some whisky to steady his nerves, before dialling Juliet's solicitor's number. The solicitor's name was Jack Eisenthal. He, too, had offices in Curzon Street. Both men had known Juliet and Miranda for many years.

Rosen's most painful task of all was having to break the news to Juliet's younger sister, Miranda, who, as next-of-kin would have to identify Juliet in the Chapel of Rest. He knew she was staying in the *Hôtel Vendôme*, on the *Place de la Concorde*. He assumed she would be spending the morning in bed with his colleague, Charles de Cadanet. Cadanet was in charge of the Rosen firm's Paris offices. Rosen had introduced Cadanet to Miranda who had been having an on-and-off affair with him for two years. Cadanet had a distinctly French appearance and manner. He was a dapper man with a crew cut. He spoke English with a slight French accent which had originally attracted Miranda. The lovers were in bed in one of the *Vendôme*'s old-fashioned suites, when the telephone rang. Cadanet lifted the receiver.

Qui est là? " he asked abruptly.

"It's Ian, Charles. I need to speak to Miranda. Is she there?"

"Indeed, she is. She's underneath me."

"Who the hell wants to speak to me, now?" asked Miranda.

"Miranda, Baby, it's Ian. I'm afraid I have the most tragic news. Could you try to prepare yourself for a shock?"

"Yes? Yes?"

"It's about Juliet. I'm terribly sorry to have to tell you that she has lost her life. It happened after a domestic fire. She was running about, looking for the manuscript of a book, and refused to go outside with the firemen. She died about two hours ago of carbon monoxide poisoning."

"Get me some brandy, Charles. Hurry," she said.

Oh, Christ, Miranda, I'm so sorry," said Rosen.

"What about the poor boy? Where is he, now?"

"Jack and I are going over to collect him from St Anne's Hospital, where Juliet died. He told hospital staff members that she wanted him to come straight to my offices, as you'd gone to Paris."

Miranda's grief had not been fully released. It was like a ball of tight phlegm at the back of her throat, at the start of a virus. She said, "I remember the legally-binding agreement my sister and I made. I talked Juliet into it. She always was a bit wild and reckless. We agreed my husband and I would have custody of Ephraim, if anything happened to her."

"You're to get the next plane back to London, and come to my offices. We'll look after Ephraim until you get here. I can't have you travelling alone. Could I speak to Charles?" said Rosen.

"Charles, here, Ian."

"You know the news by now, do you?"

"What's happened?"

"Miranda's older sister, Juliet, has died after a fire. She has entrusted her son to Miranda's care. That means Miranda will have to leave for London as soon as possible. I'm afraid I must insist that you come with her and you can leave her once you get to the Curzon Street offices."

"Very well. If that's what you want me to do, I must do it."

"Could I speak to Miranda, again, please?" asked Rosen.

"Oh, God, Ian!" she said.

"You'll be OK, Baby. You've got Jack and me. Losing a sibling is about the worst thing that can happen to anyone, but time will heal it. Have you got any Valium?"

"No! Charles, have you got any Valium?"

"Indeed, I have," said Cadanet. "I always carry a supply. Paris life demands it."

"Charles has got some, Ian."

"Good. Take about three, now. Are they yellow or blue?"

"Blue."

"That's good. They're the strongest. Try to be brave, sweetie. Remember, your friends are there for you."

"What about Simon, Ian?"

"What about him?"

"Do you think he knows what I've been doing in Paris?"

"Why should he, Baby? You told him you were going to see your ageing uncle. That's the story I'll tell if he asks me, which I don't think he will. I'll have to tell him about Juliet. No doubt, he will come to my offices, as well. It would be best for Ephraim if he did."

CHAPTER 5

A feeling of cold blackness descended on Rosen. He was forced to remember a past which he had been struggling to forget. The news of Juliet's death reminded him of his unhappy childhood. His late father, Thomas Rosen, had a large, unearned income, and was the founder of a publishing firm which he had passed on to his son. It had once been a staunchly conventional establishment and had specialized only in learned, conservative publications.

Thomas's son, Ian Michael Rosen, had more of a flair for popular demand than his father, and had dramatically changed the firm's former conservative image. The firm continued to publish works of scholarship and antiquity, but became more lucrative with the inclusion of racy literary matter, biographies of sometimes insalubrious historical figures, and soft-core pornography. His profits, combined with the inheritance of his father's earned and unearned wealth, turned him into a millionaire after his father's death.

Rosen had two younger twin sisters, Naomi and Martha to whom he had been strongly attached. He had also been devoted to his mother Sara, who had died, with his sisters, in a plane crash when he was twelve years old.

Because of the difference in age, Rosen was more of a father-figure to his sisters, than a brother. He could not conceal his paternal devotion towards them and was loving and kind to them. He was adoring and helpful to his mother, whom he looked up to and obeyed. As a young boy, he had little affection for his father. Even before the tragedy, Ian had been highly-strung and advanced for his years, and his father had found him hard to control.

Thomas Rosen was too distraught to care for his wayward, emotional son. He sent the boy to live in the country, outside Cardiff with his maternal Welsh grandmother. These years were lonely for a boy of Ian's liveliness and precocity, but she treated him kindly. He was devastated, on a sweltering day, when he returned from school and found her dead on the dining room floor. She had had a heart attack. It was only the night before that she had invited neighbours to the house to celebrate his fourteenth birthday.

His bereavements occasionally caused him to think a curse had been put on him, and he wondered, if illogically, whether they had occurred because he had forgotten to throw spilt salt over his shoulder.

He was sent to live in his father's house in Golders Green where he attended a local school. The other children were amused by his heavy Welsh accent, which he was self-conscious about. He moderated it but never managed to overcome it.

Thomas Rosen was a strict disciplinarian and a raving madman. He adhered to orthodox Judaism which he imposed on his son with an iron and relentless hand. Ian resented this from the beginning. He had never been able to come to terms with the death of his mother and sisters, or indeed that of his grandmother. The idea of being forced to worship a Supreme Being, who appeared to have allowed these things to happen, enraged him and was an anathema to him. He hated his father, almost as much as the God he forced on him.

His father's disciplinary methods of religious instruction were not simply confined to the imposition of a Supreme Being on his son. The situation was considerably more unpleasant than that. As soon as the unbelieving boy returned to London at the age of fourteen, Thomas Rosen forced him to go to his study for two hours, every night after dinner. He read long sections from books of devotion, and forced Ian to repeat what had been read to him.

He hated and feared his father, and obeyed.

"Do you believe in the words you have just recited?" asked the father.

"I've no choice but to say 'yes'. I'm afraid to say 'no'."

"I take it, that means 'no'. I thought you were aware by now, that I have methods of changing 'no' to 'yes'.

The boy knelt down on the floor and wept.

"How can I say 'yes', after what I've been put through? If

you want me to say 'yes', just so you won't make me do this again, I'll say 'yes'."

"Then, say it!"

"I'm trying to but I can't! How can I when the answer's 'no'?"

"So it's 'no', is it?"

"I'm sorry. It's not my fault. I can't control the way I think. Yes, it is 'no'. I've felt like that, since the plane crash."

"The plane crash was God's will! I think it's time you were taught a lesson. You'll sleep in this room, tonight."

"You really are a terrible bully. There's no bed in here. Where am I meant to lie down?"

"On the floor. When I come down in the morning, I shall expect a change in your attitude."

Ian did not sleep. Although he lay down, he was too enraged to sleep. He lay awake all night.

Thomas unlocked the door at 6.00 o'clock the following morning.

"Well?" he asked. "Has this experience made a believer out of you?"

"No, I can't! I can't! Why do you have to torture me, like this? Why are you so cruel to children? It's not right to be cruel to children."

"It's Friday, today! shouted the madman, startling his son.

"Friday?"

"Yes, Friday. Don't you know what Friday is? It's the day between Thursday and Saturday!"

"I know it is."

"In that case, I'm sure you are aware of what you and I will be doing when the sun goes down."

"Yes. We'll be turning the lights on."

Thomas hit his son. The boy wished he was dead. "I'm taking you to the synagogue," he said.

"Oh, no, please, anything but that!"

"You're not getting out of it. You're coming. I'm making you. It's no good resisting."

Ian thought that the only way to avoid these horrible

confrontations, would be to obey his father, implicitly. He knew that if he did not, he would go mad.

"Perhaps, you are right. I will come," he said.

Thomas put on a *yarmulka*,* shortly after the setting of the sun and asked Ian to do the same. Man and boy walked to the synagogue, which was half a mile away from their house.

Thomas guided his son, his face sheet-white, into a seat near the front of the uncrowded synagogue, and handed him a prayer book.

At the front of the synagogue, stood a gentleman known as the "Cantor". He had his back to the congregation and was facing the Holy Ark. He wore a *yarmulka*, and a black and white striped silk prayer shawl, over a white silk gown.

Near him, stood a Rabbi, also wearing a *yarmulka* and a white silk gown. The Rabbi had his back to the Cantor and faced the congregation.

Prayers were recited. The members of the congregation alternated between standing and sitting. The father made sure that his son was reciting the prayers out loud throughout, and the son made sure that the father was watching him.

At the end of the service the Cantor, the Rabbi and the members of the congregation left the synagogue and went into a social hall next to it, in which food had been laid out on a table. There was pickled herring, sponge cake, honey cake, other dishes and sweet red wine.

Ian was very hungry because he had not had lunch. He ate more of the food than he thought he could hold, and when his father was looking the other way, he tried to drown his misery with the sweet red wine.

"Are you getting any closer to your Creator, boy?" asked Thomas, aggressively. He had been talking to the Rabbi and had not noticed his son's indulgent eating and drinking.

All the child wanted was a quiet life. "I feel sure he is around us," he forced himself to remark. The lie, wrenched from him like a tooth, multiplied his pain. In an instinctive gesture, he

*Skull cap.

30

clung to the Rabbi who was standing next to his father. He put both his arms round his waist and wept.

Thomas was mortified with shame. He took Ian home and dragged him to his study. He took a cat-o'-nine-tails from his drawer and ordered him to strip naked and prostrate himself over his desk. Curiously, he found it difficult to express his fury in words, straight away. He lashed his son, put the whip back in the drawer and allowed ten minutes to pass before he spoke.

"You and I are alone in this house, Ian," he said, "and there is absolutely no limit to what I will do to you, should I wish to inflict pain on you. I'm going to ask you one question, and one question only.

"What question is that?"

"Do you believe in God?"

"Yes!" shouted the boy, fearing for his life.

"Are you quite sure?"

"Yes. Quite sure. He is the Creator of all things. I believe in him and I worship him. You were right to discipline me. To obey you is to obey God."

"Good, Ian! This problem appears to have been solved. There is no reason why we should not get on. Are we friends now?"

"Oh, yes. We are friends."

"Are you tired, Ian?"

"Yes. I want to go to my room, now."

"Then I shall bid you 'goodnight' and tomorrow, we shall pray together in the study."

Ian lay down. So great was his anger that he had been forced to lie to prevent the infliction of pain on him, that he wanted to kill his father.

Later on that night, unable to sleep, he thought seriously about killing himself. After all, there were only six more days to go until the following Friday, when the worst torture of all would be inflicted on him, once more.

He wondered how many more Fridays it would take before he cut his wrists with a razor blade, to let God and all his trappings wash themselves away from him in a river of blood.

31

However, life in London appealed to him as he grew older. He had made few friends of his own age in Wales and was happier living in a city than in the country. He soon developed an interest in girls, whose vanity and companionship delighted him. His love of the society of women was to last for the rest of his life.

He became involved with one girl when he was seventeen. She was the only daughter of his father's next-door neighbour. His attachment to her was more physical than spiritual. He met her most afternoons after school, where he had been taking his A' levels, a year early. They indulged in frenzied, youthful fornication each time they met, in the back of a disused garage, using a pile of tyres as a bed. His father had never given him advice about birth control, and within a few months of their frolicking, the girl became pregnant.

She was more emotionally dependent on him than he on her. She was afraid to tell him about her pregnancy, for fear of losing his affections. Instead, she avoided him. He assumed her non-availability was due to her embarrassment by his strange Welsh accent, which she had been continuously mimicking as their affair progressed.

It was a hot summer evening in the first week of June. Ian had just returned from school and found his father, sitting in the large garden outside their house.

"Hullo, Pop," said the boy, impertinently.

"There are one or two things I'd like to discuss with you, Ian," said Thomas, without smiling, his glacial eyes on the dry, yellow grass.

"Oh, are there?"

"Yes. I'm not particularly impressed by you. I'm not satisfied with your behaviour, all round. I thought at first you'd reformed, but it appears I was deceived."

"Why? What have I done?"

Thomas met his son's vulnerable grey eyes with a piercing, unpleasant stare.

"When did you last go to a synagogue?"

"Can't remember."

"You'd better remember. When did you last observe the Sabbath?"

"I'm past all that. It's over. Religion doesn't mean anything to me," replied Ian. "I don't believe in God. There's nothing up there. I hate the whole thing."

"I'm afraid I find this attitude nothing short of disgraceful," said Thomas.

"You can find it whatever you want. You've shoved it down my throat all my life, even before I lived in Wales. They do the same thing at my school. You've all force-fed me with it and I've thrown it up. Is that a crime?"

"In my book, it is. Not only that, I'm beating you."

Ian sat down next to his father and put his arm round him with mock affection.

"You'd be making a fool of yourself if you did. Perhaps, you've forgotten, I'll be eighteen on the fourteenth of this month."

The older man got up. Ian automatically did so, too. Thomas undid his belt and took it off.

"It's not the fourteenth, yet!" he shouted.

"You just can't get away with this."

"Shut up! Go over there and lean across the table."

"If I refused, there'd be a struggle and that would be undignified," said Ian.

His father beat him six times. The incident lasted for only about half a minute, but it caused the roots of a passionate and obsessive rage in the boy's mind, and a violent increase in his revulsion towards religion of any creed. So extreme was his intolerance of it, that he often felt ill, when called upon by anybody, to discuss it.

There were times in his adulthood when the rage was dormant, but it remained deeply embedded in his psyche, for the rest of his life.

Whenever the subject was raised, he withdrew defensively into himself, before attacking the person raising it, sometimes with restrained firmness, more often in a spirit of rudeness. His painful childhood memories of the beatings he received because

33

of his lack of religious beliefs, caused him repeated depressive attacks. These sometimes lasted for days on end.

He sought psychiatric treatment, so unsure was he whether it was his father's memory he despised, or the religion he had imposed on him. He read his casenotes, when the psychiatrist left the consulting room to take a message. He noticed that, against "Diagnosis", the doctor had written the words "paranoid atheism".

The words amused him at the time, but the matter continued to cast a weighty shadow on him which worsened with age. It was relieved only by his work, by frequent sexual activity, and the companionship of children whom he loved and who comforted him.

"And there's another matter," said Thomas. "The second matter's just as bad as the first matter."

"What's going on? What's all this in aid of? What *is* the second matter? Is there going to be a third and fourth matter, as well?"

"Please refrain from making silly jokes. It's about the girl, Ruth, our next door neighbour's daughter."

"Has she been hurt?"

"You could say that. You made her pregnant."

"How do you know it was me?"

"You've been seen over and over again in the back of that garage."

"What garage?"

"You know very well what garage. Now her parents have had to pay for her to have an abortion."

The boy looked sad. His eyes filled with tears.

"Why are you crying?" asked Thomas.

Ian wiped a stray tear from his cheek with the back of his hand.

"Because I love children," he said.

There was a long silence, broken by the father.

"Have you any idea what you want to do with your life?"

"I want to go to University, to read English."

"That shows an industrious spirit, if nothing else. How

do you feel about working in the firm and succeeding me when I get old?"

"That's what I want."

"Why?"

"Because I have a passion for the written word. I like to see how other people write things, how they handle words."

"You've been smoking, haven't you?" said the older man, suddenly.

"No, I haven't."

"You have. I can tell by your breath."

"OK, so I have. Why can't we just get along together?"

"God knows what's going to become of the firm, when you take over. I wouldn't be surprised if you turned the whole establishment into a bloody disorderly house," said the father.

Fifteen minutes passed. Neither father nor son spoke. They went back into the house and sat through a silent, three-course dinner.

CHAPTER 6

Rosen dialled the solicitor's number. "Ian Rosen here. I need to speak to Mr Eisenthal."

"I'm sorry, he's with a client at the moment."

"This is a matter of terrible urgency."

Eisenthal came onto the line.

"What's the matter, Ian?"

"I'm afraid I've got the most dreadful news, Jack."

"Yes?"

"It's about Juliet. Early this morning, a fire started. For some reason, she failed to realize the place was full of smoke. Firemen took her to a place of safety, but she re-entered the building to save the manuscript of a book she'd written. She died of carbon monoxide poisoning at St Anne's Hospital a few hours ago. Ephraim's there now. He's in the office of an odious woman called Elizabeth Hastings, who calls herself Senior Hospital Administrator."

"Juliet? Gone?"

"I'm afraid so, Jack."

"At least she had made a will. I remember going through it with her. She entrusted her sister, Miranda White, and her husband, Simon, to look after Ephraim in the event of her death. They formally agreed."

"We've both known Juliet's sister, as long as we've known Juliet. I don't know her husband all that well. He's a dentist. They're still living at 41 Lyndhurst Road, Hampstead," said Rosen.

"Yes, I know."

Both men were momentarily lost for words. Eisenthal was the first to break the silence.

"You know Ephraim well, don't you Ian?" he said.

"Yes. I saw him on many occasions with Juliet. He's a lovely boy."

"As we both know him, and he likes and trusts us, we'd better get a taxi and pick him up from the hospital," suggested Eisenthal.

"You'll have to ring the hospital first and speak to that woman. You can get her through the switchboard," said Rosen.

"My secretary will see to all that. You've told me her name and rank. I'll get a taxi and pick you up in a few minutes. I'll bring the will and the relevant papers, relating to Ephraim's custody. The whole thing will be over pretty quickly."

* * *

Elizabeth had told Allison she could leave her office and return to her duties. She thanked her in a sarcastic, patronizing manner, for her "ennobling sense of responsibility."

She had missed her lunch engagement, and her attitude towards the boy she had been forced to keep under her jurisdiction, escalated from one of irritation to hostility.

Ephraim had asked to be allowed to sit with her in her office, because he hated being alone in the tiny office adjoining it. She refused his request, and he came out of his own accord. She pushed him back into the cramped room and locked the door. His grief, combined with his claustrophobia, caused him to lose his head. He screamed and banged on the door until he was exhausted. Then he sat on the floor, crying.

Eisenthal and Rosen arrived together, soon after the news of Juliet's death had been broken.

Rosen was just under six foot and well built. His appearance was wild and not unattractive to hot-blooded, sex-starved women. He had large grey eyes, a beautiful nose and thick untidy black hair which he sometimes swept back from his face. He had the loose look about the eyes of a man with a permanent craving for women. He always wore his tie loosened at the neck, and the top two buttons of his shirt undone. He kept a gold Rolex watch on his left wrist.

Jack Eisenthal was shorter in height than his companion. He had brown eyes and light-brown wavy hair. He looked far less sexy than the other man.

Elizabeth was unnerved when the two men entered her office.

"Do you remember when we spoke on the telephone,

37

earlier?" asked Rosen, who held a lighted cigarette in his hand.

"Would you please extinguish your cigarette. This is a non-smoking hospital," said Elizabeth.

"Where am I meant to put it out?"

She handed him a saucer.

He repeated the question. "Do you remember when we spoke earlier on the telephone?"

"Why, yes."

"Where's Ephraim?"

"Next door."

Elizabeth realized she would be seen unlocking the door to let Ephraim out.

"Would you two gentlemen mind waiting in the corridor for a moment?" she said.

"What for?" asked Rosen.

"Well, it's a personal matter."

"All right. We'll wait in the room next door with Ephraim."

"I suppose it can wait."

She unlocked the door dividing the two rooms. Ephraim ran out and, on seeing the two men, whom he had always regarded as his friends, he hugged them in turn.

"Oh, Mr Rosen! Oh, Mr Eisenthal!"

"No, no. We're Ian and Jack," said Rosen.

"That's right. He's Ian. I'm the one who's Jack," said Eisenthal.

Rosen turned to Elizabeth.

"I'm going to look inside that room."

"All right, if that's what you want."

"It isn't fit to put a little bird in and you've locked him in here all this time, haven't you, you bitch?"

"It's not much smaller than my office. How do you think it feels to be kept in here for seven hours every day?"

Rosen and Eisenthal ignored her.

"I have the late Miss Silverman's will here," said Eisenthal. "I want to confirm that our visit is in order and that we are escorting Ephraim to his lawfully chosen foster-parents."

"You can take him anywhere you want, for all I care."

"Our first port of call will be the Headquarters of the N.S.P.C.C.," said Rosen.

"Yes. You've locked up a terrified, bereaved child and confined him to a room little bigger than a TV set," said Eisenthal. "We're also making a formal complaint about you to whoever runs this hospital."

Ephraim clung to Rosen.

"Come along, my boy," said the publisher. "We're all going back to my offices, where you shall have something to eat."

"Oh, Mr Rosen!"

"No, my boy. It's Ian. If you call me 'Mr Rosen' again, there won't be anything to eat!"

The two men and the boy passed Accident and Emergency on the way out of the hospital. Row upon row of stretchers serving as beds, were occupied by patients who had been waiting interminably, to be admitted for treatment for serious illnesses.

The scene reminded Rosen of a cartoon he had once seen, depicting victims of the Crimean War.

"Fucking, bloody Blair!" he muttered.

The publisher and the solicitor held Ephraim's hands, while taking him into the building containing Rosen's offices. The main office was a cheerful, airy room on the fourth floor. It had a wall-to-wall window, overlooking Curzon Street, whose old-fashioned buildings intrigued Ephraim and temporarily distracted him from his grief.

Rosen's desk was presidential in size. On it, was a computer and three British racing green telephones. There was a big glass table in the centre of the room, surrounded, on all four sides by white sofas.

"Are you cold, my boy?" asked Rosen.

"No, I'm OK, thank you, Ian."

"Now, we'll have to think about finding you something to eat. Have you had any breakfast?"

"No."

"Didn't they give you anything at the hospital?"

"A nurse took me to the canteen, when she found me in the corridor. She offered me biscuits but I wasn't hungry."

39

"Were biscuits all she suggested?"

"Yes."

"In that case, I shall have to get a proper hot lunch prepared for you. Because of what you've been through, you shall have a glass of red wine with it. Have you ever had wine before?"

"Oh, yes. Mother gave me a glass of wine with my meals. It was just as well because she wasn't much of a cook. She said it was good to have a little wine. French children have it with their meals, too, she said. She was an admirer of French customs."

Rosen was struck by the formality and solemnity of Ephraim's speech, and by the low pitch of his unbroken voice.

"You may only be twelve years old, but you talk like a proper gentleman, don't you, my boy? How do you feel about a nice hot lunch, eh?"

Ephraim lowered his head and pondered for a while. The two men thought he was about to cry.

"I do hope you won't mind," he began, "but I'd much rather have the sort of thing Mother gave me for tea."

"What did she give you for tea?" asked Rosen.

"A nice lot of sandwiches. She never gave me wine for tea, but I would like a glass all the same, please. I'd be grateful for some sandwiches, if you've got them."

"That's all right. What sort of sandwiches do you like?"

"Well, anything you have."

"In this place, we have everything. What are your favourites?"

"I like honey best, so it had better be that."

"Honey? Is that all you want?"

"Yes, thank you."

"Come, now. Honey sandwiches aren't enough to keep a growing boy alive."

"I'm afraid it's all I'll be able to hold down."

Rosen sat at his desk and picked up the intercom receiver.

"Could you bring some honey sandwiches and a glass of Claret. Bring them into my office, please."

"Yes, Mr Rosen."

"Now, my boy, where would you like to sit for your extraordinary lunch?"

"On the sofa by the window, please."

A servant brought in a tray, with a glass of Claret on it and some honey sandwiches. She was a stout, red-headed woman, and wore a dowdy black dress. She was from Yorkshire and spoke with a heavy, northern brogue.

"Where would you like me to leave the tray, Mr Rosen?" she asked.

"On the table, in front of the sofa, by the window, please."

Ephraim crammed one sandwich into his mouth after another. He became less inhibited after the glass of wine and spoke spontaneously to Rosen and Eisenthal.

"Mother was fond of the soundtrack of *Oklahoma*, Ian. Before the poisonous gases killed her, you should have heard her singing in the ambulance. She sang *The Farmer and the Cowman Should be Friends*. It drove the ambulance driver mad."

Rosen was sitting at his desk. Eisenthal sat next to Ephraim on the sofa. Both men were laughing. Ephraim was like his mother, in that he yearned for an audience. He, too, laughed, but unnaturally. He was no longer amused by the memory of Juliet's singing, because he knew he would never hear her sing again. He only went through the motions of laughter, to show the men he knew he was appreciated.

Rosen rose to his feet.

"If you think about it, Ephraim, *Oklahoma*'s funny without intending to be," he said. "All these euphoric men in hats, two sizes too big for them, singing about their State! Can you imagine a load of gaffers on a railway platform in Derbyshire, swaying backwards and forwards, singing, *'Derbyshire! Hey, hey, Derbyshire! 'Ain't it just smashing in Derbyshire?'*"

Rosen left the desk and went over to where Ephraim and Eisenthal were sitting. "Go and sit somewhere else, Jack. I want to sit next to him," he said. He sat down next to the boy and put his arm round him.

"*Derbyshire! Hey, hey, Derbyshire! Ain't things just smashing in Derbyshire?*" Ephraim laughed, this time with the

41

natural laughter of a healthy child.

The servant interrupted them to collect the tray. She looked baffled. She carried the tray outside to the kitchen.

"I hope all publishers don't carry on like this," she muttered to herself. "If they did, there wouldn't be any books in the shops at all."

"I've got a bag here," said Ephraim. "The sad things is, Mother needn't have gone back. I'd brought her manuscript down before she'd left the building."

"Manuscript? What manuscript?" asked Rosen, urgently.

"It's in the bag. I'll get it out for you."

"Then do so, my boy. Hurry!"

Ephraim passed a thick wad of printed sheets to Rosen.

"I know this book," he said, "Your mother showed me the first draft. I told her it had excellent potential to be a blockbuster, once she tidied it up. I recall there was no title, though."

"There *is* a title," said Ephraim. "It's printed on the front sheet."

Rosen held the front sheet to the paucity of the November light, coming through the window. The title suddenly rekindled Juliet's memory and caused a pleasant, tingling sensation in his genitalia. He felt himself go hard.

"Her titles were always first rate," he said. "Let me ask you this, Ephraim, when you buy a book, what do you look for first? What makes you decide whether you're going to buy it or not?"

"Its title."

"You're absolutely right. It's the title which hooks the reader. Most buyers don't even bother to open the books they buy. They just look at their covers."

"What *is* the title of the book, Ian?"

"Your mother chose a beautiful title, like all her others. She called the book *'Come, Sweet Sexton, Tend my Grave'*. She couldn't have thought of a better title than that," said Rosen, adding under his breath, the inaudible words, "Oh, Christ, Juliet, what a rare, fabulous woman you were! I don't know which was the finest or loveliest, the ink which flowed from your pen, or the hot juices from your body!"

The boy noticed the sad look in Rosen's eyes.

"Are you all right, Ian?"

"Sure, I'm all right. We're both suffering. You've lost a mother and my heart goes out to you. She was also a friend of mine for many years and I miss her, too. There's a lot of you in her, and you and I are united in mourning. Perhaps you'd like to write books for me, one day. You may inherit your mother's gift."

"I've never thought of it. There's a question I want to ask you both. Is it true my father was a serial-killer?"

Rosen and Eisenthal blanched. It was Rosen who answered the question in a stiff, guarded tone.

"Jack and I knew your father very well. So did Miranda and Simon White, who are going to look after you. He and your mother had been together for two years, until he died. Your father was a gentleman, Ephraim. He was kind and had wonderful manners. I'm sure he would be proud if he could see you now, with your nice manners and formal grown-up speech."

"Please tell me, was he a serial-killer?"

"In this life, there are certain things you will never know, my boy," said Rosen.

"Why do you say that?"

"Because there are things that are best left to rest. Knowledge can destroy us, and can do even worse things to someone your age."

"Even so, I must know. What *is* a serial killer?"

"I might answer that, when you tell me where you heard that phrase."

"I overheard that woman in the hospital asking someone if I were the son of William Rendon, the serial killer?"

"I'd like to see that bitch hanged," said the publisher. "I'm already looking into ways of having her disciplined."

"What does the expression mean, though?" asked Ephraim. "I want to know what a serial killer is."

"A serial killer," replied Rosen, after some anguished thought, "is a type of mischief-maker who goes into

43

supermarkets, and injects water into packets of cereal with a syringe. This makes the cereal uneatable, so it can't be sold. Hence, the cereal is in effect 'killed'."

Eisenthal looked at Rosen, who stared at the floor. He turned to Ephraim and sensed that the boy was dissatisfied with the information he had been given.

"I've already told your aunt, about the tragedy," said Rosen. "She had gone to Paris, to visit an uncle, apparently. She's taking the earliest plane she can get. She won't be more than a few hours, but you'll have Jack and me to amuse you in the meantime. Once you've settled down, you'll be a different person. You'll see. You'll be stronger and happier.

"Miranda and her husband, Simon the dentist, knew your father very well. The time will come, one day, for you to find out a lot more about him than I have been able to tell you."

"Can't you tell me the truth about him?"

"I'm sorry, Ephraim, we can't," said Rosen. "We want you to stop worrying about him. If it's of any consolation to you, Jack and I will be visiting Miranda and Simon most days, so that our friendship with you can be maintained. We want you to look upon us as uncles, and if ever you're feeling lonely, you're to ring us up. Will you promise not to lose touch with us?"

Ephraim felt temporarily more comfortable.

"Of course, I promise."

CHAPTER 7

Rosen, Eisenthal and Ephraim played dominoes as they waited for Miranda to arrive, hopefully with her husband.

It was 5.15.

"I'm nervous, Ian. I'm so sad I can't even cry," said Ephraim.

"No need to be, my boy. We've got to get you laughing, again. How about the *Derbyshire* song, which amused you so much, earlier?"

Rosen's tortured pity for the boy, and his devastated reaction to Juliet's death, had upset him so greatly that his original unhappy state metamorphosed. Somehow, his role as the bereaved boy's new friend and protector, dignified and ennobled his misery, and turned it to a twisted form of joy.

His sorrow momentarily mixed itself with happiness and a mild insanity. His shock turned to a sea of elation.

All he knew was that he had a duty to make the child laugh. He did not care whether his own pain would return but suspected it would. Apart from sex, nothing gave him greater pleasure in life, than making a child happy.

He referred, once more, to the Derbyshire gaffers on the railway platform, this time making more noise.

"Derbyshire! Hey, hey, Derbyshire!
Ain't it just smashing in Derbyshire!"

Ephraim laughed. Rosen continued to put his arm round him. He sang a different song, to the tune of a barrack-room ballad, making the words up as he went along.

"Derby-Derby-Derbyshire,
Derbyshire! Derbyshire!
Derby-Derby-Derbyshire's
Got loads and loads of coal.

45

Loads and loads and loads of coal,
Loads of coal, loads of coal,
And clothed-capped gaffers on the dole.
Gaffers on the dole.

Gaffers spitting in their hands.
In their hands, in their hands,
Hoiking up on paper stands,
Hoiking up on stands. "

Workmen lugging sacks of coal,
Sacks of coal, sacks of coal, say
'Stuff your profits up your hole,
Up your bleeding hole!' "

Ephraim raised his head and saw a man and woman standing in front of him. They had been shown into the room by Joan. She was so mortified by her employer's uncharacteristic behaviour, that she wanted to go home to bed.

The lady visiting had coiffed, blonde hair, parted at the side. Her hair on the other side, fell onto her face, making her look French.

Despite her unsupportable loss, she was wearing cheerful, gay colours, in a selfless attempt to cheer Ephraim up. Her eyes were red and her face grief-stricken.

Her husband, Simon, looked strained and disgruntled and was conventionally dressed in a dark blue suit.

Although he had originally supported Miranda's agreement to look after the boy in the event of his mother's death, he had felt uncomfortable about his commitment, soon after consenting. He had consoled himself with the assumption that nothing would happen to Juliet, and that he would not be called upon to take on the awesome responsibility.

Rosen and Eisenthal sprung to their feet and greeted them.

"Why, it's Miranda and Simon!" said Rosen. "We'll sit down and have a drink, first. Will you have some whisky?"

"That will suit us both," said Miranda. "Simon and I were

enjoying your most unusual performance. What's happened to Ephraim? He was here, just now."

"I'll find him," said Rosen.

Rosen left the room and found Ephraim hiding in the bathroom.

"Come on. You've nothing to be afraid of. Hold Ian's hand and come out into the office. Your aunt, Miranda is devoted to you. Surely, you remember how often she played with you when you went to her house. She's a sweet lady. If she wasn't, your mother wouldn't have wanted her and Simon to look after you."

Rosen led Ephraim into his office. Miranda was warm and forthcoming towards him, almost to the point of embarrassment. She was close to tears but she controlled herself. Simon was stiff, formal and polite. Ephraim leaned against his aunt.

"Oh, my poor, poor, motherless boy!" she said. "Look how he's nestled up to me, the little sweetheart."

Simon was a Harley Street dentist who had inherited a lot of money from his father and grandfather. He introduced himself, his speech clipped and staccato, like a Dalek.

"I'm Simon. I'm most struck by your resemblance to your father. We'd known him for some time. Oh, I should have mentioned this earlier, I'm sorry to hear about your mother.

"As Miranda and your mother were sisters, you should be content that you have at least one blood relation left."

"Oh, I see."

"We're having tea, sandwiches and cakes in a minute," said Rosen. "I'll tell you something. Ephraim loves honey. He can almost eat it neat."

"I'll remember that," said Miranda. "Did you hear that, Ephi?"

"Yes, thank you. Is it all right if I have a word next door with Ian?"

"That's all right with me."

"You go ahead, Ephraim. Come next door with me and we'll have privacy."

Rosen and Ephraim sat down in an empty secretary's office.

"What is it, old fellow?"

"It's that dentist, Ian. I don't like him."

"There's no need to worry. I'm at the other end of a telephone, whenever you need me. What's all this about the dentist?"

"He's so strange. I don't like anything about him."

"I don't see any reason why you and he can't become friends. If Miranda married him, he must be OK."

"He isn't OK, Ian."

"How do you know? You've only just met him. I know he's rather a funny chap, but I don't see how he could harm you."

"In what way is he a funny chap?"

"His problem is, he's very heavily into religion. He believes in God. He's a bit of a nut. I don't see there's any way he can harm you, though. Just don't get into a conversation with him about the subject."

Ephraim put his arms round Rosen, and cried.

"It's OK, my boy, it's OK. All you have to do is come to me if you're down."

"I don't want to go with them. I want to stay here with you."

"You *are* staying here, in a sense. You've got my number. You can come here whenever you want. That's just as good, isn't it?"

CHAPTER 8

It was 7.00 when the Whites' chauffeur, a devout Catholic convert, called Becket, arrived at Rosen's door in a silver Rolls-Royce, to collect Ephraim, Simon and Miranda. Becket had been with the Whites since they were married.

Miranda took Rosen aside, before they left.

"You and Jack *will* come to lunch on Sunday, won't you?"

"Of course we will, Miranda. Of course we will."

"I don't think I'd have any strength, if you weren't around," she said.

He kissed her lightly on the cheek. "You know I'll always be there for you. You look far too much like your sister, for me to be capable of letting you down."

She burst into tears and threw her arms round him. Unlike many Englishmen, he was unembarrassed and held her. "It's OK, Baby. It's OK."

Apart from the fact that he always shaved every day with an electric razor, he was looking dishevelled that day and his appearance and unwashed odour attracted her. His tie was loosened at the neck. In fact, she had never seen it knotted even when he was clean. The pale blue shirt he wore had not been changed for several days and she could tell that he had not taken a bath for the same amount of time. His unkempt state was at variance with the expensive, gold Rolex watch he wore on his left wrist and matching gold cufflinks. The contrast between extreme expense and sloth enthralled her to such an extent that she longed to be violated by him.

"You haven't changed your clothes for some time," she said, smiling.

"There are times when I don't feel like it. I don't go round like this, all the time. Only occasionally, when I get down in spirits."

"Perhaps, you should get down more often."

"Why, Baby?"

"Because you're more exciting when you don't wash."

CHAPTER 9

A log-fire in the drawing room, greeted Ephraim when his guardians brought him to their house. Miranda asked him if he wanted anything to drink.

"I'd like that. I'm thirsty," said the boy.

Simon poured himself some whisky. Miranda made herself a cocktail.

"If you come with me to the fridge, you can see what's on offer," said Miranda.

The fridge was half the size of a telephone box and so heavily stocked that it might as well have belonged in a dictator's bunker.

"What will you have?" asked Simon.

"Lemonade, please," the boy answered, in the formal tone which Juliet had taught him.

They sat down. Ephraim was so thirsty, he drank the lemonade in one go. Miranda took another bottle from the fridge and gave it to him.

They were sitting on a soft, bright green sofa which matched the other furniture in the room.

"There's something we need to know, Ephraim," said Simon, still making no effort to introduce an element of warmth into his voice, "It's about your school. What's it called and where is it?"

"It's called the Robert Browning School. It's in Vincent Square, near where my parents used to live, before my father died."

"Are you happy there?"

"No. I'm wretched in that place."

"Why is it so awful?" asked Simon.

"Word got round that my father had been in some kind of scandal before he died. I've never understood what happened. At break times, different boys ran up to me and opened *The News of the World*. They opened it in the middle pages and pushed it in my face. Sometimes, I saw the word, Rendon, in big letters. I could never read what was thrown in my face because they took the newspaper away again, and ran off.

"Many of the boys taunted me because my parents never married. I don't want to go back there."

"Nor shall you." said Miranda. "I've made a new plan for your schooling. That Browning dump, is it State or private?"

"Private."

"We'll settle the fee for the rest of your term. I think I'll be able to fit you in to a school near here as I know the Headmaster, well. It's a nice school but it's very strict. The academic standards are good. If a new boy starts mid-term, a tutor is made available for him during the holidays, so that he can catch up with his studies. If a boy is unhappy or wants advice, he can see that tutor at any time."

"What's the name of the school?" asked Ephraim.

"King David's School for Boys."

"Do you think they'll let me in?"

"There's a good chance. The Headmaster, Mr Lawrance, is a childhood friend of mine. I'll ring him and I'll ask him if Simon and I can see him to discuss your schooling."

Miranda was no longer able to hold her grief. She said she was going upstairs to re-arrange her hair. Instead, she went into the garden and wept.

CHAPTER 10

EARLIER YEARS

Juliet and Miranda Silverman were the daughters of Philip Silverman, the proprietor and owner of two widely-circulated national newspapers. The family lived in Golders Green. The sisters were close but their personalities were dissimilar. Juliet was three years older than Miranda. Though not of bad character, she was aware of her good looks and was outrageously flirtatious, mischievous and trouble-stirring. There was no malice behind her behaviour, however. Her motives were joke-orientated. She was a tease, a practical joker, and naughty but not wicked. She loved to attract attention to herself, and had passed this trait to her son.

Miranda, on the other hand, was a slightly easier child to raise than her sister. In her teens, she was shy, self-deprecating and sensitive. She lacked her older sister's wildness, compulsive promiscuity and *penchant* for mischief. Juliet kept her hair its natural colour but her sister dyed hers blonde. Juliet, was so clever, she hardly bothered to revise for her A' Levels and while taking them, drank and chased men, and passed almost all her exams with distinction.

Miranda was known by her contemporaries at school as a "swot". Despite her hard work, her grades were only tolerable. It did not take her long to realize that unless she married, she would probably end up being a shorthand typist or an office dog's body.

She was not devoid of a sense of dry humour and an ability to make intelligent conversation. Nor was she an ignoramus. She read a lot, not so much for pleasure, but to keep up with her sister, whom she admired and looked up to. She was her father's favourite daughter because of her industry, lack of mischief-making and abstinence from disruptive conduct in the household. Added to that, Miranda was docile and gentle, the latter two qualities endearing her to her father most of all.

Philip Silverman's wife was called Jeannette. She was a controversial character and a woman with a multi-facetted personality. She was besotted by her husband and was famous for the *soirées* she hostessed for him to promote his image and trade. Although aware of the time and trouble she took on his behalf, as well as the favourable results of her labours, Silverman disliked these *soirées*. While Jeannette vivaciously kept the parties going, he hovered uncomfortably in the background.

He was a workaholic, and an outstanding genius in the newspaper industry. He was an introverted and retiring man, so much so, that if he saw one of his employees entering a lift in the building containing his offices, he would step backwards, to avoid verbal contact with the employee.

Silverman sometimes dispelled his diffidence with his dry, robust sense of humour and razor-sharp wit.

He was cultured and erudite, even outside the field of newspapers He did not suffer fools gladly and showed occasional outbursts of spluttering Colonel's grumpiness but had a kind heart. It was his kindness, combined with his good manners and quiet friendliness, which earned him the reputation of a man with no enemies.

Jeannette was thought by some people to have a petulant and spoilt streak, but was dedicated, unreservedly, to her husband, whom she loved passionately. Their personalities were opposites. She had striking looks and her auburn hair caused her to look like an older version of Juliet.

Her temperament was not easy. She was feisty and boisterous to the point of being overwhelming. Her preoccupation with her husband's career, extended to his health. The strain of running two national newspapers with little sleep, caused her to live in permanent fear that he would become ill. Her anxiety veered towards obsessive neurosis and magnified her already short-fused personality.

Jeannette bitterly resented the fact that she had been denied a decent education, and spent as much time as she could on bettering her mind. She read all the national newspapers each day, to be able to discuss the intricacies of Silverman's trade with him.

Another *soirée* was taking place. Seventy guests were present. They consisted mainly of politicians, publishers, and columnists from the two Silverman newspapers, as well as writers of fiction and non-fiction.

One of the columnists was a man called Nicholas Butler. He was a tall, arresting man with a mane of thick red hair, swept back from his face. He had written an unusual article, in which he complained about a man who had bumped into him in a church, without apologizing.

The article started by examining the way in which manners in England had fluctuated from the Norman Conquest to the present day.

He dwelt on manners in Elizabethan times and commented that an apology would definitely have been forthcoming, had someone bumped into a man in a church during that epoch, of courtesy and courtly love.

The history of manners in foreign countries was also examined around the theme of what a person would do after bumping into another person in a place of worship.

Jeannette moved angrily through her thick circle of guests to speak to Butler, who was standing alone, a drink in one hand, and a plate of lobster in the other.

"This won't do, Nicholas," said Jeannette.

"What won't?"

"That article last Sunday about a man who bumped into you in a church. Who in the world is likely to be interested in whether or not you were bumped into in a church? All right. You happened to be in a church and a man bumped into you. So what?" she shouted.

Occasionally, Juliet and her younger sister, Miranda, attended these *soirées*.

Juliet, then aged nineteen, had become interested in Butler and was amused by the effect that his article had had on her fiery, excitable mother. Juliet advanced towards him, carrying a glass of champagne which had just been re-filled.

"Hullo, Nicholas," she said.

"Ah, good evening to you, Juliet. How are you keeping?"

"Well, thank you. There's no need for us to stand up, is there? Let's go and sit in the corner."

"I say, what a jolly idea!"

They sat down in the far corner of the L-shaped drawing room, out of Jeannette's eyeshot. Juliet talked to him at length, gaily and flirtatiously, mischievously encouraging him to write other articles, complaining about bad behaviour in places of worship.

Silverman was looking the other way. He was using the telephone on the table by his chair to ring up the Night Editor on one of his newspapers. Jeannette was interrupted by a gardening correspondent, a smartly-dressed woman in yellow silk.

Jeannette came over. "Juliet, darling, I really do think you're monopolizing Mr Butler, far too much. Do leave him alone and allow him to circulate round the room!"

Juliet drank the contents of her glass and asked one of the hired hands to refill it. She saw Alec Dugdale, a radio interviewer, distinctly the worse for wear.

Dugdale had light-brown hair, conventionally parted at the side, and wore dark glasses and a pale blue tie. He was sitting alone at a table. Juliet noticed that whenever a man approached him with conversational overtures, he responded with acidic personal questions. If his visitor were a woman, he made fresh, verbal advances towards her.

Juliet recognized him.

"Good evening, Mr Dugdale."

"Oh, good evening, madam, or Salome, I should say. Oops! I can't say anything, can I? You're the bloody daughter of the house!"

"So?"

"I really must ask you to leave me alone. That's all I ask, all I ask..."

Juliet heard Jeannette raising her voice to a timid-looking hired hand, a girl in her teens.

"What did I say to you about Mr Dugdale?" shouted the irascible hostess.

"Mr Dugdale?"

"Yes. I told you you weren't in any circumstances to refill his glass, didn't I?"

"I'm sorry, madam. I didn't hear you."

"In that case, you should listen. In the course of the last

fifteen minutes, I saw you giving him three great big brimming *beakers* of neat whisky!"

"Yes, madam."

"Then why did you do so, after I told you not to?"

"I didn't hear you, madam. I'm very sorry. He did keep asking me for more."

"Whether he kept asking for more has got nothing whatever to do with it. If I see you administering alcohol to him in any form, I shall make a formal, written complaint about you to your agency."

"Yes, madam."

Juliet waited for Jeannette to go to another part of the room. The radio interviewer was making beckoning gestures to her and pointing to his empty glass. She found him odious and repulsive and wanted him to humiliate himself by being sick.

She made sure that neither of her parents could see her, and filled his glass with more neat whisky. She observed the speed with which he drained the whisky, followed by the pallor which clouded over his face, the inevitable goldfish movements of his mouth, accompanied by his loud, swallowing noises. She knew what was going to happen and rushed from the room.

A procession of bustling skivvies, their shoulders draped in towels and cloths, carried clanking, brimming buckets of hot water up the stairs to the drawing room. Juliet watched them from the hall, convulsed with laughter. Conversation had stopped. She could hear her mother's irate voice, shouting, "It's all over here, dear. You're missing it out. He's done a whole lot more, over there, as well, blast it!"

It took twenty minutes to rectify Juliet's mischief. Guests mopped their brows. Silver buckets continued to clank. Windows were thrown open and loud, hissing aerosol sprays, gripped by hands rotating like overworked windmills, raged up and down the room, making it look like a steam-laden battlefield. Four brawny journalists, also somewhat the worse for wear, carried the slobbering radio interviewer down to the street and threw him into a waiting taxi.

Juliet waited for the conversation to start, once more and went back to the drawing room. Her mother was sitting on an upright, leopard-skin covered chair, talking animatedly to a younger man, sitting on the floor at her feet. Juliet was struck by his looks and by the fact that he was overtly happy in her presence and seemed to savour every word she uttered.

Miranda, whom Juliet had not seen earlier, came up to her sister.

"Where have you been?" asked Juliet.

"I've only been here for half an hour. I was in my room. I couldn't get my hair straight."

"It looks as if it's been giving you some trouble. God, wasn't it funny when Dugdale was sick?"

"You may think it was funny. Our parents certainly didn't think so. Nor did I."

"Who's that man over there, sitting on the floor?"

"I would have thought you'd know who he is. His name's Ian Rosen. He's a well-known publisher. He has offices in Paris as well as London. The books he publishes are often serialized in the two papers."

"Is he married?"

"I don't think so, but I'm sure it wouldn't make much difference to you if he were."

"No. I don't think it would."

Juliet walked over to where her mother was sitting. The lady in the yellow silk dress had joined her and was standing by her chair. Rosen stood up.

"I don't think you've met my daughter, Juliet, have you, Ian? Juliet, this is Mr Ian Rosen, the publisher. We serialize a lot of the material he brings out."

"Good evening, Mr Rosen."

"No, please. Ian."

"Good evening, Ian."

"And this is Mrs Barrington, the gardening correspondent. I'm sure you've seen her column in the Sunday magazine."

"How do you do, Mrs Barrington. I have, indeed." Juliet was unable to look Mrs Barrington in the eye. She looked sideways at Rosen, and the more she did so, the more she became inundated with lust. She had no interest in gardening and felt, instinctively that the lady, whose hand she had shaken, was a bore.

Jeannette, too, was irritated by Mrs Barrington's approach to her chair. She felt comfortable speaking to Rosen on his own. She forced herself to speak attractively and entertainingly to her husband's gardening correspondent.

Mrs Barrington was put off by Juliet's failure to look her in the eye. She turned to Jeannette, inadvertently liberating Rosen for Juliet, and gave her a list of the flowers she would be writing about in her forthcoming column. Jeannette listened to her without smiling, her eyes angrily moving from one part of the room to another.

Juliet walked away. Rosen followed her. She took two glasses of champagne from a silver salver, carried by a caterer, and handed one to him. They drained the glasses without speaking, and drank two more. They stared at each other's eyes, united by a violent, magnetic chemistry. Juliet broke the silence.

"Let's go and sit somewhere, out of sight."

"We can go where you were sitting with Nicholas Butler."

"There's no-one in that part of the room, now. I'll get two more glasses."

They sat down, continuing to look at each other's eyes.

"How long have you known my mother?" asked Juliet.

"Five years, and your father for the same amount of time. Your father is a remarkable man. I can't think of anyone who doesn't look up to him and respect him. He's very kind, isn't he?"

"Yes. He gets a bit irritable, sometimes but he's a fair man and a good father to us."

"Tell me a bit about him," said Rosen.

"He's got a very dry sense of humour."

"Yes, I know."

"I was once in bed with a cold. I wrapped myself up in towels because of the sweats. It's possible I made myself out to be a lot iller than I was. I was listening to one of Sir Winston Churchill's speeches on a ghetto-blaster. It was the 'We will fight on the beaches' speech. There were tears on my cheeks.

"My father came into the room. He thought I was making unnecessarily heavy weather of my ailment. He said, 'Would you like me to get you a Rabbi?"

Rosen laughed. She noticed his teeth which were tiny, white and jagged.

"Do you always cry when you hear Sir Winston Churchill's speeches?" he asked.

"Sometimes I do."

"How charming. How very attractive. Tell me another story."

"I play the piano but I can only play by ear. I was trying to learn the Chopin Funeral March on the piano in the library. I played the first two bars over and again. I had to get it right, but I couldn't manage it. My father came into the room to find a book. I was getting frustrated and I had my foot on the loud pedal.

"Oh, shut up!" he shouted.

"Then, there was an occasion when we were dining alone on a Friday evening. He offered to pour me some wine.

" 'I don't drink on Fridays,' " I said.

" 'Why not?' "

" 'Because I like to give my liver the day off then. Friday is always Liver's day off.' "

" 'Is it indeed?' said my father. 'Do you dress it up in its best clothes and send it to the seaside with a bucket and spade?' "

"You really are quite some woman," said Rosen. "Were you in the room when that bastard, Dugdale, evacuated the entire contents of his stomach?"

"I went out just before he did. Why don't you like him?"

"Because of his lewd conversation, mainly. He has no regard for the feelings of others, and whether they might be uncomfortable or nervous. There's no compassion in him and I can't abide someone who lacks compassion," said Rosen.

Juliet looked to see if either of her parents was nearby, and lifted her dress above her knee. Rosen put his hand on her thigh.

"Did you know there'd been a tragedy in Dugdale's life?" she asked.

"No."

"He had a daughter. She died of leukaemia."

"Christ, I didn't know that," said Rosen. "I know he has a

reputation for being good to children. Perhaps, he's not really as bad as he appears. Tell me more about your father. Is he strict about the kind of men you meet?"

"He is if he finds out about them. I was turned out of the house for a month last year, because of them. He sent me to stay at the Y.W.C.A."

"What does that stand for?"

"The Young Women's Christian Association."

"Who the hell would want to live in a place with a name like that?"

"I was thrown out."

"That doesn't surprise me. What did you do?"

"I fell out with the woman running it. I was so angry with her that I filled in a form, using her name, saying she wished to join the Communist Party. They turned up like wasps, buzzing round and round a plate. She couldn't get them to go away."

"What had the woman done to merit your extraordinary wrath?"

"She said I was a 'godless, brazen hussy'."

"Well, you are a brazen hussy. That's what makes you irresistible."

Their desire for each other's bodies was mutual. She checked, once more, to make sure her parents were in another part of the room, and leaned against him.

"If I can't go to bed with you within the next few minutes, I think I'm going to go mad," she said, aggressively.

"We can't possibly do anything in this house. You'd lose your board and lodging and I'd lose my serialisations. There's nowhere for us to go."

"Yes, there is. There's the basement lavatory. Go downstairs to the basement. It's at the end of a narrow corridor. I'll follow you in ten minutes."

Rosen got up. As he walked across the room, he bumped into Jeannette.

"Why, Ian! I was wondering where you were."

"Could you tell me where the cloakroom is, please?"

"It's the next floor down. Juliet!"

"Yes."

"Instead of just sitting there, will you please show Mr Rosen where the cloakroom is."

"I've already told him."

"It's no good just telling him. Take him there in person. Where are your manners?"

Juliet's excitement had overwhelmed her. She temporarily lost control, and spoke with the exaggerated accent of a Southern belle.

"I'll show him with the very greatest pleasure!"

"There's no need to show off."

"This way, please, Mr Rosen," said Juliet. They left the room. "There's a steep, spiral staircase leading to the basement, it's quite dangerous. When we get down there, I'll show you where it is."

The kitchen was in the basement. Servers walked up and down the corridor, carrying trays of lobster and other seafoods.

"It's that door at the end," said Juliet.

There was a lull. The corridor was temporarily empty.

"Go straight in. Don't lock the door. I'll wait for five minutes, so if anyone comes along, they'll get the impression I'm waiting, in the normal way."

She came out in a cold sweat. A server was carrying a tray of empty champagne bottles down the corridor.

"Are you all right, Miss Juliet?"

"Fine. I'm waiting to use the lavatory."

"This is the staff lavatory. I would have thought you'd prefer to use the one upstairs."

"I can't. Someone's in it."

The server left the corridor to go upstairs. Juliet opened the lavatory door and locked it behind her. It was quite a big room with a basin in the corner. She turned on both taps.

"Don't you know there's a bloody drought?" said Rosen. "Why did you turn on the taps like that?"

"I had to, just in case I scream."

He looked at the pink and white design, on the lavatory lid, showing eighteenth-century milkmaids.

"Quite some lavatory!" he muttered.

He sat down and unzipped himself. She pulled up her dress and sat astride him.

"Christ, you're not wearing any underwear!"

"I often don't." She leaned forward and kissed him on the mouth, gripping the lavatory tank to give the sex act better support.

At least twenty-five minutes passed. He put his arms round her waist.

"Are you going to tell your mother?" he asked, in jest.

"Bloody hell, no!"

"Did you bring Nicholas Butler down here, as well?"

"No."

He had fallen in love with her and didn't believe her.

"What was Nicholas Butler like when you brought him down here?"

"I've just told you. I didn't bring him down."

"I'm sure he'd have come down if you'd asked him."

"You're a fine one to talk! What is it about him you don't like?"

"The fact that he fancies you."

"How do you know he does?"

"Any man can tell when another man fancies a woman."

"I don't intend to seduce him. He's such a nice, sunny, pleasant sort of person, but that doesn't necessarily mean I want to screw him. Besides, his wife's here."

"What about your other men?"

"Stop it, Ian. Do you fancy my mother?"

"I did until I met you. You're just the same, except you're younger."

"Did she do this to you?"

"No."

"Would you have liked it if she had?"

"If I hadn't met you beforehand, yes."

"I'm so pleased she didn't."

"Why?"

"Because my father would not have liked it."

"I was hoping you'd say you wouldn't have liked it."

"Nor would I, either."

"What you said just then was very fine, Juliet. I won't forget it."

"What? About my father?"

"Yes. Your loyalty to him."

Juliet got up. She wiped herself with some tissues and turned off the taps.

"Wait there, for a few minutes, Ian. Then come back upstairs."

"When am I going to see you again?" he asked, urgently.

"Not for another ten days."

"Christ! I can't hold out that long."

"Yes, you can. We'll meet on Thursday week at 6.00 in the evening, in the reception area of a two-star hotel, called the Queen Mary, in Elizabeth Street."

"There you are Juliet!" said Jeannette. Her daughter was coming into the drawing room. "Where have you been?"

"I was feeling faint. I went out for some fresh air."

"Where in the world is Mr Rosen?"

"Mr Rosen? I've no idea."

"He's been gone for over half an hour."

"Oh, has he? It's no good asking me. I don't know where he is."

"You did show him the way, didn't you?"

"Oh, yes, I showed him the way."

"Then surely you'd know where he is."

"All I did was show him where the lavatory was. It's hardly likely I'd have gone in there with him, is it?"

"There's no need to be vulgar. Do you think he may have left the house, without saying 'goodbye'?"

"I shouldn't think he'd have done that."

"Then *where* is he?"

"I've told you. I don't know. Do you want me to go down to see whether the lavatory is still occupied?"

"Yes."

As Juliet was walking downstairs, Rosen was on his way up.

"I was getting worried about you, Ian. I was wondering where you'd gone," said Jeannette.

"I'm so sorry. I got talking to one of the caterers. She used to be my cook. We were talking about old times."

Jeannette turned to Mrs Barrington, who had irritatingly locked herself onto her once more.

"Dear, sweet Mr Rosen! He's such a wonderful social mixer, isn't he? Have you enjoyed yourself this evening, Ian?"

"Very much, thank you, Jeannette. I was able to have a short talk with Juliet. She's a particularly nice girl. She has such good manners."

"I know. That's the way I brought her up. You will call again, won't you? My husband holds a very high opinion of you."

"I hold a very high opinion of your husband. I'd like to call, again."

The Silverman household was plunged into a deadly atmosphere of gloom two days later. The printers on the weekday paper had staged a strike. The unions on Silverman's papers were governed by militants. When they staged strikes, they sometimes demanded that their views be reflected in the editorials and threatened to stop work indefinitely, if their demands were not met.

Unofficial aggression was not uncommon. It only took an unseen ill-wisher to throw an umbrella into the unfolding racks of papers, for a million copies to appear with a blank front page.

The words "printers' strike" were common parlance in the Silverman family. They were sometimes used in jest, even when newspapers were not being discussed. If a member of the Silverman family disliked someone, that person would say, "Oh, so-and-so's a right, regular printer's strike!"

CHAPTER 11

Juliet kept her appointment with Rosen at the hotel in Elizabeth Street, ten days following the *soirée*. He had arrived before her. So hopeless was his infatuation for her that he thought he would die of misery if she failed to turn up. He calmed his nerves with whisky and Valium and paced up and down in the reception area.

She arrived at 6.15, provocatively dressed. He embraced her with the desperation of a war-time husband united with his wife.

They sat down. His laboured breathing impaired his speech.

"What would you like to do, first?" he asked.

"Go out to dinner but let's go to bed and screw first," she said, vulgarly.

Juliet was as stiff as she might have been, had she ridden a horse for a week without rest, following two and a half hours of violent carnal activity with Rosen.

They were walking down the street, neither touching the other.

"Is there any particular food you like?"

"Italian's best," she said.

The restaurant they went to was nearly empty and well air-conditioned. Operatic arias and the songs of Edith Piaff (Rosen's favourite) were played quietly over loudspeakers.

Neither of them was hungry. They drank two bottles of wine and ate a few cream-filled dishes from the sweet trolley.

"I'm sorry to hear about the strike," said Rosen.

"Thank you. It's made my father quite ill. They reached a settlement in the end, though."

"Those print unionists are evil bastards," he said. "They're. They're not like the Jarrow marchers, with starving wives and children, begging for justice and the right to eat. These people are different. I know what they earn and it's not far short of their employers' wages. It isn't justice they're after. They're Nazis. All they're capable of doing is hating, and bringing people like your father to their knees."

"I know you're right," she said, "but this subject upsets me. I don't want to talk about it."

"That's OK. Shall I get you some whisky?"

"Yes, get me plenty!"

The waiter brought whisky to the table. She drank two measures in one go. She undid her companion's shirt and rubbed his chest.

"I'm crazy about you," he said. "I'm not happy about you seeing other men."

"The men I see are nothing to me."

"In that case, why can't you drop them?"

"Because I need them when you're not around."

"Is that all you feel for them?"

"Yes. You're the only one who's ever brought me out of myself."

"If they mean so little to you, and you have to see them when I'm not available, I could accept it, provided I know that you have some love in your heart for me."

"It's more than that," she said. "You're the most sexually attractive man I've ever met. Could I ask you a question? I wanted to ask it, earlier. I didn't want to embarrass you."

"What's your question, sweetie? You won't embarrass me."

"How is it you speak with a Welsh accent?"

"I spent some of my childhood in Wales. I've tried to get rid of the accent. I even had elocution lessons, but I still can't shake it off."

"I'm pleased you didn't. It's very sexy. Did you have a happy childhood?"

Rosen lit a cigarette, his eighth since he had entered the restaurant. It was often his habit to hold a cigarette in his left hand, while shovelling food into his mouth with his right. He put his arm round Juliet.

"No, I didn't," he said, in a depressed tone.

"Were you unhappy in Wales?"

"No. Not particularly."

"Where were you unhappy?"

"Sometimes, when I was in London," he said.

"What happened to you?"

"It's so unpleasant, I don't like discussing it. It wasn't

66

a whole lot of things. It was just the recurrence of one particular thing."

"What thing?"

"Do you know George Orwell's book, *1984*?"

"Of course, I do. I'm an educated woman."

"Do you remember that Room 101 contained the worst thing in the world, and that O'Brien's Thought Police took prisoners there so that they could be tortured by that thing?"

"Yes."

"Do you remember when Winston Smith was taken to Room 101?"

"I've just told you I've read the book. It wasn't a particularly easy incident to miss."

"What did Winston Smith hate more than anything else in the world, Juliet?"

"Rats. Were you exposed to them, or something?"

"No. It was more subtle than that. With Winston Smith, it was rats. With me, it's religion."

"Well, I must say, that's a right anti-climax!"

"It wouldn't be if you knew what I was put through. It was forced into every orifice of me. I couldn't take it any more. When my mother and sisters were killed in a plane crash, bastards queued up to say it was 'God's will'."

"I'm so sorry. Who did?"

"My sadistic bigoted father, for one. My school. You're not religious, by any chance, are you?"

"No. I gave it up a few years ago."

"Was it force-fed to you?"

"No. My parents aren't religious. I just decided I didn't want it any more, but I never went through all this hoo-ha, years after the event, like you. Forget it. That was then. This is now. You seem absolutely obsessed by the subject."

"I do try. The anger's still there, sometimes. It's like a cancer. I can't hack it out."

She kissed him lightly on the cheek. He put his hand under her dress.

"Christ, you're nice and wet!" he said.

They stayed there for another hour, drinking black coffee.

"How old were you at the time of the tragedy?" she asked.

"Twelve."

"And your sisters?"

"Both five. They were identical twins. I was more of a father to them, than an older brother."

"How awful! What were their names?"

"Naomi and Martha. They didn't have dark hair, like mine. Their hair was fair."

"What about your mother?" asked Juliet. "Were you close to her?"

"Yes. She wasn't like my father. She was benevolent and loving. Christ, Juliet, I want to talk about something else!"

"I'm in no hurry to go anywhere. Talk about anything you like. I don't care what."

He waved to the waiter and made impatient writing movements in the air with his right hand.

"Yes, sir?" said the waiter.

"I want the bill," Rosen said, peremptorily.

He sat in silence for a few minutes before speaking. He suddenly grabbed Juliet by the hand.

"I want to marry you," he said in the same tone he had used to address the waiter. "You're the only woman who's suitable for me. I love children. I want a lot of them and I want them to be brought up to be happy and free."

"I'm moving into a flat of my own where we can live," she said. "I don't want to commit myself to marriage, yet but I want to, one day. We'd still be living together."

"What about these bloody men?"

"If we're living together, I won't need them, will I?"

Juliet moved from her parents' house, to a flat financed by her father. Miranda stayed at home, and hoped that one day, a man would propose to her.

CHAPTER 12

Rosen and Juliet had been living together for several months. Miranda was still living with her parents whose house was frequently plunged into doom with printers' strikes. She wished she had the power to sit by her father's chair and comfort him, but all her efforts to instill optimism within him were in vain. She felt impotent and wished she could live anywhere but in that house, even if it meant her living in a youth hostel.

Juliet had a *penchant* for blood and gore and trained to become a medical secretary so that she could work in London's hospitals. Temporary medical secretarial work was rife at the time. Temporaries were paid more highly than permanent secretaries, which caused the permanents to look for other work.

It took her a month to train, and master medical terminology. A lot of the time, she was sent to a different hospital each week, but sometimes she lasted in any given hospital for up to three months.

Her agency rang her up and told her to report to the Department of Pathology at the Hammersmith Hospital at 9.00 o'clock on Monday morning.

It was here that she met William Rendon, whose cherubic looks instantly attracted her and whose unstable personality called upon her to act as a mother figure.

It was Rosen whom she loved most. Indeed, she was in love with him, but Rendon appealed so much to her maternal instinct that she softened towards him and felt she might be in love with him, as well.

After a few drinks, she lost control of herself and went to bed with Rendon. She made a habit of doing so but her guilt, caused by her deceit of Rosen, troubled her so much, that she broke down in front of him and confessed her infidelity.

"Just who is this bastard, Juliet?"

"He's a doctor at the Hammersmith Hospital."

"A lot of women fall for doctors. It's their white coats that turn them on. These doctors don't often have much intelligence beneath them. What's his name?"

"William Rendon."

"I suppose you think that's a very pretty name. Do you love him?"

Juliet burst into tears.

"I'm in love with both of you. Can't you understand?"

"No, I can't. I'm not losing you! I want you to tell Rendon, when you go to work tomorrow, that it's over between you. Has he asked you to marry him?"

"No."

"I want to marry you. If he doesn't, which is clearly the case, he's got no right to monopolize you. What does he look like?"

"Fair hair. Blue eyes."

"Have you got a photograph?"

Juliet took a photograph of Rendon from her wallet and showed it to the publisher.

"Christ, Juliet, you don't fancy *him*, do you? He's effeminate. He looks so bloody immature."

Juliet sobbed more violently.

"He's screwed up. He needs me as a mother figure."

"I'm screwed up and I need you as a sister figure, so where does that get us?"

"I love you most, Ian but this man needs me."

"Are you going to live with him?"

"Only until I sort him out."

"If I had any self-respect, I'd say I never wanted to make love to you again, if you decided to live with Rendon. I'm afraid I have no self-respect."

"Does that mean we can still meet?"

"It shouldn't, but it does. I'd rather have some of you than none at all."

"Rendon works until late at night. We can meet, earlier every weekday."

"Is that what you want?"

"Yes. I'm in love with you, more than I am with Rendon. I'd go mad if I couldn't come home to you first, before seeing him."

"The situation's not ideal but it could be worse. You've hurt me very much, Juliet. It's going to take a long time for me to come to terms with that."

Rosen went to Juliet's flat every evening after the close of his business. Most evenings, she came home to spend a few hours with him, before leaving him for Rendon.

His nerves, on waiting for her, not knowing when she would arrive, were unsupportable. He paced up and down the room, chain-smoking and eating crisps.

One evening, he took a chance and decided to surprise her. He bought caviar, smoked salmon and champagne. It was 7.00 o'clock and she still had not arrived. He took some Valium and lay down on the bed, until he heard the key turn in the lock.

Juliet was back. She was in floods of tears. He went into the living room with her, sat down and took her on his knee.

"What is it, Juliet? It's that dreadful Rendon, isn't it? It must be something he said to you. Ditch him. The bastard makes you cry. I don't make you cry."

"It's not what he said. It's what he asked me to do?"

"What the hell did he ask you to do?"

"He asked me to go to his father's house in Harley Street."

"Yes? So?"

"He took me up to the nursery. He asked me to dress up as his old nanny and go through the motions of knitting."

"Are you quite sure?"

"Yes. His nanny's dead. He wanted me to act out the role of a replacement figure."

"He's sick, Juliet. He's round the bloody bend."

"He also said he likes to pay prostitutes to sing *God Save the Queen*."

"Why?"

"I don't know."

"If I hear much more of this, I'm going to throw up," said Rosen.

"But I love him. I love you most but he needs me."

"He needs a bloody live-in nurse. Turn round. Look what I've prepared for you."

"How did you know that's what I like?"

"Never mind. I have ways of finding out certain things."

She wasn't hungry but she shovelled the smoked salmon into her mouth to please him.

"I want to make love to you, Juliet," he said.

They did so, on floors, over chairs, against walls, and when they finally wished to be gentle, they used the bed.

"What's Rendon like where this sort of thing is concerned?" asked Rosen, abruptly.

"Oh, stop it, Ian. I need you but he needs me."

Rosen did all that was in his power to come to terms with his rival's monopoly of Juliet's company and did not mind the situation so much. She was to live with Rendon for the last two years of his life.

CHAPTER 13

The Silverman sisters hadn't seen each other for a while. They arranged to meet in a pub. It was Juliet who suggested they meet. She was worried about her sister, remaining in her parents' house, and her misery caused by her failure to ease their father's suffering.

They met in a pub called *The Duke of York* in Mayfair. The pub was crowded. The sisters ordered double gin and tonics and sat down in a corner. Juliet waited for her sister to drain her drink, and drank her own. The gin made her aggressive.

"Why don't you ever go out with men? Are you a lezzie?"

"No, I certainly am not! It's just that men never ask me out."

"Have you *ever* had a man?"

"No, I'm afraid I haven't."

"Why don't you get your doctor to give you the Pill?"

"What's the point? Men don't ask me out."

"Those who wait to be asked, never get taken. Join clubs. Go out. Look for them. And get some decent clothes. Low necklines. Short skirts. Your blonde hair's attractive but get it done before you go out. You've got good features. For God's sake, Miranda, behave like a normal woman. Go out and get laid.

"There's that party at the Dorchester in two nights' time. We've both been invited. Big Sister will be there with you. Big Sister will give you a few lessons about how to pick up men, and don't forget to go to that doctor."

Miranda was ashamed of her virginity and was determined to please the sister she admired and wished she could emulate.

"There's another thing. Before we go to the Dorchester, you're to come to my flat so that I can make up your face."

Miranda had a 'phone call from her sister on the morning they were due to go to the Dorchester.

"I think I'm starting 'flu," said Juliet. "You'll have to go, alone. Ian's been staying with me for two days. William's gone to a conference. Ian's got a pretty bad dose of it. He's throwing up all the time and coughing up gunk.

"You're to come over and see us at about 6.00 o'clock this evening, like I said, and I'll do your face."

The two sisters were sitting at the dressing table in the only bedroom in the flat. Rosen was in bed. He was fully dressed because of the shivers and was wearing the same clothes he had worn when he first became ill. Juliet had started to put a thin, pale foundation on Miranda's face, when Rosen suddenly leaned over the side of the bed, holding a lighted cigarette, and was sick into a bucket.

"Must you do that in here, Ian?" said Juliet.

"Give me a break, will you. Christ, I feel rough!"

"This wouldn't happen if you had the injections."

"I can't stand injections. I hate doctors. I'd rather go through this, than have needles rammed into me."

"And I'd rather go through having you do that in the bathroom, instead of in here," said Juliet.

CHAPTER 14

Miranda was driven to the Dorchester alone by her father's chauffeur. She had made up her mind to find any man prepared to seduce her, be he attractive or unattractive, to be able to boast to Juliet that she had made a sexual conquest. She was determined to prove herself to her sister, whose teasing about her virginity humiliated and sickened her.

The chauffeur left her outside the Dorchester. Although she was nervous, his departure gave her a sense of freedom and craving for adventure. She went in and seized two glasses of champagne from a silver salver and drank them, quickly. She took two more, undeterred by the curious stare of the bow-tied waiter, bearing the salver.

Lights flashed and saxophones blared in the hot, crowded room where the dancing took place. She found the noisy room oppressive and unpleasant, but she was comfortably inebriated. She stayed in the outer room and leaned back on a sofa, having raised the bottom of her dress above her knees. She moved her head from side to side, watching the guests walk past her to the dance floor, and giggled at nothing.

"I say, are you all right?"

Miranda looked up and saw a ginger-haired man, a little older than she. He had the look of a superficial "chinless wonder". He spoke with an upper class accent. He did not smile. There was a cold, friendless, Gentile gravity in his features. There appeared to be nothing passionate, hot-blooded or forthcoming about him, simply an air of mild boredom and unpleasantness.

Miranda feared he might be the only man prepared to speak to her. She was so anxious to impress Juliet the next day, that she decided to flirt with the unprepossessing *goy*, standing imposingly in front of her.

"I wasn't all right until I saw you," she said, her speech slurred.

"Nice fair hair, eh," said the man, abruptly, still not smiling.

"Oh, do you think so?"

"Yes. What are you doing in life?"

"A' Levels. Yourself?"

"I'm at Barts. Training to be a dentist."

"Barts? Where's that?"

"St Bartholomew's Hospital. I would have thought you'd know that."

"I'm afraid I'm rather ignorant."

"So it would seem. You look nice, though, not half bad at all. That lilac dress of yours goes with your hair. Want to dance?"

"I don't see why not."

"My name's Simon White. My family owns a farm or two in Herefordshire. The Whites have been holed up there, as far back as Elizabeth's reign. I'm into cricket, if you're interested. Country life's not for me. That's why I came to London. There's a lot to be made in Medicine. I'll have rooms up Harley, one day."

"Eh?"

"Harley Street."

She fixed him with a questioning stare.

"Don't you know what Harley Street is? It's the place the medics go to when they hit the Big Time."

Miranda had no idea what he was talking about. Her thoughts centred on what she would tell Juliet.

"I'd like to go and dance, as you so kindly suggested," she said.

White's hold of her on the dance floor was close but stiff. She hated the sound of the deafening saxophones.

"I'm bound to say I don't mind you," shouted White, above the noise. "Got a place?"

"Only my parents' house."

"Where?"

"Golders Green."

"Pretty bloody far out! My parents gave me a house in Hampstead. Lyndhurst Road, if you're interested."

"Oh, indeed?"

"Oh, indeed, yes. Fancy buzzing by?"

"What for, if I might ask?" Miranda was relieved Juliet wasn't there to witness her immaturity and gaucheness.

"You want to get laid, don't you? I know it's what you wanted of me, all along. That's why you were sitting there, giggling."

"What do I say, Juliet?" said Miranda, half to herself and half out loud.

"What, dear?" shouted White.

She looked him in the eye, not an easy thing for her to do. He had icy, glacial, Russian Steppes eyes. She smiled.

"Yes, I think I'd like to visit your house," she said.

He drove her to his house in a noisy red MG, his hand on the grinding gear lever, throughout the journey. He disliked driving and hoped to hire a chauffeur, one day.

"Are you on the Pill, dear?" he asked, abruptly.

Her thoughts turned to her promiscuous, outrageous sister, once more, the brazen hussy she had tried to copy.

"I've got an IUD fitted. Saves me having to take the pills every day." (a lie).

"Aren't you a bit young for that? I'm told it's very painful for a woman who hasn't had children."

"Not at all. I can hardly feel it."

He took out a cassette, on which a Jazz festival had been recorded. He pushed it into the machine. She hated Jazz. It had always depressed her.

"Do you like Jazz?" he asked.

"Yes, very much," she said. The champagne was beginning to make her feel sick.

White's house in Hampstead was dingy but immaculately tidy. It seemed as if it were inhabited by a much older man, well set in the ways of advanced age. The walls in the poorly-lit hall were covered with photographs of cricket teams, their captains holding cups, Jazz musicians blowing into saxophones and small paintings of flowers in gilt-edged frames.

The library adjacent to the hall, contained books about Dentistry. A giant-sized tooth cut in half, in a glass case, occupied most of the desk, on which dental journals were stacked in neat piles.

"Come up to the bedroom," he said, briskly. That room, too, was dark and dour. A large Crucifix was nailed to the wall. It made her feel uncomfortable and she looked the other way. The carpets, curtains and meticulously-arranged bed cover, were of a dull brown colour. The objects surrounding the bed, could have belonged to a melancholic widower in the autumn of his years.

"Do you want me to help you take off your dress?" he asked, curtly.

She nodded. He removed his clothes, which he folded up neatly and put on a chair. He guided her to the bed and pushed her onto her back.

"Ever done this before, dear?"

She felt embarrassed and degraded. She longed so greatly for Juliet's approval and respect that she forced her sister's voice to speak through her.

"Yes, of course, I have. Dozens of times. What makes you think you're my first?"

"Because you're so young. You don't have the sophistication other women have, once they've had lovers."

She was so grateful that Juliet was absent and therefore unable to laugh at her coyness, that she cheered up. She was determined to finish what she had gone to his house to start.

His performance as a lover was weak, brief and abrupt, like his conversation.

She was half awake, "You can't tease me any more, Juliet, I've scored. I'm your equal, now," she muttered.

"Who the hell's Juliet?" asked White.

"My sister."

"Why are you talking to her? Don't you think you're a bit simple?"

"I was talking to myself."

Miranda failed to ring her parents to say she would not be going home that night. White had asked her to stay. He made her toast and coffee. They were sitting in the kitchen. It was 8.30 a.m.

"I'm a lonely man," he said, "I need a woman, knocking about the place. Do you want to move in here?"

Miranda wished to copy her sister by living with a man whom she was not married to. She felt no affection at all towards White who lacked sensitivity, chivalry and warmth, but he seemed devoid of cruelty and provided she had plenty to read, she assumed she would be content, living with him. Doing so, was a relief to her. She needed an outlet from the funereal atmosphere at home, where one printers' strike followed in the wake of another.

White felt similarly about her. All he wanted was the opportunity to share the bed of the same woman who cooked and cleaned for him.

They had lived together for three weeks. His habits, like his conversation, were drab and lacklustre, but he did not bully her or make many demands on her.

He had been going to church every Sunday and on one of these days, he invited her to accompany him.

She felt his intrusiveness threatening. "I'm afraid I'm not into this sort of thing," she said.

"You'll be sorry when St Peter refuses to let you pass through the Gates of Heaven."

"I haven't the faintest idea what you're talking about and I don't want to discuss this subject with you, again," she said. He never mentioned it after that.

Miranda's parents were dissatisfied by her decision to move in with White, but they thought that the relationship was one of mutual love, and came to accept their daughter's situation. When she introduced White to her parents, they were struck by his humdrum appearance and inordinate dullness, but respected him for his apparent seriousness, industry and sobriety.

Their relationship continued, with neither sexual nor conversational harmony, only a mechanical tolerance of each other's company. White's manner remained patronizing as the weeks went by. It was only the *kudos* of living with a member of the opposite sex on both their parts, which united them.

Miranda became pregnant. She boasted about her condition

to Juliet who advised her to abort the unborn child, because of the lack of love between its parents. Miranda knew that the only way to gain her sister's further respect, would be to defy her.

"Why haven't you introduced me to this dentist?" asked Juliet.

"Because he's so bloody dull."

"Why do you live with him, then?"

"Well ... er ... He's easy enough. He gives me the chance to get away from home, and all this newspaper talk."

"One doesn't move in with an uninteresting dentist, just because one doesn't like hearing people talking about newspapers," said Juliet, adding, "If he's the way you say he is, why are you having his baby?"

"Because I want a baby more than anything else. It doesn't matter whose."

"If all you want is a baby for its own sake, without having any interest at all in its father, you're a silly cow," said Juliet.

Miranda was even more determined to defy her sister. She let the pregnancy continue and when White proposed to her, she accepted.

White had had a conservative upbringing, and felt it would be "proper" to marry Miranda, regardless of whether he felt emotionally towards her or not.

He had been a devout man all his life, and his devotion bordered on bigotry. He feared divine punishment if he fathered a bastard.

The relationship was made bearable by the fact that they hardly saw each other, except in the evenings. Simon continued his studies and eventually graduated. Miranda spent her time visiting her friends in Golders Green.

Miranda was slightly injured in a car crash one day, and miscarried. White was driving after a few drinks too many. The accident made him feel guilty, and for a short time, he showed consideration and paternal concern for her. He began to mollycoddle her. The possibility that the accident could have been fatal, made him grateful that she was alive.

The accident and its ensuing shock had a mellowing effect on

Miranda. She matured, became a little less retiring but remained shy and quiet in contrast to her sister. She became vainer and more fastidious about her clothes and hair.

The Whites continued to live in 41 Lyndhurst Road, which Miranda modernized and redecorated. They lived like Derby and Joan for the first few years of their marriage. She never grew to love him but felt mild affection for him and accepted him as part of the furniture.

He had developed an obsessive, if unlasting love for her, which had begun after the road accident. He said very little to her, however, and his selfish trait caused him to hate other men being around her, even making light-hearted conversation to her.

*   *   *

Her previous contentment was shortlived. She became bored and oppressed. Her boredom turned to misery. She wanted her husband to have rooms in Harley Street so that she could boast about his status. This did not happen when she wanted it to. He complained of being fed up with staying in London at weekends, and repeatedly told her he wanted to get away, to stay with relatives and friends of his family in Herefordshire.

She felt happier when White was away at weekends. She invited Juliet to the house, regularly. Sometimes Rendon accompanied her. Eisenthal stayed a few times, but not as frequently as Rosen. Miranda was secretly attracted to Rosen, but hid her feelings because he was one of her sister's lovers. Though not as mischievous as her sister, a mild, playfully wicked streak in her caused her to allow Rosen and Rendon in the house at the same time, in the hope that they would come to blows. Juliet, too, welcomed the arrangement to gratify her reckless vanity.

Whenever Rosen and Rendon stayed at the same time, occasional minor friction occurred between them, but on the whole, they were coldly polite to each other. Rendon refrained from using the other man's first name, and puzzled everyone by addressing him as "Mr Rosen". Rendon remained unaware of

Rosen's affair with Juliet and was unable to understand the cause of the publisher's offhand manner.

Rosen tried to hide his jealousy of Rendon, but secretly despised him. There were times when guests visited 41 Lyndhurst Road, even when White was not away, and in his unwelcoming, irritable way, he grudgingly tolerated their presence. The atmosphere was not improved when the friction between Rendon and Rosen worsened one afternoon, after they had both drunk a lot of wine at lunch.

Miranda and Juliet had left the table and gone upstairs. It was then that the older sister spoke at length of her simultaneous affair with Rosen and Rendon.

Juliet told her sister about Rendon's myriad of peculiarities, including what she knew of his bizarre family background. She had no idea at the time that her contraceptive device would tear and force her into an accidental pregnancy with his child.

It would not be until the passage of a few years, before she regularly brought Ephraim to the house, and proudly introduced him to her friends and allowed Miranda to play, tirelessly, with him.

"Where are Ian and William, now?" asked Miranda.

"Still in the dining room."

"What, alone?"

"Yes. I find it rather funny. I'd love to overhear their conversation."

"They're probably sitting in silence, glaring at each other. Do they both know?"

"Ian does. William doesn't. Which of them do you prefer, Miranda?"

"If I had to choose between them, I'd go for Ian. He's bloody attractive. He's got everything any woman could possibly want in a man. He's so easy and natural, and there's a sort of abandoned, liberated earthiness about him. He's sympathetic to the underdog, to those who suffer. He's obviously got brains, but there's more soul to him than mind."

"I see," said Juliet. Her sister's words made her feel rather uncomfortable, more so, because she wasn't sure why. "I'm more in love with him than with William, although William's so vulnerable and unhinged, I feel I have to look after him, all the time. What do you think of him?"

"Who? William?"

"Yes."

"I find him totally incomprehensible. He's very sweet, like a teddy-bear, but, there's something a bit creepy about him. He's like someone tortured by a guilty secret which gives him childish pleasure and pain at the same time. He's a gentleman, all right. He has nice manners but he's so stiff and stilted. I don't like his speech mode, much."

"Why? What's wrong with it?"

"It's that accent of his. It seems contrived, as if he were trying to disguise his natural brogue. He sounds like a disgruntled foreigner, doing a *vaudeville* imitation of a stereotype Brit. I'm sure he's a nice man, but he's so typically and exaggeratedly English in the way he speaks, dresses and talks. Not only that, I don't like neat, tidy men with fair hair. I prefer men with darker hair who look a bit unwashed and dishevelled."

"Oh? Would you describe Ian as looking like that?"

"Yes, in a way. He turns me on the way he always wears his tie loosened at the neck. He seems like the sort of man who'd be just as happy to have sex in a barn, as in a five star hotel. I'm attracted by his mixture of spontaneous chivalry, and roughness. I wouldn't go so far as to describe him as crude, but he's a walking gift to a sexually hungry woman."

Rendon and Rosen remained alone at the dining room table. Rosen was fidgeting and staring angrily into space. Rendon was overtly sensitive to behaviour in others. As he had no idea whatever that Rosen was in love with Juliet, he wondered whether he had said something earlier to upset his companion.

Rosen leant nervously across the table and threw some spilt salt over his left shoulder. He was the first to break the uneasy silence.

"Oh, Christ, I'm out of fags!" he said, in a depressed, blunted tone.

"I say, do please take one of mine," said Rendon. "Isn't this a coincidence? I notice we both smoke the same brand. Have you always used *Benson and Hedges*?" He spoke with a pronounced upper class accent. There was something almost theatrical about the correctness and exacting delivery of his words.

"Yes," said Rosen.

Rendon separated a cigarette from the others and offered the packet to Rosen, with a deft, delicate movement of his hand, as if to a prospective employer. Rosen took it and was about to light it.

"Thanks."

"Oh, do please, allow me, Mr Rosen." Rendon offered him his initialled gold lighter, a gift from his father, and rotated its wheel with a stylish flick of the finger. An abnormally tall flame jetted into the air, irritating the publisher.

"There's no need to do that. I can do it, myself. I am not a woman," said Rosen.

"I was merely endeavouring to be helpful. I don't see why you need to be quite so disagreeable."

Rosen pulled on the cigarette and exhaled, filling the room with a cloud of smoke.

"What do you feel you have to offer Juliet?" he asked, confrontationally.

"I need her," said Rendon, taken aback by the directness of a question from a man he hardly knew.

"Do you think she needs you?"

"Well, I must say, I don't see that that's any of your business, Mr Rosen."

"What I choose to make my business becomes my business. It's also my business to mention that I don't think she's very happy, living with you, and putting up with your weird habits."

"What do you mean?" asked Rendon.

"Just a few foibles of yours I've heard about. A certain business about a ball of wool. Incidents when prostitutes have been paid by you to sing *God Save the Queen*."

"Oh, did Juliet tell you this?"

"Yes. Do you think it's either kind or fair to impose your mental problems on her? You made her cry the other day."

"Cry? Why?"

"Oh, just the little matter concerning the ball of wool, and your old nanny, of course," said Rosen, "and the other things you asked her to do."

"Mr Rosen, I am beginning to find your manner somewhat familiar. That was a private matter between Juliet and myself."

"What about Juliet's tears? Maybe, they are also a private matter between her and *myself*, since she came to me, and it was my shoulder she shed them on."

Rendon still failed to suspect Juliet's affair with Rosen, but it did not take him long to realize that the publisher disliked him, without his being able to understand why. He replaced his former sweetness and gentility with a sudden outburst of hostility. He gave an exaggerated imitation of Rosen's Welsh accent.

"Weel, eed be better off, getting back to them nice green valleys, boyo."

Rosen thought it would be undignified to involve himself in a cheapening verbal brawl. He forced himself to smile at Rendon. It irritated him to have to look at the face which Juliet ogled whenever she saw him.

"Oh, I say, my dear chap! A jaunt to the jolly old green valleys would be absolutely topping, hey what. Gung ho's what I say to that, my dear fellow!"

Rosen was angered by the fact that he had found it more difficult to mimic Rendon's Sloaney vowels, than Rendon had found it to use a perfect, comically-delivered Welsh accent.

He had finished the cigarette which Rendon had given him, and his pride prevented him from asking for another. He was about to rise to his feet.

"Juliet's not happy with you," he said, "Would you be prepared to let her go if I were to stand up and sing *God Save the Queen*?"

"I fail to find that a particularly poignant witticism, Mr Rosen. Juliet's not shackled to me. She can go whenever she wishes."

"It's not that easy," said Rosen. "She's a very moral, public-spirited girl, who feels you'd become more mentally ill than you are already, if she were to leave you. You are taking advantage of her kindness and goodwill, which makes her feel obliged to stay. You're aware of that. That's why you're a selfish bastard."

Rendon stood up. "I do not wish to continue this conversation with you, in the light of your most singular insolence and hostility. I intend to take a short walk in the garden to see what has come into blossom."

"Christ, how effeminate!" muttered Rosen.

He went upstairs to the guest room which Juliet was sharing with Rendon. He locked the door, undressed and got into bed with her.

"I wish you'd leave that bloody Rendon fellow alone. I can't bear his face. I can't stand his speech and his odious Sloaney intonation," said Rosen.

"What does it matter, Ian? He's a basket case and all I do is keep him intact. I've told you before, my love for you exceeds my love for him."

The more frequently he heard this argument, the more he forced himself to accept her affair with Rendon, and there were occasions when he was able to appreciate his rival's sweet, gentle manner. He was also beginning to see a lot of Juliet in her younger sister and felt protective affection towards her, mixed with extreme sadness for her, because of her loveless marriage.

CHAPTER 15

The pedestrian childless lives of the Whites were unchanged over the years. Miranda had few reasons to respect her husband, but she appreciated the *kudos* of being a successful dentist's wife. He had done well in his field and had found elegant rooms in Harley Street. Before his increase in status, she had underestimated his professional abilities and had given up hope of being what she referred to as a "Harley Boy's wife".

It gave White pleasure to be seen walking up and down the Street on his way to and from his rooms. His pride caused his boorish behaviour to worsen. He became overtly pompous and conceited and even more intolerant of the feelings of others.

It was during this period that Ephraim was brought into his house, when, as an almost sinister coincidence, he received a letter from his father's solicitor, belatedly disinheriting him for having married a lady raised under Judaism, and even more upsettingly, for failing to bring a child into the world after years of marriage.

The father had even reclaimed the Deeds of the house.

Miranda's parents were incensed by the behaviour of White's parents and bought the house for her, letting her have the Deeds.

Instead of being thankful, White was deeply embarrassed by the Silvermans' kindness. His embarrassment turned to shame and resentment, which manifested itself in cutting remarks, many of them anti-Semitic, and violent outbursts of temper.

CHAPTER 16

BACK TO THE PRESENT

Maria, a Philippino servant, knocked on the drawing room door. She was answered by Miranda.

"Is it tomorrow that Mr Rosen and Mr Eisenthal are coming to lunch?" asked the servant.

"Yes. Did you hear that, Ephi?"

"I did hear it. I'm looking forward to it," said the boy, with characteristic stiltedness.

Ephraim was tired after dinner.

"I'll show you your way round the house before you go to bed," said Miranda. "You can't stay up too long. You're exhausted."

It took her fifteen minutes to show him round the big, multi-gabled house, before taking him to his bedroom. The room was warm and its walls covered with paintings of sailing boats. There was a double bed in the centre.

We'll have to get you plenty of clothes this week, won't we, Ephi?" said Miranda.

"You're very kind," said the boy, mechanically.

"If there were no kindness in this world, there'd be no joy, no trust and no laughter. Your mother won't rest in peace until she knows you are happy."

* * *

The Whites were eating breakfast in dressing gowns. Ephraim was wearing the clothes he had worn the day before. The abrupt change in his life and surroundings had confused and depressed him. It was because his mind was clear after sleep, that these unpleasant feelings invaded him so vehemently.

Miranda sensed his discomfort and stoically hid her grief.

"I know it's strange being in a new place after all this has happened to you," she said, "but you're going to settle down and be happy. Are you looking forward to Ian and

88

Jack coming to lunch?"

"Yes. They've been very good to me," said Ephraim, stiffly.

"I know how it feels. I went to boarding school as a child. I thought I'd never settle down but my sad mood passed. In the end, I didn't want to leave."

"Where were you at school, Miranda?"

"A public school. Wycombe Abbey. We had a music teacher who wore a bright yellow wig. Every time she conducted, it went askew. Miss Copplestones was her name. The more we baited her, the angrier she got.

"All that's nothing in comparison with the trouble we gave the Latin mistress. Her bedroom was just over our dormitory, and was approached by a creaking flight of stairs.

"A gentleman used to visit her bedroom every night." (Ephraim smiled). "The acoustics were so bad, we could hear every sound in the bedroom."

Ephraim laughed, another sign that he had inherited his *penchant* for insalubrious humour from his mother.

"Do you *really* think your conversation is suitable, Miranda?" asked White, unpleasantly.

She ignored him.

"You should have heard it. The creaking bedsprings made so much noise, none of us could sleep.

"This woman's name was Miss Taylor, Miss Stephanie Taylor. We made up a poem and one of us wrote it on the study room wall:

> *"Please put a penny in the old man's hat.*
> *Miss Taylor's having triplets in the upstairs flat."*

Ephraim was laughing, convulsively. White remained cold and glared at the boy, as he listened to Miranda's mild ribaldry. Miranda hoped so passionately that the boy's mood would continue to improve, that she felt pain within, a pain which was almost worse than her grieving for her sister.

"Was Wycombe Abbey a nice school?" asked Ephraim.

"It was a nice school and a very good school, but some

things about it, weren't ideal. There was too much of an emphasis on religious devotion."

"Is there anything wrong with that?" asked White.

"Yes. There was so much of it, I don't think any of the girls were believers, when they left."

White got up to get a drink. "Children ought to be made to be devout, to save their souls."

"From what?"

"Hell, stupid!"

"Hell? I'm not letting Ephraim be exposed to that. I'm bringing him up to feel free and happy."

White sat down and read a transcript of a debate at the British Dental Association, about whether electric toothbrushes scoured the enamel off molars. Ephraim, whose non-belief had been instilled in him by his mother, had begun to dislike him even more.

"Tell me more about your school," said Ephraim.

"It was a good school from the point of its high academic standards, but it fell short on compulsory, current events classes and there were no end of term exams in current events, either. There should have been newspaper-reading classes, instead of all this religion. Newspapers are an integral part of anyone's education. Do you know, Ephi, that when I was fifteen, I didn't even know who the President of the United States was?"

"Didn't you, really?"

"No. I feel very strongly about that. That's why I'm going to encourage you to read newspapers, every day. It's not only a question of knowing the news. We should have been made to study each newspaper's editorials."

"Editorials? What are they?" asked Ephraim.

"An editorial is a passage of prose which states what a newspaper thinks, how it feels."

"How can a newspaper have feelings? It's only a newspaper, after all," said Ephraim.

"Put it this way. If there's a major front page story, for example, a terrorist bomb, killing hundreds of people, a member of a newspaper's editorial staff is paid to give an opinion about the event, and that opinion represents that newspaper's policy."

"Do all newspapers have the same policies about things which happen?"

"No, of course, they don't. Newspapers are like humans. They are all different. They tell the same stories, but the journalists who interpret them, all think about them in a different way."

Maria came to the table to speak to Miranda.

"Mr Rosen rang to say that he and Mr Eisenthal had been held up outside London and might not be able to get here for lunch."

Miranda was saddened, but her feelings were more for Ephraim than herself. She failed to come to terms with the unlikelihood of their coming and sat with her head lowered.

CHAPTER 17

They came, however. The road into London was clear. Eisenthal and in particular, Rosen, forced themselves to be jubilant throughout lunch, in order to cheer Ephraim and Miranda up. Rosen's contrived manic behaviour amused Ephraim and Miranda, but it had an irritating effect on White, who was becoming bored with his trade as a dentist. His negative feelings were not improved by the fact that one of his patients had bitten him two days earlier.

After coffee, he offered his guests cigars and port, with unwelcoming reluctance, as if he resented their presence in his house. Ephraim sensed his attitude and disliked him even more.

"Would you mind doing me a favour, Ian?" asked Miranda.

"For you, Baby, anything!" said Rosen. "Name the favour and I'll do it."

"Will you sing that song which cheered Ephraim up so much, the other day?"

"Of course, I will. Do you want me to sing it, Ephi?"

"Yes, please."

"OK, come and sit next to me. Which one do you want to hear, the first song you heard, or the one which is a bit rude?"

"I like the one which is a bit rude, best."

White got up, to go upstairs for his rest. He looked contemptuously at Rosen.

"Why don't you ever do your tie up, properly?" he barked.

"Because women find it sexy, when I don't."

"Even so, it's a bit much when you visit someone's house, isn't it?"

CHAPTER 18

The extroverted publisher and the solicitor played games with Ephraim all afternoon and did not leave the house until after tea. White had woken from his rest. He, Miranda, the two guests and Ephraim, sat at the dining room table, to discuss Juliet's will.

Eisenthal did the talking.

"You have come into an enormous inheritance, Ephraim," he began.

"Oh, he likes to be called 'Ephi'," said Miranda.

"I'm so sorry — Ephi. Now, to come to your mother's will. She has stated that all money saved from the earnings of your father, the late Dr William Victor James Rendon, together with the money he inherited from his father, the late Dr Rowland Rendon, is to be passed to you.

"Not only that, the money gained from the sale of number 79 Harley Street, the late Dr Rowland Rendon's house, and the money gained from the sale of Dr William Rendon's flat in Vauxhall Bridge Road, is also to be passed to you."

"How much money am I getting, altogether? How many pounds?" asked the boy, peremptorily. He felt at that moment that he would be happier, had his mother lived, with no money to be passed to him at all.

Eisenthal jolted. He quoted a massive overall total. Even the Whites were surprised.

"I'm afraid I have to give you a very serious warning, Ephi," said Eisenthal.

"Oh?"

"Does the name, Kate Rendon mean anything to you?"

"Yes. My mother mentioned her to me just before she died."

"What did she tell you?"

"I was so frightened, I didn't really take it in."

"Then hear me well, and don't ever forget what I say. This person's full name is Kate Alice Rendon. She is your aunt and apart from Miranda, your only surviving relative. She is a danger to you. As I understand it, you have never met her. She is the daughter of Dr Rowland Rendon and his second wife, Dolly, who is also dead. Your father, Dr William Rendon, was the son of Dr Rowland Rendon and his first wife, Mary, which means that your father was Kate Alice Rendon's half brother.

"There was a particular bond between your father and Rowland Rendon. The latter died by his own hand.

"I understand, through my long friendship with your mother, that, her sister, your aunt Miranda, was exceptionally close to her and that she gave her intricate details about Rowland, your father, and other members of the Rendon family.

"Much of the story is extremely strange, but your mother wanted you to know of every happening in the family, when you were old enough to understand."

He turned to Miranda.

"Do you know all these details? Did Juliet tell you about the origin of the strange bond between Rowland Rendon and his son, William, and the matter of Kate Rendon?"

"Yes, she did. Towards the end of her life."

"Did she tell you about William's childhood?"

"Yes."

"Did she tell you why Rowland Rendon took his life?"

"Yes. She was terribly upset because his son, William, her common-law husband, was involved with his father's suicide."

"Did she tell you that his suicide was triggered off by the sound of someone singing the National Anthem?"

Miranda started to giggle nervously. "Yes," she said.

Eisenthal turned to Ephraim.

"I'm so sorry, my boy. There's something I have to say in private. Would you mind leaving the room, just for a minute or two? Then, you can come back."

"I don't mind. All this legal talk is boring me absolutely shitless, anyway."

Rosen stifled a laughing fit. Miranda struggled to keep a straight face. White was appalled to hear such language on the lips of a twelve-year-old boy.

Miranda put her hand on his shoulder and led him to another room.

"Come with me, Ephi. It won't be long."

"This, for me is the most difficult part of the matter," said Eisenthal, once Miranda had taken her seat at the table, once more. "Did Juliet tell you about the three women William murdered in the nursery at his father's house?"

"Yes. I knew, anyway. It came out at the Inquest."

"Did she tell you why he killed them?"

"Yes."

"She gave evidence at the Inquest, didn't she, after William's death?"

"Yes. I was present. It was later on that day that Juliet found out from her doctor that she was pregnant. The scan, performed later, showed a male foetus."

"Did Juliet know about the murders before William's death?"

"No."

"Did she know there was something seriously wrong with him?"

"Yes, but it wasn't until after his death that she found out something particularly strange about him, from a relative — not a blood relation. It was that thing which made him commit the murders," said Miranda.

"Are you prepared to admit that Juliet confessed to you that William, Ephraim's father, was a serial killer?"

"Yes."

"Did she tell you she was in love with him, up to the time of his death?"

"I think she was still very excited by him but she was becoming wary of his wild, excessive behaviour."

"Did she ever tell you she meant to leave him?"

"She mentioned it on one occasion but I'm not sure of the extent to which she meant it."

"In what way did she say his behaviour had been wilder than it usually was."

"There'd been this incident in Harley Street."

"What incident in Harley Street?"

"William took Juliet to his father's house, shortly after his death, and asked her to accompany him to a room which had once been his nursery. His nanny had died there suddenly when

95

he was eight years old, and he asked Juliet to dress up as his nanny, and knit. Although she did so, William went off his head in some way and told her that if she didn't leave the house, she was in danger of being killed."

"Killed by whom?"

"By William's other self," said Miranda.

"So he was definitely psychotic?"

"Juliet thought he was."

"How did she feel when she heard she was having a baby?"

Rosen seemed restless and was chain-smoking throughout the meeting. He had already developed a dislike for White and felt uncomfortable in his house.

"Can't you cut your bloody smoking down?" snapped the fiery dentist.

"What kind of host are you, if you complain about your guests smoking? Let's say, I'm a bit on edge. Suppose we leave it at that."

"Come on, Simon," said Eisenthal. "Leave Ian alone. Now, I've got to repeat my question, How did Juliet feel when she heard she was having a baby, Miranda?"

Rosen was unable to take his eyes off Miranda's crossed legs.

"She had conflicting thoughts which upset her so much that she consulted an analyst. Part of her wanted another William. The other part was terrified that the child would inherit the gene and become a psychotic, like his father. Sometimes, she came here, sobbing hysterically, saying she wanted an abortion, but did not have the heart to go through with it. There were times when she was happy and looking forward to having the baby. As the pregnancy progressed, so did her optimism and her awareness that she was going to be a mother."

Eisenthal tapped his cigar ash into the ashtray. White didn't appear to mind him smoking and made no comment.

The lawyer turned to Miranda. "Could you please go and fetch Ephi, for me. As far as I am concerned, this business is far from being finished."

"Come and sit in the empty chair next to me, my boy,"

said Eisenthal.

"When we spoke earlier, do you remember me talking about your aunt, Miss Kate Alice Rendon?"

"Yes, yes, yes! What about the old bag?"

Eisenthal cleared his throat.

"Your grandfather, Dr Rowland Rendon, made a will a few months before his death. He stated in it that all his money, including his property, was to go to his son, in other words, your father, and that after your father's death, it was to go to whatever lady was living with him at the time of his death."

"Bloody hell! You've told me this, already."

"I know I'm boring you, but you *must* be told. Your grandfather left nothing to his daughter, Kate Rendon. I've been told that she is following your case, intensely. When she heard your mother had died, she apparently started to make enquiries. She is trying to find you and wants to get her hands on your money.

"She is not above prostituting herself to raise money to hire a private detective. She is a woman of fearsome and relentless determination. She will not give up until she gets what you have lawfully inherited. I think you'd better have a look at this. Look at it very carefully."

"What do you want me to look at? Get on with it."

"Don't be rude, Ephraim," said White.

Eisenthal handed the boy a coloured 6″ x 6″ photograph of a woman in her thirties. She had shoulder-length, blonde hair, cold, penetrating eyes, a small, slightly retroussé nose and premature furrows on either side of her mouth.

There was a streetwise, hardness about her face, combined with a look of hatchet-wielding cruelty. The picture was passed to White, Miranda and Rosen.

"That photograph makes me shudder!" said Miranda. "It's not just a case of her looking hardened by circumstance. This woman looks evil. Would you have a copy made, please, Jack?"

"I can do that for you. I'll get more copies, for anyone who wants them. Now, Ephi, you're to take what I say, seriously. Do not, in any circumstances, speak to strangers. Do not open the door. Do not answer the 'phone. How will he get to and from school, Simon?"

"I won't know until tomorrow whether he'll be going to the school of our choice. If he does, Becket, the chauffeur, will take him there and pick him up at the end of the day. I can't see how he should have problems with strangers at all, with that kind of lifestyle."

"There's something else worrying me," said Eisenthal.

"Perhaps, it's the time," said White.

"I know Ian and I have stayed here quite long enough but I want another word in private with Miranda before we leave," said Eisenthal.

"Very well," said White. "Go out into the hall, and get it over with as soon as you can."

Eisenthal was pacing up and down in the hall. Miranda was standing with her arms folded.

"What is it, Jack?"

"There's the problem about telling Ephi the whole story, Miranda. There's a risk that he might be told by someone at his school. When are you going to tell him who his father was?"

"For God's sake, Jack, the boy's only twelve years old. He's simply not of an age to hear dreadful things like that. "

Eisenthal walked nervously to an umbrella stand and tapped the floor with one of the umbrellas in it.

"He's advanced for his age," he said. "If I didn't know his height, I'd mistake him for a sixteen-year-old. He's got an extraordinary way of saying things. One moment, he's prim and proper like an ex-Etonian. Another, he uses the coarse language of the gutter."

"That comes from my sister, not his father," said Miranda. "William was the perfect gentleman, when he wasn't bumping people off. You knew what she was like, just as I did. For all her literary brilliance and erudition, she could be very crude."

"You've got to tell that boy," repeated Eisenthal.

"Tell him what?"

"Who his father was. Don't you understand the urgency and the risk of him hearing it from someone else? Tell him, now,

Miranda. Tell him, tonight."

"I'll talk to Simon about it. If he thinks it's all right, I'll tell him."

Ephraim was sitting on the drawing room floor late the following afternoon. He was feeling sad and missing his mother. White was reading one of the Sunday papers.

"Hullo, Ephi."

"Hullo, Miranda. I apologize for some of the foul language I used in front of the two gentlemen."

She ignored his words.

"I want you to go upstairs and soak in a nice bubble bath before dinner."

"All right. I'll do that. May I wash my hair, as well?"

"Yes, of course. You don't need to ask permission to do something like that."

Ephraim suddenly turned to his aunt. "Do you think Simon dislikes Ian?" he asked.

The question startled her.

"Perhaps, you'll find out the answer to that question, one day," she said.

CHAPTER 19

"A word, please, Miranda," said White.

"God, those men were here for a long time! Jack is just about tolerable. It's that Rosen fellow I can't abide. I can't stand the way he keeps looking at you as if there were something between you. I don't feel comfortable with him. I can see how he'd be attractive in a raw sort of way, and repellant at the same time. There's a wild, louche electricity about him, a sort of commonness, a contemptible earthiness, and yet he inspires so much love, everywhere he goes, particularly in women and children."

"He's good company. He's got a very kind heart."

"Is there something between you?" the dentist asked.

"No. But even if there were, I'd still say 'no'. The subject's boring. As soon as Ephraim goes to school, he's at risk of hearing who his father was. I know he's only twelve but he's precocious for his years. I've decided to tell him after dinner. Whatever you say, please don't tell me you disagree with me."

"Bloody women! They all say that," said White.

"Of course, it's all right for someone like me to tell him. He trusts me," she said.

White threw a log on the fire and stoked it. He was brooding about Rosen and wondering whether Miranda had deceived him. He remembered Juliet's and William's frequent visits to the house, and William's tendency to sit on the floor, staring at the fire.

"I suppose you'd better tell him, Miranda," he said.

Neither the Whites, nor Ephraim were hungry, and much of the food the cook gave them, was left uneaten.

Ephraim returned to his place on the floor in front of the fire. The Whites joined him. Neither of them had sat on the floor for some time. They felt awkward and ridiculous.

"Nice blaze, isn't it?" said White, stiffly, breaking the long silence. He felt stupid after uttering the words and was relieved that the unpleasant task ahead would be Miranda's rather than his.

"Whenever your father came here, he used to sit on the floor, looking at the fire, just as we are, now," she began. She put her hand in front of her mouth and uttered a discreet, little cough.

"How well did you know my father?"

"Oh, very well, quite well, that is."

"Did you like him?"

"Of course, I liked him."

"What's a serial killer, Miranda?"

"A serial killer is a person who kills, well, not just one person, but a number of people. That's right, isn't it, Simon?"

White was rolling a cigar backwards and forwards in the palms of his hands.

"Yes, yes, indeed. That's about right."

"My father was a serial killer, wasn't he, Miranda?"

"Whatever your father was, he was a very sick man who did not know what he was doing."

"I want a direct answer. Was my father a serial killer?"

"You'd make a good barrister, Ephraim," said White, without smiling.

"I must know, Miranda. Was he?"

"Yes, Ephi. He was a serial killer."

"Why?"

"If I told you the whole story, you'd be able to understand why he turned out that way. I'm afraid it's going to upset you. I decided you were to be told, in case some stranger tells you."

"I don't care what you tell me," said Ephraim. "I'm used to anything. I used to read my mother's books. If you can read one of them without fainting, you can face any adversity in life. Go on, tell me. I know a few of the things which Jack spoke about, Rowland Rendon, his son, William, my father and Kate Rendon, who's after the money. Is there a lot else I should know?"

"There is. I'm afraid it's not very nice."

"In that case, I want to hear it."

"Your grandfather, Rowland Rendon, was a very rich man. He had a younger sister called Kate Alice, and he adored her. When she died of pneumonia at the age of fourteen, his

101

mourning took the form of twisted rage. He named your wicked aunt after her.

"Kate senior had a passion for things which were red, and after her death, your grandfather disliked the sight of anyone wearing the colour.

"He trained to become a doctor and years after he qualified, he met a woman, known as a clinic clerk, at the Maudesley Hospital. Her name was Mary. They got married."

"What's a clinic clerk?" asked Ephraim.

"Oh, just some dog's body who collects patients' files, so that the doctor can refer to them when the patients visit him."

"That certainly doesn't sound very interesting!" said Ephraim.

"Nor indeed is it. Rowland took her out, one evening. They had had quite a lot to drink. He took her off somewhere, I think the back of his car, and, well, caused her to become pregnant."

"Do you mean he fucked her?"

Miranda felt as if she had been lashed across the face with a wet towel.

"Ephraim! In no circumstances whatever, will I tolerate the utterance of that disgusting, vulgar word in this house! Where did you hear it being used?"

"My mother was always using the word. I apologize for having offended you when you are being so kind to me. I had no idea it was a word one was not supposed to use. I thought it was just like any other word."

"Well you thought wrongly, didn't you?" said White. "Miranda, continue the story."

"Rowland wanted a daughter to replace his sister. He was furious when Mary gave birth to a son. That son was your father and Rowland named him William Victor James.

"Rowland couldn't bear the sight of him. He hired a nanny and confined her and her charge to the nursery wing at the top of the house.

"Rowland was in a permanent state of foul temper. He was cruel to Mary, mentally and physically. He beat her. Her fear of him caused her once good looks to disappear. She twitched all the time, fearing another attack. She became mentally ill and hideously ugly. The uglier she became, the crueller he was to her."

"Jesus, what a shit!" exclaimed Ephraim.

"Language, boy, you've been told, before," said the dentist.

"I'm sorry, Simon. I didn't mean it."

Miranda continued.

"Your father was spending all his time in the nursery with his nanny. She was the only security in his life. He adored her and was completely at peace in her presence.

"One day, he saw her making clothes out of red material. The colour enchanted him. He told her it was the only colour he wished to wear, so she dressed him in red, every day. Your father had obviously inherited Rowland's sister's passion for the colour. He couldn't bear the sight of it, and he told the nanny he would sack her if he ever saw your father wearing red again.

"She obeyed him. The boy only wore red in the nursery. One Remembrance Sunday, your father and his nanny were sitting, watching the Whitehall parade on the television. The nanny was knitting him a red sweater.

"So enraged was Rowland, that he sacked her. She had a bad heart and the shock to her system was too much for her. She collapsed and died. Rowland walked out of the nursery, leaving your father alone with the dead nanny. He was only eight at the time. He lay by her side, willing her to come back to life, and was still with her at the end of the parade.

"Rowland came back to the nursery, for some reason and found his son lying on the floor. The National Anthem was being played. He kicked your father in the ribs and ordered him to stand up."

"Did he stand up? I certainly wouldn't have," said Ephraim.

"He had no choice. Rowland continued to be cruel to him throughout his childhood and often beat him, savagely. After the nanny's death, he locked him in the nursery and only let him out to go to school.

"Then things gradually began to change. Mary's body was found in the Thames. Her death was thought to be suicide.

Rowland fell in love with his pretty, young secretary whose name was Dolly. She had a positive effect on him and turned him into a much nicer, kinder man. He felt terrible remorse about his treatment of your father and treated him, decently.

"Rowland married Dolly, and a bond of love was formed between him and your father.

"Rowland and Dolly had a daughter called Kate Alice, as you know, but Rowland was so guilt-stricken about his former cruelty to your father, that he later made a will, leaving everything he had to him, and making her little more than a pauper."

"Surely, that's not really fair," said Ephraim. "I'm so rich, I won't know what to do with what I've inherited. Don't you think it would be nice if I shared some of it with her?"

"I understand what you're saying," said Miranda. "What you don't see is how evil she is. A share is not enough for her. She wants the whole lot.

"Your father went to medical school. He trained at the Hammersmith Hospital. It was at about this time that something happened to his personality. His memory of his childhood was too much for him. He started to go out with girls, some of whom he took to his father's house. He persuaded them to accompany him to the nursery. He needed to invoke his nanny and sometimes asked these women to dress up like her and sit in the chair, knitting.

"Your mother was the only one who agreed to do as he wished. I think the others refused. Without even knowing he was doing it, he killed these women and left their bodies in an alcove in the nursery.

"He confessed his actions to his father. Rowland was so desperate to atone for his former cruelty, that he covered up for him. He did everything he could to persuade your father to stop this habit, but failed.

"One night, your father picked up two prostitutes and brought them to the nursery. He asked one of them to sit, knitting while singing the National Anthem."

Ephraim had a giggling fit.

"Was he particularly fond of the tune, then?"

"I don't think so. He lay on the floor and asked the other prostitute to kick him and insult him and order him to get up and stand to attention, just as Rowland had done."

"These women, did they do as my father asked?"

"I've a feeling they were difficult. It's understandable that they would have been disinclined to co-operate.

"How much did he pay them?" asked the boy, his general attitude one of amusement.

"I've no idea."

"What happened to them?"

"Your father killed them. In all, he killed three women."

"I must say, I don't think three's a very big number. Think of how many people Hitler killed."

"I know you find some of this funny, but are you upset by what I've told you?" asked Miranda.

"Not in the least. He may have killed three women, but he still brought me into the world. The only thing which makes me sad is the fact that I never met him. It would have meant so much to me to have a father."

"I know, my boy, I know."

"One evening, can I be driven to the red light areas to see prostitutes, waiting to be picked up?"

Miranda lit a cigarette. White looked downhearted. He resented being obliged to have any part in the boy's upbringing.

"You're only twelve, Ephraim," said Miranda. "Twelve-year-old boys have no business, being interested in prostitutes."

"I don't want to pick them up, Miranda. All I want to do is look at them. Sometimes, my mother took me, on evenings when she wasn't writing."

"Your mother?" asked White, in a flabbergasted tone.

"Oh, yes. She told me all about them, what they were asked to do, how much they were paid, everything."

"I think it's time we all went to bed," said White. "This conversation has gone on for long enough."

CHAPTER 20

It was 4.00 o'clock in the morning. Miranda was woken by a strange, wailing noise. It took her about a minute to realize that the sound was coming from Ephraim's room and that he was singing. His voice became louder and louder, as if he were trying to drive something away. The singing was accompanied by the sound of weeping.

"I'd like to say a word for the farmer..."

Miranda got out of bed and put on her dressing gown. Her sudden movement woke White up.

"What the hell's going on?" he demanded.

"The poor boy's having a nightmare. I must go to him at once."

"Do you think mollycoddling's going to make a man of him?"

She ignored the question. Ephraim was lying on his back, still singing with his arms crossed in front of him, like a cadaver.

"Are you awake, darling?"

"Yes."

"You were having a nightmare, weren't you?"

"No. I've been awake all the time. That's not all. I heard a woman singing outside. I don't think I was imagining it."

"I think you were. What was she singing?"

"This song to the tune of *The Minstrel Boy*."

"What were the words to the song?"

"They were,

'The Rendon Boy to the Grave will go
If I don't get my money.'"

Miranda covered her head with her hands.

"You're making that up, aren't you?"

"No. It's what I heard."

"I'm afraid I don't believe you. If you're thinking of Kate, she wouldn't be able to climb up to your window. You shouldn't tell tall stories. It's naughty."

"But it's true," said the boy. "It's not only that. I have nightmares a lot of nights about my mother being wheeled off and me never seeing her again."

As they were speaking, Kate disappeared from outside the house, with the agility of a cat-burglar.

"I know, my boy, I understand. Whatever you feel now, it won't last. That's the most important thing you need to know. Do you want to come and sleep in our bedroom?"

"No, Miranda. Simon wouldn't want it."

"I'm not concerned with what he wants. You come first. You always will."

"It's all right. I'll stay here. Perhaps, I shall get off to sleep. I'm sorry I woke you."

CHAPTER 21

White had been pacing up and down the bedroom like an expectant father, when Miranda had been talking to Ephraim.

"Sit down on the bed. I want to talk to you," he said.

"What about?"

"That boy's going to be nothing but trouble," said White. "It was really high-handed and presumptuous of Juliet to dump him on us like this."

"You've forgotten, we reached a legal agreement. Would you have preferred it if he'd been put in an orphanage?"

"Of course, I would. What a bloody daft question!"

"I thought at first you would grow to love him, just as I have. You really are a hard, cold man." She breathed in, as if intending to add to her statement.

"Unlike Ian Rosen? That's what you were about to say, wasn't it?"

"That wasn't what I was going to say, but at least, Ian's warm and loving towards him, and able to make him laugh, when laughter and love are what he needs."

White ran his hand impatiently through his hair.

"That man is only capable of arousing laughter by the use of lewd language and the repetitive singing of that common, vulgar song."

"What common, vulgar song?"

"You know very well. That dreadful song I overheard about the unemployed in Derbyshire, spitting into their hands."

"I think it a bit far-fetched to say that references to spitting are either common or vulgar. It is vulgar to spit but not to speak or sing about someone else spitting."

"That's not really the point. Next Sunday, Jack can come over for lunch but I don't want Rosen here. In fact, I don't wish to see him again. Any man, prepared to publish Juliet's sickening, repulsive, black-humoured books, is most certainly not welcome in my house."

"Juliet was my sister, Simon. Besides, what knowledge do you have of books? You can barely even read, except your

108

crappy dental journals. You've never read the classics. I don't even think you know any Shakespeare, let alone the works of famous French or Russian novelists.

"You are a professional philistine and could not possibly hold any respected authority on those who have had the courage to handle the written word. Juliet's works are among the finest ever written. Her handling of the English language and its very intricacies are unique. Dozens of journals regarded her manipulation of her pen as that of a colossus. It was her pen which made her a giant."

"I'm not getting into a literary discussion at this bloody hour of the night," said White. "All I'm saying is, I don't want Rosen coming here."

"Are you jealous?"

"A man like that is too crude to merit another man's jealousy. I'm sickened by the way he keeps looking at you."

"It's not my fault if he looks at me."

"It is your fault because you condone it. It's partly because you feel something for him. I may not be literary but I'm no fool. It's also a matter of your extraordinary vanity."

"How can you expect me not to be vain? I'm a woman! It is only natural that I present myself well. Do you expect me to receive guests in a dressing gown, my face unpainted and my hair in curlers, like a music-hall caricature of a Glaswegian battered wife?"

"Shut up! Has something been going on between that Rosen fellow and you?"

Miranda turned away from her husband.

"Well, has there?"

"No," she answered quietly.

"Are you quite sure?"

"Oh, yes, Simon. I'm quite sure."

"I hope you are, because if you aren't, there is absolutely no limit to what I will do. I can give you an example of what I am capable of, when someone is foolish enough to cross my path. Not long ago, one of my patients, a rather insignificant little man, started an affair with my secretary whom I was a bit soft on. He thought I had no idea what was going on. He needed some heavy dental work done. I gave him a general anaesthetic and I took all his teeth out."

Miranda felt a sudden drop in her blood pressure. Her love for her husband had died and had turned to dislike, ever since she had first noticed his coldness towards Ephraim.

"You're a bit vicious, aren't you? It's not a likeable trait in a man. Viciousness is a feminine characteristic. I tend to associate vicious men with homosexuals."

"There's another thing I hate about Rosen and that's his horrible Welsh accent. Where did he get it from, if he's from Golders Green?"

"He spent some of his childhood in Wales, with his grandmother. Anyway, his accent's only just noticeable. I find it rather attractive."

There was a long pause. The unhappily-matched couple got into bed.

"I'd much rather talk about Ephraim and his quality of life, than about you, Simon. You say you think he's 'going to be nothing but trouble.' Would you mind explaining that?"

"For a start, I don't care for his cavalier attitude towards his father's crimes. He seems to regard them as a joke. I'm also repelled by his unwholesome interest in prostitutes. As for his repeated use of disgusting language, he makes me feel quite sick."

"How unfortunate for you to be so easily nauseated, Simon! He had no idea that 'fuck' and 'shit' were swear words."

"No doubt, that mother of his used language like that in his hearing, all the time. It's such a shame you weren't able to persuade Juliet to have an abortion when she kept coming here, asking you for advice."

Miranda sat up and rested her weight on her elbows. She could feel her body shaking.

"How dare you!" she shouted. "That boy is more to me than you are, or were, or ever could be! If I ever witness an act of cruelty towards him on your part, I'll put a knife in you, Simon White, and I don't care if I have to rot in Holloway for it!"

White did not take her words particularly seriously, and attributed her behaviour to that of a stereotyped, hysterical woman. He hoped, for the sake of his own pride, that she was not having physical relations with Rosen. He rolled onto his side and spoke once more, his voice unintentionally raised, his mind oblivious of the thinness of the wall, dividing his room from Ephraim's.

"I'm sure you know that that little brat's father was the biggest necrophiliac in London. He's going to turn into a replica of his father. I can smell William's genes in him."

"Don't be disgusting!" shouted Miranda. So intense was her venom that she felt herself capable of killing her husband then, had she had a weapon to hand.

CHAPTER 22

White put on an act of being reasonably friendly towards Ephraim during the next few weeks. He and Miranda accompanied him to the study of Mr Lawrance, the Headmaster of King David's School for Boys.

Lawrance was well-known for his overtly verbose way of expressing himself, to such an extent that he might have just stepped out from Queen Victoria's reign. Ephraim sat solemnly in one of the study's upright chairs, with his head lowered, his hands clasped on his knee and his golden curls tumbling loosely onto his face.

"Have you any Latin, Ephraim?" asked Mr Lawrance, kindly.

"I did a little Latin at the Browning, sir. I am afraid I am not very good, though, because I only studied it for a few months. That is, before I left the school when my mother died."

"What a smart, grown-up way, you have of speaking, young Mr Rendon. It is your kind that turn into industrious, professional men."

"I am indeed indebted, sir," replied the unusually precocious twelve-year-old."

Mr Lawrance raised his eyebrows and lifted his arms in an expansive gesture of bemused affection. White smiled, rather snidely. Miranda beamed with adoration and pride.

"Tell me, young man, and this is about your Latin. Could you give me some idea how much you know. How far have you got, eh?"

Ephraim remained motionless in his chair. He did not even move his head while speaking. Mr Lawrance had already formed the impression that his pupil-to-be was most singular.

"We'd all been told to learn *Bellum*. Well, that was the afternoon, just before the fire which claimed my mother's life. I went straight home. After my mother had provided me with my evening meal, I retired to my room, where I committed it to memory."

"Indeed? Please understand. I know you've had a dreadful

112

time and I'm aware how difficult things have been for you. Would you mind reciting *Bellum* for me?"

"No. I do not mind at all, sir."

"Then would you care to do so?"

Ephraim recited both the singular and plural of *Bellum* in Latin, and, without being asked, said which each case meant in English.

"Very good, my boy, very, very good. However, the Latin class for twelve-year-olds, although divided into three streams, is quite some way beyond *Bellum*. This means you will have to have extra tuition in Latin from our tutor, Mr Penman. Is there any subject, Mr White, that you feel Ephraim could get by without, so that he could bring his Latin up to date during that time?"

White looked at the timetable which Mr Lawrance had given him. He was disinterested in his foster-son's education and was more preoccupied with the possibility of his wife cuckolding him with Rosen.

"I dare say the boy could easily do without carpentry classes," he said.

"I see. How do you feel about singing classes?"

"I'm afraid Ephraim likes to sing from time to time, sometimes even during the night. His voice is pretty terrible to behold. It would be a trifle more bearable for all concerned, were he to be taught to sing in an acceptable manner. I feel, he must attend his singing classes."

"Very well, Mr White. As carpentry is only taught once a week, one hour's tuition on a weekly basis, will not be enough to bring his Latin to the level of the other boys. Could you choose one other subject which you feel is unnecessary."

"I certainly don't see why he should learn French," said White, assertively. "There's no need. Because of all this Euro rubbish, every French child is forced to learn English. What's the point of an English child learning French?"

"Are you quite sure that is what you want, Mr White?"

"Quite sure. No two ways about it."

Mr Lawrance turned to Ephraim.

"Did you learn any French at your last school?"

"No, sir. I don't speak any French at all."

He scanned the large, imposing Headmaster, with his innocent wide eyes. "I do know one thing, sir, and that's something my mother told me. When a gentleman approaches a particularly low-grade type of whore, the whore often says, 'How do you like your French?' Perhaps, you'd care to tell me what that means, exactly, sir."

Mr Lawrance whitened and gaped at Ephraim, looking like an owl waiting to be fed. He ripped his glasses off, in a subconscious attempt to blur his vision of reality.

"Your *mother* said this to you?" he spluttered.

"Oh, yes, sir. She and I often talked about this sort of thing, and I saw passages in the books she'd written, too. My mother used to take me out some nights. She took me to red light areas in London. She loved to point out the whores to me. It was ever so fascinating, sir. Do you do what most of the other gentlemen do, after hours? Do you go up the disorderlies?"

Mr Lawrance was beginning to think his encounter with Ephraim was no more than a dream. He responded mechanically.

"What do you mean by your use of the words, 'up the disorderlies'?"

"You must know, sir. Do you ever frequent disorderly houses, or brothels as they are sometimes called?"

Mr Lawrance was under the impression that his pupil-to-be was actually mad. It did not occur to him that his mother had been the only person he had been influenced by in his earlier life. He assumed that his insanity was due entirely to his inheritance of his notorious father's genes.

Because he was an exceptionally kind man, he decided he would help the boy in any way he could, to find peace and sanity as well as academic knowledge. He turned to White, then to Miranda, and to White, once more.

"Mr and Mrs White, would you mind leaving me alone with Ephraim for a few minutes? I feel he will be less likely to show off, once he is deprived of his audience. Not only that, he may be maladjusted at the moment, but he has a most brilliant mind, which, if shaped by the right hands, will turn into the mind of a genius when he becomes a man."

"May I ask you a question?" said Miranda, who had been silent, until then. Even in her grief, she had found it hard to keep a straight face, when Ephraim was innocently questioning the conservative Headmaster about whether or not he consorted with prostitutes.

"Yes, certainly, Mrs White."

"Does corporal punishment take place in this school?"

"No, of course, it doesn't. Surely, you should know that corporal punishment in schools has been illegal for quite some years."

"I see. Is there any bullying in the school? Ephraim's such an obvious misfit, I fear he might easily be targeted."

"We are most strict about bullying, Mrs White. We have prefects who patrol the grounds and corridors all the time. No-one knows who they are. They are like plain-clothes policemen. If a boy is caught bullying another boy, either physically or psychologically, we summon the guilty one's parents to the school. We then ask all the boys to assemble in the school hall, and we expel that person, in the presence of the other boys, the masters and the offender's parents.

"This is a most unpleasant, psychological punishment, and all the boys here are told that this is the procedure when an act of bullying takes place. In fact, we haven't had a case of bullying for well over ten years, now. That's because of every boy's fear of the punishment he would receive if he broke that rule."

"What about ordinary discipline?" asked White. "If a boy disgraces himself, how is he taught a lesson?"

"We set about this in a way which not only corrects the error, but also improves a boy's education. We make them learn things by heart — material of a mind-improving nature."

"I see, Mr Lawrance. We'd like to leave you for a few minutes with Ephraim, so that you can get to know each other better, alone," said White.

"That will be no problem. Go and sit in my secretary's office next door. I'll ask her to make you tea."

115

Ephraim had not moved at all since he had been asked to sit down. His arms, legs, hands and head had remained so motionless that an onlooker would have mistaken him for a waxwork. It was only his eyes which had moved, straying from Mr Lawrance to Miranda, but not once focusing on White.

Man and boy were alone in the room.

"Ephraim, do you think you could try to relax a bit," said Mr Lawrance. "I am not going to be unkind to you and there is no need to be tense or frightened."

"I am not frightened, sir. I am not frightened of anything. I miss my mother very much. I never met my father. I love Mrs White almost as much as my mother, but Mr White isn't always very nice to me."

"In what way, not nice, Ephraim?"

"He snubs me a lot of the time. He's very cold and unloving. I overheard a ghastly row one night between him and Mrs White. He said he wished I'd been put in an orphanage. He also said my mother should have aborted me. He shouted to her about my father in rather a nasty way, but I can't remember exactly what he said. I did what I could to erase it from my mind."

"What interests me most about you, is the advanced way in which you speak," said Mr Lawrance. "You use the sort of words a fully-grown man would use. Have you any idea why that is?"

"I think so," said Ephraim. "My mother encouraged me to read a great deal. She once said she wanted me to be a writer, like her. It's true, she didn't like me reading her books. She said I wasn't old enough. It was because she told me not to read them, that I often got up in the night and read sections from them."

Mr Lawrance turned round in his swivel chair.

"I'm sorry to learn that you have a tendency to be disobedient," he said, sternly. "When you come to this school, it will be expected of you to obey your teachers, implicitly. When you are told to do something, you will do it. Likewise, if there is something you are told not to do, in no circumstances are you to do that thing, whatever it may be."

"I understand you entirely, sir, and I will do my utmost to ensure that I give you complete satisfaction in all ways and at all times."

"Good," said Lawrance. "You've just said your mother encouraged you to read a lot. Do you enjoy reading?"

"Yes, sir. It's only from books that I meet the people I wish to know. They take me into another world, away from Mr White, and away from my mother's death."

"Tell me a bit about the books you've been reading. What books were they?"

"I couldn't name all of them, sir, but I shall endeavour to name a few. They were *Jane Eyre*, *Wuthering Heights*, some of the books written by Charles Dickens, Samuel Richardson's *Clarissa* — oh that was all set out in the form of tedious letters, mainly written by a most unfortunate young woman who was pressurized by her family about whom she was to marry. I disliked the book, and, had I written it myself, I would have been deeply ashamed of having bored my readers beyond oblivion."

Mr Lawrance stared at the child, aghast. He was beginning to fear him. Instead of simply finding him singular, he saw him as being unnatural, threatening and surreal.

"What other books have you read?"

"Certain of Thackeray's works. They do not really appeal to me, because they appear superficial. Jane Austen — I don't like her, either. Fielding's *Tom Jones* and Defoe's *Moll Flanders*. I like those better. I've also read *Dr Jekyll and Mr Hyde*, Stevenson, that is."

"Yes, I do know that, actually. Perhaps you'd like to tell me a bit about that."

This time, it was Ephraim who suddenly looked frightened, rather than his thunderstruck superior.

"If it is all the same to you, sir, I would be terribly grateful if you would refrain from asking me to speak about the contents of that book."

"Why?"

"Oh, please, sir." The child looked like a dog about to be

savagely whipped.

"Go on, Ephraim. Why do you refuse to tell me about that particular book?"

Ephraim burst into tears.

"Oh, no, no! Please, I beg of you, sir. I'm even prepared to go down upon bended knee!"

"You shall not have your own way. You shall obey me."

"I will not be persecuted," the boy suddenly shouted, adding the words "fuck you!" still not appearing to accept that he was using a forbidden word, and continuing to assume that, because his mother had done so, he, too, was entitled to do so, whether he had been reprimanded for it, or not.

"Ephraim," began Mr Lawrance, "You will gain absolutely nothing, nor respect from anyone, if you use that word. You will be shunned. Those, who love you, or come to love you, will cease to do so. I know that love is something very important to you. No-one in the world, and I repeat, no-one, will love you if you utter that word. There are certain people who will pretend to love you, simply through the pleasure of making a fool and laughing stock of you, but their love, so called, will be false. Secretly, they will despise you."

"But, sir, my mother used the word all the time, and she loved me, even when I used it, myself."

Mr Lawrance wiped his brow with his handkerchief.

"I understand what you say. Your poor mother has passed away. She was a wonderful mother to you and you will never meet anyone quite like her, again. She was unique. Shall I say, she was an exception to what we call a rule. I know she would not have liked it, if you emulated one particular thing she did, and in so doing, made enemies.

"I wouldn't go so far as to say your mother was at fault. All I am saying is that, wherever she is, now, she passionately wants you to be loved, and if, by refraining from the use of that word, you stand a fairer chance of being loved, I can assure you, she would not wish you to use it. Do you understand?"

"Yes. I understand, sir. I apologize for having made you angry. I will do my best not to use the word, sir."

"Good. I'm sure you will. However, I wish to get to the bottom of the matter concerning that book, and will do so. These two characters, do they remind you of Mr White, who might be nice to you sometimes, but not at other times?"

"No, sir."

"Then why were you so upset when I asked you about it?"

"Well, it's my father, sir. All the things I've heard about him are either very good or very bad."

"You are *not* your father, Ephraim. You are you. You have the right to choose between good and evil. You are so grown up, I'm sure you know the difference between right and wrong. You know when you are doing right and when you are doing wrong. Do you want to do right?"

"Yes, sir. I want to do right."

"And are you ever tempted to do wrong?"

"If you mean stealing, inflicting cruelty and other similar things, I think I can say that I would not do any of these things."

"You are already showing promise, Ephraim. There is one thing you must never do, not because it is wrong but because it is incorrect."

"What would that be, sir?"

"Never, ever again, are you to address me in an impertinent manner. During our conversation, you have been unacceptably impertinent to me, more than once. I am senior in rank to you, and for that reason, you will always defer to me and address me respectfully and courteously.

"Once you are officially a pupil in my school, you will be punished if you are rude, either to me or to any of the masters. You know very well, you will not be beaten but you will still be made to accept psychological humiliation, to ensure that you behave in a reasonable, proper and decent manner."

"I will do absolutely everything in my power to ensure that I please you every day in every way, sir."

"I think we've covered most of the important issues, Ephraim. Do you have any questions?"

"Well, the thought keeps coming into my head. It's about my mother. On her way to the hospital, she said something to the

119

ambulance driver." Ephraim could not conceal a secretive smile because he longed to be asked what she had said, knowing that he himself would be exempt from blame.

"I know very well what your mother said to the ambulance driver," said Mr Lawrance. "In fact, I was informed of the matter by Mrs White. There is absolutely no point in repeating her words to me. I dare say you wish to shock me but my function in your life is not to provide you with an audience. It is to make a man out of you."

"All right, sir."

"Before you leave, are there any further questions you wish to ask me? If there are, they must be intelligent questions, and not stupid, attention-seeking, or discourteous questions."

"There is just one question, sir, and to the best of my knowledge, it is an intelligent question," said Ephraim.

"Well, what is your question?"

"It's well, er ... it's ..."

"Yes? Get on with it. I haven't got all day."

"What is a necrophiliac, sir?"

Mr Lawrance had already risen to his feet. He suddenly felt faint and allowed himself to fall into his leather-studded chair.

"A necrophiliac, Ephraim, is plainly and simply, a filiac which is necro. There is nothing whatever that I can add upon this matter, and I would be grateful if you would leave my study, find Mr and Mrs White, who are in my secretary's office next door, and ask them to come in."

"May I go, then, sir?"

"You must learn to listen when a superior addresses you. I have already told you to go, and that means you are to go. It doesn't mean that you are to remain in this room. It means that you are to remove yourself from this room."

"Goodbye, then, sir."

"Goodbye, Ephraim."

Ephraim was confused and humiliated, following his conversation with Mr Lawrance. He realized that he had formed some reverent, awed respect for his future Headmaster, something he had never experienced towards any other individual, even his mother. He wondered whether he would ever be able to confide in him and gain some awareness, through talking to him, about precisely who he was and how he would ever live with himself.

The Whites returned to Mr Lawrance's study.

"I'm pleased to have the opportunity of talking to you both, once more, Mr and Mrs White. Would you kindly sit down."

"Let's have it, Mr Lawrance. What's your opinion of this boy?" asked White, curtly.

"He is a boy of quite extraordinary brilliance, Mr White. He has the mental age of one far older than his years. I feel that under my strict supervision, he will be shaped into a man who might even attain global fame as a genius. That could take the form of a man of letters, a scientist, a discoverer, a politician or even a towering figure in the field of medicine.

"That is if he is not led astray and the risk of that happening is of some concern to me. Unless he is watched, it will not be easy to control him. It is true that he is a prodigy and is almost as well-read as a university undergraduate, but there has been certain, shall I say, mutating material fed into his brain, and he is unable to tell the difference between the significance of unwholesome and unnatural knowledge, and advanced academic knowledge."

"My wife and I have been hanging about here for some hours, now, Mr Lawrance," said White, his voice raised. "Suppose you come to the point and stop being so damned pompous."

"This matter doesn't call for rudeness, Mr White."

"All right. Perhaps I shouldn't have said it that way. What do you mean by such words as 'mutating material fed into his brain', and 'unwholesome and unnatural knowledge'?"

"You, yourself witnessed an example. I'm much more concerned about something he said to me once you had left the room."

"Get on with it then, man! What did he say to you?"

"Don't be so rude, Simon," said Miranda.

"Mr White," began the Headmaster, "As I understand it,

Ephraim had been living alone with his mother until the fire. I don't think he had much contact with other children, because, as you told me in the beginning, he could not get on with them as they teased him about his father.

"From his mother, he went straight to you and your wife. Has he been in contact with anyone you know since staying in your house?"

"Oh, God, Mr Lawrance, what are you on about, now? Is this some bloody diphtheria enquiry?" said Simon.

Miranda gave him a hard kick in the shin.

"Your manners are vile, Simon. You ought to be ashamed of yourself. I apologize for his behaviour, Mr Lawrance. I think I should be answering the questions, now."

"Mrs White, have you ever taken Ephraim out to meet other people? Has anyone visited your house."

"Ephraim's not been out, Mr Lawrance, but he enjoys the company of two gentlemen we have known for some years."

"And who are they?"

"Ian Rosen's one. He's a publisher. He brought out all Ephraim's mother's books. The boy is particularly devoted to him and is to a great extent, emotionally dependent on him."

"I see. What about the other gentleman?"

"That's Ephraim's mother's solicitor. His name's Jack Eisenthal. I've known both of them for a considerable amount of time. They are good men and have been exceptionally kind to Ephraim."

"And there's been no-one else?"

"No. Perhaps you'd be good enough to tell us what Ephraim said to you when he was alone with you."

"He asked me what a necrophiliac was."

"Did you tell him?"

"Indeed, I did not. I wish to know how he came to be exposed to this word."

Simon touched the knot of his tie and moved it like a self-important senior civil servant.

"Come on, man! It's obvious where he picked up the word," he said. "He got it from one of his mother's filthy books."

"Now, just you wait a minute, Simon White," said Miranda. "And, if you know what's good for you, you'll refrain from speaking ill of that boy's mother. She was also my sister.

"I can explain exactly what happened, Mr Lawrance, and will do so. My husband and I had a violent argument in our bedroom one night. Ephraim sleeps in the room next to ours and the wall, dividing the two rooms is thin enough to hear shouted words. I, in fact, was not doing any of the shouting. It was my husband. He was out of control."

"What was he shouting about?"

"Ephraim's father. His exact words were, 'That little brat's father was the biggest necrophiliac in London.' It was from my husband that the boy heard the word, but to escape blame, he has accused innocent parties, such as Ephraim's dead mother, of polluting his mind, when in fact he is the author of the very pollution he complains of."

"What also concerns me," said Mr Lawrance, "is the fact that you and your husband are his lawful guardians, and it would be an understatement to say that your relationship is extremely stormy. How can you expect him to be mentally stable if you quarrel in this horribly unpleasant manner, and shout about such matters as necrophilia? If I am to take responsibility for his education, it is essential that his mind be at rest. If it is not, how can it possibly be fed with academic knowledge?"

Miranda looked briefly at Simon, then she faced Mr Lawrance.

"I am boss in my household. There is a special bond between Ephraim and me. My husband is not an easy man but he can't upset him. Ephraim has made it plain that he doesn't like him. They ignore each other."

"Even so, I would appreciate it if you would restrain your husband from making statements about the boy's father and exposing him to words which he should most certainly not be allowed to hear. A considerable amount of my time has been wasted by the use of that word and its consequences," said Mr Lawrance, his tone exhausted.

"I know. Don't blame me. He was responsible."

"You really are a right little trouble-maker, Miranda," said White.

"I'm glad I am. It's my duty to protect that boy's psyche. You haven't been any help at all, except on the evening we first brought him home. I admit you were reasonable towards him, then. It never lasted. You're a cold, harsh, heartless bastard, and I'm proud of being able to say this before a witness."

Mr Lawrance got up and opened a window, and walked slowly back to his chair.

"Mr and Mrs White," he began, "I am running a school with intent to turn boys into gentlemen. You have given me enough trouble, today, and it is only my belief in Ephraim and my hope for the development of his remarkable mind, that I have agreed to take him.

"I am *not* running a disorderly house! I am not running a mortuary! I am not a funeral director, and I am of far too lofty a status, even to be spoken to about necrophilia, let alone to be questioned about it by a twelve-year-old boy.

"I have had enough of both of you, and, to use the language to which this boy has been exposed, I am ordering you to piss off! Ephraim's waiting in the secretary's office next door. Take him away and have him delivered here on Monday morning."

Becket drove White, Miranda and Ephraim away from the school. Miranda was depressed and embarrassed by her husband's behaviour and asked to be dropped outside her hairdresser's.

As White and Ephraim walked up the gravelly path to their house, White noticed something peculiar which startled him.

"Go straight in, Ephraim. Don't hang about, waiting for me. I'm just going to look at the shrubs." The boy went in. White left the path to see the thing startling him, more closely.

On the soggy grass, on the right of the path, the letters K.R., at least six inches high, had been engraved deeply into the ground, possibly with an umbrella handle.

He knew who had done it but was so indifferent to Ephraim's welfare and safety, that he twisted his foot on the two letters, making them illegible. He knew that if he had not done so,

Miranda would have called the police.

Sometimes, he wished secretly that he could kill Ephraim, but his strictly-brought-up moral instincts reminded him that murder, particularly of a child, was not "quite the thing", even if the murderer escaped undetected. He also feared that he might go to hell as a result of his obsessively-held religious beliefs.

There was one isolated occasion when he was tempted to stray from his fear of celestial punishment. Ephraim was standing at the top of a steep flight of stairs, without holding the bannisters, musing. White was standing behind him, thinking he was alone. He raised his hand and was about to push his palm into the child's shoulder, hoping he would fall to his death and break his neck.

Just before he was about to do so, Miranda came out into the corridor.

"What are you two standing there like that for?" she asked.

"Oh, I was waiting for Ephraim to get a move on. He was just standing there and I'm trying to get downstairs," said White.

CHAPTER 23

Miranda had been sitting on Ephraim's bed, reading *Tom Brown's Schooldays* to him.

"Haven't you got anything else?" he asked.

"What do you want me to read to you?"

"I'd like you to read one of Edgar Allan Poe's poems to me. I derive quite a degree of comfort from them."

"Has anyone ever told you that your father loved the works of Edgar Allan Poe?"

"Yes. My mother."

"It means you've inherited one of your father's genes. You've got his looks, as well but I've already told you that."

Ephraim ignored her words.

"I want you to read *The Raven*, please, if you would be so kind. I know it's unusual to read to boys as old as twelve, but I'd like you to, all the same."

"This is even more extraordinary. That was one of his favourite Edgar Allan Poe poems. Have you read it, before?"

"Yes. Many times. I know it so well, I can recite most of it."

A feeling of uncanniness descended on Miranda.

"Your father knew the whole poem by heart. Before I get it out for you, would you mind explaining exactly what you said to Mr Lawrance when you were alone with him?"

"We talked about, well, just general things — why?"

"You asked him a particular question, just before you left, didn't you?"

"Yes. That's right."

"What did you ask him?"

"I just asked him what a necrophiliac was. He answered me but I didn't understand what he said. I didn't want to go on asking because he said the matter was closed. He's a very strict man, isn't he? I think he has a kind heart, though."

"In what way did he answer your question? It is very important that I know."

"If I tell you what he said, will you promise to explain what his words meant?"

"That would depend on what he said. The sooner you tell me, the sooner you will know whether I'll be prepared to make things clearer," said Miranda.

"His exact words were, 'A necrophiliac is plainly and simply, a filiac that's necro.'"

Miranda had a nervous giggling fit.

"What did Mr Lawrance mean? What does the word mean?" bleated the boy.

"A necrophiliac, Ephi, is a person who is unwell in mind. He does a certain thing, without knowing that that particular thing is, well, unwholesome."

Ephraim sat up and rested his weight on his elbows.

"Well, what does that person do?"

"He tampers with dead bodies and does things to them that, in normal circumstances, a man would do to his wife when they want a baby."

"Does that mean he strokes them, fondles them, kisses them and gets inside them?"

Miranda looked away from the boy.

"Yes. That's about right."

"I heard Simon shouting at you the other night. He said my father was the biggest necrophiliac in London."

"Simon had no business saying that. Anyway, since he doesn't know any, how can he have the authority to say who has done this sort of thing the most?"

"Did my father do that, Miranda?"

"Yes. Yes, he did. Don't think less of him for it. He wasn't well. The cruelty he suffered during his childhood, unhinged his mind."

"Do you think he did this because he knew a dead body would not reject him?"

"That's a very intelligent question, Ephi. No-one really knows."

"Did he do it to those three women after he'd killed them?"

"I don't know if he did it in all three cases. Are you upset?"

127

"No. Not upset. I just think the whole thing's so terribly funny."

"Why?"

"Because the sight of someone doing that to a motionless body, obviously not reacting or responding, would seem absolutely hilarious to an onlooker."

"At least, it's nice to see you are so easily amused. Do you want me to get the book?"

"Oh, yes! I want to hear *The Raven*, even more than I did earlier."

Miranda went to the drawing room, where White was sitting, and poured herself some brandy, before going to Ephraim's room.

"You've caused more trouble than you know, you bastard," she said. "Ian thinks you're a shit, as well. I've told him what you did. I'd rather be with him than you, any day."

"Not a chance, Miranda. It's true I can't bear you but I'm not suffering the indignity of letting him take you from me. I'd rather kill him than let that happen. What have you come down for, anyway?"

"For something to read to Ephraim?"

"Tips for stiff-fuckers' sons, I suppose?"

Miranda went up to White and slapped his face, with such ferocity that she hurt her hand.

"I'll nail you, Simon White! By God, I'll nail you, one way or another!"

White tried repeatedly to light his cigarette but his lighter had run out. He tore a strip of skin from his thumb, which put him in an even fouler mood than he had been in already.

"Go to the little brat, then! Just don't hang about in here, because there's a chance I'd do something which would land me in Wormwood Scrubs."

CHAPTER 24

The White family's chauffeur was known as Becket. No-one appeared to know what his first name was. He played a major part in Miranda's life, since her move to Hampstead, and later would play a significant role in Ephraim's life. The circumstances of his personal life, culminating with his motives for becoming a chauffeur, were extraordinary. One could describe his life and his eccentricity as unique.

Becket was a very English sort of man, with dark, brooding features, a stern mouth and haunted almond eyes. He came from an upper class family, and was a personally convinced, and devout religionist. The most remarkable thing about him was his chosen station as chauffeur to a wealthy family, when he was actually the son and only child of the late Lord Chancellor, the Earl of Blexted, a brilliant wit, scholar and statesman, who had been born, simply, as Richard Becket.

Becket felt painfully inadequate, following his father's death, shed his inherited title, immersed himself even more fervently into his religion, and converted to Catholicism. Although he was extremely erudite, his self-esteem was pitifully low because he felt that, no matter what he did, he could never live up to his father's image. He adopted his servile rank to punish himself.

He dedicated all his spare time to the betterment of his mind, in an attempt to achieve academic excellence. He was ignorant of the supreme fineness of his mind, and was misguidedly convinced, in failing to match his father's achievements, that he was a man of no worth.

His knowledge of certain subjects, and in particular, of Russian literature, was of an extreme that might even have overtaken the erudition of an Oxford Don. Although his knowledge was almost boundless, he saw its attainment as being no more than a coincidence and permanently chastised himself for not equalling his father.

He was happily married to a bouncy, but morally very strict woman, called Betsy. They had a son called Peter, aged sixteen, and he was continuously pressurised by his father into reading intellectual material.

Becket, Peter's father, was a dry-humoured, dry-tongued, melancholy man who sometimes indulged in harmless, mischievous jokes, when he was not rocking backwards and forwards in his chair, in a desperate attempt to shake off his gloom.

It was his soft streak which endeared him to those who knew him well, and who tended to accept, with good grace, the displays of boorishness, brought on by his depressive fits which sometimes ate into his brain like a slow cancer.

He was sentimental towards animals, of which his favourites were Collie dogs. He was the owner of such a dog. It sensed when its master's soul was trapped at the bottom of a well. It would spring onto his lap and lick the tears of hopelessness from his cheeks.

Becket was a masochistic lover of the film, *Lassie, Come Home*, about a dog touring Yorkshire, in a pathetic attempt to be re-united with its previous owners in Scotland.

Each time he saw the film, Becket wept. Peter scanned the TV Times most days, and if he found that the film would be showing, he made a point of staying out, so horribly embarrassed was he by the sight of his father weeping.

Becket's multi-facetted personality caused others to see him as something of a character, even in his younger years.

It was the time of his Confirmation. As he was kneeling, being confirmed, a ping-pong ball fell from his pocket, and went bang bang bang bang, all the way down the marble aisle of the Eton College chapel.

Later in his youth, at the age of eighteen, he had been invited to stay in the multi-gabled residence of His Grace, the Duke of Sandwell. Becket stayed awake until the small hours, reading one of Seneca's axioms in the original, and was committing it to memory. Its theme, that it is a law rather than a penalty to die, intrigued him so much that he became reckless and threw his finished cigarettes over the room, instead of putting them out in the ashtray by his bed.

He was woken by a puzzled fireman, staring him in the face.

He asked him if he were a drunken Oxford undergraduate, disguised as a Roman centurion.

This strange behaviour did not prevent him from receiving a second invitation to the Duke of Sandwell's residence, however.

It was 3.00 o'clock in the morning. Becket turned his bath taps on and retired to his bedroom, where he read an account of Socrates's death in the original, as the tears poured down his cheeks. He had forgotten about the running bath.

By 8 o'clock that morning, the luckless Duke's residence was awash, and uninhabitable for six months.

Becket spoke with a slow, drawling, heavy upper class accent. When alone with his family, and not too depressed to speak, his conversation alternated between the utterance of dry, subtle anecdotes, many with an academic *dénouement*, and quips towards his son, Peter, if he found any gaps in his knowledge.

Peter loved his mother, despite her exacting standards and strictness, but was in awe of his father. His mother had left the house for a few days, to stay in a hostel in Rome, so that she could visit her friends, members of an English community on the outskirts of the city. Many of these people earned their livings, doing menial jobs and tried to learn Italian in their spare time.

Peter would be having lunch, his first meal alone with his father. He wrote out a list of the subjects he would discuss with the older man, so anxious was he not to be unprepared for an onslaught of questions he could not answer.

Peter was aware of Becket's love of Russian literature. He took out a book on the subject. The book specialized, not so much in straight-forward story-telling, but in axioms of certain Russian writers. Some of the axioms were succinct and to the point. Others, were complex and profound, and hard to memorize.

The father and son were on their way to a gloomy, almost windowless room, where the son had laid out cold food on a table, covered with a white cloth.

The telephone, in the corner of the room, rang loudly, grating Becket's nerves and making him jump.

"Answer it, will you," he said, dourly, as if he had just lost all his relatives in an air crash. "I don't want to speak to anyone on the 'phone."

Peter lifted the receiver.

"It's a bad line. I can't hear you," he said.

The caller spoke more loudly, and said the call was from Rome.

"It's Rome on the line," said Peter.

Becket's lugubriousness deepened. He spoke with an angry drawl. "Well, if the call's all the way from Rome, I suppose I'll have to take it, won't I?"

It was his wife, Betsy. She tried to persuade him to get time off for a few days, to stay there with her, and meet her friends, forgetting he had met them already and been perilously bored by them.

"No, I won't come to Rome," he said. "Those friends of yours are the most ghastly bores. I don't want to see any of them." He hung up.

"So what's going on in Rome?" asked Peter, if only to make conversation.

Becket put pieces of cold chicken, potato salad and lettuce on to his plate, as he spoke, his voice like that of an out-of-work funeral director.

"Rome stands where Rome stood, on the Tiber!"

When they had taken what they wanted, they sat down. They each had a beaker of cider by their plates.

Becket took a few sips of cider, laid down his napkin and began to eat. A mood of depression was on him, stilling his tongue. Peter had no idea what tortured thoughts were passing through his father's mind. His own thoughts raced feverishly to his morning's reading.

"I took out a book about Russian writers," he said, his voice raised, almost to a bark. His awe had made his tone sound menacing.

"I don't recall suggesting you didn't," replied the depressive.

There was a pause, lasting for three minutes.

"Well?" asked Becket.

"The book wasn't about their lives. It was about some of the things they thought."

"Oh, axioms?"

"That's right. Axioms."

"Say so, then! Was there something in particular which interested you?"

Peter passed his napkin from his right hand to his left, and then from his left hand to his right.

"Yes. Something Tolstoy said."

"What did he say?"

"He said, and these were his words; in fact they were quite extraordinary. He said, *'If you have a vice, be sure to name that vice in others, in order that others might see you to be without that vice.'*"

Becket swallowed half the cider in his beaker, wiped his mouth, sighed and tilted his head backwards.

"That's not Tolstoy, you ass," he said, failing to conceal the irritation in his voice. "That's Turgeniev!"

There was another pause, this time lasting for ten minutes. Becket stared abstractedly into space, slowly shovelling food into his mouth, with his fork. Peter drained his beaker of cider, and nervously introduced the subject of J. R. R. Tolkien, a writer, whom, astoundingly, Becket had not encountered on his scholarly travels.

"I've been reading *Lord of the Rings*," said the boy, his voice abnormally raised, once more.

"There's no need to shout. What is it about?"

"Well, it's three volumes. It's very long."

"I said, 'What is it about'?"

"It's a bit hard to explain. It's about these sort of funny creatures, trying to find a ring, so that they can throw it over the top of a mountain, into a kind of furnace."

"I say, you're not making much sense, are you?" said Becket, whose depression had worsened, since he had started eating the unappetising, cold lunch.

"What I'm really trying to say, is, it's about all these, well, for want of a better word, dwarves."

"Dorgs?"

"Dwarves."

"*Dorgs?* Do make yourself clear!"

"No. I said dwarves. You know, very small people."

"Oh, dwarves. Try looking at me when you're speaking to me. That way, I'd understand you better."

Peter's fear of his father did not in any way mask the love he felt for him. He remembered one particular incident all his life.

Betsy was adamant that Peter should not take up smoking. Becket, on the other hand, believed the practice to be harmless, and mischievously invited the boy to smoke during her occasional absences. It was not long before Peter became addicted to cigarettes. He bought two packets of the same brand that his father smoked.

The father, the mother and the son had just finished eating. Becket pulled out a cigarette and lit it and blew a thick cloud of smoke across the table at Betsy, who fanned the air, furiously.

Becket leant across the table and offered Peter one of his cigarettes, knowing that the boy yearned for a cigarette at that moment, more than anything else in the world.

"I won't, thanks," he said quietly.

"Go on!"

"It's very kind of you, but no thanks."

"Go on! Don't be so wet!"

"No, really, no thank you."

Betsy was unaware that her son had taken up smoking. She got up from the table and said she had some ironing to do.

Becket and Peter were alone in the room. Peter was feeling more at ease because Becket had been joking, in a slightly ribald manner, about Gorky's rough and ready methods of propositioning peasant women.

Peter accepted Becket's offer of a cigarette, this time. Becket leaned conspiratorially across the table.

"I say, that was dashed droll, don't you think? That business about the cigarettes, eh? Really dashed droll, that's what I call it!"

CHAPTER 25

It was Ephraim's first morning at King David's School for Boys. He had just had breakfast and was feeling ill at ease in his sombre grey school uniform.

Miranda walked out into the street with him.

"Morning, Becket," she called out.

"Good morning, Mrs White."

Becket had been warned repeatedly about the possibility of Ephraim being exposed to suspicious-looking strangers. He stood, bolt upright by the silver Rolls-Royce, looking almost military in his chauffeur's uniform.

He opened the back door for the boy, who had just said "goodbye" to his foster-mother. He was thinking about *The Brothers Karamazov*, a book he liked to read over and over again. He thought it was over-crowded, that only one brother (in his opinion, Alyosha), was essential to the book's structure, and that in general, Dostoievsky had bitten off more than he could chew.

Ephraim got into the back, and sat, leaning against the left hand door. Becket was in a relatively low mood that morning and hoped the boy would refrain from serenading him with meaningless chatter.

"Not too bad a day to start at a new school, Ephraim," he forced himself to remark.

"No."

Ephraim stared at the immaculately polished floor of the Rolls. He sat motionless and hoped with all his heart, that he would be popular with the other boys, that they would provide him with the audience he craved, laugh at his outrageous jokes and stories, and regard him as the central core of their interests. He wanted to be a cult figure to them, someone they would flock to and follow like a film star.

He stopped thinking, abruptly. The smell of the inside of the Rolls, was making him feel nauseated. He wondered whether he should say something to the smartly-dressed man who was driving him, or whether to do nothing at all and simply hope that it wouldn't happen, and even if it did happen, it crossed his mind that there was a chance he might not notice it.

He wound down the window and put his head out of it, letting the full force of the wind blow in his face. It musn't happen, he told himself. No, of course, it won't happen, but there's still the possibility that it might just happen. Oh, dear, it is possible. It really is possible. I think it's worse. It's probable. I think it's going to happen. I will definitely have to say something to this man. I can't delay it. All right, I'll tell him, now.

Ephraim tapped Becket who was still ruminating about the jumbled, authorial structure of *The Brothers Karamazov*. He tapped him a second time. Becket looked at him through the driver's mirror.

"I am afraid I want to be sick."

The devout Catholic crossed himself. He indicated left and swerved the silver Rolls to the side of the road, its front left wheel brushing against the pavement.

Becket bounded from the Rolls, raced round to the front and hurriedly opened Ephraim's door. He eased the boy out and rushed him to a wall, linking a row of terraced houses. Ephraim leant over the wall and brought up everything he had consumed that morning, into someone's proudly tended garden.

Becket could not tolerate the sight of someone being sick. When his son, Peter, was small, the child often suffered from car sickness. Betsy had been driving on one of these occasions, when Peter was sick without warning. Becket found the experience so horrific that he threw himself out of the moving car, rolled down a bank and broke his collar bone.

Ephraim had a great deal to bring up. He had eaten a heaped-up bowl of cereal, a plate of bacon, eggs, sausages and tomatoes and three to four pieces of toast, mounded with his beloved honey.

Becket held his head and looked the other way. He tried to immerse his thoughts in the unknown matter of Gorky's sex life.

Ephraim finished, wiped his mouth with the back of his hand and stood up straight like a soldier.

"I'm pretty sure I've got everything up, now. Thank you, Becket," he said.

Becket's immediate reaction was to speak to him in the way he spoke to his son.

"*Mr* Becket to you!" he said, his voice raised.

"I don't understand. I thought I was supposed to call you 'Becket' because Miranda calls you 'Becket'."

"That has nothing to do with it. Mrs White is entitled to call me 'Becket' because she and her husband employ me. You do not employ me. Therefore, when you speak to me, if you wish to use a name, you address me as 'Mr Becket'."

"Very well. I give you my word that I shall always address you, not as 'Becket', but as '*Mr* Becket'."

"All right. Are you quite sure you aren't going to be sick, again?"

"Yes. Quite sure. I've got the whole lot up, now, thank you, Mr Becket, like I said."

"Good. You must see it from my point of view. It would be the end of the world if you were sick in the Rolls."

"Why?"

"Because I'm the poor peasant who has to clear everything up. It takes me several hours a day to clean this car. If you were sick in it, it would break my heart."

"It won't happen in the car," said Ephraim.

"I'm glad to hear it. Hurry back into the car, now. Otherwise, you'll be late for school."

Ephraim did not feel at ease with Becket. The dry, sardonic delivery of his words, combined with his insistence on protocol, daunted him. At the same time, there was something he liked and admired about him and found quaintly intriguing.

He got into the back of the car and was feeling a lot better. Becket was now thinking how intensely irritating Gruzhenka* was and felt grateful that he didn't have to drive her. He eased himself behind the wheel, belted himself, and started the Rolls.

"Mr Becket?" asked Ephraim.

---

*Female character in *The Brothers Karamazov*.

"Speaking, dear!"

Once more, the boy felt the conflicting emotions of fear and dry amusement.

"I really want you and I to be friends. I love to have friends."

"Don't we all, my good man?"

"Can I ask you a question?"

"Provided you keep it brief."

"As I say, it's important that you become my friend."

"Well, what's your question?" Becket's slow, dour, upper class accent was more apparent, because he was becoming very depressed, again.

"Do you ever go ... what I mean is ... in your spare time...?" He intended to ask the older man whether he frequented prostitutes, but lacked the boldness required to.

"What the devil are you talking about?"

Ephraim saw a warning light in his brain. He wanted this man to be his friend. He had no wish to offend him.

"What I really want to know is, are you a descendant of Thomas à Becket?" he shouted, without meaning to.

"That's a start, if ever there was one," said Becket. This time, his tone was so dry, it could have mopped up a heavily-flooded house in seconds.

"Well, are you?"

"Perhaps, if you were more attentive to your history, young man, you would know that this man died in 1170. Far, far too many centuries have passed since then, for any link to be maintained. Apart from that, he had been ordained, and was unable to marry and raise a family. Did you not know that the King had had him ordained?" This time, the melancholy drawl was so extreme that it might have suggested drunkenness to an ignorant ear.

"I didn't know."

"Now, you do, you young ninny. Every time there is something you don't know, you must ask questions. That is the only way you will ever find out. In fact, that is exactly what you were doing when you asked your question, just now. You were doing as you should do. There is nothing more irritating than a person who is ignorant. If you fail to ask questions, you will turn from a shy boy, into a dull, ignorant man. What woman would have to do with an ignorant man? Questions, questions, questions, young man! When in doubt, ask a question. Never be afraid to do so."

"I asked the Headmaster at King David's a lot of questions. He seemed rather cross."

"That surely would depend upon the nature of the questions you asked him. I have no doubt at all, they were damn silly questions."

The intriguing, almost appealing dryness of Becket's words, inspired Ephraim to show his exhibitionist streak.

"There was one particular question I asked him, when he and I were alone. I think it was that question which made him cross."

"I'm sure it did, because it was probably a damned silly question."

"Do you want to know what I asked him, Mr Becket?"

"I neither know nor care what you asked him. Had it been an intelligent question, you would have received an intelligent answer. This doesn't seem to have been the case. It transpires that you either asked him an utterly fatuous question, or you asked him an extremely personal question. That's why I have no wish whatever to be told what you asked him."

Half of Ephraim's pride was crushed, as if trampled on by a herd of elephants. The other half was unaffected. The chauffeur's acidic tongue somehow refreshed him and opened a new world for him, a world exposing him to the utter boundlessness of language and the notion that English was not simply one language, but a countless number of languages, available to any English-speaking person.

He knew he would become a talented writer, one day. Becket's handling of the spoken word, had made him aware of the richness of language, and had brought him closer to his mother.

"I suppose you're thinking about that question you asked the Headmaster," Becket said, suddenly. Ephraim was indeed thinking about it. He was startled by Becket's apparent ability to read his thoughts, and was impressed by his daunting knowledge of psychology.

"That's what you were thinking about, wasn't it?" asked Becket.

"Yes, Mr Becket."

"I was wrong when I told you I had no idea what your question was. I know perfectly well what you asked him."

"How do you know?"

"The way I found out, concerns you not in the least."

"May I ask what you thought of my question?"

"You want me to give you an entertaining, saucy answer, but I won't."

"Maybe, you won't. Just tell me. Was it a silly question?"

"As a matter of fact, no."

"Did you know my father?"

"Yes. Extremely well. You know that I have served in the White household since Mr White gave up driving. Your father, and your mother, too, visited the house on more occasions than I can remember."

"Did you like my father?"

"He was a hardworking, gently-presented, outwardly pleasant, courteous, knowledgable, articulate individual," said Becket, who had temporarily drenched the boy so much with his string of adjectives, that he felt he was drowning.

"I know he was said to be all those things, but did you actually *like* him?"

"I am a professional man, Ephraim. That's all I can say."

"So you know that he practised necrophilia, don't you?"

"You will kindly understand that I am a chauffeur. I am not a person who discusses, or who ever will discuss that subject. Dashed weird, is what I call it, dashed weird."

"But I want you to. Why do people go in for it?"

"What did I just tell you?"

"Never mind, I still want to know."

"I'll tell you one thing, and one thing only," said Becket. "A boy who goes on and on about a subject, which his companions do not wish to discuss, is known as a shattering, thundering, crashing, paralysing bore!" This time, the chauffeur's cacophony of adjectives felt like cricket balls being hurled from a machine at the boy's head.

"Jesus, Mr Becket," said Ephraim, impertinently, "why do you use all those adjectives before you get to a noun?"

"Oh, for God's sake, Ephraim!" muttered Becket.

A silence ensued. Neither man nor boy spoke until the end of the journey. Becket got out and opened the back door, his expression subservient. Ephraim got out and looked the older man in the eye.

"Thank you, Mr Becket."

"And thank you, Ephraim. Don't you forget what I said."

"No. I won't forget it. I hope we'll be able to talk again when you collect me."

"Indeed, we will. You may ask me more questions, provided they are intelligent. I shall also wish to know what, if anything, you have learned on your first day at your new school."

CHAPTER 26

There were fourteen other boys besides Ephraim in the classroom during his first lesson. His cheeky, innocent smile attracted many of the boys, most of whom were welcoming and friendly. He introduced himself, unselfconsciously, as Ephi Rendon and the boys responded by giving their first names. Some of them shook his hand, one of whom was a boy called Paul Wise.

"Want a toffee?" asked Paul.

Ephraim thanked him and started to unwrap it.

"Is it true you were last at a *goy* school, called the Browning or something, near the Thames? I heard they weren't very nice to you."

"Nor were they."

"Is that why you left?"

"One of the reasons. I had to move, anyway. My mother died in a fire."

"Your mother, eh? I'm sorry to hear that, Ephi. Here, have another toffee."

"I haven't finished this one, yet."

"It doesn't matter. Put it in your pocket. Save it for later."

"Thank you, Paul."

"Is your father still alive, Ephi?"

"No. That's why I'm being looked after by foster-parents."

"Are they nice to you?"

"Miranda is. She's my aunt, my mother's sister. She's nice, like my mother. She's not strict or anything. I'm comfortable with her and she doesn't mind dirty jokes."

Paul laughed. Three other boys, Ben, Jacob and Jonathan, joined Paul and Ephraim. The group formed a circle round Ephraim, making him feel the centre of attention.

"What's that foster-father of yours like, Ephi?" asked Ben.

"I hate him."

"Why."

"Because he hates me. He's a horrible man. He's a dentist up Harley."

"Harley Street, eh?" said Paul. "Sounds pretty smooth.

142

Know any swear words?"

"I *will* tell you. I know quite a lot of them, but I don't want to tell you, now. I'm saving them for the masters."

"The Masters?" exclaimed the boys in unison.

"That's right. I don't want to do that on my first day but I will in a week or two. You'll see."

Ephraim felt happy. He had managed to round up an audience in minutes. The knowledge of his ability to attract, reminded him of his mother and made him feel safe.

At nine o'clock, a bell rang. The literature master, Mr Green, a stout, grey-haired man, entered the classroom.

Some of the boys were already standing. The others rose to their feet. Mr Green sat at the sloping desk in front of his class.

"I understand, we have a new boy, today," he said, gently. "Would the young gentleman please be so good as to raise his hand."

Ephraim did so.

"Am I to understand your name is Ephraim Rendon?"

"Yes, sir."

"It's a lovely name. Can you tell me a few things about yourself, Ephraim?"

"I used to live by the Thames. I live in Hampstead, now, sir."

"Why did you move?"

"I had to. Well, my mother died in a fire, recently. I've no father. I had to move to my foster-parents' house."

"Why, you poor soul! My heart goes out to you. What else can you tell me about yourself?"

"My foster-parents are called Mr and Mrs White. They've got this most unusual chauffeur called Becket. He drives a Rolls. Mr White's a *goy*. He's a dentist. He's got rooms in Harley Street."

"That is all very well," said Mr Green. "So far, you have only told me about others. What about you? What are *your* interests?"

"I like the poetry of Edgar Allan Poe, sir."

Mr Green opened his arms in an expansive, baffled gesture.

"Edgar Allan Poe, Ephraim? While a highly commendable and enterprising choice of reading matter, the man was an American, and this school concentrates on English writers. Do you know of any?"

Ephraim gave the names and works of all the English writers he had mentioned to the then, over-strained Mr Lawrance.

"Your knowledge for a boy of your years is quite staggering," said Mr Green. The other boys stared at Ephraim in amazed admiration. "Who is your favourite writer?"

"Edgar Allan Poe," said Ephraim, assertively.

"But he is not an *English* writer, is he, dear?"

"I still love his poems, whether he's an English writer or not, sir."

"Try to give me the names of other English writers you like."

"I can certainly tell you one thing. My chauffeur reads Dostoievsky. He keeps a well-thumbed copy of *The Brothers K* on his dash."

The boys giggled. The sound of the gentle, rippling laughter warmed Ephraim. His audience, if only small, felt like a junky's first heroin injection.

"I'm not interested in what your chauffeur reads," said Mr Green, irritably. "I'm asking you what you read."

"I like Fielding's *Tom Jones*, sir."

"Why?"

"Because of the big-bosomed, buxom-buttocked wenches, sir. I like the feel of over-painted whores, touting on cobbled streets. I like the smell of hot sex and debauchery, hitting you in the face on almost every page."

Mr Green was silent for a while, while the boys stared and tittered at Ephraim.

"Your attitude is insolent and precocious, boy! What worries me is the fact that you don't speak in this manner to show off. You do so because you think it is quite normal. This term, we are doing Shakespeare's *Romeo and Juliet*, simplified for children. We are also doing *Oliver Twist*. Do you know those two?"

"Yes. My mother taught me a lot of things out of school. Those works were among them."

"I am very glad to hear it, young man. What do you want to do with your life when you get older?"

"I want to be a writer. I feel I will be. My mother always wanted me to be a writer."

"Your mother was a writer herself, wasn't she?"

"Yes. That's right, sir."

"All I can say is, her books certainly wouldn't be suitable for even the most advanced boys in a conservative school such as this."

The bell rang at the end of the class. The other boys struggled to keep up with Ephraim as he hurried down the corridor. They begged him to find copies of his mother's books. They praised him for his remarks about *Tom Jones*. They touched his clothing and many of them said he had brought a ray of light into their dull lives. The roots of the Ephraim cult, though only in embryo form, had begun to grow, and it would not be long before they turned to an oak tree.

Ephraim had been at the school for two weeks. Miranda and White were continuing to quarrel, about her interest in Ian Rosen, and her pampering love for Ephraim. The boy heard every word uttered during these quarrels, and because White made it clear how much he resented him, he enjoyed leaving home and going back to school each morning, where at least he knew he was popular.

His loathing for Simon turned into an obsession, which goaded him into showing off even more to the other boys, to feel gratified.

CHAPTER 27

It was nearly 9 o'clock. The class in Religious Instruction, taught by Mr Paulden, was about to begin. Mr Paulden was a tall, thin man with a pointed grey beard. He was scheduled that morning, to speak about Abraham, and God's testing his reaction to his request that he sacrifice his son, Isaac.

Mr Paulden entered the classroom. He was rather a frightening man, and the action of the boys rising to their feet, was swift, respectful and almost military.

He ordered the boys to sit down and open their Bibles, at the verses describing Abraham's ordeal.

"Just before we begin, we have a new boy here, I'm told. Would the new boy care to raise his hand," said Mr Paulden.

Ephraim did so, content that the eyes of the other boys were focused on him, in anticipation of whatever outrage he would commit next.

"What is your name?"

"Ephraim Rendon, sir."

Mr Paulden was having trouble with his hearing aid. It enabled him to enjoy perfect hearing, but when it was maladjusted, he couldn't hear anything.

"Fred, from Leicestershire, dear? I can't hear you."

"Ephraim Rendon, sir," repeated the boy, loudly.

"Tell me a bit about yourself."

Ephraim had had this question put to him so many times that it bored him. He took advantage of Mr Paulden's deafness, to amuse the boys.

"I'm a serial killer's son, sir. My father murdered three women and hanky-pankied about with them after they'd snuffed it.

"My father used to pay prostitutes to sing 'God Save the Queen'. My father *loved* Edgar Allan Poe. My mother said I was conceived while my father recited *The Raven*. My father loved to have intercourse with dead bodies. My father was the biggest necrophiliac in London."

Mr Paulden heard nothing. The other boys became convulsed

146

with uncontrolled, hysterical giggles. They rocked about on their chairs.

Mr Paulden managed to adjust his hearing aid.

"I demand discipline in my class!" he shouted. "Kindly explain what you find so funny." He turned to Ephraim, who continued to sit up straight, his face in repose.

"What did you say, just then, when I asked you to tell me about yourself? How is it that you have managed to evoke this extraordinary amount of merriment among your class mates?"

"All I said was that I used to live by the Thames but had since moved to Hampstead. I am an orphan and I am being looked after by my foster-parents, whose names are Mr and Mrs White. I also said, and perhaps this is a trifle less interesting, that Mr White is a dentist with a practice in Harley Street."

"Harley Street, eh? Good, good. I can't say I find anything particularly funny about that."

Ephraim's hatred for White radiated to his anger with any party, forcing a man to kill his son to test his loyalty. The story of Abraham, as it was being read aloud by Mr Paulden, sickened and disgusted him, to such an extent that he refused to listen. He raised his desk a few inches, to enable him to gain comfort from his beloved Edgar.

Mr Paulden looked up from his Bible.

"Rendall!" he called out.

"It's Rendon, sir. Ephraim Rendon."

"Stand up when I speak to you!"

"Yes, sir."

"What are you doing?"

"Nothing, sir."

"That's an untruth, boy, and you know it. You were reading a book, and you will kindly bring it to me, as I intend to confiscate it."

Ephraim handed the book to the master. Mr Paulden expected such a book as *Lady Chatterley's Lover* to be handed to him, and was staggered by the notion of a twelve-year-old boy reading Edgar Allan Poe for pleasure.

"All right, all right, back to your desk."

147

Ephraim sat down. He knew he remained the centre of attention and felt relaxed and elated.

"Rendall!" called Paulden a second time.

"No, sir. It's not Rendall. It's Rendon."

"I thought I told you to stand up every time I choose to address you. On your feet, boy, at the double!"

Ephraim continued to find the situation comic. He leapt to his feet and resisted the temptation to give a mock salute to the master.

"You are probably unaware of this," said Mr Paulden. "I have been reading about Abraham and Isaac."

"Yes, I know you have, sir."

"Perhaps, you can enlighten the class on the matter. Do you know the story?"

"Yes, sir."

"In that case, could you please give an opinion about Abraham's trauma."

"I'll tell you what I think," said Ephraim with unexpected rage in his otherwise sweet, gentle voice. "In my view, God's an absolute shit! He's a bludgeoning, blustering bully! He's so bloody conceited and full of himself that he brutalizes and harasses Abraham, just to find out whether his victim is sufficiently loyal to him, to kill his own son. Who the fucking hell does he think he is? Besides, what moron would sacrifice his son to a God that probably doesn't exist anyway?"

Mr Paulden turned white. He looked as if he had been bitten in the private parts by a rat. He eased himself into his chair, while the boys ogled Ephraim, like an over-excited crowd, waiting for a pop-star to come out of his dressing room.

When he eventually managed to speak, Mr Paulden sounded saddened.

"We might as well all be as dead as nits, if we cannot recognize a Supreme Being, Ephraim. Without Deity, we are lost, destitute, alone. We are cast out into an eternity of darkness and misery. Our souls suffer the tortures of the damned. They are desolate and empty."

"Crashing, thundering bollocks, sir! My father had no belief in a Supreme Being. Nor did my mother. Their souls weren't desolate and empty. It's true my father wasn't a happy man, but he wasn't cast out into an eternity of darkness, as you call it. He lived a full and glorious life. He made love to women. He was hot-blooded. He was alive!

"Besides, if you're convinced there's a Deity, you'd live in permanent fear of punishment. If that's happiness, I'm the King of Siam!"

Mr Paulden's facial expression had turned from shock and outrage, to torment, not so much as a result of Ephraim's disturbing words, but because they had been so vehemently uttered by an angel-faced twelve-year-old boy.

The most dreadful thought to hit Mr Paulden, was that he suddenly felt his own faith drain from him, without warning. He could not come to terms with the fact that, after relying implicitly on it all his life, he, and all he stood for, had been crushed to the ground, not by an elder, not by a relative, but by a child.

"I declare the class over," he said. "I'm expecting an overseas telephone call from a colleague." He was rising slowly from his chair, his head turned away from the boys.

"Psst! Ephi," said Paul Wise, who was sitting next to him."

"What is it, Paul?"

"I dare you to run up to him, just before he leaves the room, and tell him the back of his head looks like a chicken's ass!"

Ephraim was incapable of refusing a dare, so desperate was he to cling to his image, and enjoy himself when he was away from White.

He accepted the dare, just before Mr Paulden left the room, in the hope that the outrage would be reported to White. He felt as if he were floating in space, surrounded by stars, each one focusing its brilliance on his face. He felt the silvery wine of adulation flow into his stomach, as he and his friends walked from the classroom, into the playground.

He hadn't really meant to hurt Mr Paulden and knock the bottom out of his world, and suddenly became ashamed of accepting the dare. All he sought was personal glorification, and

149

the love he had lost when his mother died.

He was unaware that Mr Paulden had been to see Mr Lawrance and tendered his resignation from the school, because he had just lost his religious faith. Worse still, the traumatised master had reported Ephraim's foul language, which would mean his being given a detention.

Mr Lawrance's secretary found Ephraim in the playground, performing like a prize circus monkey before his adoring friends, all of whom worshipped him, because he dared to do the things they were afraid to do themselves.

"Mr Lawrance wishes to see you in his study, Ephraim."

The Headmaster's main preoccupation was with replacing the master in Religious Instruction. He had already consumed half a glass of whisky by the time Ephraim came into the room.

"Sit down, Ephraim," he said. The boy obeyed.

"I'm sure you are aware why I sent for you."

"I am aware, sir."

"The incident you have involved yourself in is of such mind-blowing and horrifying severity that I am at a loss, even to put it into words, so I'll be brief.

"Contrary to my orders, you have been using that word again, and other words equally as disgusting. You frighten people, Ephraim. Do you realize that?"

"I don't mean to frighten them. I don't do it on purpose, sir."

"I'd like you to know that Mr Paulden has just handed in his resignation."

"Why's he done that, sir?"

"Because he has lost his faith in a Supreme Being."

"If everyone stopped working, just because they'd become non-believers, there'd be no industry, no newspapers, no factories, no banks, no schools."

"You worry me, all day, Ephraim. You worry me, all night. Reason goads me to the act of expelling you, not just because you are disruptive, but because of your influence on the other boys. You are a cult figure."

"Yes, I know, sir."

"Had any other boy behaved so appallingly and persisted in insulting my masters, I would not have hesitated to expel him. However, I can't do that to you, Ephraim, because you are not of this world. You are incomprehensible. It is because I have insight and intuition that I allow you to stay here.

"You will be something so extraordinary when you grow up, that not a soul on earth will fail to have heard of you. It's for that reason and that reason alone that I'm keeping you. Like yourself, I am vain, and I could not pass by the opportunity of going into history by your side, as having been your spiritual guide.

"I shall not be giving you a detention, but next time, I hear a report of foul language, or any other form of disgraceful behaviour I shall, and it will be a *strict* detention."

"Incidentally, Mr Paulden said that, in addition to your other insolence, you passed a personal remark as he left the classroom, but, fortunately for you, he refused to tell me what you said."

The boy remained motionless in his chair.

"I hope you appreciate that poor Mr Paulden has just suffered a terrible loss. He has lost his faith, the very thing he leaned on in adversity."

"What sort of a loss is that, sir? He hasn't lost a wife or a child. What he's lost is nothing in comparison with the loss of my mother. She brought me up to have no faith. Perhaps, I don't really know what it feels like to lose it, or why losing it should feel so bad."

"All right, Ephraim. Put it this way, when you are rude to the masters, for the amusement of your friends, doesn't it occur to you that they are human beings, and they have feelings, just as you do? You hurt them, Ephraim. That's not a very kind thing to do."

"I realize that, sir. Believe me, I do understand. I wouldn't like to think I'd hurt anyone."

"All right. You may go now."

"I apologize for any distress or inconvenience I might have caused you, sir."

Ephraim walked towards the door. Near it, was a small

151

painting he hadn't noticed before. It depicted a fire-blowing devil, holding a pitchfork. An arrow had gone through his back and exited on the other side.

"An arresting picture, isn't it?" said Mr Lawrance.

Ephraim looked for a few seconds at the picture and turned his head to the Headmaster.

"Whoever painted that picture," he said, "must have derived a considerable amount of influence from Hieronymus Bosch."

"Goodbye, Ephraim," said Lawrance.

The boy returned to the playground to give his friends an exaggerated account of his encounter with the Head.

Mr Lawrance drank the other half of his glass of whisky and poured himself another. His shaking hand reached for the telephone.

CHAPTER 28

Miranda was wallowing in a bath, scented with an expensive Jermyn Street essence, given to her by Ian Rosen. She was treating herself in an abortive attempt to assuage her grief. The portable 'phone resting on the edge of the bath rang, which disappointed her. She had wanted her peace and solitude to remain undisturbed for at least another hour.

"Whatever's the matter, Mr Lawrance? Has something happened to Ephraim?" she asked. Although she and Mr Lawrance had been childhood friends, they had begun to address each other formally, since Ephraim became a pupil at King David's School.

"Ephraim's all right, Mrs White, "but he is causing us all nothing but trouble."

"What sort of trouble?"

"In the first instance, despite the fact that he's been told not to, he persists in using that word."

"Oh, you must mean 'fuck'?"

"Precisely. I do mean 'fuck'. It simply must not go on."

"I agree, it's awfully naughty of him, but he only does it because he's been told not to. I'll give him a serious talking to. He always listens to me."

"That's not the worst of it, Mrs White. He's a rabblerouser. The boys come flocking to him. That's why he won't stop showing off."

"All right. I'll talk to him about that, too. Anything else?"

"Yes, and this is the gravest matter of all. We had a master in Religious Instruction here for fifteen years, name of Mr Paulden. This luckless fellow was taking a class this morning and speaking about Abraham and Isaac.

"When asked to give an opinion about the story, Ephraim said, and these were his words, 'I think God's an absolute shit! Who the fucking hell does he think he is?'"

Miranda covered the receiver and had a giggling fit.

"Are you there?" asked Lawrance.

"I'm here. Oh, dear, I've just lost my beautiful bar of soap.

153

It's in the bath somewhere. I can't find it, blast it!"

"Do please, try to understand the seriousness of this matter. Ephraim went on to state, using particularly aggressive language, that he was a non-believer and that religion did nothing other than cause misery, because it left one in permanent fear of punishment."

"I'm sorry if he was tactless. I'll speak to him about that as well. Are you quite sure he spoke like that to a religious buff?"

"Quite sure, Mrs White."

"I appreciate your having kept him on, seeing he's so difficult. Perhaps, you should ask yourself why he is like that.

"He's been through a terrible experience, losing his mother. Can you really blame him for denying the existence of a Supreme Being? I have no faith, either. Both Ephraim's parents rejected God. I have no intention of encouraging him to accept religion because I don't believe in it. What if I did encourage him? What do you think would happen to him when he gets older and finds out God does not exist? He'd go off his head."

"But the boy was actually upsetting the master. He was so angry."

"Who was angry? Ephraim or the master?" asked Miranda.

"Ephraim."

"That's because he was being forced to accept and condone the behaviour of a vicious God, a God driving a man to utter distraction, simply to test his loyalty. Ephraim was angry because he was being invited to worship this mythical entity himself, whom he doesn't believe in or wish to be bullied into doing so. That, added to his mother's death, and the absence of a father, was too much for him to bear.

"In fact, I am quite adamant that he be excused from any further religious instruction, and be encouraged to work hard at his studies."

"You want me to take him out of religion?" gasped Mr Lawrance."

"Yes. That is what I want. That way, such classes would not be disrupted. The religious buff in charge would no longer be interrupted or interfered with, and, what is most important of all,

154

Ephraim would stand a greater chance of finding peace of mind."

There was a pause, broken by Miranda.

"Dammit, the water's getting cold, and there's no more hot water coming out of the tap. Could we wind this up, do you think?"

"All right, Mrs White. I must insist on your having a serious talk with Ephraim. At the moment, he's a loose cannon and a damned nuisance. It's only his huge intellect which has enabled him to stay here."

"I understand you, Mr Lawrance. When our chauffeur brings him home, we'll talk the whole thing over."

CHAPTER 29

Miranda felt shivery because of the lack of hot water. She put on a bathtowel dressing gown and went downstairs to see if the afternoon mail had been delivered. She found there were no letters, but she suddenly noticed something strange in the letter box. She picked it up and looked at it closely. It was an unused condom containing a lock of poorly conditioned blonde hair and a chip from a red-varnished fingernail.

She felt sure that the object had been delivered by Kate although she was ignorant of the engraving on the lawn. She decided not to tell White because she suspected that he was on Kate's side and that the two were united, for their own reasons, by hostility towards Ephraim. She knew that if she called the Police, they would say that a lock of hair and a chipped nail were insignificant and a waste of their time. Miranda did her duty. She made sure someone was with Ephraim all the time, but feared for her sanity, not only because of her bereavement, but also a matter she feared was beyond her control.

CHAPTER 30

Miranda and Ephraim were sitting by the fire. She opened the conversation.

"I've just had a 'phone call from Mr Lawrance. I hear you've been behaving very badly again, and I'm not amused."

"I'm sorry, Miranda. I was so angry."

"Why were you angry?"

"Because a master was trying to throw all this Bible stuff into my face. It's against everything my mother taught me. We were going through Abraham's potential sacrifice of Isaac. It was horrific. Then, this crappy old git was trying to get me to believe in God. Why the hell should I, after what happened to my mother, who brought me up to believe he doesn't exist, anyway?"

"Ephi," began Miranda, quietly, "it is not your disbelief, but your manners which are being called into question. Why did you have to be so rude? Have you no sense of diplomacy or tact? Are you incapable of arguing with these nuts, such as the religious buff, in a calm, restrained and reasonable manner? I know you'll go a very long way in life, but I hope to hell you won't go for the Diplomatic Corps!

"I want you to do this, just to please me. I want you to be polite to everyone. Also, in no circumstances are you to say 'fuck'."

"I promise, Miranda. Will they shun me because I reject God?"

"Will who shun you?"

"The boys."

"No. That won't happen. We live at a time when hardly anyone believes in a Supreme Being. I stopped when I was fifteen, just about the same time your mother stopped. As for your father, I don't think he ever believed in his life. It is the evoking of laughter, the act of giving love to others, of being loyal to your friends, and of being kind, which makes you a good person. And it is dedicated, hard work which gives you

157

fame, respect and recognition."

White had come home ten minutes ago. He had listened to their conversation through a half-open door. He waited for it to finish before he came into the room.

"I heard all that, so don't try to cover up for him, Miranda! What's all this talk about you being a non-believer?"

"Don't interrogate him, Simon! I've just ticked him off and he's said he'll behave better in future."

"He's been playing up again, hasn't he?"

"We've talked it over. He's agreed to come to heel, and moderate his behaviour."

"I'm not stupid, Miranda. He told his religion master he thought God was an absolute shit. That bloody Lawrance got to me on my mobile. The whole thing's outrageous. I was trying to bridge a loose wisdom tooth to a cavity-ridden molar, on the insistence of that dreadful man, Felix Drake who's always jamming my bloody switchboard!"

"God is a shit, Simon. I'll stand by that because of the way he treated Abraham," said Ephraim.

"I'll teach you not to be insubservient, you bastard, whom your mother should have aborted!"

He went over to Ephraim and wrenched him to his feet. He held his arm with his left hand, and gave him a resounding slap on the ear with his right.

"I'm not scared of you and never have been, not when Miranda's with me," shouted the boy.

Miranda followed White into the kitchen. She took a carving knife from the drawer and held it to his throat.

"That's it, Simon White. You're a coward. You sank so low as to brutalize a boy half your size. I hate you more than I've hated anyone in my life. I don't want to share this house with you any more. You're unkind to a boy who has just lost his mother. You've gone too far, and there'll be a price tag for it!"

White's attack on Ephraim had released his rage and he was calm.

"Oh, don't forget, Miranda, we're due to attend a conference about advancements in dentistry, at the British Dental Association

158

at 8.00 o'clock. It's a special do, which means we bring our wives. Becket's collecting us at 7.15."

Becket's task of driving the Whites to the British Dental Association, was unpleasant. They quarrelled perilously, screaming and shouting in the back of the Rolls, mainly about Ephraim's behaviour. So distracted was Becket that he inadvertently went through two red lights, causing a lorry to screech to a halt, and narrowly miss a pedestrian.

CHAPTER 31

"Good morning, Mr Becket," said Ephraim, when the chauffeur was due to take him to school the following morning.

"Good morning, Ephraim."

Becket was depressed that day because his black thoughts about his supposed failure to equal his father, had been particularly vicious.

To make things worse, this was one of those days when he felt his devout Catholicism shaking a little, and he was terrified of losing it. His misery had also increased on witnessing the fight the Whites had had in the back of the Rolls, the night before.

"I understand you've got a copy of *The Brothers Karamazov* up there in front of you," remarked Ephraim.

"You understand right."

"I've been trying to read it in my spare time for the past two weeks."

"Have you, now?"

"Yes. Although it's not easy to read, with its long words, I tried to force myself to understand parts of it."

"It's a bit young for you, isn't it?"

"Well, perhaps. What do you think of it?"

"I think it's too crowded. The ridiculous number of characters has ruined the book. All that's needed, apart from the father, is one son, and one son only, not three."

"What son would you have chosen, Mr Becket?"

"Alyosha," replied the chauffeur, firmly. "There are enough facets in him to cover ten characters, let alone needing to put in two more brothers."

"Miranda's been going through the book with me. It's too hard for me to read it, myself. She's explained the personalities of the three brothers. That's all I understand about the book, the differences in the three brothers. There was only one brother who appealed to me."

"Name him, Ephraim," said Becket, who was still so gloomy, he wanted to slit his throat.

"Ivan Karamazov," said the boy.

"I knew all along you'd say that," said Becket, in a despairing tone.

"Why?"

"Because of your godlessness. Your foster-parents were arguing about it in the car last night, if arguing is an appropriate word. Godlessness is a terrible affliction, Ephraim. My own faith wavers occasionally, and on those days, I feel so ashamed, I want to die."

"Why feel ashamed? It's not your fault."

"I feel ashamed because a person with no God, is a person who has allowed himself to be morally and spiritually unguided."

"I don't feel like that. I feel free without God."

"You say that because you are a fool," said Becket. There was a long pause, broken by the lugubrious chauffeur. "I wish you and I had been the same age and at the same school. I, too, was an absolutely ghastly boy!" he said.

CHAPTER 32

White was suffering from a throbbing hangover, when his first
patient was ten minutes late for her appointment, the next
morning. His spirits were always at their lowest in the mornings.

His patient's name was Mrs Yates. She was about thirty. She
was thin, fidgety and had an irritating, overwhelming
nervousness about her.

"You rang us up late, yesterday afternoon, to say you had
lost a filling, in your back, right molar. You said it troubled you
so much that you wished to be fitted in between patients as a
matter of, to quote your own words, 'extreme urgency',"
said White.

"Yes. That's the part of my mouth I do most of my
chomping with," replied Mrs Yates.

"Chomping?"

"Oh, I meant chewing."

"I suppose you'll want a local injection."

"Of course, I will!"

White barked a few peremptory orders at his nurse, an
unalert agency temp. She put a suction pipe into Mrs Yates's
mouth, to drain her saliva, while White prepared the syringe, his
loathing for Ian Rosen and passionate resentment of Ephraim,
seething through his brain.

"Do open your mouth, Mrs Yates. Do you think I'm doing
this for my own amusement?"

The agitated patient obeyed. She flinched as she watched the
needle approaching her gum. White, too, flinched, because he
wished he were about to push it into Rosen's eye.

"I do wish you'd keep still, dear!"

"I'm so sorry. I know I'm irritating you."

"You are so right, Mrs Yates. You are just so right!"

"I'm afraid I'm awfully edgy and jumpy. It's difficult to
relax. I've only just got over a pretty bad attack of influenza."

"Do you mean 'flu?" rasped White.

"Yes."

"Then, say so, for God's sake!"

Mrs Yates's gum took a few minutes to go numb. White started drilling the recently decayed surface enamel, in the tooth needing to be re-filled. Mrs Yates hated the suction pipe being in her mouth. She covered the nurse's hand with her own and timidly pushed it away. The nurse sheepishly held it by her side.

"Put that back!" shouted White. "I don't want a bloody waterfall on my hands!"

The gum was not numb enough. White hit the nerve. Mrs Yates screamed.

"I need another injection. The nerve's not dead," said Mrs Yates.

"I've had enough of this," said White. "You know perfectly well, the nerve's dead. It's all in your mind. Either you want the tooth filled, or you don't. You're wasting my time and your money."

By this time, the patient was even angrier than the bitter, aggrieved dentist.

"I don't understand why you have to be so bloody rude!" she shouted.

"Suppose, you allow me to get on with my work?"

"Perhaps, I shouldn't have sworn."

"No, perhaps, you shouldn't."

"Even so, may I have another injection, please? That way, I won't scream."

White sighed. He pushed the needle into her gum and pretended, once more, that it was Rosen's eye. Mrs Yates let out a slight cry of pain.

"A lot of your problems are due to the fact that you don't use dental floss," said White.

"I do. I've been struggling with it, like an unhatted cotton-picker from the deep South. Honest to goodness, I have!"

"Hatted or unhatted, your gums are a shattering thundering disgrace!"

He finished his work on Mrs Yates, pressed a lever to ease the chair into an upright position and curtly told her he would be sending her a bill within a few days.

Mrs Yates walked to the door. She turned round and faced White.

"Mr White," she said, "I have been to more dentists in Harley Street than I have had lovers. Never, in my life, have I encountered such a disagreeable and foul-mannered dentist as yourself!

"You're the sort of man who would tie one end of a piece of string to a rotten tooth, and the other end to an open door, and slam it. Your methods of dentistry smack of something out of a Laurel and Hardy film."

"How dare you!"

"I wondered when you'd ask how dare I? I intend to tell all my friends with dental problems about my sickening experience on your hands. I'm astounded by the fact that you practice in Harley Street, when your rightful place of trade is on Brighton Pier, or in a back room at some Victorian fairground."

"Would you kindly leave my surgery, please, Mrs Yates," said White, quietly.

"I'm familiar with this street and its stringent rules of professional protocol. I'm compiling a report about your disgraceful behaviour to the General Dental Council," said Mrs Yates.

White blanched, as if at gunpoint.

"Oh, Mrs Yates! Perhaps, I was a little remiss in my treatment of you. I've not been feeling too well, myself, of late. I apologize. In fact, I will refrain from sending you a bill."

Mrs Yates paused to think, while the dentist's heart crashed against his ribs.

"No-one shuts my mouth with a panicky bribe, Mr White. How many other patients of yours have you tried to silence? I have a witness, namely your nurse." She turned to the nurse, "Are you prepared to stand before the General Dental Council as a witness?"

"Yes, Mrs Yates. I am indeed. You are not the only patient I've witnessed him being rude to."

White waited for Mrs Yates to leave. He went out into the hall, where a trim, white-overalled receptionist was sitting.

"Would you please cancel my appointments for the rest of the day. I've got a virus coming on," he said.

He left the building. He walked a few yards down Harley Street, turned into Weymouth Street and then into Marylebone High Street. He staggered into a noisy public house called The Red Lion, where he slumped into an uncomfortable, wooden chair. He remained there for a few hours and got systematically drunk. He planned to go home in the early afternoon, when he assumed Miranda would be out, buying clothes. He looked forward to lowering the blinds in the marital bedroom and sinking into a stupor.

*   *   *

Ephraim was allowed to go home early that day as he had been excused from his Religious Instruction class. He went to his room, and studied his Latin declensions.

It was 1.00 o'clock. White was slumped, unconscious, his head and shoulders resting on a table at The Red Lion. Although the pub had a reputation for attracting rough, shady characters, who trafficked in heroin and crack cocaine, the barman was unhappy about the sight of a drunk out cold. He knew he risked losing his licence, if a customer were found to be plastered with liquor from his own pumps.

He waddled over to White and shook him. White stirred. He raised his head and focused his bloodshot eyes on the barman.

"When is the new set of burs* coming for my air rotor drill? They're overdue, blast it!" he said, his speech scarcely audible.

"You're legless, Guv'nor," said the barman. "I'm getting you out. I'll get bleeding nicked if the Law finds you in here."

"Bugger all that! When am I getting my burs? I hope you know you're talking to a Harley Street dentist."

"Blimey mate! I wouldn't want you touching *my* bloody teeth!"

The barman stood behind the dentist and wrenched his head

*Bur: A metal pin at the end of a dentist's drill.

165

and shoulders from the table. He picked him up in a fireman's lift and took him outside into the street. He sat him on the pavement and left him leaning against the wall.

An hour and a half passed. White came to his senses. He staggered to his feet and hailed a taxi whose over-exhausted driver failed to notice his drink-reeking breath.

He was home within half an hour.

The only thought in his head was not the undelivered burs for his air rotor drill, but the knowledge that he would soon be in bed with the blinds closed.

He heard nothing in the house. The drink had made him deaf and partially blind. He poured chilled water from the fridge into a jug and filled it with ice cubes which he planned to put on his bedside table. He dragged himself up the stairs, clinging to the banister, with the hand not holding the jug.

The door of the matrimonial bedroom was closed but not locked. He turned the handle and walked unsteadily towards the double bed. He put the jug down on the bedside table, and realized, in his semi-comatose state that the blinds had already been pulled down. In his drunkenness, it did not cross his mind whether it was normal for them to be down in the middle of the day. Apart from the thin shards of light coming through the slats of the blinds, the room was almost dark.

He drank some water, straight from the jug and put it back on the bedside table, the side of the bed he slept on. He rolled onto the bed and lay on his back. Within minutes, he was asleep, and snoring, making the hideous noise that drunks make when they doss down on floors in rough pubs, no longer able to stand. White's mouth gaped open like a cadaver's and a stream of saliva trickled down his chin and onto his neck.

He began to dream and for the first time for several weeks, his spirits soared. He felt like a gull gliding through a cloudless sky over an azure sea. The pleasant sensation was caused by the dream he was having.

White had Mrs Yates in his chair. Her arms were secured behind her back by a strait-jacket and her legs bound to the base of the chair with metal strips embedded with nails, which would

166

dig deeply into her flesh, if she tried to move them.

The dentist had refused to give her a painkilling injection. He held his drill, boring through the nerve of each tooth in her head. Occasionally, he drilled holes in her tongue and the roof of her mouth. She was screaming so loudly in agony, that White was satisfied that her shouts of excruciating pain were radiating down the whole of Harley Street. The screams he derived sexual sadistic pleasure from hearing, sounded almost like those of a satisfied woman having one screaming orgasm after another. The screaming was continuous and was as gratifying to his ears as the rarest music ever composed.

Suddenly, he became puzzled as the dream progressed. What he felt was even more curious, as he was on his feet, bending in ecstasy over his victim. He felt some strange movement going on behind him. It was as if something were touching his body and rocking him. The almost static screaming went on and continued to emanate more from pleasure than pain. He wondered if Mrs Yates were actually a masochist and revelling in her experience in the dentist's chair. He began to feel disappointed, as a child does when told it can't go to the funfair.

The rocking became more pronounced and the screaming louder. He found that he was not standing at all. He was lying on his back. It was not until he rolled off the bed onto the floor, that he knew he had been dreaming.

The darkness confused him but his vision was no longer impaired. He could see well enough to realize that something unpleasant was happening to him. He dragged himself to his feet and walked to the other side of the bed and raised his eyes. He saw the well-built, almost fully-clothed figure of a man, lying face downwards, making violent, thrusting movements, increasing in speed.

He looked in the oval mirror just above the bedstead and saw Ian Rosen's face, his grey eyes lovingly looking downwards, his thick black hair dishevelled.

Beneath him, rocked the naked body of the dentist's wife, Miranda. Rosen alternated between kissing her mouth and breasts, with the same intense ferocity as his fornication.

167

White watched, initially too shocked to speak or act. He stood there for over five minutes, while Miranda let out loud screams of demented joy.

She pulled away from underneath Rosen and lay on her back. He turned onto his side and lit a cigarette. He seemed sad, because his love for her was so overwhelming, and because of the melancholia from which many men suffer after orgasm.

The lovers looked up simultaneously and stared blankly at the cuckolded dentist. Miranda laughed nervously, like an East End washerwoman.

Rosen stared White in the face. His eyes fixed him with contempt, because he knew of his cruelty to Ephraim, the boy he thought of as his own son.

White's hangover and accompanying nausea turned into the rage of a bull, approached by a picador, in the midst of a clapping crowd, maniacally clacking castanets.

He threw himself onto Rosen and hit him. His words were sparse in comparison with his physical attack, and at that moment, were limited to the bellowing of "Get back to your murky presses where you belong!"

His words amused Rosen.

"Why don't you get back to teeth, starting with your own? Your breath stinks like a heap of rotten meat. I'm at a loss to understand how your wife could bear to lie by your side, all this time."

Rosen was physically stronger than White, and Miranda felt there would be no danger of her husband harming him. She sprang from the bed, put on a dressing gown and left the love-sick publisher and the livid dentist alone in the bedroom, fighting with comic indignity.

Miranda went to Ephraim's room and found the boy working on his Latin declensions, writing them out over and over again, to commit them to memory, in his meticulously neat, copperplate hand.

"It's going to be all right, isn't it, Miranda?" he said.

"What is, my boy?"

"You and Ian. Simon's going, isn't he? Ian's taking his

place, isn't he? I'm pleased, Miranda. I love Ian."

"I know you do. And Simon is going. It won't be easy, at first. There will be technicalities, divorce proceedings."

"Will all that be over, quickly?"

"Not the divorce proceedings, but I'm not having Simon living here any more. Ian's coming to live here, instead."

"Are you going to marry him?"

"Yes, once the proceedings are over. He is very much in love with me, and I with him. We're going to live together but we won't officially be man and wife, yet. That needn't affect you. All I want is for you to be happy, and that wouldn't be possible if Simon stays here."

"When's Ian moving in?"

"He already has. Simon has no rights to this house. I'm the one who holds the Deeds, now."

A wave of euphoria surged through Ephraim. He got up and rushed into the marital bedroom. He was amused by the sight of two men in combat. He leapt onto the bed and jumped up and down, while the fighting continued. His thoughts turned to his mother. He continued to jump up and down and broke into song, making up the words as he went along.

The dentist and the printer should be friends!
The dentist and the printer should be friends!
The dentist likes to pull out teeth, the printer
prints the written word,
But that's no reason why they cain't be friends.

Rosen rolled about on the bed, momentarily convulsed with giggles.

Something broke within White. His hands leapt to his rival's throat. He suspected the General Dental Council would strike him off the register, and had suddenly come to terms with the loss of the woman he despised.

He decided that the murder of Rosen would lead to life imprisonment and welcomed the idea of prison, which would relieve him of his responsibilities. All his financial obligations

169

would disappear, once he became a convicted murderer.

He took advantage of the fact that Rosen was distracted by a further nervous, giggling fit. He felt his hands tighten round his neck, and probably would have killed him, had it not been for the second diversion Ephraim created.

The boy seized the jug of iced water from the bedside table. He approached White from behind, and emptied it over his head. White removed his hands from Rosen's throat and jumped backwards.

Ephraim prodded him in the ribs, convinced that his mother was watching over him.

He stood up straight, staring defiantly at White and broke into song once more.

"I don't think very much of the dentist!"

White ignored Rosen's presence and slapped Ephraim's face repeatedly, until the publisher intervened.

Rosen grabbed White's private parts and twisted them. Ephraim was afraid and fled from the room.

"Worse than this will happen to you, White, if you inflict one further act of cruelty on this boy. Lay so much as a finger on him, and I'll destroy you, even more than I've destroyed you, already. I could go to the police and tell them you were foolish enough to try to murder me in front of a witness.

"Miranda despises you. Ephraim can't bear you because you're cruel to him. You even went so far as to hit him, when his only crime was to say he didn't believe in God."

"I felt I had no choice," said White. "I was trying to exert a decent influence on him. As his foster-father, I was trying to get some religion into him, to stand him in better stead, later on in life."

"You just don't get it, do you?" shouted Rosen. "Atheism sets a child free. Religion is a bundle of threatening oppressive blackmail. It screws him up. All he needs to know is the difference between good and evil and right and wrong. A non-believer knows that, but very few believers do. If you'd known the difference between right and wrong, you wouldn't have tormented a bereaved child.

"Apart from that, I am in love with Miranda and she's in love with me. No-one wants you here."

"Where do you imagine I'm going to live?" asked the dentist, mildly.

"The Y.M.C.A. of course! It's cheap. It's central. It's convenient. It's true you won't be allowed women in your room, but what difference could that possibly make to you? No woman would want you. Try blowing into a polythene bag. Then open it and smell the air inside it. You've got bad breath, old boy. Bad breath! And you're a bloody dentist. That's the equivalent of a publisher being dyslexic."

CHAPTER 33

White had thought all along that he would defy Rosen and forcibly keep Miranda. He was unaware of the extent to which their affair had progressed. He also hoped he could continue to use Ephraim as a scapegoat, to dignify his dissatisfaction with himself and his life. He liked hitting the boy, if only to cause himself shame and further unhappiness afterwards.

The dentist's disturbed thoughts were also centred round his insignificant and unprepossessing appearance. He realized that he could not possibly compete with the aura of animal attractiveness, which he believed surrounded Rosen.

The aura, which radiated from his rival belittled him further, and made him hate Rosen even more intensely.

He had been hit harder on the few occasions when Rosen had visited his house, recently, in an unkempt, unwashed state, which he suspected, made him even more irresistible to women, than he was when he took time and trouble with his ablutions.

The ablution issue played a curious part in Miranda's and Rosen's relationship. His standards of personal cleanliness vacillated from one extreme to the other. The dominant part of him was fastidiously clean, but he sometimes went through phases of refusing to wash himself, sometimes for as long as a week at a time. These strange episodes of self-degradation enhanced his sexual appetite and fed the *nostalgie de la boue*, in which he liked to wallow, as a form of rebellion against his obsessively clean, disciplinarian father, whose memory he despised.

"Do you do this, just to please me?" Miranda asked on one of these occasions.

"Yes. I suppose that's one of the reasons. It's also part of my rebellion against my father. He was an obsessive cleanliness fanatic. Although I'm clean, I sometimes want to break out and go to the other extreme."

"Is your fanatical loathing for religion, also a form of rebellion against your father?"

"Yes. He was a sadist. He tortured me all the time because

I was incapable of believing in God. Anyone doing that to a child, should be locked up."

"Did your father also tell you that sex was evil?"

"Looks like it, doesn't it? Why else have I turned out to be what I am?"

"Do you often get depressed, Ian?"

"Not a lot. I'm not the type, but if I start thinking about religion, the mood hits me for days. I feel life isn't worth living."

CHAPTER 34

Miranda's and Rosen's plans worked. White collected the belongings she felt he needed. He refused to wait in the living room while waiting for the removal van to arrive. He sat on a window-sill in the hall, looking furiously through the window, swigging from a flask of whisky.

The removal men arrived two hours late. White opened the door for them to pick up the boxes in the hall.

"These need signing for," said one of the removal men. "It was Mrs White who made the arrangements, so we'll need her signature on the consent form."

"You aren't going to get it," said the dentist, aggressively.

"What the hell do you mean, we ain't going to get it? She on the premises?"

"Yes," said White. "She's upstairs in bed with her fucking lover!"

CHAPTER 35

The shock of White's expulsion from the marital home, took a few days to sink in. He started off in a comfortably financial state and wandered with a suitcase round the streets in London's West End, aimlessly staring into shop windows. He had left most of his possessions in lockers at Victoria Station. Often, he loitered outside restaurants and Wimpy bars and was discontented with their drab appearances.

At first, he was anxious not to spend too much money, as he was aware that funds were no longer coming in. This was the first time in his life when he felt hunger. He had always been used to three meals a day, without wanting more.

He did not care where he went, as he had no goal or obligation. He was wandering down Oxford Street, in the direction of Charing Cross Road. He was attracted by the plush, green, velvet curtains of a London Steak House. The thought of pulling the curtains aside to watch others with meaningless lives, shuffle past, appealed to him.

He went in. The ground floor level of the restaurant was empty, apart from a couple in punk clothing who were about to leave.

A disinterested waiter, with a paunch and blood-shot eyes, sauntered towards him.

"Yes, please?" said the waiter, aggressively.

"Table for one. By the window," said White in staccato blasts.

"You can't eat up here. You'll have to go downstairs."

"If I did that, I wouldn't be able to look out onto the street."

"You eat downstairs," said the waiter, as aggressively as before.

"In that case, I'm afraid you'll have to lose my custom. As I see it, you're pretty short of that."

White regretted his lack of co-operation. It was 8.00 o'clock in the evening. He hadn't eaten anything since early that morning. He went to a Pizzeria next door, where he ordered iia bottle of wine and a pizza. He drank all the wine and felt artificially optimistic.

He knew he had enough money to last him for a few weeks and instead of being fastidious, he went to the other extreme and indulged in reckless spending.

He decided to stay in five-star hotels. His mood had deteriorated and he lay in bed, brooding every morning, until the cleaners told him they needed to do his room. At night, he took his evening clothes from his suitcase and rang Room Service so that they could be ironed. He went to casinos, regularly, in the hope that he would win double the costs required by the hotels he was staying in. He was unlucky at the tables, almost every night, but assumed, misguidedly, that the more he played *Roulette*, the more likely he would be to win a fortune in the end.

This did not happen. When he went to his PO box to collect his mail, he noticed an envelope, ominously marked "General Dental Council". He knew this would not contain the generous cheque he so needed. Instead, it contained a summons to the offices of the General Dental Council. He was aware that he had been reported for rudeness, incompetence and professional slackness, on countless occasions and that his future, as a dental practitioner, was doomed. He shuddered as he remembered one occasion, when he had been blind drunk, on wielding his air rotor drill, which he drove through a horrified patient's tongue, mistaking it, in his intoxicated state, for a cavity.

He was in a state of advanced drunkenness when he was summoned to the sobering surroundings of the General Dental Council's disciplinary court, and struck off, without being verbally capable of defending himself. He accepted that he had been struck off the dental register and had to rely on the Job Centres who offered him various positions. One was that of lavatory cleaner, which he turned down. Another was that of Night Porter in a block of flats which bored him beyond oblivion. The third and last job he was offered, was that of driver of a furniture van, which he inadvertently drove across an old lady's lawn.

He had gambled away his money and become a pauper. Each

day, he became gloomier than he had been the day before and the prospect of suicide was never far from his mind. He was cheered, if only a little, by the news that, because he was incompetent at every job he was offered and thought to be subnormal in some way, he would finally be eligible for full State benefits. He moved into a bedsit on the top floor of a drab, poorly-maintained building at the Trafalgar Square end of Charing Cross Road. There was a small balcony outside his room. Each night, he went out onto it and leaned over the edge, but couldn't summon the courage to kill himself.

He left his room at 11.00 o'clock one Saturday morning, to empty a bag of rubbish. His path was blocked by a neatly-dressed man of about twenty-five, who was sitting on the top step of the perilously unsafe metal spiral staircase, leading to the bottom of the building. He was smoking.

"I'd like to get by, if I may," said White, not politely, but considerably less rudely than the manner in which he had addressed his patients.

The man had on a tailored denim suit and trainers. He sprung to his feet.

"Oh, sorry. I didn't hear you coming," he said. He spoke with a London SW3 accent. White wondered why a man with such an accent should be living in humble circumstances. He was enlightened by the man's pleasant smile and noticed that his gums were swollen and in need of dental floss. He was about to tell him so, but an unpleasant twinge in his stomach reminded him that he wasn't a dentist any more.

He had been out of social contact with others for such a long time that he felt an urgent need to start a conversation with someone, even a stranger.

"Do you live here?" he asked.

"Yes. I moved in two days ago. I live in the room next to yours. My girlfriend's staying with me. She doesn't like me smoking. Every time I want a cigarette, I have to come out here. It's a bit much, isn't it?"

White suddenly looked bitter and angry.

"I used to know a man who smoked all the bloody time. He

177

was a publisher. He nicked my wife. I was a dentist once. I had rooms in Harley Street. Just imagine that — Harley Street! I lost everything, my wife, my livelihood, all my money."

"I'm sorry to hear that. I think it's time we introduced each other, don't you? My name's Rupert Milton. I live here because I work in the bookshop across the road. I hate having to get up early to go to work. All I have to do is walk ten yards."

"Well, I never," said White, who was comforted in a strange way by Milton's presence and sunny manner. Because he had not had a conversation with anyone for so long, even his mother tongue had become rusty and had lost its fluency.

"I'm Simon White," he said, after a long pause.

"You said, to quote your own words, a 'publisher had nicked your wife,' began Milton. "What's his name? It's possible we sell books published by him in our shop. I've worked there for over a year. I know most of the publishers' names."

"His name's Ian Rosen," said White.

"Ian Rosen? He's very well-known. He publishes stuff on every subject you could think of. He's the most undiscriminating publisher I know of."

White suddenly became acutely downhearted. He felt he had made a friend, and, like a foreigner, he struggled to find his words.

"Is he, now?" was all he could think of saying.

"I hope you won't mind my saying so," said Milton, "but you do speak in an awfully strange way, as if saying things tortured you. I'm not usually as familiar as this, but I'm struck by the fact that it seems to hurt you to speak, as if words were being dragged out of you against your will."

White sat down on the top step.

"I haven't spoken to anyone for so long, that I feel I'm speaking another language." His speech was slow and deliberate and he kept waving his hand in the air to help him utter his words.

Milton appeared to be a kind-hearted man. He thought the best way to get his staccato-voiced companion to speak his mother tongue fluently again, would be to take him out and buy him a few drinks. He assumed that it would only take an hour or so of concentrated conversation, to restore his power of speech. He told White to wait. He unlocked the door of his room. White heard him speaking to his girlfriend.

"You'd stay in bed all day, Helga, if you had a chance, wouldn't you?"

"That's what Saturdays are for," said a female voice, with a strong German accent.

"I'm going out for a while. You don't mind, do you?"

"No, I don't mind. I'm tired. I'm going to sleep for the rest of the day, anyway."

Milton came out and pushed the door shut. He and White walked down the spiral staircase and out of the building. Milton took him to a nearby pub. He ordered a pint of beer and bought White a double whisky. The two men sat in a corner, furthest away from the jukebox.

"Are you sure we're talking about the same Ian Rosen?" asked Milton.

"Yes, the same, all right."

"You couldn't have liked him, I know, but you knew him well enough. What sort of a man is he?"

"He's very wild-looking. He's a most un-British sort of fellow. He's emotional, passionate and vibrant. There is something common, and childish about him. He is often clean in appearance, but he sometimes goes for several days without washing. I think it was that which turned my wife on most."

Milton drank a little from his second glass of beer.

"I'm sure no woman would be turned on by a man who didn't wash," he said. "My girl-friend wouldn't stay with me unless I went to the public baths every day."

"My wife's different," said White. "She likes her man to be unwashed. What confused me most was my own attitude to Rosen. He has the most beautiful face I've ever seen in any human being, either male or female, and I'm not even gay. There's an animal attractiveness about him that might attract even the hardest of heterosexual men. It was those frightening feelings he inspired in me that helped to made me hate him so much.

179

"Regardless of his unwashed state and scruffiness, he inspires love in almost everyone who meets him. He has a devastating effect on women. They crane their necks to stare at him in the street, and he has a pied piper effect on children. I have none of those qualities which is why I resent him, but underneath the jealous hate, I get some inexplicable carnal urge which torments me and makes me despise him even more."

Milton drained his second pint of beer.

"Please don't mind my saying so but I suspect you're fighting the fact that you're bi-sexual and haven't the courage to come out of the closet."

"I know that's not the case," said White. "Despite my hatred for him, he comes over as a sweet, loving man and from what I saw, when I came home and found him copulating with my wife, he appeared to be a fantastic, vigorous and virile lover, unlike myself. I could feel the extent of his skill by my wife's screaming orgasms.

"He also knows so many things. He knows everything there is to know about books..."

Milton interrupted him.

"That's not surprising, is it, if he's a publisher?"

"There's another thing I hate him for," said White. "Apart from his periods of dirtiness, he wears his collar and tie loose, everywhere he goes. Women get knocked sideways by that."

"Why didn't you do the same, then?" asked Milton.

"Because, at the time, I was a flaming Harley boy, and I'd have looked an idiot," said White, adding, "there's something else about Rosen. He chain-smokes all day. For some reason, that's another thing which makes women go for him like a magnate. There's something about his commonness and vulgarity which turns them on. Perhaps, they think it's his way of being human, and interpret these traits as a form of bestial warmth. He's a ladies' man. He's sweet and charming towards women and children but he's rude and cutting towards other men."

"In what way is he common?" asked Milton.

"He's a slouch. He's got rather a black sense of humour and likes to make jokes about the unemployed in Derbyshire spitting into their hands. He refers to cigarettes as 'fags'. He uses slang words to describe sexual functions. He's always stuffing potato crisps into his mouth and he is an aggressively militant atheist."

Milton's mouth was full of beer. He suddenly started laughing and spat some of it into the air.

"What's so funny?" asked White.

"You may not know what you said, but you used two statements, just then which had no link whatever. There is no connection between eating crisps and godlessness. I can give you an example of your weird speech mode. I saw a film the other day about the Irish Troubles. An IRA man said to a man, who had no IRA connection, 'I think you ought to join the IRA because both our fathers are ill.' Do you understand the joke?"

"Having thought about it, I do," said White.

Milton took some tobacco from his pocket and rolled himself a cigarette.

"Have you got any children, Simon?" he asked.

"Yes. An adopted child called Ephraim. He's twelve."

"Do you get on with him?"

"Not a lot. He was lumped on us when his mother died in a fire. Rosen was soft on the boy's mother and got soft on Ephraim, too. Rosen often came to the house. A loving bond developed between him and Ephraim who absolutely worships Rosen.

"It so happened that Ephraim's mother brought him up as a religious non-believer, but I did all I could to reverse this."

"Why?"

"Because I thought it was right. One day, at school, he had an anti-religious outburst, and stated to everyone he came across, masters, pupils, alike, that God did not exist. Apart from being his mother's son, which inspired Rosen's love, the man and boy were united by their rejection of a Deity.

"One day, I completely lost my head. I was so fed up with Ephraim's attitude towards this, that I hit him. That finally turned my wife against me. She threatened me with a carving knife. My action enraged Rosen, because of the atheistic bond between him and Ephraim and their love for each other. Rosen

181

accused me of cruelty to the child, because I could not accept that he was a non-believer. They threw me out."

"Are you saying you hit a twelve-year-old boy because he didn't believe in God?"

"Yes. That's about it. Are you a believer?"

"No," said Milton. "I can tell you something about yourself, which you may not necessarily wish to hear."

"Oh? What's that?"

"If what you say is anything to go by, it sounds as if you're not a very nice person. Ian Rosen comes extremely well out of your story, whether he goes round unwashed or not, whether he is a womaniser, or whether in your eyes he appears common or vulgar. Whatever his flaws are, he sounds an attractive, strong, golden-hearted, man, a very human man, a man of rare decency and nobility. No wonder, you were thrown out."

White was jolted by the words of the man he thought he might befriend. "Why do you say that?" he asked, his tone embarrassed and subdued.

Milton took his empty glass back to the bar and returned to the table to collect his jacket.

"Because you're a shit, Simon," he said. White turned his head, slowly, uncomprehendingly. Milton was already outside in the street.

White bought a bottle of whisky from an off licence and returned to his room. He lay on his back, and drank a quarter of the bottle, and slept until Saturday evening. He woke up deeply depressed and brooded for a few hours. He decided that he was faced with little choice but to take his life. His black mood was intolerable and was worsening, causing him to feel as if a fast-moving cancer were eating into his head. Even five minutes seemed too long a period of time for him to wait.

He drank the remainder of the whisky and left his room, locking the door and leaving his key on the inside, to make sure he wouldn't lose his nerve and go back in.

He stood on the top step of the spiral staircase and was reminded of his meeting with Milton whom he thought might become his friend. He looked down at the vast, winding, black metal which reassured him by its beckoning, if chilling appearance. He knew that once he jumped, the despair would be annihilated, and, in view of his religious beliefs, he expected to wake up, surrounded by fluffy clouds and angels tweaking lyres.

He took a few steps backwards and ran to the top of the staircase, raising his arms in front of him, as if diving into a swimming pool. As his feet sprung from the top step, he felt a few seconds of complete happiness, as his body bounced from rail to rail, before being embraced in the Reaper's comforting, skeletal arms.

CHAPTER 36

Rosen and Miranda were already married when they heard the news of White's death. No-one was sad when they heard the news that he had died by his own hand, because word had got round that he had been unkind to an innocent, bereaved child, and had even gone so far as to call that child's late father names, and state in his hearing that he should have been aborted.

Rosen suggested that some respect be shown. He, Miranda and Ephraim picked spring flowers from their garden, and laid them on the recalcitrant dentist's grave.

Ephraim backed away from the grave. Rosen laid his hand on his shoulder.

"He was cruel to you but you have still shown goodwill. Not many people think like that," he said.

"Simon was a very unhappy man," replied the boy, "and he was punished enough by that alone. I always try to see good in everybody, even if they are wicked."

* * *

Ephraim's life was unchanged. Becket drove him to and from his school each day. He still enchanted boys of all ages. They were attracted to him because he continued to show off, without any signs of mockery or malice.

He once spent two hours repairing the broken wing of a pigeon, with Sellotape, but that, for his own private reasons, was an act he performed alone, devoid of an audience.

Ephraim was sitting down to dinner with Rosen and Miranda.

"How was school today, Ephi?" asked Rosen, as he re-filled his wine glass."

"Lovely, thank you, Ian."

"Lovely? Well, I must say that's the funniest word I've heard, to describe a day at school. Go on, my boy. Tell Miranda and me what you got up to, and how those studies of yours are getting on."

"I got an A grade for my Latin test."

"You did? Very well done. Anything else to tell us?"

"I got A for English composition, too."

"Now, you're talking! We could make a writer of you yet, like your mother. What was the composition about, my boy?"

"It was about this really stupid doctor. He calls himself a consultant. He's into hearts. He has to identify one of his patients in a hospital mortuary. The patient had thrown himself from a lavatory window. I meant the composition to be funny. There's a lot of dialogue between the doctor and the man in the mortuary."

"There is? Have you brought the composition home?" asked Rosen.

"Yes."

"Do get it and let me have a look at it."

"Are you sure you want to see it?"

"Of course, I am. I wouldn't have asked you, otherwise, would I?"

Ephraim went to his room and found the composition. The fact that Rosen was invariably kind to him, dispelled his selfconsciousness about showing him his carefully thought-out creation.

Dinner was over. Miranda and Rosen were sitting by the fire. Ephraim brought the two-sided piece of paper into the room and handed it to Rosen. The first thing Rosen noticed was his neat, italic handwriting.

"Beautiful writing!" he said. "Have you seen it, Miranda?"

"Of course, I have. Why don't you read his work?"

Rosen read the composition, intently. As his eyes moved over the page, his reaction was one of mild laughter which turned to disinhibited giggles.

Ephraim had overlooked the rank of his main character. The 'doctor" he had described, was a consultant cardiologist, and a man of great seniority, due to his age and his distinguished career.

He was accounted for as swigging from a bottle of whisky, while talking to the mortuary attendant, using a torrent of outdated slang words. It was stated that he lit up a fat Havana

185

cigar. In his frustration to find his dead patient, he wrenched open all the drawers, one by one, and left them open.

Ephraim's dialogue between the doctor and the attendant, was ribald, pompous, loaded with strings of adjectives and interspersed with schoolboy slang. Because the story had been penned by a twelve-year-old boy, his work had been warmly commended by his English master.

Much of the dialogue was nonsensical. The doctor kept complaining about the attendant's inability to find the right drawer. If illogically, given his distinguished rank, the revered, Etonian-voiced doctor was accounted for as addressing the man as a "right flipping, bleeding, half-witted spastic."

In turn, the attendant called him a "frigging, four-eyed nancy boy," an inappropriate choice of words because, apart from his almost God-like status in the medical profession, the senior consultant had been described by Ephraim as a respectably married man with four children.

By the time Rosen had finished reading, tears of laughter were flowing down his cheeks. He was encouraged by the child's developing gift for the written word. He was sure he would continue to write such original, if desperately eccentric compositions, and improve his penmanship over the years.

"He's going to be another Juliet, when he gets older, isn't he, Miranda?" he said. "And he's going to do Black Comedy, like his mother. There's one thing you must understand, though, Ephi. A consultant cardiologist would not be likely to speak like that to a mortuary attendant. Nor, indeed, would a mortuary attendant speak like that to a consultant."

"There's no doubt he's got the gene in him," said Miranda.

Rosen turned to Ephraim who had returned to his chair, after putting a log on the fire.

"Would you like to be a writer, when you grow up, old fellow, like your mother?"

"Yes. I like being told to write imaginative passages. When I do it, I feel happy. I'm in a beautiful world that I've made, myself. I like writing things on paper, writing my thoughts, anything."

"You're Juliet's boy, all right. We were very close. Now, I've got you, and I feel she's living in you. You've got her outrageous sense of humour. It means a lot to me to look after you as a father," said Rosen.

"I feel like that, too," said the boy.

"You look worried, all of a sudden. Have you got a question for me?"

"Yes. It's on my mind. You knew my father, William Rendon, didn't you?"

"Yes, of course, I did."

"Did you like him?" asked Ephraim, cautiously.

"Yes, Ephi. He was a sweet, gentle soul."

"Do you know he was a necrophiliac?"

Rosen paused. "Yes. Yes, I do."

"Then, do you still like his memory?"

"I've just told you, Ephi, I had a lot of respect for your father. I know what Miranda told you. I know everything. Despite my respect for him, I am aware that he was, through no fault of his own, a very, very sick man. Once, whatever it was, took him over, he had no control over the things he did and no memory of it, afterwards."

"How does that happen?"

"He had a recognized illness. He was a psychotic. Sometimes, if you have gone through terrible suffering or trauma, you are vulnerable to it. There are many forms of it, but your father had the most commonly recognized form. In his case, there were times when half of his mind shut down completely. The other half worked, but because the old half had turned off, he did things he shouldn't have done, when he went through this phase, and didn't remember anything after he'd done them."

"I think I understand. He was like Jekyll and Hyde, wasn't he?"

"Yes. That's it. Jekyll and Hyde. Wherever your father is now, in space, in this room, in areas around you, I know he sees you."

"I'd like to believe that. How do you know?"

"I can't say how I know. I just know. There are no such

187

places as Heaven and Hell, but one thing I do believe, is the fact that the dead can come back to watch the living."

"But I'd see my father, if he came back."

"No, you wouldn't. The dead are invisible, but they still see. Your father hated White, from beyond the grave. When White had to go, I feel sure your father was behind his falling fortune, because he treated you badly. Your father dotes on you and is very proud of you. I want you to remember that, just in case you feel lonely at any time, when Miranda and I are out of the house."

"Thank you, Ian. I'll remember. I've got another question."

"Well?"

"Do you know the book, *Dr Jekyll and Mr Hyde*?" began Ephraim.

"Of course, I do. Books are my trade. You make me laugh, you do. What you just said was the equivalent of asking White if he knew what toothpaste was. What about the book?"

"Well, I read it. In fact, I read it several times but I was a bit confused and frightened by it. What did Jekyll do when he turned into Hyde?"

Rosen picked up a log and threw it onto the fire, unsure how to word his reply.

"Oh, he was just generally beastly to the women in the streets," he said, vaguely.

Miranda giggled.

"Yes, that's right, he went up to them, and said things like, 'If you don't get out of my way, immediately, I'll steal your bonnet,'" she said.

"We mustn't forget, Ephi's very advanced for his years," said Rosen. "I don't know why we're talking to him in this babyish way. I didn't mean that, exactly, Ephi. When Jekyll turned into Hyde, he was sexually violent towards these women. He beat them. He raped them. When he turned back into Jekyll, he was civilized and respectable. In the end, his Hyde side took over. Instead of only being a bastard once in a while, his bad side took over more frequently, until he became a bastard for good."

"That wasn't the case with my father, was it?" asked the boy.

"Oh, Christ, no! When your father did the things he shouldn't have done, it was only on a few isolated occasions. He was a sweet person, most of the time and that was the way he was until he died."

"Did he commit suicide?"

"Certainly not, no. He died by accident. He took too many pills, underestimating their strength. He had too much to live for, to want to take his life."

"What had he to live for?"

"His work, for one thing ... women." Rosen winked at Miranda. "Your father was an exceptionally highly-sexed fella."

CHAPTER 37

At break, the following day, Ephraim was surrounded, as always, by a thronging flock of boys, whom he referred to as his "disciples". They stood back to give him space, while he cracked jokes, told attention-seeking anecdotes and sang ribald, barrack-room ballads.

The bell rang and the boys returned to the school building. Paul Wise, Ephraim's best friend, was the only boy who remained outside. He went over to Ephraim.

"Where were you, Paul? You weren't at History, earlier. I looked everywhere for you. I was hoping I'd be able to sit next to you."

Ephraim noticed that his friend was upset about something. "What's the matter?"

"I'm afraid the doctor had to come out, last night. It's my mother. She's got cancer. It's too advanced to be cured."

"You shouldn't be too quick to believe that. A lot of very bad cancers can be cured, these days."

"The doctor said she only had three months to live."

Ephraim was distressed by his friend's sadness. He tried to instill a mood of hope and optimism within him. He told him a fictitious story, making up the words as he went along. He believed that true kindness manifested itself in being economical with the truth and telling the listener what he wanted to hear.

"I had this uncle, once," he began. The act of lying was so natural to him that he believed, at that moment, that he had had an uncle. He continued, "He had cancer, too. All his doctors told him he only had two months to live. They were wrong. Six years later, my uncle was killed in a car crash."

"So there is hope, after all?" said Paul.

"Yes, of course, there is. There always is. All you have to do, is remember what I told you, just now, about my uncle. How's your father taking it?"

"Terribly badly, I'm afraid."

"Have you any other family?"

"Three sisters. They're all older than me."

"Do you like them?"

"I like them, all right. They're always very nice to me."

"Then it's not so bad, is it? Do your sisters live at home?"

"Yes. They play games with me a lot, Dominoes, Monopoly, games like that."

"Which is your favourite?" asked Ephraim.

"Monopoly. I have dreams about owning the whole of London when I grow up. They're only dreams, though. A dream is only a dream."

"I don't agree," said Ephraim. "It's dreams that keep you alive. They give you hope. I make myself dream all the time when I'm awake. Sometimes, I don't know the difference between what is real and what isn't."

"I hope you're not referring to what you said about your uncle."

Ephraim altered his eye contact, and instead of looking his friend in the face, as he had been during the conversation, he looked away.

"I wasn't making up what I told you about my uncle's death, Paul. It's true, all of it."

CHAPTER 38

Rosen, Miranda and Ephraim were sitting in the kitchen, having breakfast. Rosen had made a point of having a crate of honey sent to the house as he knew that Ephraim liked to eat tablespoonfuls of it on its own.

The family had been eating in a silence broken by Rosen.

"There's something worrying me, Ephi," he began.

"Oh, what's that?"

"Why don't you ever bring your friends home?"

"I suppose I've never thought about it."

"You're not ashamed of something, are you?"

"Ashamed? No," replied the boy. He was confused and unsure of his thoughts. Although unaware of it, he wished to be divided, to have his school and home as separate entities, and not to allow his home self and school self to meet.

"Then, what is the problem?" asked Rosen.

"When there are two lives, there are two people," began Ephraim. "I wish I could understand it, but I can't. Somehow, I feel peculiar about bringing someone from one life into another life, a boy from school, to my home."

"Why?" asked Rosen.

"I feel awful about it. Other boys keep asking me, as well. I want to cut myself in half. I want to close one side down when the other is in use. Sometimes, I think it's my father in me."

"I can understand that," said Rosen. "I'm not going to force you to do anything. Miranda said you had a favourite friend. His name's Paul someone, isn't it?"

"That's right, Paul Wise."

"Is he Saul Wise's son? Saul Wise is one of my best-selling authors."

"Paul did say his father wrote books. He never said you'd published them."

"That's because he probably doesn't know that my name's Rosen when yours is Rendon. Did your friend say his father's first name was Saul?"

"He did say that, a while ago. Paul's mother is very ill.

Cancer, he said."

"I was wondering why Saul had been taking so long to finish his latest book. His son must be very unhappy. Why don't you bring him home for the weekend, eh?"

"Well, er, can I think about it?"

"No," said Rosen. "The sooner you bring your friend home, the sooner you'll get over your discomfort. Once you bring the two sides of yourself together, it won't be unpleasant any more. When your two selves meet, you'll forget you ever felt this way. Go on. Ask him. Do so, for your own good. It's possible Paul won't want to leave his family while his mother's so ill. You never know, though, he might want to get away from a morbid household."

Ephraim was anxious to please Rosen because of his love for him, but he didn't believe he would feel comfortable when his two personalities would be forced to meet.

"OK, I'll ask him," he said.

"You don't have to if you don't want to," said Miranda. "Don't pressurize him, Ian."

"No. It's OK. I'll do it," said Ephraim.

* * *

English Literature was the first class the following day. The boys were studying *Julius Caesar*. Ephraim and Paul were sitting next to each other at the back of the room.

"How's your mother?" asked Ephraim.

"She's worse. The doctor's giving her morphine, now. I really hate it at home. I can't bear being in a house of death. I want to go away, anywhere, I don't care where."

"I suppose you could come to my house for the weekend," said Ephraim, in an abrupt, thoughtless tone, which was unintended.

"You don't really sound as if you want me."

"I didn't mean it like that. Of course, I want you. It's just that I've never brought anyone home before."

"What, never? That's pretty odd."

193

"You said your father wrote books, didn't you?"

"Yes. What of it?"

"What's his publisher's name?"

"That's a weird question," said Paul. "My father's publisher is called Ian Rosen."

"I thought so. Ian Rosen is my stepfather."

"You never told me that."

"He's my second stepfather. My first stepfather's dead. I hated my first stepfather but I love Ian Rosen. My natural father's dead. The more I hear about him, the sadder I am I never met him."

"Oh, that's right. William Rendon, the necrophiliac."

"I beg your pardon?"

"Don't you remember? You told the whole class he was a necrophiliac."

"I know. I was showing off."

The English Literature master clapped his hands.

"Rendon and Wise," he called out.

"Sir?" said the two boys, in unison.

"Stop talking, damn you! Where had I got to in *Julius Caesar*? Rendon, you answer."

"Cassius is trying to persuade Brutus to have hostile feelings towards Caesar," said Ephraim.

"That is correct. If you want to have a private conversation, in future, kindly wait until break."

* * *

Ephraim felt sick, when Becket arrived at the school, to pick up the two boys, the following Friday afternoon. The melancholy, book-read chauffeur, too, was feeling apprehensive. He had only to look at Ephraim, to be terrified that he was going to be sick in the Rolls.

"Are you two boys all right to travel in the car?" he asked.

"We're fine. It's all right, Mr Becket, neither of us is going to be sick," said Ephraim. "If I feel it coming on, I'll give you plenty of notice."

194

"You certainly will. You're so right!"

The traffic between the school and the Rosens' house was heavy. Ephraim and Paul felt sick, Ephraim, because the merger of his two selves, was an anathema to him, Paul due to the imminent loss of his mother, and pity for the father he felt unable to comfort. He was the first to break the silence.

"It's not only my mother I'm worried about, Ephi. It's my father. He's been in writer's deadlock for some weeks, now. He's behind with his work and is frightened of being sued for breach of contract."

"Does he know you're spending the weekend in his publisher's house?" asked Ephraim.

"Yes. I told him. I know how close you are to Ian Rosen. Is there any way you can explain this to him?"

"I suspect you may be using me," said Ephraim, his tone angry and paranoid. "Is it possible you're not valuing me for what I am, but as a potential go-between to sort out your father's problems?"

"That's not a very nice thing to say," said Paul, "when you know I'm suffering because of my mother dying. I've been friends with you, long before I found out that your stepfather published my father's work."

Ephraim opened his window the whole way. He leant out of it, to dispel his nausea, which was replaced by a wave of guilt.

"I didn't mean what I said. I'll tell Ian. You don't realize what a nice man he is. He'll understand."

"OK."

"What does your father write?" asked Ephraim, in an attempt to be friendly. "Does he write novels?"

Paul failed to reply.

"Please talk to me. All I did was ask you what sort of books he wrote."

"He's written a few thrillers for your stepfather. They sold well. He gave up fiction a while ago. He's been doing biographies over the last few years."

"Would you please stop the car, Mr Becket," said Ephraim, urgently.

An agonized look clouded over Becket's face. He swerved to the side of the road, and embarrassed Ephraim by the exaggerated formality with which he sprung from the car, to open the door for him.

Ephraim was sick into a trimmed, box-like laurel hedge, whose irritated owner was making noisy, cutting movements on the other side. At least, the boy was relieved by the fact that Becket refrained from holding his head. He was already mortified with the shame of travelling in a chauffeur-driven Rolls-Royce, while Paul was driven to and from the school each day, by his financially-burdened father, in a second-hand Ford Escort.

Ephraim got back into the car. As Becket returned to the driver's seat, the boy looked briefly at the mirror and noticed the look of resignation and despair on the chauffeur's face. He wondered what unexpressed thoughts plagued him and was surprised by his ability to disguise them with his occasional outbursts of sardonic humour.

"Are you all right?" asked Paul.

"I am, now. What biographies has your father written?"

"Are you putting me to the test?"

"No, I only want to know, for my own interest."

"He did one on a Victorian narrative painter, whose name I've forgotten. He did another on a pretty boring Swedish playwright called Ibsen. At the moment, he's trying to write about a man he refers to as 'de Soggins'. He's very secretive about it and often locks the door of his study. On the few occasions he forgets to lock the door, I sometimes walk in, and he bundles a pile of papers under his arm, like a criminal."

"Why?"

"He said I wasn't to read what he'd been writing."

"Is that because he thinks he writes badly?"

"At it again, aren't you, Ephi?"

"At what?"

"You're trying to look down on my father, just because your stepfather employs him."

"And you're trying to look down on my stepfather, just because your father is employed by him."

"You're lording it over me."

"I'm not lording it over you. It's not my fault I'm rich. There are times when I wish I had nothing. If I didn't live the way I do, I wouldn't be embarrassed about taking friends to the house. I wouldn't need to get out and be sick, either."

"You'd be sick, anyway. You're always being sick."

Ephraim's eyes wandered to the driver's mirror, once more. He noticed Becket's dry-humoured smile.

CHAPTER 39

Rosen and Miranda were effusively welcoming towards Paul, and put the sad, suspicious boy at his ease. They were in the garden, having tea. Rosen noticed Ephraim's fast breathing and the uncharacteristic, jerky movements of his eyes, from one object to another. When nervous, he had a tendency to speak rapidly, abruptly and unnaturally loudly.

"Paul's father's worried because he's behind with his book. He's worried about money. He's afraid you'll sue him for breach of contract. He's writing about a man he calls 'de Soggins'! he shouted.

Rosen had hysterical giggles. He turned to Paul.

"Why on earth does your father call him 'de Soggins'?" he asked.

"I don't know. Isn't that his name, Mr Rosen?"

"No, Paul. Your father's writing a book for me about the Marquis de Sade."

"Who's he? My father won't talk about it, you see."

Rosen had realized that Paul was not as precocious and advanced for his years, as Ephraim. He felt able to relate to his stepson as an adult, and had to make an effort to treat Paul as a child.

"He was, well, er, a ... French gentleman," he muttered, adding, "There's absolutely no need for your father to worry about the book being overdue. I'm so sorry to hear about your mother's illness. Ephraim told me about it. It's a terrible thing to have happen in a family. Tell your father to take his time. Jolly old de Soggins will just have to wait. Tell him, it's bon swoggins, de Soggins, until he feels able to take up his pen."

* * *

The boys were in Ephraim's room, sitting on the bed.

"Had you heard of the Marquis de Sade?" asked Paul.

"Yes, I had." Ephraim's tone was even more abrupt than it had been during tea. The idea of being the stepson of his guest's father's employer, and the suspicion that his friend resented his riches, made him feel ill. He tried to convince himself that Paul was feeling equally as uneasy about being the poorer of the two, and having a father who was beholden to Rosen.

"Who was he, besides just a Frenchman?" asked the guest.

"He was what they might call a ladies' man," replied Ephraim, stiffly. He continued, his voice like that of an exhausted tourist guide, his sentences clipped and staccato.

"He was an aristocrat, much richer than me, of course. He was forced to marry. He was in love with his wife's sister. He had three children, two sons, one daughter. He liked his valets to whip him and he whipped them. He whipped prostitutes and asked them to whip him."

"Why?"

"How the bloody hell should I know?"

Ephraim got up and looked out of the window.

"Our next door neighbour is mowing his lawn. He owns a big black dog and he drives a German car." The delivery of the dull, unsolicited information sounded like a declaration of war.

"Why are you behaving like this?" asked Paul. "What's the matter with you? You're a different person at school. You're always cheerful, entertaining and jolly. Here, your whole personality's gone missing. You look exactly the same but your mind seems to have been taken over by a robot. You're so cold and unfriendly."

"I'm sorry, Paul. My right hand doesn't know what my left hand is doing."

"Why not? It should do. Both your hands are controlled by you, aren't they?"

"No. They are not."

"You frighten me, Ephi. Why are you like this?"

"Because I like to keep my wounds well bandaged up, at all times, Paul, at all times."

"What wounds? Wounds inflicted by whom?"

"Perhaps, one of the worst, is my guilt about yearning for my natural father, when my love for Ian is so great."

"Your father was a necrophiliac."

"So what? Your father writes about a man who asked prostitutes to whip him."

"Even if your father were to re-appear, he'd never value you while you lived. He'd prefer to wait for you to be dead," said Paul.

"I don't understand your remark."

"Yes, you do. You like to show off in front of an audience, but if you get carried away, and let something out, that you think is funny and sensational at the time, you haven't the guts to take it, when someone throws it back at you."

The insult was too much for Ephraim. He walked towards Paul until he was only an inch away from him.

"I want you out of my house, Paul, and that means, now," he shouted.

CHAPTER 40

Ephraim came down to dinner, alone. He looked sheepishly at Miranda and Rosen, and helped himself from the sideboard.

"What's happened to your charming friend?" asked Rosen. "Why isn't he here?"

"Because he's somewhere else!" shouted Ephraim.

"What kind of dotty answer is that?"

"I told him to go."

"Why, Ephi?"

"Because he tried to break into my head."

Rosen got up and walked over to his stepson. He put his arm round his shoulder.

"I've a feeling your quarrel was a misunderstanding, coming from you, not him."

"Ian's right," said Miranda. "I know you were feeling terrible. I sensed it at tea, but however much you were suffering, you could have forced yourself to be a bit nicer to the poor boy, particularly as his mother is dying. Those barked remarks you made, weren't addressed to him. You weren't polite enough to even bark *at* him. You were barking about him, as if he weren't there."

Ephraim let out a nervous laugh.

"It's all right, my boy," said Rosen. "I'll soon make a whole boy out of you, not a divided boy. He who lives divided, divides others. That's a dangerous thing, so we'll have to do some work on it. The more frequently you bring other boys home, the sooner this problem will be solved. I'll come to your room, later and we'll have a talk. I bought a mouth organ, yesterday. There's something I want to play to you — after our talk, not before."

Ephraim was in bed, lying on his back. Rosen came in and sat on the bed.

"So what's this nonsense really in aid of, eh?"

"Although I like the boys to flock to me in droves, to give me the audience I need, within me, I only relate to them at a distance. You're the one person I can get close to, even more so

201

than Miranda. I live in permanent fear of being insulted, of someone trying to get into the vault I prefer to keep locked. It's only the front window I want the world to see, not what I keep at the back of the shop."

"Something's happened recently, hasn't it, Ephi?"

"Yes. It wasn't anything to do with Paul."

"Let's have it."

"A boy called David invited me to have lunch with him on the lawn at the school. David had just had his *Bar Mitzvah*. His father and sister were there. His sister was fifteen. Her name was Rachel. She had long, straight, red hair. She was very beautiful. I fell in love with her, as soon as I saw her."

"Oh, you're so like your father!" said Rosen. "What happened, or are you too shy to tell me?"

"I started talking to her, in a frank manner. I don't believe in moderating words."

"Out with it, Ephi. What did you say to her?"

"I got carried away. She had on a pretty dress and had a nice bosom. I said, or maybe I shouted, 'You've got a fantastic arse. I want to go to bed with you'."

"Oh, Christ, Ephi! Did you say that in front of the father?"

"Yes. He said something in reply, as well."

"I bet he did. What did he say?"

"He said, 'Those manners of yours, Rendon, could do with a lick of paint.'"

Rosen tried not to laugh, but failed. "As you're so grown up, I'll talk to you like a grown up. If you want to attract a young lady, you should use more delicate language. What would have been wrong with, 'If I may say so, you are very beautiful?'"

There was a silence.

"Just how well did you know my mother?" asked the boy, his tone obsessively inquisitive."

"If you really want to know, I knew her a lot more than I let on. I was in love with her. We were lovers."

"Is there a chance you might be my natural father?"

"No. All this happened a while after your father's death."

Ephraim sat up, supporting his weight on his elbows.

He smiled, cheekily.

"What was she like as a lover?"

Rosen turned briefly away from the boy.

"She was quite out of this world," he said, in a voice scarcely above a whisper.

"Have you had other lovers?"

"I have, yes, but not since Miranda."

"Is sex very important to you?"

"Yes. It's the equivalent of religion."

"Are you religious?"

"No. I love life too much to need God. That sort of thing is abhorrent to me. I'm like you."

"I don't understand."

"Don't you remember that furore you caused about Abraham and Isaac? Miranda told me about it. You nearly brought the whole bloody school to a standstill.

"Miranda had me in stitches when she told me you'd said to that master, 'I think God's an absolute shit. Who the fucking hell does he think he is?' But even so, I'd like it if you'd make some effort to be a bit more polite to your teachers. Don't use the word 'fuck', either.

"I know just how much you hate having God thrown at you, though. I hate the way he's shovelled down any child's throat. That's why I said I was like you. I know what it's like. I understand how you feel."

"What, about God?"

"Yes. I don't think there's anything up there, either, Ephi. The idea of God existing is a myth, something no-one wants to be burdened with. I know your father and mother felt the same."

"When did you first start thinking like that, Ian?"

"When I was about your age. I'd had an orthodox Jewish upbringing. I believe in the humane values I was taught and am grateful for that. What I couldn't support was the way God was rammed down my throat. It turned me against religion for the rest of my life. That doesn't mean I don't value the need for compassion, but the very last thing we need is some unseen Being, which we are taught exists, but doesn't."

"Have you ever had children?" asked the boy.

"Yes. I had a daughter, but she was run over and killed at the age of six."

"What, my mother's daughter?"

"No. Another woman's daughter."

"I'm very sorry."

"Don't be. At least, I know where she's buried. I visit the grave, sometimes and I feel comforted."

"The sex act, Ian, what is it really like?" asked the boy, suddenly.

"It's the most beautiful thing, the most wonderful thing in the world," replied the lady-killing publisher. "You'll know about it in a few years, and you'll laugh at anyone trying to tell you there's a bloody Deity." His tone was almost angry.

Rosen paused. He took the mouth organ from his pocket.

"Would you like me to play?"

"Yes."

Rosen played a piece of music, the like of which the boy had never heard before. A wave of heat passed through him.

"That's wonderful, Ian. What is it?"

"*Voltava*. Its composer's name is Smetana. When extreme beauty is mixed with suffering, the suffering takes on a grace of its own and becomes dignified. It should ennoble you. When you go back to school on Monday, I want you to go to Paul, and say you're sorry you hurt him."

"I never meant to, but I'll say I'm sorry."

"Good lad. That way, you'll get liked, and not just used as a performer."

Rosen left and went to Miranda's room where she was waiting. The boy heard their violent act of love through the thin wall, and wept because he was too young to know how a lover felt, when he loved.

CHAPTER 41

In a rough, noisy pub in Hampstead called The Swan, sat a man and woman, in their mid thirties. The man was well-dressed and flashy-looking. He had untidy dark hair, bloodshot eyes and a lean, calculating face. His hands were small and clumsy, and he wore a signet ring on his left little finger. He was in the jewellery trade, although his profits were at a loss. His name was Jethro Pendary.

The woman at his side looked old for her years. She had long, curly, naturally blonde hair which was in poor condition and looked as if it had been dyed that colour. Her eyes were slanting and of a glacial blue. She had lines on her forehead and deep furrows on either side of her mouth. She looked washed-up and lush, as if she earned her living by commercial promiscuity.

She had on a tight, black silk dress, secured by thick black straps of a different fabric, as if they had been sewn on to replace the delicate straps which had originally belonged to the dress. Her legs were shapely and bare. She had on a pair of black stiletto heels.

Her name was Kate Alice Rendon and she was drunk. She was leaning against Pendary and rubbing her head against his arm.

"How did you know my son's at King David's?" asked Pendary, his voice blunted and his accent regionless.

"I wanted to know. I asked around, didn't I?" she said. "Someone I know, asked the barman, here. Apparently, you go round telling others, that your son's at the school." Despite her common appearance, her voice was cultivated and refined.

"Why should that be of any interest to you?"

"It's not only of interest to me. It could be of interest to us both. You're in debt and I want to live comfortably for the rest of my life."

Pendary drained his glass of Newcastle Brown Ale. He went to the bar and ordered another, and a fourth double gin and tonic for Kate.

"What did you mean by the remark you made, just then?" he asked.

"I suspect you're not a man of grandiose principles, if the other women you associate with, are anything to go by. How low do you think you'd be prepared to stoop? Well, you know, where getting your hands on big money is concerned?"

Pendary drank more Newcastle Brown Ale. The alcohol caused him to find Kate's loose appearance, combined with the smell of gin on her breath, attractive.

"I don't have much of a conscience," he said. "Right and wrong doesn't bother me. The only thing that troubles me, is ending up in jail."

"What if I were to suggest something, and that thing were fool-proof? What if I had a plan which meant neither of us would be caught?"

She rubbed his arm with her hand. Her chipped nail varnish added a further dimension to the seediness of her appearance, and excited him.

"Come on, Kate. Let's have it," he said.

"Oh, Jethro, don't be in too much of a hurry. This is something which can't be rushed."

"I'd still appreciate it if you'd tell me what you had in mind," he said.

"It's about this nephew of mine. I'm bloody incensed, Jethro. All my father's money went to my older brother, and not one penny came to me. When my brother died, it all went to his son."

"Is that because you'd done something to upset your father?"

Kate forced herself to cry and widened her slanting blue eyes, allowing her tears to fall down her cheeks, unchecked. She put on a frail and waif-like act, aware that a fast-living, sparsely-moralled man, such as Pendary, would warm further to her.

"I never did wrong, Jethro. I was always loving, loyal and respectful to my father. It's just that he had treated my brother badly as a child, and made up for it by giving him all he had."

"Is this true?"

"Yes, Jethro."

"What happened to your mother?"

"She was killed in a car crash, on her way to my boarding school, to pick me up."

"I'm sorry to hear that. Where did you go to school?"

"I went to Godstowe, in High Wycombe."

"*You* went to Godstowe? I don't believe you!"

"Why?"

"Because it's such a strict school, or so I was told. Its academic standards are about the highest of any prep. school in the country.* I hope you don't think I'm rude, but you don't seem the product of a school like that. Where did you go after that?"

"I was going to go to Wycombe Abbey. I'd passed my Common Entrance, but because of the transfer of funds after my father's death, the fees couldn't be paid. I went to an awful school instead, where I didn't learn anything. I wasn't even allowed a decent education."

Pendary felt she had been unjustly treated. He loved her at that moment and prepared himself for whatever crime she wished him to commit, provided he would benefit from it.

"A man can get away with being denied an education, but it's tough for a woman," he remarked. "What's your plan?"

"My nephew is at King David's. He's the brat with all the money, the money I should have shared. The only way to get what is morally, but not legally mine, is to abduct him, hold him to ransom."

"I suppose you think we could get away with it, do you, just like that?"

"Yes, if we work it out. Think of the hundreds of people you read about in the newspapers, who have been kidnapped. Take Suzy Lamplugh. Her body was never found, nor was her abductor. The police are really slow about kidnapping offences in this country. They're pretty slow all round. They institute a search, slap up a picture of the missing person in all the nicks, drag a few lakes. Then they say they've done their best, and they're too bone idle to carry their enquiries through.

"Did they find Lord Lucan? No. They were too lazy to look for him, except for raking a couple of beaches. They weren't

*The Author attended this school.

even able to find the bodies of Myra Hindley's victims. Because they were so incompetent, they had to get the old bag out of jail and ask her to identify most of their graves."

Kate rubbed Pendary's thigh and spoke in a seductive, drink-sodden whisper.

"I'd like to take this boy to another country. Marseilles's the place I have in mind, because I know it so well and the layout of its streets is familiar to me."

"Are you suggesting we just turn up at the school, find him in the playground and cart him off, just like that?"

"No, stupid," said Kate. "There's only one way to do it and that's the easy way. Talk it over with your son. Get him to befriend my nephew. Develop the friendship. Then, invite him to stay with you for the weekend. Put him at his ease over a forty-eight hour period. Invite him to come for a walk, say after lunch on Sunday. Knock him unconscious. Bind him and gag him and sling him into the boot of your car.

"As for your son, offer him a share of the ransom money, to give him a motive, but there's no need for you to keep your promise. The money should be shared by both of us. Once the Rendon boy's guardians have paid, and the heat is off, we could settle down in a warm, sunny place, like California. What do you think?"

"It's a perfect idea," said Pendary. "The more I think about it, the better it sounds. I've never felt comfortable since my wife died, five years ago, but since we've been in here, I've felt more attached to you than I was. I want you to move in with me, and when this is over, I want to marry you."

"OK," she said. Her tone was awkward and stilted. "If we get this right, I wouldn't say 'no'."

"I need more details about the boy," said Pendary. What's his name?"

"Ephraim Rendon."

"Where does he live?"

"Hampstead. Five minutes away from the Royal Free Hospital."

"Who looks after him?"

"A wealthy man called Rosen, and his wife, Miranda. She

208

used to be married to a dentist called Simon White."

"I'm not interested in who she was last married to," barked Pendary. "What sort of man is Rosen?"

"A most devoted man. He adores Ephraim. Rosen's a good-humoured, well-adjusted, stable sort of person. He's very rich, as I said. He's said to be devastatingly sexy."

"Do you think I want to hear that?" said Pendary, irritably. "How did you find all this out."

"Through a private detective."

"How were you able to afford one?"

"I've saved up," she replied, vaguely. Apart from her earnings as a more sophisticated class of prostitute, she had robbed a number of people, including a woman whose signature she had forged on cheques.

"What does the Rendon boy look like?"

"He's got an angel's face and fair wavy hair. Take a look at this. Here's his photograph."

Pendary observed a small, frayed photograph of Ephraim sitting on a garden seat, holding a football.

"How old is he?"

"Twelve."

"He's exactly the same age as my Rodney. They'd be in the same year, but I don't know about the stream."

"Ephraim's in the A stream. What about your son?"

"I'm not sure. I'll ask him when I next see him."

"Will he be hard to persuade, do you think?" asked Kate.

"No. He's got no values. He's like his father in that way. He loves money, and would sink to any level to get it. He's a cold boy. He's capable of being friendly and affable but he doesn't form relationships, easily. He's a loner. He respects me very much, and when I tell him to do something, he does it."

"So you think he will be prepared to put on an act of befriending Ephraim, knowing what's going to happen to him?"

"Oh, yes," said Pendary. "He'd think nothing of it, not if he was obeying my orders."

209

CHAPTER 42

Kate, Pendary and his son Rodney, were having tea, in the kitchen in the Pendarys' airy, top floor flat in Arkwright Road, Hampstead. Kate reminded Rodney of his late mother who looked like her, as well as being of similar brazen mien.

"Well, Rodney, what do you think of our plan?" asked Pendary, in a domineering tone. "Remember, you'll be rich, as well. You'd like to move to somewhere bigger, wouldn't you?"

"Anywhere's better than this. I won't have any trouble getting in with Ephraim. I know him vaguely, anyway. He's easy, enough."

"Would you mind, not leaning over the table like that, when you're talking to me. Take your spoon out of your cup, when you're finished stirring your tea," said the father.

"Oh, sorry."

"When will you be starting your work on him?"

"Next break, as long as he's not entertaining his audience."

"What do you mean, his audience?"

"The crowd he always has around him. He loves to be the centre of attention. He cracks jokes. Sometimes, he sings dirty songs. He makes everyone laugh."

"Then, you must get through the crowd. Get to his heart. Offer him something more than an audience. Flatter him. Don't dither about. Get on with it. Are you in the same stream as him?"

"Yes."

"He's something of a show-off, isn't he, or so I've heard?" said Kate.

"He never stops showing off. He's the boy who knocked the Religious Instruction Master's faith, during a class about Abraham and Isaac, when he said God was a shit."

"Oh, he said that, did he?" said Kate.

"He's also into necrophilia."

"What on earth do you mean by that?" asked Pendary.

"He jokes about it."

"Why?"

"Because he knows it shocks everyone."

210

"How would a boy of his age know about a subject like that?"

"He's very advanced for his years. His mother was Juliet Silverman, the writer."

"Juliet Silverman? Why the hell wasn't I told this before, Kate?"

"Juliet Silverman's hardly been dead for a year," said Pendary. "I can't stand her stuff. It's too vulgar, sick and black for my tastes. I wonder if Ephraim's read any of it."

"He told us all he wasn't supposed to. He often hunted out his mother's manuscripts, and read them without her permission."

"Hence his disgusting conversation," said Kate.

She began to varnish her nails and painted over the chipped pieces already on them.

"I hate this boy even more vehemently, after hearing all this," she said. "Jethro, go to the London Library tomorrow. Make photocopies of sections from his mother's books and show them to Rodney. That way, he'll have something to start on."

Ephraim was alone when Rodney found him in the playground. His audience had deserted him. His conversation about the monotonously over-exercised subject of necrophilia, had reached such an outrageous extreme that those of his followers, who were not nauseated, were bored beyond oblivion.

He felt betrayed, and the only antidote to his misery, was the knowledge that Rosen would be there for him when he went home. Rosen would listen to him, would not be bored by him and would not be nauseated by him. Miranda, too, was there for him, but although she almost suffocated him with her love, it was Rosen he adored and depended on, most.

He felt someone's hand on his shoulder.

"Hullo, Ephi," said a friendly voice.

"Why, it's Rodney Pendary, isn't it?" said Ephraim.

"That's right. I thought you knew me. I know you. In fact, it would be impossible *not* to do so."

"Why?"

"Because you're a star. Not knowing you would be like not knowing who Morecombe and Wise were."

"Am I as famous in the school as that?"

"Oh, more than that, so much more than that!"

"That's very nice of you."

"I've been reading sections from some of your mother's books, Ephi. She's a brilliant writer."

"Oh, do you think so?"

"I know so. Did she allow you to read her books?"

"No, but I read some of them all the same, whether she said I could, or not."

"She was so clever. Although I've never had the honour of talking to you until now, I've heard you speaking to the other boys, and I've never heard such wit in my life. You get this gift from your mother. I heard your essay about the consultant cardiologist who went to pick up a body in a mortuary, that day it was read out in class. It was wonderful. Is there any chance of your having a copy made for me?"

Ephraim leant against the wall and ran his hand through his hair, smiling, looking like a painted illustration of *Le Corbeau et le Renard*.

"I don't see why not. I really do think you're awfully nice."

"'Nice' isn't the word I'd use. I see you for what you are, not just as Juliet Silverman's and William Rendon's son."

"I sometimes think the others are only interested in me because of my parents."

"I'm afraid they are," said Rodney. "Not me, though. I'm not like the rest of them. Even if I didn't know who your parents were, I'd still find you fascinating."

"Are you sure you mean that? You're not just saying it, for some reason, are you?" said Ephraim.

"Of course, I mean it. Why do you think I'd say it if I didn't mean it?"

"I don't know. I don't really understand others, oh, except Ian."

"Who's Ian? Is he a boy at the school?"

"No. He's my stepfather."

"Are you very fond of him?"

"I adore him. I'd die for him, if I had to."

"He's a lucky man, to have you thinking of him like that."

"What's your father like?"

Rodney was startled. Although a hard, calculating boy, he felt momentarily ashamed.

"He's a bit bossy," he said. "He drinks a lot. He's very fussy about table manners. Is Ian like that?"

"No. I've never really thought about it. I don't think he is, particularly."

"Is he strict?"

"Not in the least. Mind you, I don't know what the parents of other boys are like, compared with him."

"Haven't you been to their houses?"

"No. I've never been invited."

"That's very rude of them," said Rodney, "particularly as you give so much of yourself, all the time. The boys here stay in each other's houses, regularly. Don't you feel left out?"

"Yes, I do, in a way."

"Do you want to sit next to me, at lunch, today?"

"I would like that."

"I'll keep a place vacant for you."

The school canteen was noisy. The pleas of the master supervising the boys, begging for order, were ignored. The lunch was simple and consisted of chicken, potatoes and vegetables.

Ephraim was amused, and was struck by Rodney's poor table manners. He ate with his fingers, and his elbows on the table. Occasionally, he leant across Ephraim and poured salt into his mouth, from its container. Ephraim formed a picture in his mind, of Rodney's father, complaining about his son's habits, and imagined him to have Rodney's dark hair, cut short and parted neatly at the side, like a stockbroker's.

"What are you thinking about, Ephi?"

"I was thinking about your father."

"Why?"

"I was just wondering what he looked like."

"What do you think he looks like?"

"I should think his face is like yours, and his hair is very neat and cut short, with a side parting."

"He doesn't look like that, at all," said Rodney. He's a scruffy-looking man, except when he dresses up."

213

"What does he do?"

"He's in the jewellery trade. When he's not working, he likes to drink."

"Is he an alcoholic?" asked Ephraim.

"No. Not as bad as that. Why are you so interested in him?"

"Because I like you, so it's understandable that I should be curious about him."

"Why not come and stay with us? It won't be possible this weekend? We're going to the seaside. Come next weekend. Then you can meet him and see for yourself. I'm an only child, like you. I've got no-one to play with at weekends, and no-one to talk to."

"What about your mother?"

"She's dead, I'm afraid, but I've got a stepmother."

"Do you like her?" asked Ephraim.

"Yes, well enough."

"What does she look like?"

Rodney poured more salt into his mouth, from its container. He was unnerved by the question.

"If you want to know what she looks like, you'll have to come and stay. Promise you'll come? I hate being alone when my father and stepmother are out, drinking."

"Of course, I'll come, as long as Ian says it's all right."

CHAPTER 43

"Who is Jethro Pendary, Ephi?" asked Rosen.

"He's in the jewellery business."

"I've never heard of the fellow. Does he own a shop?"

"I don't know. All I know is, he's in the business."

"Hasn't his son told you exactly what it is he does do?"

"Not in any detail."

"I'm not all that comfortable about your staying in a household, when you're unsure about your host's trade."

"Rodney's a nice boy, Ian. He's the only boy in the school who's invited me to his home."

"That's because you never have anyone here. Those who don't invite, don't get invited."

"Rodney's invited me, hasn't he?"

"All right, Ephi," said Rosen. "Of course, I want you to see your friends. There's one condition."

"What's that, Ian?"

"I want Rodney and his father to come here, first. I need to meet them, to make sure they are respectable."

* * *

The Rosens did not expect the Pendarys to arrive at exactly 7.00 o'clock. Rosen was sitting in an armchair with Miranda on his knee. Ephraim was upstairs, studying. Maria opened the door and showed Pendary and his son, Rodney, into the living room.

The first thing Rosen noticed was Pendary's neat, tidy appearance and his son's clean clothes and well-brushed hair.

"You must be Mr Pendary," he said, his tone mildly amicable but suspicious.

"I am. I'd prefer it if you'd call me Jethro."

"I am Ian Rosen. This is my wife, Miranda. Jethro's an unusual name. Is it your real name or a nickname?"

Pendary ran his hands through his slicked-back hair. He was ill at ease with Rosen. His host's spirits were low that day and his appearance was unkempt.

"No, no. It's my real name, Mr Rosen."

215

"You can call me Ian, if you want. The young man with you, is he your son?"

"Yes. Come on, Rodney, shake hands with Mr and Mrs Rosen. Look sharp. This is one of your dopey days, I see."

"He's shy," said Rosen. "There's no need for him to be. Sit down, both of you. What do you want to drink?"

"Have you got any beer?" asked Pendary.

"Yes. There's beer. Is there any kind you want, in particular?"

"*Larger*, if you've got it. I'd like it with lime, if possible."

Rosen thought that men who drank *Larger* with lime, were either vulgar and loutish, or homosexuals.

"We've got *Larger* and lime. You can pour the lime in, yourself. What would you like, Rodney?"

"A glass of milk, please, Mr Rosen."

"Miranda, could you go to the fridge and get some milk for Rodney," said Rosen.

As she went into the kitchen, Rosen lovingly watched her neat behind and swinging hips. He felt saddened by how quiet she always was. She never spoke about her sister's death and he wished she would share her grief with him. His thoughts turned to Pendary who struck him as being "naff". He was disappointed by Ephraim's friendship with Rodney, whose rough, nondescript accent worsened his mood. He poured two glasses of whisky for himself and Miranda. She was taking an abnormally long time to bring in the milk.

He wondered whether she was shedding secret tears. He hated her crying in private. He preferred the few occasions when she did so in front of him, because of the pleasure it gave him to comfort her.

Rodney sat on the edge of an upright chair and fiddled with his hair, his fingers turning it round in circles. He avoided eye contact with Rosen. Pendary stared into space and occasionally gave a secretive smile.

There was an uncomfortable silence. Not one of the three occupants of the room knew what to say. Rosen's nervous discomfort worsened. He lit his fourth cigarette since the arrival of the Pendarys. His concern about his wife's long absence turned to anxiety. He got up. "I want to know what's happening to the milk," he said.

"What do you think is happening to it?" asked Pendary, smiling enigmatically.

"You'll soon find out. You seem amused. Someone who smiles for no reason is a bit simple. Maybe, you're just in a good mood."

"I am. There's no reason why I shouldn't be."

Rosen left the room, without excusing himself. The Pendarys waited for his return, and spoke in conspiratorial whispers.

"What do you think Mr Rosen's profession is?" Rodney asked his father.

"No idea. He's as rich as Croesus. Maybe he's got an inheritance and doesn't need to work. Perhaps he's a writer. He looks like a writer."

"Why?"

"Because most male writers look slovenly. It's not unusual for them to have dirty fingernails and behave in a surly manner towards outsiders. They get melancholy a lot of the time and it's not uncommon for them to leave their guests alone in a room for long periods, without apologizing."

"What do you think they're doing?" asked Rodney.

"I've no idea. I've never got on with writers. I'm not interested in books. Nearly all the writers I've met are pretty bad-mannered. I think that Rosen fellow's just wandered off. Perhaps his wife left through another door and he went to look for her."

"I don't agree," said the boy. "I think they're in some kind of trouble."

Pendary let out a lascivious laugh.

"Not half as much trouble as is coming to them!" he said.

*   *   *

Miranda was kneeling on the kitchen floor when Rosen found her. There was half a bottle of milk by her side. The rest of the milk had been poured into a glass which was standing on top of the fridge.

Rosen knelt beside her.

"It's Juliet, isn't it, Baby?" he said.

"Yes, I've tried to suppress it, ever since she died. I've tried to appear cheerful and jolly for Ephraim's sake. I want to see him happy. I've forced myself not to cry, either in front of him, or otherwise."

Rosen held her. His unwashed state excited her.

"Why don't you cry, now? You're on the verge of tears, already."

"I mustn't."

"He won't know. He's upstairs, working. You *must* cry. Otherwise, you'll go mad."

"No. I can't let myself, Ian. Once I start, I won't stop. It would be like alcoholism."

"Rubbish! Cry, just to please me. A woman's very sexy when she cries. It would mean I'd be able to lick the salt tears off your cheeks. In fact, it would be rather mean of you to refuse to grant me such a simple request. Go on. Prove to me you're a woman. No-one will witness your tears, but me."

Miranda did cry. Her body shook like an epileptic's. She undid Rosen's shirt and let her tears fall on his chest.

"Good girl. When I see you do that, my love for you is terrifying and I almost want to die," he said.

"I feel so lucky to have you that I'm sometimes frightened you will."

He had a sudden wish to do everything he could to cheer her up. He lowered his voice and spoke seductively into her ear.

"Do you want a fuck?"

"What, now? In here? That's impossible. The bloody Pendarys are sitting next door."

"Does it matter?"

"Yes, of course it does. One of them might come in, wondering where we are."

"That wouldn't bother me much. It shouldn't concern anyone who really wants it."

"I do want it, she said.

"OK, Baby, promise you won't scream?"

CHAPTER 44

Miranda and Rosen returned to the living room. She was carrying a glass of milk for Rodney. Neither of them apologized for their lengthy absence. Rosen sat down. Miranda handed the milk to Rodney and sat by her husband. Pendary leant forward in his chair and let out a discreet little cough. Rosen broke the silence.

"Ephraim told me you were a jeweller," he said. "I haven't seen your name outside any jewellers' shops in this neighbourhood."

"That's because I haven't got one, Ian."

"Where is your place of work?"

"There's a workshop in our flat. I make jewellery. Other times, I sell ready-made stuff in stalls."

"You *make* it? How do you sell it?"

"By advertising. Mainly by word of mouth."

"Does this ensure you make a profit?"

"I'm never skint. I've got a modest, unearned income. Also, a lot of ladies come to me with offbeat requests. I get asked to design pendants, broaches and bracelets, that sort of thing. As they're all of individual design, they're not available in shops."

Pendary's rapid speech unnerved Rosen. Although the publisher failed to warm to his guest, part of him felt that Pendary was law-abiding and respectable. The other part doubted and mistrusted him.

"Give me an example of the type of bracelet a lady might ask you to design for her," said Rosen.

"Very recently, a lady asked me to design a gold-plated *Clockwork Orange* bracelet."

"What the hell's a *Clockwork Orange* bracelet?" asked Rosen, irritably."

"The bracelet the lady wanted me to design, was modelled on the poster, advertising the film. Did you see the film?"

"Yes," said Rosen.

"Did you enjoy it?"

Rosen suddenly felt in the mood for temporarily animated,

less confrontational conversation.

"I wouldn't go so far as to say I enjoyed it, but it was beautifully done and quite funny in places. Neither the film, nor the book, showed the leading character to have any common sense. It's a weakness on the part of the author to show his main protagonist to be dumb. It was pretty dotty of the man, just out of prison, to go straight back to the house where he had disgraced himself, and expect his host to give him dinner. I thought the funniest part of the film was the Bible-fantasy scene."

Pendary appeared shocked. "Am I to understand that you are not a very devout man, Ian?"

Rosen became stiff, like a watch-dog being caught off guard.

"You could say that. I don't go in for that sort of thing, much."

"I do," said Pendary. "It's a pity you don't. It helps me feel I'm being guided. It gives me the moral code I think we all need."

"Does it, now? My own sense of judgement gives me a moral code. I'm not unstable enough to need what you think you need. I'd rather do without it. I believe in myself. I don't need guidance from some invisible force," said Rosen, in a blunted, defensive tone, which Pendary considered rude.

"Are you an atheist?" asked the jeweller, if somewhat unintelligently.

"Yes, I am!"

There was a silence. Rodney fiddled with his hair, once more. Rosen put his arm round Miranda and stared angrily at Pendary who was looking the other way.

"When did this lady ask you to design the bracelet?" asked the publisher.

"Like I said, very recently."

"I don't understand. Stanley Kubrick, who directed the film, banned it from being shown in this country, quite some years ago, because of 'copycat' violence. That would mean the poster would not have been advertised either, but you say the lady asked you to copy the poster 'very recently'. How could this have been possible? What do you mean?" asked Rosen.

Pendary crossed and uncrossed his legs.

"The lady was so attracted to the film when it first came out, that she bought a poster, advertising it. She said she'd kept it rolled up for some years, before deciding to have a bracelet modelled on it."

"I also don't understand how a poster of such intricate design could have been copied in the form of a bracelet," said Rosen. "As I remember, it shows a man, holding a long, sharp knife, coming out of a triangle, and a naked woman. Do you expect me to believe that such a design could be reconstructed in plated gold?"

Pendary bent over and opened his briefcase. In it, were photographs of some of the jewellery he had made. Among the photographs, was one of the bracelet. He handed the photograph to Rosen.

"You'll realize you've proved yourself wrong when you see this, Ian," said Pendary.

Rosen saw a photograph of a detailed, gold-plated bracelet, showing a man's face, a knife protruding from a triangle, and a naked woman with her legs parted, forming a clasp on the inside.

He stared at it, aghast, acutely embarrassed by his aggression towards his guest.

"I'm so sorry. I owe you an apology. You were right. I shouldn't have cross-examined you in that unfriendly way. Why don't you and Rodney stay to dinner?"

"We'd like to but we've got to get back. My wife will have supper ready at home, and Rodney has got homework to do."

"Why didn't you bring your wife here, tonight?"

"Because she's got a bad cold. I know you asked her to come, but she didn't want to go out."

"You don't have a photograph of her on you, do you?" asked Rosen.

"Yes, I do. Why do you ask?"

"All I wanted was to see whether Rodney looks like you, or his mother."

"My wife's his stepmother. Here's the photograph, if

221

you still want to see it."

Rosen looked casually at the photograph, aware that Pendary had already built up a dislike for him, and found his request peculiar. The woman had well-groomed, glossy black hair, so neatly arranged that it could have been a wig. Her facial features were blurred by the length of time the picture had been kept, folded in Pendary's pocket.

"Hasn't she got lovely hair?" said Pendary.

"Yes, it's nice, isn't it?" said the publisher.

"Does she remind you of anyone?"

"No. Not that I can think of."

"We must be going, I'm afraid. Thanks for the drinks, Ian. I hope we meet again. Up you get, Rodney. Drink up the rest of your milk."

Rosen turned to Pendary. "I must insist on having your telephone number for when Ephraim stays with you on Friday week. I might want to ring him during the weekend, and provided he reverses the charges, he will want to ring me. He's not used to being away from home."

"It's 794 6998," said Pendary, quoting the first number which came into his head. "Do you want me to write it down?"

"Yes."

Pendary passed a tattered piece of paper, giving the imaginary number, to Rosen who suddenly fixed him with a steely glare. Pendary was outraged and returned the stare. Rosen was still ambiguous in his judgement of him. Part of him sensed an overall shadiness. The other part respected him for his artistic talent and his spontaneously-proven truth-telling about the time the bracelet had been designed.

He smiled. "I hope you'll come again, and that we will have the honour of meeting Rodney's stepmother. Goodbye, Jeffrey."

"My name's not Jeffrey. It's Jethro. If I come here again, I hope you will be a slightly more genial host, rather than a boorish cross-examining barrister."

Rosen laughed. "That will depend on whether you give me reason to, won't it?"

Rodney drank the milk, hurriedly and crossed the room to

Pendary who was standing by the door.

"Where are your manners, Rodney?" said the father. "Go and shake hands with Mr and Mrs Rosen, immediately, and thank Mrs Rosen for the milk."

The boy obeyed, his head lowered, his eyes on the floor.

"Raise your head when you're about to speak to someone," commanded Pendary.

Rosen laughed, once more.

"Goodbye, Rodney. I notice that father of yours is licking you into fairly good shape. A bit of a tyrant, isn't he?"

"Well, no, not really. Only a little bit."

"All right, all right," said Pendary. "I didn't hear you thanking Mrs Rosen for the milk."

"Thank you so much for the milk, Mrs Rosen," said the boy. He sounded like a drugged robot.

"Was it the kind of milk you like?" asked Miranda.

"Yes, thank you. I prefer milk with a lot of cream."

"In that case, I'll make sure there's plenty of it, next time you come."

Pendary turned away from his host and hostess, and laughed, muttering inaudibly to himself. Only Rodney heard his words.

"The next time I come here, I shall probably be delivering a wreath," he said.

CHAPTER 45

Maria had gone out to buy a crate of cigarettes for Rosen. Miranda was washing glasses in the kitchen. Rosen came up behind her and put his arms round her waist. He kissed her lightly on the cheek. They went next door and sat down.

"What do you think of Pendary?" he asked.

"He's OK, Ian. He seems harmless enough. Rodney's very well brought up. I judge a parent by his children's manners. I feel quite safe about allowing Ephraim to stay with him."

Rosen put out his cigarette and lit another. He said, "It's possible you're right. Even so, I've got a feeling there's something not quite right about him. He was excessively smartly dressed, like someone attending an interview for a senior job in the Foreign Office, instead of coming on an informal visit to the guardians of a boy his son had invited to stay."

Miranda fiddled her hair in knots, just as Rodney had done.

"Just because he was overdressed, it doesn't necessarily mean he'd be a danger to Ephraim," she said.

"I understand that but I don't feel I can trust him. I feel awful about it because Ephraim would be terribly upset if I didn't let him go. I don't know what would be worse, letting him go and fearing he might be in untrustworthy hands, or telling him the whole thing was off."

Miranda leant against him, drinking in his unwashed odour as if it were wine.

"What's the worst thing Pendary could possibly do to him?" she asked.

"Obviously, nothing sinister, but other things, such as allowing him and Rodney to go out unaccompanied in the evenings, exposing him to matter, unsuitable for twelve-year-olds," said Rosen.

"Do you mean, allowing him to watch 18 Certificate videos?"

"No. That doesn't worry me. I could tell by the man's breath that he's a heavy drinker. That could make him careless, with two twelve-year-olds on his hands. I know he drives. He left his heinous heap of flashing sky-blue metal outside the house.

Another thing I'm not happy about is the idea of him driving Ephraim when he's incapable.

"It's possible he might be keeping bad company. Ephraim would do anything for a dare. For all I know, Pendary might fill his house with drug-users. I thought he looked a bit glazed about the eyes. Ephraim's not above accepting things he knows he shouldn't have. If in the wrong company, he's quite capable of being attracted to the glamorous side of what is forbidden," said Rosen.

"Don't you think your fears are far-fetched, Ian?"

"I wish they were. It was an accumulation of things I didn't care for about the man, his inappropriate clothes, his weird, secretive smile, his eye contact, the unnatural way he sat on the edge of his chair, his son's rough accent, his asking for *Larger* and lime, all minor things, I know," said Rosen.

"It's not surprising he sat, unnaturally. You made him nervous with your aggressive behaviour towards him," said Miranda. "Also, he's on the telephone and if Ephraim becomes unhappy or ill at ease, all he has to do is ring us up and reverse the charges."

"Well, I certainly feel comfortable about that, if not about anything else, but I just haven't got the heart to say 'no' to Ephraim. He's never been invited to stay with anyone before, and I feel he thinks it's a great honour to be asked to another boy's home. If I said he couldn't go, I'd dent his pride. I only wish Pendary's overall presentation had been more satisfactory."

"I thought you were dreadfully rude to him, Ian." Rosen shovelled crisps into his mouth. He finished eating before he spoke.

"I'm not aware of the fact that I was particularly rude. When was I rude?"

"That business about Stanley Kubrick."

"What about him?"

"When you said he'd banned the film."

"Well, he had. So what?"

"You were trying to trip Pendary up about the bracelet. You didn't call him a liar but you got pretty close to doing so. It must have been very embarrassing for Rodney to listen to you berating his father like that."

Rosen pulled Miranda from her sitting position and took her on his knee. He put on an act of boyish, mock contrition.

"Did I do anything else naughty, Miss?" he said.

"I'm afraid you did. You were referring to an incident in the film and Pendary said you didn't strike him as being very devout."

Rosen went to the fridge in the kitchen. He opened a fresh bottle of milk and drank some of it from the bottle. He wiped his mouth on the back of his hand and carried the bottle into the living room. He sat down next to Miranda.

"I remember Pendary saying that," he said. "It was a bloody intrusive thing to say. I don't expect anyone to come to our house and start talking to me about something I can't stomach."

"You also implied that a religious person is that way inclined because he's unstable," said Miranda.

Rosen had another swig of milk and wiped his mouth with the back of his hand, once more. He scratched his shoulders and arms. They were itching because his body had not seen water for five days.

"Christ, Miranda, I said that because it's true!" he said, angrily.

"Even if it's true, do you have to hurt someone's feelings?"

"I wouldn't want to hurt anyone. You know that. I had the impression the man was a bigot and at variance with humanity. Because of my childhood, I'm sickened by anyone who has faith."

"Don't you think you are bigoted, yourself, if you're sickened by views which don't correspond with your own?"

"Perhaps I am." He put his last cigarette out and lit another. "I am a flawed human being. You see me as some kind of saintly fantasy figure. I'm afraid I am not. I'm no more than a desperate sex maniac who publishes books which I probably wouldn't be capable of writing, myself. I am an angry, idiosyncratic person who is so insanely in love with you that all I feel is pain. I love you even more than I loved your sister."

"Take me upstairs," she said.

CHAPTER 46

Miranda was exhausted and went to sleep straight away. Rosen lay awake, thinking and chain-smoking.

He thought of the number of times he had told others that he was happy and loved life, and concluded that his dominant mood was one of merriment and well-being, but when he was feeling depressed, as he did, then, he feared the mood was static and representative of his natural state. He wondered if he really was as humane as he tried to be, and asked himself if there was any merit in his humanity when it was only displayed to those he loved, as opposed to mankind in general.

It crossed his mind that his behaviour was thoughtless on occasions when religion was mentioned. He felt there were times when he contradicted others in too vehement and flamboyant a manner, but that he was not entirely unjustified because of the unhappy childhood which haunted him. If he had genuinely hurt Pendary's feelings, he hadn't meant to, as he had taken into account afterwards that Pendary knew nothing of his revulsion for religion, or the reason for it.

It was 4.00 a.m. Miranda was having a nightmare and woke up, shouting.

"Please don't, Frederick. I can't take any more of this. I want to leave you but I can't."

Rosen shook her awake.

"Who the hell's Frederick, Miranda?"

"It's nothing. I was having a bad dream."

"Evidently. Just who the hell is he? If I caught the bastard crawling into bed with you, I'd beat him up."

"Would you make him look worse?" she asked.

"I always make the other guy look worse. You've got some explaining to do. I want to hear it."

"I don't see him any more. Nor have I for many years. He was an odious, sadistic person."

"What were you doing with him, then?"

She thought for a while. "It started after I married Simon. I had a road accident and I miscarried."

"What, with White's baby?" asked Rosen.

"Yes."

"Christ! Why didn't you tell me, before?"

"Because I wanted to forget. I was in a private ward for a few days."

"Where?" asked Rosen.

"The Royal Free."

"This man, Frederick, what had he to do with all this?"

"He was a hospital volunteer. He visited me a lot every day and read to me. He seemed nice, at first. He helped me to get some form of relief from Simon. I got very dependent on him."

"Oh, you did, did you?" said Rosen.

"It finished quickly, though."

"What did?" asked Rosen.

"Well, the whole thing. He had a trolley of books with him whenever he visited. I liked him to read to me."

"What did you ask him to read to you?"

"*Jane Eyre.*"

"Just *Jane Eyre*?"

"Yes. It was all I wanted to hear at the time."

"Is it your favourite book?"

"One of my favourites. Ephraim's very keen on it, as well."

"Do you have a *penchant* for Mr Rochester? He wasn't a very nice man, was he, locking up his mentally-ill wife, in the attic, like that? In all the films I've seen of that book, I can see a bit of Pendary in Mr Rochester, the secrecy, the impression he's trying to hide something."

She evaded his remark. "I've always been attracted by the melancholy in Mr Rochester, although Ephraim says how much he hates him."

"Perhaps, Ephraim's got more insight than you," said Rosen. "Anyway, what's all this got to do with this man, Frederick?"

"I asked him to read to me about the re-union of Mr Rochester and Jane."

"Did he do so?"

"Yes," she said. "I could never hear enough of it. Frederick gave me his address, after I left the Royal Free. He lived alone. I went to his house every afternoon when Simon was working."

"Was Frederick very good-looking?" asked Rosen, angrily.

"I thought so at the time."

"What did he look like?"

"Staring eyes. Brown hair. Central parting."

Rosen took a handful of crisps. He always kept them on the table, on his side of the bed.

"Oscar Wilde type, eh? Did he go on reading to you?"

"Not after I left the hospital. Then, things went wrong. I left him," she said.

"Why?"

"The relationship became sexual and the physical side became more intense. The spoken side of the relationship stopped and I started to fear him. The fear was due to my blinkered infatuation and the possibility of him rejecting me. I felt worse every time I visited him but I couldn't stop myself because I was physically addicted. I felt even more wretched because I didn't have a child and I wanted a child more than anything."

Rosen put his hand on the lower part of her stomach. "I know you do, Baby. That's why I'm going to give you one. I want one, as well. I want lots of them, and Ephraim will have plenty of company and be happy."

He kissed her on the cheek and held her.

"Was Frederick cruel to you?" he asked.

"Yes, but only verbally."

"Christ, what a bastard! What did he say?"

"Oh, he said things like, 'There is no elegance in you. You've got no self-respect. Your parents must been shits to produce someone as gutless and boring as you. You lack the femininity to love and look after a child'."

"That last statement's a bloody lie for a start," said Rosen. "Look at the wonderful mother replacement you are to Ephraim. What else did he say?"

"He said I had nothing to offer any man besides sex, and even in that regard, I had no subtlety..." She tailed off, as if not wishing to remember."

"Poor Baby! If any of this was true, I wouldn't be here. Did he say anything else?"

"He said it was impossible to have an intelligent conversation with me, that I was halfwitted and if I didn't want to make a fool of myself, I should say nothing, except 'yes' and 'no'. That's why I don't talk much, unless I've got something definite to say. I feel more confident when I'm looking after Ephraim because I've proved to myself how easy and natural I am with children."

Rosen continued to light one cigarette after another. "I've always tried to understand why you say so little. You're all right when we're alone, but if other people are there, you hardly say a word. You said nothing whatever when Pendary and his son were here, except at the end when you talked about milk and cream.

"You're capable of saying far more than you do. Until you told me about your past, I thought it was just shyness on your part. After all, you come from a pressurized family background and you have a very domineering mother. I thought it was something to do with that."

"I'm sure it's that as well," said Miranda, "but it was Frederick who did the worst damage."

Rosen rolled closer to Miranda and put his arms round her waist.

"I bitterly resent the fact that you failed to tell me about Frederick, earlier on. You shouldn't have left me in the dark. Now that's over, I'd like you to speak more than you have up to now. Why don't you try?"

"Because none of the words I utter are worth hearing."

"Your listeners will decide whether or not they're worth hearing," said Rosen. "Frederick is history. Who cares what he said? In those days, you didn't have Ephraim, who is getting more and more like Juliet every day and lessening your grief."

"Why do you think he delivered all those insults to me?" asked Miranda.

"Because of something he hated in himself. Those who hate themselves are sometimes cruel to others."

"Then it's quite clear you don't hate yourself," she remarked.

"Of course, I don't. I'd say I was very happy most of the time. I occasionally get depressive fits that last for a few days, and sometimes during that time, I feel too dejected to care about cleanliness."

"I think you were in one of those moods when Pendary visited," said Miranda.

"I was feeling down. I still am. I took an instinctive dislike to the man. I couldn't stand his unfathomable brain chemistry and his bloody religious beliefs. I also felt awful about my conflict."

"Conflict?"

"Yes. Not wanting to hurt Ephraim, as well as not being happy about him staying in that man's place. Perhaps, I've been misguided because Pendary's a man, and I've never been cut out to get on with other men," said Rosen.

"Why?"

Rosen had not taken his shirt off before going to bed and had not changed it for several days. He scratched himself, once more and the itching made him irritable.

"Most of them bang on about their possessions, the maximum speeds of their cars, and boast-about their amorous conquests. On the whole, I find them shallow and depressing. I'm more interested in ideas, words and language. I'm far happier in the company of women. They are incomprehensible and mysterious and I love their soft skins. Apart from you, it's in the presence of children, like Ephraim, that I am completely happy."

"Why don't you find a woman more exciting than me?" Miranda asked. She had become almost as depressed as Rosen.

"Because you're a warm and fantastic lover. You're a welcoming house on a winter's day. You make me feel as if I'm coming home out of the cold. I come back to you over and over again and the miracle is unchanged."

"Frederick was right, then," she said, sadly. "He said sex was all I had to offer any man."

"I don't want to hear any more about bloody Frederick," said Rosen. "He was wrong. It isn't just sex, in your case. There is a lamb-like gentleness about you, a frailty which stimulates me by making me want to protect you. Somehow, having Ephraim with us, makes me want to, even more. There is so much dignity and courage in you. Your stoicism after the tragedy, moves me

231

and puts me to shame.

"There's also a reticence and modesty which makes you irresistible. Your movements are those of a cat sensing danger. You're always just a little out of my reach and beyond my understanding. You have that gambolling colt-like grace about you which makes words superfluous.

"I don't think I can find clearer language than this to paint your portrait, other than to say that whenever you come into a room, I feel myself go hard."

Miranda was silent but kept her feelings about his words to herself, to enhance the mystery he admired.

*　*　*

They were having breakfast in the kitchen the next morning.

"You mentioned my reticence last night," said Miranda. "Earlier on, you commented on my silences when we're in company."

Rosen poured himself coffee. It was his fourth cup. He was almost as dependent on coffee as on nicotine.

"Can you not understand ambiguity of thought?" he said. "On the surface, I'd like you to grow up and take an intelligent part in conversations. Underneath, I'm turned on by the very qualities I criticise. They are childlike. They remind me of my love of children and closeness to Ephraim."

"Do you know the works of Ed McBain?" she asked. As she did so, she buttered a piece of toast which she didn't realize was burnt.

"Yes. They're all the same. I don't like them, much. That's burnt toast you're about to eat."

She ignored him.

"Then you'll remember the policeman called Steve Carella?"

"What about him?"

"He is happily married to a woman called Teddy, a deaf mute. They adore each other but they never speak to each other."

"Are you comparing yourself to her?" asked Rosen.

"Yes, in a way."

"So you see yourself as a deaf mute, do you?"

"I think that's how others see me."

Rosen laughed. It was a tortured, rather than happy laugh.

"I love your self-deprecation but I hate it at the same time. Can you understand that?"

"I think I can. I have no feelings of self-worth. When Juliet and I were living at home, and there were printers' strikes, threatening to kill off the two papers, my father went into such a state of despair that I often found him sitting alone in the dark, when I came home. Juliet knew how to deal with him. She used to put the light on and kneel by his chair and feed him with optimism. I was no good at that. I had no idea what to do. I never put the light on, the way Juliet did. The gloom was too much for me. I didn't even say 'hullo'. I just went to bed. Perhaps, Ephraim doesn't know the extent of my love for him, either."

Rosen lit his third cigarette that morning and inhaled deeply on it, filling the room with smoke.

"It's not so much a question of what you did when you found your father," said Rosen. "All that really matters is where your heart was. Do you know who I see in you, the more you tell me about your alleged inability to express your love for your father?"

"No. Who are you thinking of, Ian?"

"You're like Cordelia."

"I do hope you didn't think my sister was like Goneril or Regan," said Miranda.

"Don't be silly. That character is a replica of you. Some women are capable of love, but that love makes them so fragile that they are not robust enough to let it out and let it be seen by the loved one.

"It's different where I'm concerned. You show the enormity of your love for me, maybe because it has a physical side. That doesn't apply in your father's case. Perhaps, in your subconscious, you feel that there would be an element of incest in your expression of love, and because that horrifies you so much, you know you have to confine yourself to the spoken word. So when you find your father in a dreadful mental state, caused by

Q

fear of bankruptcy, you feel pathetic and impotent. You may even come over as being cold. You might just as well be saying, in answer to your father's unasked question, '*Nothing, my lord*', when you really do mean that your love is '*dearer than eyesight, space and liberty*'. You don't like saying what you really mean. When you're with others, except for Ephraim and me, you lock yourself in."

"Why do you think I do that?" asked Miranda.

"Because you're so bloody British, that you're a music-hall caricature of the British."

"I hate myself for that," she said. "I'd give anything in the world to say to him '*We two of us shall sing like birds i' the cage*', but I've been so repressed, my tongue would refuse to utter them."

"I shouldn't think he'd have the faintest idea what you were talking about if it did. He'd think you were raving mad," said Rosen.

"I'm still no use to anyone. My mother's gone to America for a while to do research for someone writing about J.F.K.

"Oh, him," said Rosen. "It was only because he distinguished himself over Cuba, that everyone thought he was bloody God. Fancy saying to taxpayers, 'Ask not what this country can do for you, but what you can do for this country'. Women thought he was fantastically good-looking. I think he had a face like the back end of a broken-down bus. Anyway, enough of him. How is your father managing while your mother's away?"

"He's alone in the house. He is still grieving for my sister and I'm incapable of comforting him," she said.

"You've no idea whether he gets comfort from you or not. Why don't you ring him up and invite him to lunch this Sunday? I know he'd be pleased to see Ephraim."

"Could I leave it until the following Sunday, Ian?"

"You've forgotten Ephraim will be staying with the Pendarys, then."

"My father might not want to come," said Miranda.

"You won't know if you don't ask him."

"Oh, Ian, this is such a terrible burden to bear!"

"If you're saying that the act of picking up a telephone is a terrible burden, you must have less intelligence than a village idiot. Prove to me you're not a village idiot."

"It would be a great strain to have lunch with just you and my father, even if Ephraim were there as well."

"Why would it be a strain? I get on all right with your father."

"I'd want someone else there, as well."

"All right. Charles de Cadanet's in London, at the moment. Ask him if he wants to come," said Rosen.

"I'd feel better if he were there."

"I don't mind him being there, but I wouldn't feel particularly at ease, myself," said Rosen.

"Why?"

"Because I'd be in the presence of a man who's slept with you. I'd also have to be with two men who love you."

CHAPTER 47

Cadanet irritated Rosen by arriving an hour early on Sunday. Rosen didn't feel up to entertaining him. Miranda had gone for a walk. She was saddened by the fact that Ephraim had woken up with a sore throat and a fever and that her father wouldn't be able to see him.

Rosen beckoned Cadanet into the living room and offered him whisky.

"How are you doing, Ian?"

"OK, thanks. I wish you hadn't arrived an hour early, at a time when I like to read the Sunday papers."

"Oh? Oh, dear."

"I still intend to read them. Is there a particular paper I can give you?"

Cadanet felt disgruntled and wished to irritate his host.

"I'd like *The News of the World*, if you've got it," he said, aggressively.

"We don't take it. What do you want that for?"

"Because it's rubbish. It takes my mind off my work."

"Do you want another paper, or would you prefer to sit here, looking at the fire?"

"I'd rather look at the fire."

"Perhaps, that's because you're a man with the makings of a fine mind," said Rosen, without smiling.

Miranda came back from her walk, five minutes before Silverman arrived in a red mini which he drove himself. He was averse to ostentation and because he was living alone, he had offered his chauffeur early retirement.

Rosen opened the front door when he rang. The younger man had taken trouble with his ablutions, and received his guest, his clothes clean, his tie knotted, his teeth a little whiter than usual and his breath exuding the smell of rose-scented mouthwash. His thoughts were still focused on Pendary and whether he should allow Ephraim to stay with him the following weekend.

"Good morning, Mr Silverman. Do come in. Let me take your coat."

"There's no need to call me 'Mr Silverman'. My name is Philip," said Silverman, smiling.

He was a tall, well-built man with thick, white hair. He was wearing dark glasses because his eyes were hurting. The glasses made him look rather sinister, and unnerved Rosen.

"I shouldn't have worn a coat. It's not cold enough. I do feel terribly hot," said Silverman.

"Come through into the living room. Would you like me to open the windows for you?"

"Yes, Ian, if you would."

Rosen walked round the room, opening all the windows in turn. He faced Silverman.

"Perhaps you'd like some whisky and ice."

"I'd rather have a glass of water."

Miranda came in and said "hullo" to her father and kissed him reservedly on the cheek. She introduced Cadanet to her father, in the stiff, stilted tone of an old-fashioned housekeeper. Silverman fixed Cadanet with a friendly smile which suddenly took on a mask-like appearance. His skin turned to a greyish white colour, but Cadanet was not observant enough to notice. Rosen looked at Silverman and realized his guest was ill.

"Are you all right, Philip?"

Silverman sat down and took off his dark glasses. His face had become paler and his eyes looked glazed. Rosen leant over him and held a glass of water to his lips. Miranda whitened and looked terrified, not knowing what was wrong with her father.

"Stand back, Miranda," said Rosen. He understood her terror so completely that it pained him.

"Lean forward, Philip. Put your head between your knees. That way, you'll feel better," said Rosen.

Silverman leant heavily to one side of the chair. His head fell loosely on to its side.

Miranda thought her father had died. She knelt down, clutching his arm, screaming.

"For Christ's sake, look after her, Charles! You really are a slow-witted man," shouted Rosen. "Can't you see she's screwed up?" He held Silverman's head between his knees for a few minutes, after checking that he was breathing. Then he eased him into an upright position. Silverman opened his eyes.

"What happened?" he asked.

"You fainted, Philip," said Rosen. "You'll be all right in a few minutes."

Cadanet was sitting, comforting Miranda in another part of the room. She was still screaming and her body was shaking.

"Get over here, Charles," said Rosen. "You're to hold this glass of brandy to his lips. I need to look after Miranda."

Rosen sat down on the sofa with her and held her, while she continued to shake convulsively.

"It's OK, Baby. Your father's recovered. It was only a fainting fit. Juliet told me he had them, sometimes. I would have thought you'd have known, instead of thinking the worst the way you did."

"I know but it was such a shock because I'd never seen it happen before."

"I think you should go up and lie down. I'll get you some tea for the shock. Becket's going to take your father home and I'll drive the Mini. Who's looking after him?"

"Mr Potter, his valet."

"I'll ring Mr Potter and tell him what's happened. Is he a good valet?"

"Yes. He's very supportive. My father's always trusted him."

"Good. So he'll know what to do. Your father will be able to sleep it off. When I get back, would you like me to cheer you up the best way you know?"

"I think so."

"You only think so?"

"I'm so terribly shocked. I thought he was dead."

"Well, he isn't, so what are you bothered about?"

"This business has altered something in me," she said.

"It's all right. You've had a nasty shock. It's not static. It will pass in a few hours. Once I've taken your father's car to .his house, I know you'll want me to cheer you up the best way. You'll see."

He went downstairs to see Silverman.

"Would you like me to get you a doctor, Philip?"

"Certainly not! It's not serious. I always recover quite quickly when I faint. One thing I can't stand is doctors."

"I'm the same as you. I can't stand them, either," said Rosen. "Are you sure you'll be all right?"

"Oh, I'm all right. I know this isn't the kind of thing that one fellow should say to another, but after Juliet died, you couldn't possibly have married a kinder, more stoic or more self-sacrificing girl than Miranda. There's no selfishness or self pity in her. She's very shy and inclined to under-estimate herself. Because she thinks she's useless company, she might even create a false impression of being a bit cold, but she's such a good girl, such a very good girl."

"Yes, I know she is," said Rosen.

"What a comfort Juliet's boy must be to you both!"

"He is, Philip. He's taken the sting out of our grief. I'm sorry you couldn't see him, today. He's got a sore throat and a temperature. You'll be able to see him next time you come."

Silverman patted his son-in-law on the shoulder. "I'd like to see more of him than I do. He lessens my terrible loss. He's so like his mother."

CHAPTER 48

When Rosen went into Silverman's house, he was filled with nostalgia, as he had rarely been there since his first meeting with Juliet. He guided the older man upstairs.

"Do you want me to help you undress before you get into bed?"

"I'm not going to bed," said Silverman, irritably. "I shall sit down and finish reading the papers."

Rosen was startled by his father-in-law's abrupt behaviour.

"Miranda told me a gentleman called Mr Parker looked after you," he said.

"No! Not Parker. Potter."

"Oh, sorry, Potter. Shall I tell him you're here?"

"When I need him, I'll ring for him."

"Can I get you anything?"

Rosen could tell that Silverman was struggling to keep his temper. "You've been very kind, but no."

Potter hurriedly entered the room without being summoned. He was an overweight, red-faced, hearty-looking man. Rosen knew that his over-zealous stance would irritate his boss and was grateful not to be in his position.

"I 'ear you was taken ill, yet again, sir," said Potter, his voice raised, his accent Cockney. "Another of them funny turns of yours, was it?"

"Yes," said the newspaper magnate, in a stiff, impatient tone.

"Dearie me! I'll soon get you into bed. Close weather always seems to bring them nasty attacks on. Best to stay at 'ome on days like that, says I."

Rosen was amused by the valet's provocative manner and seeming ignorance of his boss's short-temper. He struggled to keep a straight face.

"Er, Mr Potter..." he began.

"Blast you, Potter, I don't want to go to bed!" said Silverman. "Just get me some brandy and stop rattling about like a maddening old hen!"

Potter stood with his head lowered like that of a boy, walking behind his mother's hearse. Hot tears were rolling down his cheeks. At first, Silverman thought he had spoken too harshly to him.

"Damn it, Potter! Whatever is the matter? Not something I said just now, eh?"

"Oh, no, sir. This is obviously the very worst moment to broach the subject, sir..."

"What subject?"

"I know you was taken ill, and it's not the moment..."

"Come on, Potter! Out with it!"

"I don't know if I'll be able to look after you, much longer. I'm thinking of tendering my resignation."

"*W-h-a-a-t*?" shouted Silverman.

"It's Mr Wilkes, the gardener, sir. I just can't take any more. Either he goes or I'll have to go."

"Oh, for Christ's sake, Potter! What's happened between you and Wilkes?"

Potter began to sob convulsively, while Silverman stared at him, exasperated. Rosen found the situation comic, and felt his depression lessen, temporarily.

"Well, Potter?" said Silverman.

"It happens every single night, sir."

"What does?"

"I can't take any more. Wilkes can't seem to stop himself. He *cheats* at cards!"

Silverman was uncomprehending, for he was facing the incomprehensible.

"Oh, bloody hell, Potter!" he shouted. "Find Wilkes and bring him here, immediately, and we'll get this rubbish cleared up. As for you, you can't stand here blubbing, just because someone cheats at cards."

Rosen tried to suppress a hysterical giggling fit. He felt happier because he knew the anecdote would cheer Miranda up. He was sensitive enough not to hover obsequiously over Silverman. He folded his arms and spoke to him at a distance.

"Do you need anything else, Philip, or would you prefer me

to leave you in peace?"

"I'll be better off on my own, now. Thank you so much for all your kindness. I don't usually say this to other men but I'll say it to you. You're a perfect gentleman. There are very few men about, like you. My only happiness lies in the fact that you have married my daughter. There's just one thing that's worrying me, though."

"Which is what, sir — oh, sorry, Philip?"

Silverman pointed playfully at Rosen.

"Ha! ha! You nearly landed yourself in it, then, didn't you, my boy? On a serious note, I'm terrified by the amount of cigarettes you smoke. There's something plaguing you, I can tell. Miranda's not ill, is she? She looked half dead when I left."

"No, no. She's fine. She was just worried about you, that's all."

"Me? Why?"

"Well, the fainting attack."

"Shut up about that, Ian," said Silverman.

CHAPTER 49

Rosen hated praise. It embarrassed and belittled him, as if complimentary words were a reprimand. He felt depressed, again on his way back to 41 Lyndhurst Road. He mounted the stairs, two at a time, to shake off the mood, in his hurry to comfort Miranda by making love to her and making her laugh by telling her the anecdote about Silverman's gardener.

She was in bed, lying on her back, an empty half-sized bottle of vodka poised to her lips. She was still trembling and her eyes were glazed, just as her father's were before he fainted.

"Sorry I screamed like that, Ian," she said.

"Why be sorry? You were scared. Shock hits everyone in a different way. When did you take up vodka?"

"Today."

"How much have you had?"

"Only half of it. There's half a bottle left."

Rosen took the bottle from her hand. It was empty. He was more shocked than angry. Anger took hold of him.

"If that's half a bottle of vodka, I'm the King of Siam!" he shouted. He threw the empty bottle onto the floor.

"Don't berate me," she said. "I've never been so frightened in my life. I drank it through fear."

Rosen sat on the bed and held her hand. This time, his voice was gentler. "What you don't understand is that what happened today is the best thing that's happened to you since Juliet's death, apart from the joy of having Ephraim with us."

"What do you mean? I thought my heart was going to stop."

"You don't get it, do you?" he said. "In your mind, you saw your father dead. That means that his genuine death will hit you much more mildly than it would if you hadn't seen him faint."

"Did you think he was dead, Ian?"

Rosen got up and walked round the room before sitting down again.

"For a couple of seconds, the thought crossed my mind, but unlike you, I was observant enough to notice he was breathing. I also knew he had a fainting history."

Miranda felt a bizarre conflict of emotions. She was shell-shocked and embarrassed, but somehow stronger.

"This business has made me a lot stronger, Ian. Perhaps, you don't believe me?"

"Why do you say that?"

"Because what happened has killed my morbidity."

"Morbidity? What morbidity?"

"I've always been morbid, like my sister, but she put her morbidity into use when she finally started writing."

Rosen held her and kissed her on the cheek.

"Why are you morbid, Baby? The more you tell me about yourself, the more I can help you. Once you get happier, it will make Ephraim more emotionally stable."

"I'm morbid because of the house I was brought up in. Whenever there was a printers' strike, my mother got into the most awful state and lived in dread of my father having a heart attack. Her permanent anxiety formed an aura around her which went through the whole house. It was like living in the House of Usher. Juliet rose above it by trying her hand at writing. I wasn't bright enough and I became convinced by my mother's fears that my father's health would be effected.

"It got so bad that every time he came into a room, I feared he would fall down and die."

"Why, you maniac?" asked Rosen.

"Because of my mother's infectious fear. Did you ever fear your father would die in front of you?"

"I wish he bloody had!" said Rosen.

Miranda was half laughing and half crying.

"Once, I stared and stared at my father, willing him to stay alive. He noticed and asked me if I was all right."

"He must have thought you were absolutely bonkers!" said Rosen.

"You were right, just now, Ian. Now that I've seen him dead in my own mind, I know what it's like and I'm not scared any more. I feel strong. I feel transformed. I've grown up."

Rosen's love for her was so virulent that he longed to violate her. He restrained himself because he was unsure how she was feeling. He put his arms round her.

"You look stronger since we started talking. Perhaps it's the vodka speaking through you."

"It's worn off," she said. "I think I can take anything, now. It's not my father's death but death in general which holds no sting for me. I feel as if a terrible weight has been lifted from me. Perhaps the thing which has relieved me most of all, is that if anything happened to Ephraim, I could handle it. I'd be cool. He'd sense I'd be on top of things and he'd be confident. I'm prepared to throw every last ounce of my blood into Ephraim and restore him to his former happiness. After what happened today, I'm no longer interested in what happens to me, only you and Ephraim."

"I believe you," said Rosen, "but there's still something you're holding back, isn't there?"

"Yes. I want you to loosen your tie."

"I thought you were going to say that. I hate being the one who takes the initiative, all the time. It makes me feel I'm bullying you, on occasions you might not want to make love. Sometimes, I wish you'd touch me, spontaneously. I know it's not a thing women are expected to do, but I only wish you'd do it."

"You know very well I always want it," she said. "It's a pity you're so clean, today."

He undid his collar and tie.

"I had to clean up because your father was visiting," he said.

"All right. To make up for that, will you give it to me rough, rougher than usual?"

"Surely, you don't want me to hurt you, Baby?"

"I do. That's exactly what I do want."

"I can't do that, Miranda. You know that."

"You'd be hurting me if you didn't."

Rosen was upset by her request. His need was enormous but his wish to be a gentleman exceeded his lust.

"Do it, Ian," she said, aggressively.

He complied, with extreme reluctance. He entered her like a battering-ram and stayed within her for about twenty minutes, slapping her throughout. He felt disgusted with himself and degraded by having to do as he was asked. He sat on the side of the bed, clutching himself.

"Christ, what the hell have you done to me?" he said. "You've raped me, girl. I'm in bloody agony."

"Just wait for it to pass. Then give me more," she said.

He sat there, in a long silence and held his head in his hands.

"What is it, Ian?"

"I can't take my mind off Pendary. Do you think he's got some connection with Kate?"

"No, of course, he hasn't," said Miranda. "Ephraim made friends with Rodney in the playground, of his own volition. You must be raving mad if you think Kate's got anything to do with their friendship."

Rosen ran his hands through his hair.

"It sounds as if you're right. I always get paranoid when I'm depressed," he said.

"Why are you depressed?"

"Because I don't want Ephraim to stay with the Pendarys but at the same time, I'd never forgive myself if I prevented him from going."

He paused for a while and his breathing quickened.

"There's something else I've thought of. The way Pendary kept giving Rodney orders. It didn't seem natural. It seemed contrived, almost as if it had been rehearsed."

"That's rubbish, Ian. All he was doing was prompting him to behave. Frankly, I'm beginning to find this whole subject a trifle tedious," said Miranda.

CHAPTER 50

On Friday morning, Becket drove Ephraim to school. The boy took a suitcase with him as the Pendarys lived within walking distance from the school. Ephraim was looking forward to walking with Rodney to his father's home in Arkwright Road.

"Oh, I'm afraid we don't own the house," said Rodney, his tone apologetic. "We live in a flat on the top floor. It's a long walk up. Can you manage it?"

"I don't mind the walk."

Rodney rang the bell of the top floor flat. It was opened by Kate, whose long blonde hair was coiled under a neat, black wig. She assumed Ephraim had seen photographs of her, either in his mother's flat, or in his foster parents' house.

"What have you brought with you, Rodney?" she asked. She had intended to sound light-hearted, rather than rude.

"This is Ephraim Rendon," said Rodney.

"Good afternoon. I'm Mary Pendary, said Kate, without smiling."

"How do you do, Mrs Pendary."

"Go into the living room, and sit down. Mr Pendary is changing. He'll be out, shortly."

Ephraim was puzzled by his hostess's failure to offer him refreshments, but he was too polite to comment on her behaviour.

"Sorry, Ephi, was there something you wanted?" asked Rodney. Ephraim noticed there were no signs of tea being made.

"I wondered if I could have a glass of water, please."

Pendary had been in the bathroom, adjoining the living room. He entered the room with his wet hair slicked back and a towel over his shoulder. He was carrying a glass of water in his hand.

"Hullo, young man. You must be Ephraim Rendon. I've brought you your water. I've heard all about you. How are you?"

His pleasant manner put Ephraim at his ease.

"I'm very pleased to meet you, Mr Pendary."

Pendary, Rodney, Kate and Ephraim sat down to high tea, prepared by Kate, at 6.00 that evening. Ephraim was only accustomed to having dinner at 8.30, and was unnerved by the silence at the table. He forced himself to make polite conversation.

"This really is very nice, Mrs Pendary," he remarked, as he ate the sausages, scrambled eggs and fried bread provided.

"It's simple," said Kate. "No doubt, you're accustomed to something much more elaborate."

"Oh, no!"

Pendary looked angrily at his son.

"Those table manners of yours, again, Rodney! I can't tolerate this ghastly habit of yours, in relation to the salt. In fact, I'm confiscating it. You're not having any salt, until you learn to pour it out on the side of your plate."

"Oh, sorry. I'll try to remember."

"You're right, you will. It's such a disgraceful way to carry on in front of a guest. Do they allow you to do that at school?"

"They never seem to mind."

"Do you do it at school?"

Rodney failed to answer.

"Well, Ephraim, since I can't get an answer from my son, perhaps you can tell me. Does he seem to have this problem with his salt?"

"With his salt, Mr Pendary?"

"His salt. Does he pour it into his mouth, as he did, just then?"

"He does do that, actually, yes, Mr Pendary. Ephraim laughed nervously.

"It's not funny, you know," said Pendary. "When you grow up and have children, you won't find it funny when they embarrass you in this way."

"I quite agree with you, Mr Pendary. I'm sorry I laughed just then. It was nerves."

"Bad manners, more likely," said Kate.

After they had eaten, Pendary rose from the table.

"Mrs Pendary and I are going out for two hours," he

said. "Will you look after Ephraim and see he has everything he needs."

"I don't think he knows how to play chess. I can teach him," said Rodney.

"Good. Can you play chess, young man?" asked Pendary.

"No."

"Would you like to learn?"

"Yes, all right, Mr Pendary."

The awkward atmosphere was upsetting Ephraim. He disliked the Pendary household and wanted to be with Rosen.

"What are you crying about, young man?" asked Pendary. "Is it something Rodney said to you?"

"No, Mr Pendary."

"Dry your tears, then. I'm not a monster. I'm just a perfectly harmless bloke. There's no need to shed tears, on my account."

Rodney taught Ephraim the rules of chess. His guest was quick to learn the moves. Rodney set up the pieces and allowed Ephraim to make the first move.

It was not before long, that the guest noticed something extremely singular about the host. Although he was playing with a beginner, he was an inveterate and remorseless cheat. He made a conventional knight's move and surreptitiously moved the piece to its adjacent square, from which he took his opponent's bishop.

"That's not right. Your knight was there," said Ephraim.

"Oh, sorry, I didn't notice."

"You did notice. You noticed all along. Why did you do that?"

"I didn't realize what I was doing. I didn't mean it," said Rodney.

Ephraim told himself that it was only a game and that if his host chose to cheat, he should be allowed to do so. He did not realize, until it was too late, that Rodney went at life with the same dishonesty he applied to games.

Ephraim became addicted to chess, which fascinated and absorbed him so completely, that he no longer missed Rosen. Whenever the Pendarys went out, the boys played the game repeatedly, and continued to do so, well into Sunday.

R

Pendary and Kate returned to the flat in time for Kate to cook lunch. They were drunk. Kate was surly because she had to cook, when she would have preferred to go to bed. Pendary was exuberant and giggly.

"What have you two been doing, all morning?" he asked.

"We've been playing chess," said Ephraim.

"You want to watch Rodney. He's not the most scrupulous of players. Has he been taking your queen off the board when you haven't been looking?"

"Not quite as bad as that, Mr Pendary, but he's been pretty hot, all the same."

"Oh? So you mean he's been dishonest? I'll give him a good clip for that. Dishonesty is something I will not tolerate, not in this household, it isn't."

*   *   *

Kate smiled throughout lunch. Her change of mood from unwelcoming sullenness, to gaiety, confused Ephraim.

"It's been a nice morning, hasn't it, Mrs Pendary?"

"It has. It's been a lovely morning. If it's still fine this afternoon, perhaps you'd like to come for a walk with Mr Pendary and me."

"I would like to. That's extremely kind of you, Mrs Pendary, and Mr Pendary, of course."

"What about you, Rodney? Would you like to come for a walk with us?" asked Kate.

"I won't, if that's all right with you. I was up all night, reading, and I'd like to sleep after lunch."

CHAPTER 51

Pendary and Kate walked downstairs and into the driveway of the building, followed by Ephraim. They entered one of the garages, used by the occupants of the building. Kate unlocked the boot of Pendary's car, which contained a coil of rope and a cosh. She called to Ephraim and pointed to something in the street, to divert his attention.

Pendary came up to him from behind, and hit him over the head with the cosh, not hard enough to kill him, but enough to knock him out. He tied his hands and feet. He put a rolled-up rag in his mouth and wound some of the rope round his head. He lifted his unconscious victim into the boot and closed the door.

He took off the back and front numberplates with a screwdriver. He pulled out another set of numberplates from under the carpet on the passenger's side, and attached them to the car. He put the removed numberplates under the carpet in their place.

"Get in and drive," he said.

Kate got in on the driver's side and waited for him to install himself. She reversed into the street.

"Have you got the passports?" asked Pendary.

"They're in the bag."

"Do you remember our new names?"

"Yes. They are Julian Mark Bentley and Mildred Mary Burns. There are forged driving licences in those names, as well. We've got enough fuel to last well into France. When we get on the ferry, we'll buy food at the bar, for ourselves and the hostage. We will refer to him throughout as 'the hostage', and will not use his name, even when addressing him."

Pendary combed his hair, in a nervous, reflex gesture.

"What arrangements have you made in Marseilles, or are we just going to leave him in an underground carpark all day, and feed him when we have to?" asked Pendary.

"I've rented a small room, overlooking the Rue St Férreol, where most of the hookers are. I'll go into the business, myself. It's the only way."

"What do you mean, you'll go into it? You've been in it all your life."

"It's not the same. This time, I'll solicit from the streets, instead of five star hotels," said Kate.

"What about your hair? Are you going to wear that wig all the time?"

"I'll wear it at the beginning. I'll go back to my own hair, once I think the heat is off. No-one would ever suspect me of settling in Marseilles. It's the last place an English woman would be likely to live in."

"What's going to happen if Rosen refuses to give us the money?" asked Pendary.

"If he refuses, we'll have to go without, won't we?"

"What if they find us and we have to surrender?"

"Hold the hostage at gunpoint."

"But you haven't got a gun."

Kate took a ladies' Colt 38 from her handbag, with the hand which wasn't holding the wheel.

"It holds six bullets in its chamber, and I've got a bagful of spare bullets," she said.

"You really are a depraved woman," said Pendary.

They gave ham sandwiches and plenty of water to their hostage, during their journey to Marseilles. The weather there was blindingly hot and the car absorbed the heat and increased Ephraim's agony.

Kate parked the car at the bottom storey of an underground carpark. She got out first to unlock the boot. Pendary ambled after her. He had drunk half a bottle of whisky during the journey. Its effects were wearing off. He had a headache, which, combined with the heat, made him impatient and bad-tempered.

"I'm tired, Kate. I want to lie down. You've got a room to take your punters to. Where do you imagine I'm going to stay?"

"Use your initiative," she said. "There's a large number of two-star hotels, one on the port, Hôtel Club Meditérrané, and a few in the side streets, leading away from the port. We can't afford to be seen together, more than is necessary. I suggest the Club Meditérrané. The staff there are civil. There are wood lice

252

all over the place and a discotèque on the first floor which goes on for most of the night. There's a fine view of the harbour," said Kate.

"Who's going to pay the bloody bill?"

"That won't be difficult. It's a cheap hotel. I'll help you with my earnings."

"I'm beginning to ask myself if any of this is worth it," he said.

Kate slapped him. "You want a half share of the boy's fortune, don't you?"

"I want it, yes. Will I ever get it?"

"Not with an attitude like that. I'll take charge. You'll do everything I tell you to."

"At least, that saves me having to take any decisions, myself," said Pendary.

Kate unlocked the boot. Pendary held Ephraim steady, while she untied the rope round his mouth and limbs, and removed the rag. The boy had become petrified with shock and trauma, and was trembling. A doctor witnessing his state, would have ordered his admission to hospital as an emergency.

"More ham sandwiches and a bottle of water, for you," said Kate. "If you don't eat what I give you, you'll starve. You'll die here. You'll never go back to London."

She broke off a piece of bread and pushed it into his mouth. The heat had given him a headache which nauseated him.

"Come on. Chew it up. I suppose you think I've got all day, to make sure you eat."

"I'm sorry. I can't swallow it, Mrs Pendary."

"Don't you dare address either me or my husband as 'Pendary', down here. If you use that name, I'll beat you."

"What am I to call you?"

"You don't call us anything. We won't use your name, either. If necessary, we'll simply address you as 'you'. If you can't eat the bread, you're to drink at least half of that bottle of water."

Ephraim was thirsty. He did as he was told.

"Get out of there," ordered Pendary. "You're to come with

us, now. Walk between us, holding us by the arm, as if things were normal, and we were your parents."

Ephraim burst into tears.

"Stop your bloody racket," said Kate.

"I want Ian. I want to go back to London."

"You will do, when our demands are met. It's time we told you why we brought you to Marseilles," said Kate.

Ephraim didn't answer. His crying was worse.

"First, I'll tell you who I am," said Kate. She removed her black wig and let her natural hair fall over her shoulders. Ephraim had a retentive memory and remembered being shown a photograph of his 'evil Aunt Kate', and the lecture he had been given about avoiding her, should she approach him.

"Do you know who I am?" she asked.

"Yes. You're my aunt Kate, my father's sister."

"Correct. Why do you think you're here?"

"Because you want my money."

"If your guardian, Rosen, is prepared to go to the banks and building societies, where it is invested, have it converted into fifty pound notes and put it in a case, big enough to hold it, a start will have been made.

"Either he, or someone acting on his behalf, will leave it in a left luggage locker at the Gare St Charles. That person will put the key to the locker in a sealed envelope, which will be gift-wrapped and given to my partner.

"When the money is counted, and if its amount is satisfactory to both of us, we will release you and disappear.

"I will give you enough money to get a taxi to the British Consulate. The one in Marseilles employs a right, ghastly load of uncooperative louts. Their job is to help British citizens in trouble, and our taxes pay for them to sit with their feet up all day, reading bloody Harold Robbins."

"If they're like that, there's no point in my going to see them," said Ephraim.

Kate put her wig back on and jostled him, to remind him of her hostile feelings towards him, despite the frail jocularity in her description of staff members in the notorious British Consulate.

"It's possible they might be friendlier towards a child, than an adult," she said.

"I doubt it," said Pendary. "I've been to Marseilles, before. I swam in the harbour. I cracked the nerve of a tooth in two, hauling myself out on an anchor chain. Those fuckers at the British Consulate couldn't have been ruder."

"I'm bored with all this talk about the British Consulate," said Kate. "It doesn't have much bearing on the hostage. Come on, boy. Walk between us. If you try anything or make a noise, we'll see to it that you never go to London again."

The trio left the lower storey of the carpark and walked with an effort, up the steep slopes in the oppressive heat. There was no ventilation. The heavy lingering petrol fumes nauseated the three of them. Ephraim was coughing and continuing to cry.

"You should be ashamed, and you can shut up your stupid crying!" said Kate. "We'll be up to, the street, soon, so remember what I told you."

They walked through some busy side streets towards the harbour. Ephraim was struck by the flamboyant range of activities taking place in these streets. A fire-eater blew a volcano of flames into the air, as paraffin dripped from his chin. Near him, on the same pavement, a legless, silver-haired war veteran fiendishly polished people's shoes, as if an overlord were holding a whip over him.

"We'll have to wait while I get my shoes cleaned. They're very dusty," said Kate. "I'm not going round with them looking like this. Boy, stay with my partner. Don't leave his side."

The shoe-cleaning queue was long. Her head was uncovered except by the black wig in the hot sun and her temper worsened. Her turn came after a twenty minute wait.

"You'd better be worth waiting for," she said to the legless war veteran, in fluent French.

"I apologize, madame, I've had a lot of customers, today," said the veteran.

"And a lot of money from them, too, I should imagine."

"No, madame. Not a lot of money. Just enough to feed my dog."

"Where's the dog?"

"He's asleep under the umbrella. All I care about is seeing

he gets enough to eat."

"All right, all right. Clean these shoes. I'll keep them on, while you do it."

The veteran wiped them and cleaned them, using four different pots of polish. He worked with the same dedicated, frenzied industry as he had with his other customers. The black stiletto shoes shone so brilliantly, that the veteran could see his face in them.

"How much?" asked Kate.

"Four francs, please." (The rough equivalent of forty pence).

"Work it down to three," said Kate.

"I'm afraid I can't. All my customers are charged four francs. That's my fee."

Kate took four francs from her pocket and threw them on the ground in front of the veteran, instead of placing them in his hand.

"I could have thrown it further away, but you'd have needed legs to go after it," she said.

The more cruelty he witnessed, the more Ephraim yearned for Rosen. He wondered whether he would ever see him again.

"There's something I wish to say, madame," said the veteran.

"What is it? I've paid you, haven't I?"

"Do you know how I lost my legs?"

"Ought I to know?"

"They were blown off in the Second World War. My only desire then, was to free the world of tyranny, to fight for the freedom you now enjoy."

Even Kate was embarrassed by his remark.

"Bravo, monsieur," she muttered.

The partners and their hostage left the side street and came onto a wide street overlooking the harbour.

Ephraim was cheered by the beauty of the harbour, its flotilla of boats and its stone walls at its entrance, which would later look even more attractive, with the sunset shining on them, giving them a soft, pink hue.

His fear and loneliness were of such a horrendous extreme, that a reflex action pushed them to the back of his mind. He was numbed and very depressed. His misery was noticed by Kate, who took sadistic pleasure on witnessing it. She was puzzled by his apparent lack of fear.

They crossed over to the other side of the road, where row upon row of restaurants and cafés, exist. Kate wanted black coffee and steered Pendary and Ephraim to a café overlooking a sea of fishing boats in the harbour.

She drank her coffee, holding the cup in one hand and pressing the barrel of her gun into Ephraim's ribs, with the other.

She and Pendary were startled by the arrival of two elderly English ladies, who sat at the next table. They were talking loudly and Kate heard their conversation.

"I've just been reading about that poor boy who disappeared, when he went to stay with his schoolfriend for the weekend," said the first old lady to speak. Her name was Ethel.

Her companion's name was Mavis. She didn't share Ethel's interest.

"This sort of thing happens the whole time," said Mavis. "I'm not that upset about it, particularly as I'd never met the boy."

"You should take more of an interest when that sort of thing happens. It's not just a question of the boy disappearing. The parents of the friend he was staying with, also disappeared," said Ethel.

"All right, we could perhaps see this a bit more clearly," said Mavis. A boy has a schoolfriend. He is invited to stay in his house. His host's parents disappear, as well as the boy. That looks strange, I know. Why would a child invited by his friend, to his house, be abducted or harmed by his host's parents? The absence of the parents is probably a coincidence. I presume the boy was returning to his own parents, sometime on Sunday. He might have hitchhiked and landed himself with a killer.

"As for the host's parents, they probably went out to see their friends and stayed up late."

"They'd been away for two days when I read about it," said Ethel.

"Perhaps they took a short holiday, after their guest left

the flat," said Mavis.

"What do you think could have happened to the boy?"

"He's probably been murdered," said Mavis. "Perhaps, he got talking to the wrong kind of man, on his way home, a psychopath, I should think."

Ephraim was sitting between Pendary and Kate, throughout the conversation. It would have been a perfect occasion for him to shout out loud, and say he was the boy who had been abducted, which is why Kate dug her revolver even more sharply into his ribcage, and continued to put her other arm round him.

"Yes, I know it's hot," she said to Ephraim, her voice raised with artificial pleasantness. "Why don't you have an ice cream, darling? They've got so many flavours, here. Have a look at the menu."

Ephraim's mental state was so dislodged, and his hopes so reduced, that he spoke normally, like someone who has decided to take their life, and in anticipation of it, feels calm and resigned.

He looked briefly at the ice creams on the menu.

"So, what will you have, eh, my boy?" asked Pendary, loudly."

"I'd like the concentrated honey ice," please.

"So you're fond of honey?"

"I love it."

"In that case, we'll make up honey sandwiches instead of ham sandwiches. That way, you'll eat them. We can't have you wasting away, can we?"

The thing Kate had been dreading, happened. Ethel leaned over her table.

"Was there something you wanted?" asked Kate.

"Oh, I'm sorry to intrude on your family. It's such a pleasure to hear English spoken in Marseilles. Would you mind if we joined you?"

"Well, if you must, you must," said Kate.

The old ladies sat down opposite Ephraim, whose honey ice cream was an elixir, giving him the strength to face what was happening to him.

"Are you enjoying that, young man?" asked Ethel.

"Yes, thank you."

She turned to Kate.

"My sister and I are absolutely fascinated by that boy in London who never went home, after spending the weekend with his schoolfriend. There was a picture of him in the paper but it was a poor edition and too blurred to see what he looks like."

"I vaguely remember reading about that. What about it?" said Kate.

"What do you think could have happened to him?"

"I suppose he's been murdered. It's happening all the time."

"The strangest part is the fact that his friend's parents also disappeared."

"A bit odd, perhaps," said Kate. "If a boy is invited to his schoolfriend's house for the weekend, his schoolfriend's parents would hardly be likely to abduct him, would they?"

"I can't see why," said Ethel. "It's very mysterious, though. If they did not abduct him, why would they have disappeared?"

"How the hell should I know?" said Kate. "How do you expect me to know the answers to your bloody silly questions? I've never met the boy who disappeared. Nor, indeed, have I met his friend who invited him home. As for the parents, I've never met them, either. It's just possible, the boy's parents were psychopaths. They might have killed the missing boy, for kicks."

"Yes, I'm inclined to think that's what happened," said Ethel.

Kate wondered how much longer she would be able to tolerate these old ladies. Pendary sensed her restlessness and rose to his feet.

"I hope you'll excuse us. We've only arrived, today, and we all want to get back to our hotel, and rest," he said.

"What hotel are you staying in?" asked Ethel.

"You mustn't think me rude," said Kate, "but I'm not telling you which one it is. You and your friend are very intrusive. You would impose yourselves on us, and burden us with questions about that blasted boy, knowing that none of us have the answers. If you want to know of further developments, I suggest you read the English newspapers, every day."

Pendary, Kate and Ephraim continued to walk, until they

259

reached the Rue St Farréol, which was lined by prostitutes. Kate led them into a dilapidated building, overlooking the street, and took them across a filthy, foul-smelling hall, to her room. The door leading to it, had a heavy industrial padlock on it which she unlocked with a large key.

She opened the door and pushed Ephraim into a small, damp room, devoid of furniture, other than two mattresses. Its walls were covered with pealing brownish wallpaper. In the areas, stripped of wallpaper, were faded, painted slogans, saying *Algérie Française* which, in the light of their historical significance, had remained there for many years.

Ephraim noticed a tattered green velvet screen in a corner of the room by the door. It was here that Kate would be receiving her punters. She dragged one of the mattresses and the threadbare blankets covering it, across the floor, and put it behind the screen. She turned to Pendary.

"Now you know where I live, you'll be able to visit me every day. When I'm not working, I'll come to your hotel. Tomorrow, we'll get hold of Rosen on the mobile 'phone. We'll have to dial 141 first. That way, the call won't be traced. Why not go to your hotel and freshen up, before dinner."

"What about the boy?"

"I've got to keep him locked up. You know that. I'll get him a pot of honey. It's the only way we can get food down him."

Pendary turned to leave. Kate was alone in the windowless room with Ephraim.

"You're a nasty, cruel woman, Kate," he shouted. "You've no right to put Ian through this. Why can't I make a deal with you? I know my grandfather's will wasn't fair and I'd like to share the money with you."

Kate slapped him so violently that he fell to the floor.

"I don't want half. I want the whole bloody lot!" she shouted. "If anyone tries to thwart me, I'll kill you."

"Am I to sleep on the other mattress?" asked Ephraim.

"What else do you think you're going to sleep on, you little fool? I suppose you're accustomed to a four poster bed."

"I haven't got a four poster bed at home, just an ordinary bed."

"When I've unpacked a few belongings, I'll show you where you'll be sleeping."

"It seems I've plenty of time to wait."

"Watch that cheek, or I'll hit you."

Kate dragged the second mattress and its filthy blankets to another corner. She pulled a second screen towards it, so that none of her punters would see her hostage.

"There's another thing," she said. "Because my rightful money has been denied me, I've become a prostitute. I'll go out and pick men up in the street, and bring them here, for business. You'll be hidden behind the screen, and if you make so much as a sound, I'll shoot you. I won't shoot to kill. If I killed you, I wouldn't get the money. I'll shoot you in the foot, instead, and if you scream, I'll shoot you in the other foot."

Ephraim wept piteously.

"Shut up that stupid blubbing!"

"I want Ian. I want to go back to London."

"If he loves you, he'll pay up and you'll go back to London. By the way, when I go out to find punters, I'm locking you in here. If you scream, no-one will hear you. This building is in a state of disuse."

"May I have some bread, please?"

Kate threw the tail end of a *baguette* at him. "My partner's bringing a pot of honey tomorrow, to get you to eat the bread, so that you're still alive, when Rosen co-operates and takes you home."

CHAPTER 52

Miranda and Rosen had been expecting Ephraim to come home at 7.00 o'clock on Sunday evening. An hour passed and there was no sign of him. At 9.30, Rosen's shaking hand poured whisky into his and Miranda's glasses. He dialled 794 6998, the number Pendary had given him. It gave an unobtainable tone. He tried it several times and called the Operator, who told him the number did not exist.

"What's Ephraim's friend's name, again?" asked Rosen.

He pulled on a cigarette, his tenth over a fifteen minute period.

"Rodney Pendary."

"We'd better call the police," said Miranda.

"No. Not yet. I'm making preliminary enquiries, first. I'm ringing up the Headmaster of the school, at his home. It's Mr Lawrance, isn't it?"

"Yes."

"I'm finding out Pendary's address."

Rosen smoked another two cigarettes and dialled the Headmaster's home number. It rang at least twenty times. Rosen could feel his heart hitting his ribs. Finally, the telephone was answered.

"I'm sorry to ring you at home, Mr Lawrance," he began.

"It's a shame you did. We're playing Bridge."

"I'm afraid this is a matter of utmost urgency. My name's Ian Rosen. I am Ephraim Rendon's foster-father. I married Mrs White after her husband died."

"Oh, good evening to you, Mr Rosen. How can I help?"

"Ephraim went to stay with a friend of his called Rodney Pendary, for the weekend."

"I know, Rodney, the boy with the exquisite table manners."

"My wife and I were expecting Ephraim home at 7.00 o'clock this evening. He's always punctual and reliable. He would have rung us if he'd been delayed for any reason. We think he may have come to harm."

"Rodney's Jethro Pendary's son, isn't he?"

"Yes. Apparently, he's in the jewellery trade."

"The jewellery trade? That's a bit steep, isn't it? He sells trinkets at Paddington Station, and pays his son's school fees from an inheritance left by his mother."

"Ephraim never left us the Pendarys' address. I'd feel better if you could give it to me," said Rosen.

"It's not usual protocol, but in the circum-stances, I'll get it off the computer. I keep a record of the boys' addresses at home, as well as at school. Would you mind waiting?"

"OK."

A few seconds passed.

"I've found it for you, Mr Rosen. That's right. Rodney Pendary, C/o Jethro Pendary, Top Flat, 7 Arkwright Road. There's no 'phone number listed. I assume these people aren't on the 'phone. I do think you should call the police. They get hostile towards members of the public, trying to do their job for them."

"You've been very kind. Thank you for your time," said Rosen.

"There's only one thing for me to do, if I'm to find out any more."

"What?" said Miranda.

"I'm going round to the Pendarys' house, now."

"Is that wise? You're in such a state, you might blow it."

"We're both going, Miranda. I'll get Becket out. He won't resent it in the circumstances. He's very good-natured."

Becket drove them to Arkwright Road. Rosen chain-smoked throughout the journey and fondled Miranda's breasts. Their dependence on each other's bodies helped to keep them sane. Miranda undid his zip and rubbed him until he became hard.

Becket parked the Rolls outside the building where the Pendarys lived. Rosen and Miranda put their arms round each other's waists, and rang the Top Flat bell at number 7 Arkwright Road.

"If there's no-one there, I think I'll die," said Rosen.

A light was on. Rosen kept the palm of his hand pressed on the bell, and let it ring for fifteen minutes. A boy's voice, said "Yes? Who is it?"

263

"Come on, Rodney, it's the Rosens."

" My father told me never to let strangers in."

"We're not strangers. You've been to our house. If you let us in, I can guarantee no-one will harm you."

"It's difficult for me, after what my father said."

"Never mind what your father said. If you let us in, you will not regret it."

Rodney knew his visitors were persistent and would refuse to go away unless he let them in. He was tired and wanted to go to bed.

"All right, come in. Just push the front door."

Rodney opened the door of the Pendarys' flat. It was dirty and untidy, with football tackle, Monopoly boards and chessmen, lying on their sides. Rodney was dressed in dirty grey denim trousers and an Arsenal T-shirt.

"Hullo, Rodney." said Rosen, gently. The scene was too harrowing for Miranda. She sat on a chair and wept.

"Hullo. Why do I have to speak to you?"

"Because I'm giving you this," said Rosen. He pushed a ten pound note into the boy's hand.

"My name's Ian Rosen, as you know, and I look after Ephraim Rendon."

"Oh, yes, Ephi."

"I am aware that he was staying in your house for the weekend."

"That's right."

"We're most anxious to know where he is, now. When did he leave?"

"Oh, not long after lunch, this afternoon. After that, he said he wanted to go out for a walk with my father and stepmother. They haven't come back yet."

"Do you by any chance have a photograph of your stepmother?"

"Yes. Why do you ask? I remember my father showing you a photograph, when we visited your house."

"Could we see another one, do you think?"

Rodney passed over a large close-up photograph of Kate,

wearing a bathing suit. It was not the same photograph that Rosen had seen before. Her natural, long, blonde, wavy hair cascaded onto her shoulders. The photograph did not conceal her hard face, from which a pair of cynical, slanting, blue eyes, glared. She looked uncannily like her father, Rowland Rendon.

"Take a look at this, Miranda. That's Kate," said Rosen. "She must have been wearing a wig in the other picture I saw."

Miranda observed the photograph. Her face froze. "That's her," she said. "I remember the first photograph of her we saw, when Jack came to the house, after Juliet died."

"Your stepmother may have abducted Ephraim and I demand to know where she has taken him," said Rosen.

"But I don't know where they went, Mr Rosen."

"Do your parents usually go out for long periods of time, leaving you alone?"

"Yes. Nearly all the time. They go out drinking for hours."

"Surely, they wouldn't have taken Ephraim, drinking."

"Perhaps not."

"Have you any idea where they might have gone?"

"I don't know, Mr Rosen. They've been away for so long. It's possible they've left the country."

The boy looked nervous, as if he had accidentally betrayed a confidence. He looked away from the Rosens.

"My father's been very bossy of late. He's particularly fussy about table manners. He confiscated the salt on Friday. I had to go for the whole meal, without salt."

"I see. Do you think we could veer away from the salt?" said Rosen, as patiently as he could. "Why do you think your father and stepmother may have gone to another country?"

"Only because my stepmother has often said she'd like to get away from London, and settle in Marseilles."

"Why?"

"She's been there quite a few times. She likes it there. She says it's an easier place to find what she calls 'street work', and she likes the sun."

"Have you any reason to think she's taken Ephraim there?"

"No. She just says she'd like to live there."

S

"Did your father ask you to befriend Ephraim and invite him here for the weekend?"

Rodney avoided eye contact a second time. He sat down and drummed his fingers on the table.

"Did my father ask me to invite him?"

"Yes. That's the question I just asked you," said Rosen.

"No. Of course, he didn't. I got talking to Ephraim in the playground. We became friends. I like him very much. I asked him because I get lonely when my parents are out."

"Have you invited any of the other boys home?"

"No. Oh, sorry, I once asked a boy called John Pemberton, home. It was during the holidays. John stayed here for about a week."

"Was this before or after Kate moved in with your father."

"Before. At least I think so."

"Isn't this something you'd remember?"

"Well, I do remember, now. My father was by himself. He didn't go out drinking so often, until she moved in."

"Before he left, did you and Ephraim have an argument, at all?" asked Rosen.

"No, not an argument. We played chess a lot. I'm afraid I didn't keep the rules. He got a bit cross."

"Are you saying you cheated?"

"Oh, no. I wasn't cheating. I was just rearranging some of my men, so that they would be in a better position to take my opponent's pieces."

Rosen smiled. The boy was struck by his tiny, white teeth.

"It does sound as if you were cheating. Do you cheat at other games?"

"No, of course, I don't."

"Do you tell the truth when someone asks you questions?"

"Yes. Why wouldn't I tell the truth?"

"All right, Rodney. We won't keep you, any longer. We're sorry to have disturbed you, when it's clear you want to go to bed."

"That's all right, Mr Rosen. I hope you find Ephraim. I'd like to know where he is, just as you do. I'd also like to know

266

where my parents have gone."

"No doubt, there's a simple explanation. Will you be all right here, on your own?"

"Yes, Mr Rosen. I'm used to it."

The Rosens left the Pendarys' flat and went down into the unlit hall. Rosen threw his arms round Miranda.

"What is it, Ian?"

"I can't bear being deprived of children, any more! I've had enough. Take your diaphram out," he said, peremptorily.

"What, now?"

"Now. This place is empty. No-one will see you."

She started to undo her jeans and pulled them down.

"No," he said. "I've got a better idea. Let me take it out for you. It would be so much nicer."

He knelt at her feet like an old-fashioned courtesan, about to propose marriage. It was difficult for him to find what he was looking for and even harder to dislodge it and pull it out.

"Christ, you haven't cleaned this thing out for weeks!" he said.

She looked confused and embarrassed. "Give it to me. I'll deal with that when we get home."

He stood up and looked at her, his eyes saddened and excited at the same time.

"No, I think I'd like to keep it," he said.

"Why do you want it?"

"Personal reasons. I want to carry it round with me. Let's get in the car. I'm desperate for it."

"So am I, Ian," she said.

*   *   *

Becket opened the two back doors. He could tell by the expressions on the faces of his employers, that he would not be required to drive away, immediately. Rosen put his hands under Miranda's shirt. He laid her on her back and had violent, noisy tormented sex with her, while she screamed in ecstasy. An elderly lady was walking past, holding a little girl's hand. She

267

looked briefly into the Rolls and shielded the child's eyes.

Becket, already acutely depressed by the turn of events, and Rosen's embarrassing outburst of disinhibited behaviour, sat there, his aristocratic face as rigid as a board, reading *The Brothers Karamazov*.

The Rosens woke up early the following morning. Rosen rolled on top of Miranda. Her appetite, particularly at that time of day, was nearly always as voracious as his.

"I'm so sorry, Ian. It came on in the night. I can't do anything for a few days."

"Poor little girl. Do you want me to get some Paracetamol from the bathroom?"

"Will you?"

He handed her the pills and gave her a glass of water. He lifted her head and shoulders onto his chest and put his arms round her waist.

"Do you want me to rub your tummy?" he asked.

"I've got a better idea."

"Which is what, sweetie?"

"I want to go down."

He sat up and clutched her hair, and pushed her head downwards. His breathing became laboured and he let out a strange, melancholy wail.

"Oh, Christ, oh, Christ...."

CHAPTER 53

Rosen went to his local police station and outlined his circumstances to the Desk Sergeant, who asked him to keep them informed, if he obtained concrete evidence that Ephraim had been taken to Marseilles.

Rosen returned to his office to take his mind off his grief, and examined a new manuscript, impeccably presented by a gifted female author. A senior Reader had passed it to him, thinking it might interest him. Though entertaining, the manuscript's narrative was indecent. He wanted to publish it because it was wittily and skilfully written, but decided not to do so. The judgement his common sense forced him to adopt, saddened him and intensified his grief. He rang for his secretary, a slim, mini-skirted redhead.

"You wanted me, Mr Rosen?"

"Yes. I feel I ought to write personally to Marianne Parr."

"Who's she?"

"The author of the manuscript the Readers have been arguing about. The one I insisted on seeing."

"Which one?"

" *A Funeral Director's Breakfast.*"

"Ah, yes, that one."

"I can't bear having to turn an author down, particularly if it's a first book. It feels like committing a murder."

"Come, Mr Rosen, you're too soft."

"I hate having to hurt someone, but there are times when it can't be avoided in this trade. What do you think of the manuscript?"

"I think it's a bit rude. Very up front. Not badly written, though."

"It's so extreme and explicit, there's not a word of it I can lawfully print," said Rosen. "It's hilarious, though. I almost wish I'd written it myself. Would you mind taking this letter, please.

'Dear Miss Parr,

'Thank you for sending me the manuscript of A Funeral Director's Breakfast. *I really am sorry to have to inform you, that, in its present state, we are unable to consider it for publication, as regrettably, it contravenes the Obscene Publications Act.*

'This does not mean to say I do not like it. You have a most engaging and witty turn of phrase, and your obvious talent as a writer, is by no means unnoticed.

'Once you have recovered from the painful shock of rejection, I would suggest that you re-write the book. There are some subjects which should not be referred to in words, but subtly implied.

'Have courage. The book is not beyond resurrection. Give it another try. I might well be able to reconsider.'"

"Will that be all?" asked the secretary.

"That will do. I like to ask secretaries for their opinions. I don't like to see them as objects. Do you think this letter's appropriate?"

"I think you give far too much, Mr Rosen."

"You do, do you? Why don't you lock this door?"

"Mr Rosen, you're a married man!"

"If a man has an affair, he is disloyal to his wife. I'm not asking you for that."

"Just how long are you proposing to go on for?"

"I promise you, I won't ask you, again. Just this time."

She removed only the clothing necessary to make a carnal act possible, and leant over the desk.

"Very well, Mr Rosen. I will endeavour to institute the relief you require."

"Come on, there's no need to be so pompous."

She talked to him mechanically, throughout. "The Russian translator is waiting outside, to discuss Mr Fox's book, about the Irish rebel who choked to death when the hangman set up the noose, incorrectly. He is most emphatic that distribution can only take place in Moscow and Petersburg, due to management

270

problems. He says Mr Yeltsin has expressed an interest in this work, and is anxious to read it before he dies. Oh, was my performance to your satisfaction, Mr Rosen?"

Rosen got up and adjusted his clothing.

"No, it wasn't," he said. "It's unheard of to carry on a conversation while doing what we've done. I do hope you don't do this to other men. It would scare the wits out of them."

Rosen was low in spirits, after the incident and despaired of finding Ephraim. He took a full bottle of whisky from the drawer and drank half of it. He sat there, staring into space, for two hours.

His telephone rang.

"Is your name Ian Rosen?" It was a man's voice. His voice was soft and his accent unlinked to region or class. His speech sounded stifled, as if he were holding a cloth in front of his mouth. He was using a mobile 'phone and had dialled 141 first so that the call could not be traced.

"Yes, that's right," said Rosen.

"Do you want to know where Ephraim is?"

"Yes."

"He is with us. He's still alive. You want him to continue that way, I assume?"

"Yes. I suspect you are Jethro Pendary, using a disguised voice, and that you are with a woman called Kate Rendon."

"You suspect wrongly. I am someone else."

"Where the hell is he?"

"Somewhere in Marseilles. If you want him back, you'll have to go out of your way to get him."

"What do you want me to do?"

"Get hold of all his inherited assets, convert them to fifty pound notes and leave the container in a left luggage locker at the Gare St Charles. Put the key in gift-wrapping paper, and take it as far as the entrance to Marseilles Harbour. Go on walking until you find an ancient tower. You will see a man in an open-necked green shirt and white trousers. He is there every day between 4.00 and 4.30 p.m.

"You will address him in code. When you approach him,

271

you will say 'Is this the city where the Marquis de Sade asked his valet to whip him?' You see, Mr Rosen, we know a lot about you and the people who write for you.

"If the man replies, 'Yes, indeed, it is,' it will mean you've found the right person. You will give him the key and walk away from him.

"If the container is found and the money counted is reasonable to us, we will have the hostage at the tower by the harbour entrance at 11.15, the morning after you meet the man in the green shirt. If you allow the police to become involved, we will shoot the hostage."

The caller hung up. Rosen went back to the police station. He then rang Becket and asked him to accompany him to Marseilles. The chauffeur was sweet, co-operative and agreeable. He said he would do anything to secure the release of the boy he had become attached to, even if he had had to carry brimming buckets of hot water backwards and forwards to the Rolls, on the many occasions he had failed to hold his bile.

Rosen told Miranda about his intended visit to Marseilles.

"I'm coming with you," she announced.

"You can't come, Miranda. It's out of the question for you to be there, when there's likely to be bloodshed. I promise I'll ring you up twice a day."

"Why is Becket coming with you?"

"Because I need a man whom I like and trust."

"You're not taking the car, are you?"

"No, of course, I'm not. It's not the sort of operation which requires a car, and certainly not a Rolls."

"Why are you going out, again, when you've only just come in?"

"I've got to see Nick, the Doctor."

"Do you mean Dr Jacobs?"

"Yes."

"Why do you call him 'Nick, the Doctor'?"

"I just feel like referring to him as that. My nerves are smashed. If I can't get some Valium off him, I'll be as good as dead."

Dr Nicholas Jacobs had looked after Rosen's family for a considerable amount of time. Both his parents had been under his care, and he had been present when Ian was born. He was in his late sixties, and was mildly over-weight, and unhealthy-looking. His grey hair was parted half way down his head, to disguise its thinness. He had small, modest rooms in Harley Street.

Rosen was called from the waiting room into the consulting room. Jacobs had a pleasant, friendly, if intrusive manner and rose to his feet to greet his patient.

"It's been well over a year since I last looked at you," he began. "I'm so sorry to hear from Miranda about that boy. How is it you're so attached to him, if you don't mind me asking?"

"I was in love with his mother."

"I see. I really must insist on examining you, after all this time."

"It's not an examination I've come for," said Rosen. "I need Valium."

"I'm prepared to come to that. I say, that's your third since you've been in here. How many are you having a day?"

"Until now, it's been about forty. Now, it's sixty to eighty."

"In that case, I must insist on giving you a chest X-ray."

"I'll only agree to that if you give me Valium," said Rosen, in an exasperated tone.

"I'm going to give it to you. Go next door and the radiographer will do your X-rays."

Rosen went out to be X-rayed and came back five minutes later. Jacobs was sitting, waiting to see the films.

"Why do you wear your tie loosened at the neck, like that, all the time?"

"It drives women crazy," said Rosen.

"You always were a bit of a lad, weren't you?"

"You could say that. I can't get enough of the stuff. I wish I had more control but I haven't. My body seems to need it all the time."

"What you really mean is, *you* need it. You still haven't turned to religion, I take it?" said the compulsively talkative doctor.

273

"Not a chance, sorry. Could we talk about something else?" said the patient. He was so downhearted, his voice could hardly be heard.

"I'll check the rest of you while I'm waiting."

"Very well."

"Must you smoke while I'm listening to your heart?"

"Sorry. I'll put it out."

Although Rosen had been over-attentive to personal hygiene for most of his life, events had made him even more depressed, and it was now well over a week since he had bathed or changed his clothes.

"I hope you don't mind me asking you this, but when did you last have a bath?" asked Jacobs.

"Oh Christ, sorry, is it as bad as that?"

"Put it this way, it's pretty bad."

"Surely, as a doctor, you should know that, when a man's living in hell, he's not likely to want to wash. Anyway, it turns Miranda on when I'm like that. It makes her want me to screw her all night long."

The doctor cleared his throat. He appeared embarrassed and looked down at his desk, like an over-the-limit motorist who had been pulled into the side.

The radiographer came into the room with the X-rays. Jacobs slapped them onto an illuminated sheet of glass. "Your lungs — they're inflamed!" he exclaimed.

"Are they? They feel fine."

"I have never in my life witnessed a more pitiful state of self neglect in a man of your class," said Jacobs. "You'll need some antibiotics."

"I don't want them! All I want is Valium."

"Which strength?"

"I like the blue ones best."

"Those are the 10mg ones. They're the strongest. There's something loveably childlike about you, Ian."

Rosen got up to leave.

"You humiliated me about the bathing. I resented your words, because I am known everywhere for my extreme cleanliness. Your common sense should have told you this is just an aberration. You should never have mentioned it. If I'd been in your place, I certainly wouldn't have considered it a humane thing to do."

"Please believe how much I feel for you, my boy," said Jacobs.

"Thank you. I'm sorry I was abrupt with you. I can be familiar with you, because of the amount of time you've known me. You use far, far too many words. I think I'd probably top myself if you submitted a manuscript to me."

"I'm relieved to tell you, I can't write prose. I hardly know one end of a pen from the other," replied the doctor.

CHAPTER 54

Rosen and Becket arrived at Marignane Airport, just outside Marseilles. Rosen had with him a large suitcase, containing banknotes. They took a taxi to the station. Rosen left the suitcase in a left luggage locker and took away the key. They took another taxi to a five star hotel, overlooking the harbour.

It was 8.00 in the evening. Rosen took Becket to a bouillabaisse restaurant near the hotel. It, too, was at the harbour's edge. The sun was setting over the masts of the moored boats, and the sand-coloured buildings, including the tower at the harbour's entrance, were of a glowing pink. The two men ordered whisky and wine of which they drank plenty, before being able to make conversation.

"It's a tragedy that such sadness brings us to this beautiful place," said Rosen.

Becket was unaccustomed to liquor. Unbeknown to him, he replied at length in a mixture of English and Latin.

"What the hell are you talking about?" rasped the publisher.

Becket continued to speak in the two languages. He recited a few poems in Latin.

"You really are going to have to speak English, Mr Becket," said Rosen. "I can't tolerate this behaviour."

Becket said nothing. He sank into a strange, melancholic trance and rocked backwards and forwards in his chair. A furious Frenchman, dining alone at a neighbouring table, shouted at length at the head waiter because his bouillabaisse was cold. An American couple complained to Rosen about his chain-smoking. Rosen ignored them. Becket lit a Winston Churchill cigar in defiance of the two Americans. He left the restaurant without warning and walked with a lurch to the edge of the harbour. He leant over and scooped up some of the water in his hands and splashed it over himself. He went back into the restaurant, without apparent knowledge of his action, or concern about the baffled stares of the other diners.

"I don't mind eccentricity in a man," said Rosen, "but what I can't bear is eccentricity beyond my comprehension."

"It's no good complaining because I went out at dinner. I was hot," said Becket. His voice was an octave lower than its customary deep pitch and his speech had a lilting lurch like his walk. He looked enigmatically at Rosen, partly like a dog which had just been thrashed, and partly like a proud genius mounting a platform to collect a prize. His benign ambiguity of mien perplexed and frightened Rosen.

"I don't think I'll ever be able to understand you, Mr Becket," he said. "You're so different to other men."

Becket was silent. A faint smile struggled to break through his tormented features. He continued to rock backwards and forwards in his chair, while his private nightmares remained firmly sealed in the iron vault embedded in his brain.

* * *

The telephone rang in Becket's room at 10.00 the following morning.

"Are you all right, today, Mr Becket?" Rosen sounded as perplexed as he had been the night before. His confusion was mixed with concern and affection for his curious, unfathomable, intellectually brilliant companion, the only contemporary member of the male sex, he had ever warmed to.

"Ticking over, nicely, Mr Rosen. Are *you* all right?"

"I'm OK. May I come and see you in your room?"

"Of course, you may, Mr Rosen. You will be *most* welcome."

Becket was lying on his back, wrapped up in towels and smoking a Winston Churchill cigar, his facial expression betraying torment, mixed with peace and resignation. Rosen sat on the bed.

"I don't know how to say this, Mr Becket. Your personality is confusing me in a very major way. It's a sort of relief because I become distracted from my terrible grief. The other part of it intimidates me. I've never thought about anyone like this before. You may be incomprehensible, but I think you might be a better man than I am."

277

Becket's features changed like lightning, from agony of soul, to joviality, and agony, once more.

"I'm bound to say I find that remark dashed wet. Have a Winston."

"A cigar? I won't, thank you. We're to go to the harbour entrance at 4.00 this afternoon and stay there until 4.30, to see that man. Do you remember?"

"Yes."

"It would be best for you to walk about thirty yards behind me. It's too dangerous for me to be seen, accompanied."

"Why do you need me to come in any event?"

"Because I'd feel better. Because I like and trust you."

Becket shifted his eyes from one object in the room to another. He laughed to himself.

"What the hell are you laughing at, Mr Becket?"

"A French woman was woken up early in the morning by a neighbour. She didn't know his name, and addressed her complaint to 'L'homme qui se lève très tôt le matin'.*

"Is that what you were laughing at?"

"Yes."

"I don't find that particularly funny. What made you think of it, now? Is it a Freudian matter?"

Becket let out another tortured laugh and pointed at Rosen.

"Froydy-Woydy!" he exclaimed.

Rosen felt like a lost child, at a loss to understand the unreachable. He leant forward with his head in his hands. His depression was intolerable.

*The man who gets up very early in the morning.

278

CHAPTER 55

It was 2.00 in the afternoon. The two somewhat uncomfortably-matched Englishmen were sitting in a café on the port. Rosen had had nothing to drink, other than black coffee. Nervousness and edginess had added another dimension to his grief, and he yearned for the Valium which he had left in the hotel.

Becket was looking at the cathedral on top of the hill, overlooking Marseilles. He was the first to break the silence.

"Would you like to accompany me to the cathedral, to say prayers for the boy, Mr Rosen?"

"There wouldn't be any point. I have no faith."

"Not even some?"

"Not any. I don't believe in God, Mr Becket. Nor have I, since I was twelve years old. I get angry when religion is forced onto children, and they are warned about hell fire, and that sort of thing. It's a threat to them, not a comfort.

"Don't take offence, but one thing I can't tolerate is a religious person, trying to impose his God on me. Even in adversity, I don't want God in my life."

Rosen put out his cigarette and lit another. He inhaled urgently on it. It was his sixth since entering the café.

"I find your attitude dashed regrettable. Dashed regrettable, I call it," said Becket.

"You can regret it as much as you want, for all I care. All I ask is that you don't impose your God on me. I'm not up to it. I'm a militant non-believer, with humanitarian values. I'd sooner watch a blind person being helped across a road, than a lot of idiots, praying. I suppose, if I were to have any God, it would be sex. That's a thing my body needs, to stay healthy."

"You need it, Mr Rosen."

"It's easy for you to say that. It's the way I am made. I need a prostitute. As it is, I haven't had a woman since we've been here and it's making me physically uncomfortable, so much so that it's hurting me."

"I hope you don't resent my asking you, but did something extremely unpleasant happen to you when you were twelve

279

years old?" asked Becket.

Rosen was about to tell the truth but a sudden feeling he was being intruded on, prevented him from doing so. He raised his eyes to the sky, his facial expression one of defiance and arrogance.

"I prefer to keep the doors of my tortured inner chamber firmly locked,"* he said, his voice scarcely audible.

* * *

At 3.00 that afternoon, Rosen and Becket walked towards the tower at the Harbour Entrance. Rosen had returned to the hotel to collect the Valium, prescribed by Dr Jacobs. He took two of the 10mg pills, and lay on his bed shaking for half an hour before they took effect.

He 'phoned Becket's room and was pleased to find he was alert.

"It's gone 3.30, Mr Becket. It's a long walk. Are you ready?"

"I am indeed ready. Let's go."

Rosen could not have been more grateful to the Valium that day. His mind was lucid, and his personality had taken on an artificially chilling dimension.

Becket was following him. Rosen had no idea what a long walk it was from the mouth of the harbour to its entrance. Though seen as a sedative, Valium can restore physical and mental energy. He was oblivious to the sticky heat in the later afternoon. He continued to walk, his gift-wrapped key in his hand. He walked until he found the ancient tower.

He could not see the man in the green shirt. He thought there would be no chance of missing him, because he had arrived at 3.50 p.m. and stayed until after 4.30. He walked round the tower several times, fanatically chain-smoking. He scanned the entrance of the harbour. There was still no sign of him.

---

*These were the words of the late Robert Maxwell. It should be noted that they were not uttered in relation to religious matters, or prostitutes, either in Marseilles, or any other township.

In his calmer state, he reasoned that the man would be there the following day, but when that day came, he repeated his visit to the harbour entrance and still found no-one. He turned back. Becket was thirty yards behind him. He threw his arms round him and sobbed like a child.

"What are the police doing about this?" asked Becket.

"I was told by the Desk Sergeant that the *Gendarmerie* would be informed. They're said to be strong on kidnapping. I don't deny I have doubts about the competence of *gendarmes*, but they're reputed to be better than the English police. The best thing we can do, bearing in mind that the case hasn't been collected from the station, is seek Kate Rendon out ourselves. The information I have on her is that she's a prostitute, and she mentioned her desire to settle down in Marseilles, doing, what Rodney Pendary quoted as 'street work'."

"That would suggest she's a ten-bob knock. What do you think the ten-bob knocks do in this city? They stand in the streets. I've seen them. They congregate in a concentrated area in the streets behind the harbour.

"I've got Kate's photograph. She's never met me and wouldn't recognize me. Take a look."

Becket observed the hard, cold features, the unappealing slanting eyes.

"Memorize Kate's features, will you, Mr Becket. I've committed them to memory. It's evident she won't be on the streets all the time, but if we watch all these women, we'd find out more about her habits and movements, probably by putting delicate questions to them. She won't know us. We have to be dogged. We just walk round these streets until we find her. I'll pick her up and allow her to take me to her shame. I only hope that I'll find Ephraim there, too."

It was 9.30 in the evening, a time when the prostitutes would be coming out in droves. Becket and Rosen dined in another restaurant, overlooking the harbour. It was cooler and Becket's behaviour, though a trifle distracted, was more restrained than it had been the night before. Rosen was relieved by the fact that his companion refrained from interspersing his speech with Latin and leaving the table abruptly, to wash in the harbour.

The men paid the bill and went to a narrow street, leading away from the harbour. They came to the Rue Farréol, where stylishly dressed prostitutes lined the entire street, like an invading army.

"Christ, the quantity of them!" said Rosen, despairingly.

"It's only a question of walking up and down the whole beat and looking at each one, while keeping a discreet distance. A lot of other men are looking at them. There's no reason for any of them to get suspicious.

"It's a good thing that it's out of fashion for a middle-aged woman to have long peroxide blonde hair. That will make it easier to find Kate Rendon."

Becket sat in a café, reading a leather-bound tome about barges combing the Volga, called *Foma Gordyev*, by Gorky. Rosen swigged from a half bottle of whisky and walked hungrily towards the women, to ask lightly-worded questions if the opportunity arose, and to gratify his insatiable carnal appetite, which had become so demanding, it was almost an illness.

He had not bathed or changed his clothes since his arrival in Marseilles. The aroma caused by the lack of hygiene in this otherwise scrupulously clean man, excited some of the prostitutes who were used to their punters sprucing themselves before approaching them.

Rosen looked at the many women in turn. None of the peroxide blondes were as old as Kate Rendon. He wondered whether she had changed her hair and looked at each woman's face in turn. Upward slanting eyes, a rare feature in a face, would stand out and only escape recognition if their owner wore dark glasses.

He abandoned the search, but planned to go through the same procedure every night, until he found Kate Rendon, even if it meant doing so for months. His new partner at the publishing house, was trustworthy and would have been capable of running the business, unaided, for a year, if necessary.

A black-haired prostitute in a tight, leopard-skin cat suit, stepped away from the other women and pulled him by the sleeve. She was stimulated by his unwashed state and loosened tie.

"Where do you want to go?" asked Rosen, in fluent French. His accent sounded more East European than English.

"I have a room in a hotel the other side of the harbour."

"In what hotel?"

The woman guided him to the port. She barely wore any make-up. Her skin was milkmaid-fresh and she was slightly overweight. There was a cheeky spontaneity about her which attracted Rosen. He put one arm round her shoulder and the other round her waist and rubbed her protruding stomach, to tease her about her plumpness. The pair walked past the café, where Becket was sitting, reading, smoking a cigar.

Becket looked up. He pointed at Rosen and fixed him with a mischievous, charming smile.

"I'll tell Mrs Rosen!"

"No, you won't. I'm seeking information. What's that extraordinary-looking book you've got there."

Becket rocked backwards and forwards, and answered in the tone of an exhausted priest, reciting prayers. "It examines a fairly significant deterioration in industrial relations in the timber transport industry in the provinces of Nineteenth Century Russia, alongside the assessment of the mind of a young man, born into riches but unable to identify with his own class. The writer appears to lose his grip and sense of authorial presentation at the end of Chapter III."

Rosen reached for the bottle of whisky on the table and took several swigs from it. He knew the prostitute did not speak English, and kissed her lightly on the cheek, through courtesy, while a language she had no knowledge of, was being spoken.

"Christ! It sounds a right barrel of laughs," he remarked. "I hope no-one sends a ghastly, boring book like that to me."

"The book is not boring, Mr Rosen. Its prose, though deviating from its central theme as it progresses, is pure, enriching and ennobling. Might I ask if you intend to wash yourself, before you go to this lady's bed?"

"Shut up, Becket! She likes me in this state."

"Has she said so?"

"Not in words. I've felt it in her. Sometimes, I understand women, even if they don't speak."

The prostitute took Rosen to a dilapidated building, whose tattered hallway was strewn with foul-smelling litter and used heroin syringes.

"Is this place a health hazard?" asked Rosen.

"No. My room is very clean. I have nothing to do with the other people who live here."

Rosen paid her the fee for her services and smoked throughout the act.

"Do you always come, like that?" he asked. She appeared confused and embarrassed.

"I'm so sorry, I didn't mean to embarrass you. Lie down beside me and let me hold you."

He found her vulnerability, combined with the natural warmth of her performance, endearing.

"Are you able to stay longer?" he asked.

"I can stay for as long as you like."

"I won't ask you for more. I just want to talk to you, but I'll pay you for your time. What's your name?"

"Mei."

"May? How do you spell that?"

"M-E-I."

"It's a strange name."

"What's your name, monsieur?"

"It's David. How long have you been doing this kind of work?"

"Two years. Before that, I worked in a bar. I had to leave."

"Why?"

"The patron forced me to have an affair with him. I was going to have a baby. I lost it."

"I'm so sorry. Was it his?"

"No. My friend's. I was going to marry him. When he found out, he said he never wanted to see me, again."

"Poor little girl! You've had it rough, haven't you?"

"I'm all right, now."

"Have you been able to make friends with the other girls?"

"I get on with nearly all of them. The ones that are French are easy to get on with. They're straight-forward. I know where I stand with them. It's the ones, who aren't French, who cause trouble."

"You're not French either, are you?"

"No. I'm from Hong Kong. In a community in another country, foreigners don't get on with other foreigners."

"What sort of people do you not get on with?"

"Well, it's quite recent."

"What is?"

"We all know each other well. We don't always like each other."

"I've just asked you what you meant when you said it was quite recent."

"There's been a new one. Someone found out that she keeps a boy in her room and that he sees everyone coming in and going out. She's very unpleasant. She upsets everyone."

Rosen sat up, abruptly and rested his weight on his elbows.

"How old is this boy?" he demanded.

"He's about eleven or twelve."

"Is he her son?"

"No-one thinks so, because of the way she treats him."

"Treats him? How does she treat him?"

"She won't let him out. One of my customers went to her, only last week. He said the boy was too ill to go out."

"Too ill? Too ill? In what way, ill?"

"He's had a fever for a while."

"For how long?"

"I don't know."

"Was a doctor sent for?"

"No. She didn't want a doctor."

"Who is she? What's her name?"

"She's known as 'Ekaterina'. I don't know if that's her real name. We all refer to her as the 'English woman'.

"Are any of the other girls English?"

"No. Just this one."

285

"Do you know where she lives?"

"She rents a room in Rue St Farréol."

"Have you any idea what number?"

"No."

"What does Ekaterina look like?"

"The day she first started, she wore a short black wig. Now, she has long, curly blonde hair. She's older than most of us."

Rosen took the photograph of Kate Rendon from his inside pocket and showed it to Mei.

"Is this the woman you're referring to?"

Mei held it up to the light and scrutinized it. She looked puzzled by the fact that one of her customers should keep an ageing prostitute's photograph. She thought it would be unprofessional to ask him why.

"Yes. That's her."

"What time of day does she go on the streets?"

"She used to work at night."

"Don't tell me what she used to do. What does she do, now?"

"She works in the afternoon. She stops at dinner time."

"What hours?"

"I don't know the times."

"Why did she change?"

"Because the girls working at night couldn't stand her. They told her they wouldn't have her on their beat."

"Does she actually stand on the street when she works?"

"Of course. Always. Why?"

"I thought there might be a possibility of her using a telephone."

"No. She works in the street, every afternoon except Sunday."

"Tomorrow's Sunday," said Rosen.

"She's the only one who doesn't work on a Sunday."

Rosen lit a cigarette. It was his twelfth since his visit to Mei's room.

"I want you to promise me something, Mei."

"What's that?"

"Will you give me your word that you won't tell anyone at all about this conversation?"

"I won't tell anyone. I was brought up never to break promises."

"Good girl."

Rosen got up and said he was leaving.

"You will come back, won't you?" she said.

"I will come back, provided I find you standing in the street. I'm afraid I won't come here on my own."

"Then I'll see you again, won't I?"

"I don't know, Mei. I hope so, but I can't say for certain. Do you remember telling me about your baby?"

"Yes."

"I'm in a similar situation. I'm in a lot of trouble. I've no idea how it's going to end, or what's going to happen to me. That's why you mustn't get dependent on me."

"You are a very kind man," she said. "Not many men are like you."

"If it's kindness you seek in a man, you should change your trade."

"Are you going to the police?"

"No. That would cause confusion. I'd be better off sorting this out, myself," said Rosen.

Rosen woke up at 10.00 the next morning. He swallowed some Valium, ordered a pot of coffee and took a bath, as well as immersing himself in an elaborate tooth-cleaning ritual, using an electric toothbrush and two different brands of mouthwash. The drug, combined with the knowledge that he was closer to finding Ephraim, filled him with optimism and hope.

He chain-smoked with his left hand and stuffed potato crisps into his mouth with his right, as he walked through the hot streets. He went to the same café as before. He found Becket, smoking a cigar, reading. The lugubrious chauffeur was wearing an arresting turquoise and orange tropical suit. He was aware of how startling his clothing was to the eye, and smiled, secretively.

"Christ, that suit of yours is a bit sudden, isn't it?" remarked Rosen.

"You're later than I thought you'd be, Mr Rosen."

"Could we cut out this 'mister' business? Just call me Ian. I found out from that lady I was with, where Ephraim is?"

"Where he is?"

"Yes. Kate Rendon solicits under the name of 'Ekaterina'. She works in the Rue St Farréol every afternoon, except Sunday. She lives in the same street.

Becket re-lit his cigar which had just gone out.

"How do you know it's the same woman?"

"I showed the girl the photograph. She knows her. All the women know her. I'm very concerned because she told me the woman, calling herself 'Ekaterina', keeps a child with her, a boy, whom she says is ill."

"Ill, in what way?"

"I couldn't get any details out of her. All she said was that he had a 'fever'. That could mean anything. It could be just a cold. It could be something much worse. Now I know where to find her, I'll pick her up and let her take me home."

He put his cigarette out and lit another. He put his arm round Becket and wept, while the chauffeur, unable to deal with openly expressed emotions, stared rigidly into space.

"It's not the despair that's driving me insane. It's the hope I can't tolerate," said Rosen.

He ordered whisky which he drank out of the bottle. He continued to drink until his mood brightened.

"There's no hope, in a situation like this, for a godless man," said Becket.

Rosen ignored the remark. "When did you last have a woman?" he asked, confrontationally.

"A woman? What a singular question! It's hard to say, off hand."

"No man can be complete if he doesn't have a woman, regularly. His physical state makes his mental state. What the hell does he want a Deity for? Who the hell needs it? It's oppressive. It's unwholesome!" shouted Rosen who was already inebriated.

"*I* need it."

"That's because you're an idiot. Why don't you show me you're more than that? We've been in this city for quite a while. How is it you haven't scored once?"

Becket let out a shy, secretive laugh, allowing nothing of his inner self to be displayed.

"You seem to think I've had no experience with women," he said. "Come out into the street with me. Then you can watch me."

"I didn't mean to humiliate you," said Rosen. "It's a very personal thing, being able to watch a friend, and see what he does when he goes to a woman."

They paid the bill and walked out onto the Rue St Farréol. The bizarrely-dressed chauffeur was holding the publisher steady. Although it was still morning, a cluster of prostitutes stood on the street corner. Becket approached one of them, a nondescript, poor-complexioned woman with thigh-high white boots. He addressed her in theatrical, Churchillian French and kissed her hand. When she was taking him to her room, he did not put his arm round her shoulder or waist. He took her by the arm like an elderly man, walking with his wife after fifty years of marriage.

CHAPTER 56

Billy Jopp was a former Merchant Navy chef who had been invalided out of service because of arthritis. He chose to live in Marseilles because he associated it with memories of available women, good restaurants, hot-blooded street fights and rough living.

He had been traumatised by his confinement to land and was permanently in an advanced state of mania. He had made no effort to learn French and communicated with the inhabitants of Marseilles, by pulling them by their ear lobes and shouting at them at the top of his voice in English.

He was formally dressed in a pale blue linen suit and collar and tie. He wore a pair of black-framed glasses, covering most of his face. He was sitting at a table, a distance from the door of the café frequented by Becket and Rosen, and was accompanied by a woman with whom he was having a one-sided conversation. The publisher and the chauffeur had returned and were sitting by the door.

Jopp only had one eye. The other eye was a glass replica. Whenever he wished to make a point, he repeated himself and nervously took out his glass eye, wiped it on his sleeve and put it back in its socket, without knowing he had done so.

He ranted at his female companion, making a Guinness-Book-of-Records-breaking noise, and displaying a blistering West Country accent, more potent than a tropical mid-day sun.

"I've not been too well of late," he shouted, thinking he was speaking, normally. "I went up the Doc. Speaks English, does 'ee. 'Is it Big C?' I asked him. He said 'No, it's emphysema.' I'm off the fags now. When I had my cough this morning, I gunked up an 'ole 'andkerchief-full of blood."

The other customers turned and stared at him. Those, who did not speak English, were fascinated by the sound of his words and assumed he was a political fanatic.

He took his glass eye out, rolled it on the table like a marble and put it back in its socket.

"When I had my cough this morning, I gunked up an 'ole

'andkerchief-full of blood," he repeated.

"So you've said, already," remarked his female companion. "Do you normally take out your eye, roll it about on the table and put it back in its socket?"

Jopp ignored her question.

"So I went down with this emphysema, only days after I got over my meningitis, see. Then I gets my cough in the morning, too."

"Why do you keep referring to 'my' cough?" she said. "It's not as if it's anyone else's cough."

"No, but I were up the Doc, again, yesterday, because I wanted to know where all this blood was coming from, see."

Jopp continued his monologue. Hitler's utterances at a Nuremburg rally, would have seemed no more than pathetic, bird-like bleats in comparison with the eccentric West countryman's delivery.

Becket wished he would leave and tried to read his book. Rosen was convulsed with mirthless, tragic laughter.

"Christ, this man's funny, Becket! I can't understand why he's not on the stage."

Jopp continued his repetitive ranting.

"I says to the Doc, 'I'm filling up these 'ere 'andkerchief-fulls of blood every day. Am I croaking'?"

"You'll have to pay me for my time," said his companion. "I can't listen to all this medical talk, unless you give me another hundred francs, and fifty francs, every time you get your eye out. Apart from that, I prefer to spend Sunday afternoons at home."

Jopp had run out of cash. "Forget it," he said, irritated by the notion that she found his conversation tedious. He got up and was about to leave the café. He saw Becket and Rosen sitting by the door and observed Rosen's compulsive chain-smoking and brimming ashtray. He slapped the baffled publisher on the back.

"Be warned, whoever you are, and I'm warning you from the bottom of my heart. Give it up! It's not too late! You're committing suicide! Them there fags'll kill you, just as they

291

nearly killed me. You should see the 'andkerchief-fulls of blood I gunk up! Next time, I gunk up, I'll scrape the blood off the 'andkerchief. I'll scoop it into a saucer and I'll bring it to you and show you what it looks like, how much of it there is, and the amount of clots there are in it!"

"Oh, buzz off," said Rosen.

CHAPTER 57

Ten minutes passed. The woman, who had been sitting with Jopp, got up and walked towards the door. Rosen had not noticed her until then. He turned to look at her. His eyes moved from her legs, to her chest and finally to her face. He kicked Becket under the table, and mouthed the words, 'It's her!'"

He turned to Kate Rendon.

"Do you speak English?" he asked.

"I am English."

"Are you free at the moment?"

"I'm on my way home. I don't work on Sunday afternoons."

"That's a terrible pity. I'm going back to London, tonight. That means I'll miss you."

Kate was in debt. Pendary did not like it in Marseilles. He had lost hope in financial gain from Ephraim's abduction, and had gone back to London. She had found out about his departure when she went to visit him at the Hôtel Club Mediterrané and was given an abruptly-worded note from the concierge. In addition, her premature age had decreased her clientele, and she found her new punter sexually attractive.

"All right, it's on," she said, curtly.

"What do you charge?"

"I want four hundred francs. I want it, beforehand."

He took a wad of bank notes from his inside pocket and gave them to her.

"Come on, girl, let's go."

Rosen looked over his shoulder and saw Becket following them down the street, at a distance of about thirty yards. They walked past a group of street women, many of whom recognized the woman calling herself "Ekaterina". They were surprised by the sight of a woman attracting a man in daylight, when the bright sun accentuated the furrows on her face, brought on by bitterness, heavy drinking and debauchery.

Rosen's mobile 'phone rang. The Valium he had taken earlier had worn off. Although he had it with him, his self respect prevented him from taking it in front of Kate. His initial reaction was of fear that Miranda had come to harm. His chest hurt and his heart banged against his ribs.

"Bloody hell, yes!"

"Sorry to have rung your mobile. We didn't know where you were, Mr Rosen."

"Who's calling?"

"It's the Reader's Department. James Crawford speaking."

"Is something the matter?"

"No. I rang because you said you were most particular about being informed of the titles of every strangely-worded manuscript which comes in."

"Get on with it. What about it?"

"We've just received another manuscript from Marianne Parr."

"Who?"

"Marianne Parr's the one who sent in *A Funeral Director's Breakfast*, which you rejected."

"Oh, her? She couldn't have done another one, already. She's only just turned one out. I couldn't take it because it was so far out, it was a thousand feet in the air. I told her to re-do it."

"Whatever you told her to do, she's done another one, instead."

"What's the title?"

The reception on the line was poor.

"I said, what's the title? repeated Rosen.

"*'Maggots and Blood on the Carving Knife'*."

Two of the street women hurled abuse at Kate. They resented the fact that they had been left standing for most of the morning, while an older, seedier-looking woman had been picked up by a seemingly wealthy, attractive client with a mobile telephone, speaking another language, probably to someone in another country.

Rosen couldn't hear. He gesticulated to the two women to stop shouting.

"Let's have it, again," he said. "There's background noise on the line."

Crawford repeated the title.

" *'Maggots and Blood on the Carving Knife'*."

"Christ, that's a bloody stupid title! Tell her she's capable of doing much better than that," said Rosen. "She'd stand a better chance of getting her books published, if they were less sick and sordid. That woman carries her stuff to ridiculously unheard-of extremes. There's no bloody subtlety in her titles."

He put the mobile 'phone back in his pocket.

Kate leaned against him. Her touch disgusted him.

"Are you in publishing?" she asked.

"Yes."

"What do you publish?"

"Books."

"You're not very talkative, are you?"

"I haven't come out here to talk. Could you take me to where you live? I only want to do what I've come to do. I'm not made of time."

She took him to the scratched, graffiti-strewn metal door, leading to a hallway in a tenement building, which had been recently squatted in by semi-comatose drug addicts and vagrants, lying slumped on the floor and staircase.

Kate unlocked the door to her room. Rosen noticed the wallpaper, which had pealed off in places, showing outdated pro-Algerian daubings. There were two tattered, green velvet screens, one just inside the door, the other at the end of the room.

There was a foul-smelling bucket, sprinkled with disinfectant, draped with a towel, on the floor, near the screen furthest from the door. Nearby, was an array of open bottles of honey, unfit to be eaten.

Kate went behind the screen nearest to the door, to wash herself in an enamel bowl. There were no plumbing facilities in the building. Ablutions and disposal of human waste took place in the rooms the tenants ate and slept in.

Rosen waited for Kate to go behind the screen. He went to the door leading to the street, and unlocked it so that Becket could enter the building. He went back to Kate's room and left the door ajar.

Kate was still not ready. Neither she nor Rosen had spoken since entering the room. Rosen went to the screen at the other end of the room. He was prepared for Ephraim's death and was not afraid of looking behind it.

He was faced by the sight of a mattress, covered with filthy blankets and overcoats. He felt that, wherever Ephraim was, he was not in Kate's room. The thought crossed his mind that she had murdered him, probably in the room, and disposed of the body.

He took the bottle of Valium from his pocket and shovelled two pills into his mouth. He decided to wait for the drug to take effect, before moving the blankets and overcoats, to see if there was anything underneath them.

He looked out from behind the screen to see whether or not Kate had finished washing herself and had come out into the open part of the room. The only person he could see was Becket, who was sitting bolt upright in an armchair, reading a pink, satin-bound tome, his face resigned and expressionless.

A pleasant feeling of drowsiness descended on Rosen. He looked at the pile of blankets and coats, once more and realized that they were no longer in the same position, as if movement had taken place. He was about to lift them and look underneath them, when they were thrown violently onto the floor.

Ephraim was alive. His fever had reached such a pitch, that he was throwing himself from one side to another. His face was a yellowish, white colour. There were black shadows under his eyes. He looked as if he were approaching death. His eyes were open and moving about like a ferret's. He recognized Rosen and lifted his arm, with such an extreme effort that he might have been lifting lead.

"Ian!"

Rosen knelt on the floor and put his arms round him.

"Yes, my boy, it's Ian. He's come to take you home."

"I am very ill," said the boy. "I think I'm dying."

"You're not going to die." Rosen was pleased he had taken the Valium. It transferred him to an altered state, and prevented

296

him from losing control in front of Ephraim.

"It's not 'flu, is it my boy?" said Rosen.

"I don't think so." The boy spoke in staccato blasts. "Epidemic here. Meningitis. Can't stand light. Bad headache. Stiff neck. Man from Cornwall came here with it. Came and talked to me. Came here a lot. Came to see the woman."

"The man who came here, did he talk like this...?" Rosen gave an imitation of Jopp's rasping voice.

"Yes."

Ephraim pointed at the floor. Rosen noticed that one of the floor boards was loose.

"For you, Ian," said the boy.

"What's for me, Ephi?"

"I tore off some wallpaper when she was out. I didn't think you'd find me, but I hoped you would, all along, so that I could give it to you."

Rosen lifted the loose floor board and found several torn strips of wallpaper underneath it. The strips were covered with neat, tidy handwriting.

"You've written for me, my boy! I knew all along, you'd write for me, one day. I'll keep these. I'm going over there to call a doctor. Then I'll come back."

"Don't go! Don't leave me alone!"

"I'm not going anywhere. Don't be frightened. I'm coming back."

Kate had brushed her hair and washed and painted her face. She was leaning over Becket's chair and offering him her services. He ignored her, despising the situation he was in, and continued to read like a depressed commuter, waiting for a late train.

Rosen shouted to him from across the room and threw his mobile 'phone at him.

"Stop your bloody reading! Call the *gendarmerie*. Tell them to send emergency medical aid. I think he may be dangerously ill. Hurry!"

Kate was not alarmed by the prospect of *gendarmes* being called to her room. Since Ephraim was her nephew, she could not see why his presence, under her alleged care, would be considered unlawful. Her services had been sought by many *gendarmes*, a few of whom had been requested from Paris to combat illicit drug trafficking. Some of the Parisian *gendarmes* had been attracted to her because of her English accent.

She went over to where Rosen was standing and put her hand on his shoulder.

"Aren't I rude, keeping you waiting like this? You're a beautiful man. Why don't you let me take you to bed?"

Something broke within Rosen.

"You fucking sadistic bitch!" he shouted. "You've pretty well finished him off, haven't you, you cheap, backstreet slut?"

He hit her hard several times about the face and jaw. He pushed her violently against the wall and ripped off her clothes.

"Don't do that. I've got AIDS!" she shouted.

He unzipped himself and pulled a frayed box of condoms from his back pocket.

"Not any more, you haven't," he said.

Becket sat rigidly, staring into space, while Rosen raped her. He waited for him to finish and nervously crossed himself, having sadly reached the conclusion that his employer's sexual needs were beyond being insatiable.

Rosen lumbered over to the flabbergasted chauffeur. "Oh, Christ, Becket, I'm still hard and it's bloody nearly killing me," he muttered, adding, "I do wish you'd stop doing that. Have you called them?"

"Yes. They're on their way."

"Good man. I'm going over to sit with Ephraim. I don't know what I would have done, if I hadn't taken the pills. That book you can't stop reading, is it any good?"

"It is informative, Ian," replied the phlegmatic chauffeur. "It is indeed most informative."

The *gendarmerie* responded to Becket's call, within ten minutes. Five cosh-wielding *gendarmes* and two paramedics spilled out of a van and accompanying ambulance outside the building. Two London officers were with them. They had been posted to Marseilles to find Ephraim. They had both been idle

298

and had wasted the taxpayer's money, loitering in bars and lying on the beach on the outskirts of the city.

Rosen saw them through the window. He went down to the street and led them, making hysterical beckoning gestures, to the room.

Kate was lying on the mattress behind her screen, recovering from Rosen's rape. She was more stimulated than traumatised by the raw, gutter treatment she had received, from what she regarded as an overpoweringly sexually attractive man. It would have broken his heart, had he found out the extent to which she had enjoyed being raped by him.

The *gendarmes* were puzzled by the sight of Becket, sitting motionless in a chair.

"Who the hell's this man, sitting here, reading?" rasped one of the British officers.

"Don't worry about him. He's a loyal friend. He's been working for my family for years," said Rosen.

The *gendarmes*, paramedics, and the two British officers rushed over to Ephraim. Rosen went after them.

"Are you off your heads? A crowd round him, could finish him off. Let me go in with the two paramedics."

Rosen stood, weeping at a distance from Ephraim and watched the paramedics examining him.

"Has he got a chance?" he shouted.

"At the moment, things don't look too good," said one of the paramedics. "He's received no treatment, so his condition's much worse."

"Is it meningitis?"

"Yes. He's got all the symptoms of it. There's an epidemic of it in the city."

"Oh, Christ!"

"If we get him to hospital, the first thing we'll do is dose him with antibiotics. It might not be too late. The antibiotics will bring his fever down."

Rosen went to Ephraim and lifted him. He carried him to the open part of the room, where the *gendarmes* and two British officers waited.

"Don't you know how infectious meningitis is?" said one of the British officers. "You're endangering yourself, holding him close to you, like this. You'll catch it."

"I don't give a fuck if I do," said Rosen. "Get him to hospital."

Two *gendarmes* found Kate and handcuffed her, while the paramedics lifted Ephraim onto a stretcher. Rosen insisted on travelling with him in the ambulance and ordered Becket to join them. He stroked Ephraim's sweating face and ran his hands through his soaking wet hair throughout the journey to hospital, as the ambulance was driven at lethal speeds along the narrow, cobbled backstreets of the city. The perilous driving held no fear for Rosen. So deep had his depression become, that he did not care whether he lived or died.

CHAPTER 58

Ephraim hovered between life and death in hospital for a few days. His condition neither improved nor deteriorated. Rosen slept on the floor by his bed-side, and wept when he wasn't sleeping.

"I think he should be flown to London," he said."

"He wouldn't stand the flight," said the doctor, attending to him.

"I don't believe that. He'd still be lying down. I insist on taking him back to London."

Kate was taken to the police station. Rosen and Becket travelled with Ephraim on a bumpy British Airways jet. Rosen had given Becket the key to the suitcase containing the money at the Rue St Charles. It was still there when the chauffeur went to collect it. Rosen kept an eye on it throughout the flight.

The stretcher, bearing Ephraim, was lain across a row of three seats in the Club compartment, which had become an isolated area. The chauffeur and the publisher occupied two of the seats facing the boy. Rosen fussed over the boy, stroked his head and played *Voltava* on his mouth organ, his aching love giving him the will to live. Becket crossed himself, once more, having prayed for his life to be restored.

"I thought I told you not to do that!" shouted Rosen. "It's scaring him to death. He's averse to religion, just as much as I am."

A crowd of newspaper photographers and reporters greeted them at Heathrow Airport. Rosen was ticked off by British Airways ground staff for smoking while getting out of the plane. He lit up once more when he came into the building. The flashing bulbs took his mind off his grief.

"How do you feel about Kate Rendon's arrest?" asked a reporter. She was a pretty, inexperienced young woman, a freelance journalist who had graduated from university three months earlier.

"I hope she never gets out of prison, alive. She's the sort of person I'd like to see strung up on a gibbet!"

"Are you praying for the boy's recovery?"

"I don't pray. I'm leaving all that to my friend, Mr Becket, here. He's a believer. I'm not."

"Doesn't that weaken you in adversity?"

"Why should it? There is no greater solace in adversity than the female sex. Has your Editor ever told you you've got fantastic legs?"

Miranda was at the back of the crowd. Becket was standing by Rosen's side. When Rosen saw her, he shed his inhibitions and kissed her on the lips with the hunger of an unfed animal. He put his hands under her dress and fondled her breasts. Some of the reporters stared at him, giggling.

"Oh, for God's sake, Ian!" said Becket.

The embarrassed police escorts, who had flown from Marseilles, cleared the crowd, to enable Ephraim to be carried to a waiting ambulance, bound for the Royal Free Hospital which had a private wing. Rosen and Miranda were allowed to travel in it, and throughout the journey, Rosen cosseted the boy, aware that his love was increasing his will to live.

The Rosens were allowed to sleep in the private wing at the Royal Free Hospital. Ephraim was in Intensive Care. The doctor, a specialist in children's disorders, was pleasant and sympathetic to Rosen. His name was Dr Page.

"Come in and see him. I'm afraid he's in a coma."

Rosen instinctively lit a cigarette which Page snatched from his hand. "You'll have to do without that, if you go into Intensive Care. That was being a bit naughty, I think."

Rosen went into Intensive Care, accompanied by Page. When he saw Ephraim, the only patient there, wired up with a heart monitor, he knelt on the floor and sobbed.

"Has he got a chance, Doc?"

"We're doing everything we can to help him. It is on his side that his will to live is very great. It's you who have made it so."

"All I want to know is, will he live?"

"The odds are fifty-fifty, Ian. That means there's a chance. Do you believe in God?"

"No."

Rosen sat in Intensive Care, weeping. He caressed and talked to Ephraim in the hope that he might come out of the coma. He played *Voltava* once more, aware that its haunting strains went straight into the boy's soul.

That night, he struggled to keep his sanity by having repeated, frenzied sex with Miranda. At first, it cheered and stimulated her. In the end, it exhausted her.

"I don't think I can take much more sex at the moment, Ian," she said. "I'm sore. My insides are getting worn out." She was in tears because she thought she was failing to support him.

"I'm so sorry. It hurts me when you cry. I'd be perfectly happy to lie beside you and hold you, just to show you how besottedly I love you. There's no need to worry about being sore, once in a while. You're one of the most sexually alive women I've ever met."

Dr Page came into their room the following morning, unannounced. Rosen was lying back on the bed, smoking, and Miranda was fellating him. She pulled the sheet over him. Page flushed and let out a discreet little cough.

"I have some promising news, this morning, Ian."

"Yes?"

Ephraim's out of his coma, which means the antibiotics have worked. His temperature's gone down. Also, and this is a delicate matter, I know. I'm aware of your shattering stress, but could you please not make so much noise when you make love to your wife, during the night. Some of the patients have been complaining."

"I'll do my best. If you've got a female partner, you will agree that it's not easy. Can we see him?" he asked.

"You can, but I feel you should go, one at a time. Ian, you'd better go first."

Ephraim recognized Rosen from the other side of the Intensive Care ward. His monitoring wires had been removed.

"I thought I'd never see you, again, Ian."

"You thought wrongly, didn't you, my boy?"

"That evil woman, is she being punished?"

"Yes, she's being punished, all right."

"How is she being punished?"

"She's been locked up. Not only that, I beat her up. In the old days, she'd have been hanged. After the way she treated you, I'd have been prepared to queue up all night and watch it happen."

"Did you cheat on Miranda in Marseilles?"

Rosen looked away from Ephraim.

"How could I have done? There wasn't time. I had to spend every minute looking for you."

CHAPTER 59

It took two weeks for Ephraim to be well enough to go home. Dr Page was with the Rosens while Ephraim, still very weak, was being helped by a nurse to dress.

Rosen's experiences, combined with his shock and the relief which followed, made it impossible for him to contain his emotion. He shook Dr Page's hand, sobbing.

"Thank you for all you've done, Doctor," he said.

"It's not me you have to thank. It was all the love you poured into the boy, as well as the music, which made him determined not to die. Without what you did, we would have lost him."

Rosen turned to leave the building.

"Isn't there something you've forgotten?" asked Page.

"Forgotten? I don't follow you."

"I'm sorry, Mrs Rosen. I need to speak to your husband, alone."

"Why? Is something wrong?" said Miranda.

"No. There's something I have to tell your husband in private. You'll find out what it's about later, but at the moment, it's a matter of great delicacy."

Miranda and Ephraim went outside, and waited in the car. Rosen went into Dr Page's office.

"Is there anything wrong with the boy? He's just recovered. What's this in aid of?" Rosen asked, urgently.

"It's about the blood."

"What blood?"

"Surely, you remember you asked me to take blood from him, and you, as well."

"I'd forgotten. It was the shock we've been through. Now, I remember. What about it?"

"You asked me to do a DNA test on Ephraim."

"Yes, I did. I can't think about anything else but him. A fit of insanity drove me to asking for it to be done."

"Your blood sample and the DNA test came through to me last night. What I'm about to tell you, will come as a serious shock to you."

"Don't mess about, Doc. Let's have it."

"Well, it is you who are Ephraim's natural father, not William Rendon."

Rosen lit his fourth cigarette since he had been in Dr Page's consulting room. He looked confused and embarrassed, before a feeling of sadness took over him.

"I do wish you'd stop chain-smoking in here, Ian. This is a non-smoking hospital."

"I've had a bloody awful shock. No-one has the right to forbid smoking in hospitals, unless it's done in operating theatres or wards. A smoker is treated like a leper, everywhere he goes."

"I don't make these regulations. Please, just be a good boy and put it out."

"There's no ashtray! You've taken it away."

Page was unrelaxed in Rosen's presence. The publisher looked about to see if he could find a saucer. His fragile patience had gone. He put his cigarette out in a geranium plant, delivered that day as a wedding anniversary present, to the beleaguered doctor.

"That's the most disgusting thing I've ever seen anyone do in my life!" shouted Page.

"Oh, Christ, perhaps I shouldn't have done that! I'm sorry. I really do mean I'm sorry."

He got up to go. Page opened the door for him.

"Are you pleased to hear the news?" he asked.

"I'm absolutely overjoyed as far as I'm concerned, but my heart is broken for the boy. He might not think I was good enough to be his father. I think it would be better if I didn't tell him."

"I would have thought he'd been overjoyed, too, if his love for you is anything to go by."

"No. I think his greatest pride in life has been in thinking William Rendon was his father."

"Why?"

"Because the exhibitionist gene inherited from his mother, has made him seek out the anti hero, not the hero."

"What was so bad about William Rendon?"

"He was a necrophiliac!" shouted Rosen.

"Please don't shout in here. This is a hospital."

Page staggered back from the door and sank into his chair. He reached frenziedly into his pocket and lit a cigarette.

"So, it's not a non-smoking hospital any more, is it?" said Rosen.

CHAPTER 60

Ephraim went to bed. Rosen and Miranda were sitting drinking, when he told her about the DNA. He also showed her a younger photograph of his Welsh grandmother, who had wavy fair hair and bore a slight resemblance to Ephraim.

"Surely, you should see that as wonderful news," said Miranda.

Rosen drained his glass of whisky and refilled it. He inhaled deeply on about the third cigarette he had smoked since sitting down, and made a slight wheezing noise.

"Those things will kill you, one day," she said.

"Oh, Christ, Miranda, I'm not interested in my bloody health. I'm more concerned about the DNA. If he found out, I'd be such a disappointment to him, after the mystique he'd built up about Rendon. His love for me is enormous, but if he were denied the opportunity to boast about Rendon's behaviour, I think something would die within him."

"I don't. I think you should tell him. He probably doesn't think so much about Rendon, any more. The news would make him happier than he's ever been in his life."

"You're wrong," said Rosen. "He'd be terribly confused. I once told him I'd had an affair with Juliet. He asked me if there was any chance of my being his natural father. I said 'No'. I told him the affair had been some time after Rendon's death.

"I didn't tell him everything. I'd been with her, before, during the last year of Rendon's life. She was two-timing me with him. She felt secure, knowing I was always there for her. She was frightened of Rendon because of the effect that palmfuls of Dexedrine were having on him.

"His behaviour was never appropriate to surroundings or circumstance. He used to go into public places, and shout the words 'Take it away, it's red!' without warning, without reason. It wasn't even as if he'd been given a steak that was too rare, or Burgundy when he wanted white.

"The man was so wacky, I was terrified he might kill her. I tried to persuade her to ditch him, but she seemed in love with his insanity.

"Whenever he came to see us, he was sweet and affable but I was never able to be friendly or warm towards him because he was screwing a woman I was in love with. You found him affable enough, didn't you?"

"Why, yes. I didn't see him as anything else, except a bit weird, maybe."

"Then, there was his other side, the side no-one ever understood. You don't know how utterly bonkers he really was. He had screaming fits every time he watched Remembrance Sunday on television. He hired prostitutes and paid them to sing *God Save the* bloody *Queen*. He had this nutty thing about his nanny. He was always asking women to dress up as her, and knit. If they refused, he murdered them and when they were dead, he screwed them. That was found out by police investigations after the Inquest.

"I went to his Inquest. I wanted to marry Juliet, but she was so insistent that her unborn child was Rendon's and not mine, I couldn't bear to live with her. I encouraged her to write, to get him out of her system. I knew she had the makings of a natural writer. She wouldn't talk about anything else and it got worse after he died.

"I told her I'd publish any books she wrote, if she polished them up and made them good. She sat at her computer every night, all night long, writing. One night, when I was kept awake by the sound of the printer, I went to see what she'd been doing. All that time, she'd been writing about him. She wasn't writing a book. It was just one interminable diary about bloody Rendon.

"I couldn't take any more of it. I said I was happy for us to be best friends, but not lovers.

"I was still in love with her, though. She was so attractive and exciting at the Inquest. It was a whole lot of things put together — the way she rejected a Bible, which had been passed to her, and angrily insisted on taking the secular oath. She was so beautiful, so cheeky, so arrogant. I wanted to drag her from the witness box and rape her."

Miranda had listened to him, so far. She lost her temper.

"What makes you think I want to hear about your blasted, bloody Ex?" she shouted.

"I told you her performance in court turned me on, but there's nothing in the world which turns me on more, than a furious, jealous woman," said Rosen.

"I see," she said. There was a silence lasting for about five minutes, broken by Rosen.

"What was unsupportable was her tunnelled vision, the way she went on and on at me about another man."

"I must say, I certainly understand your point. Was she a natural lover, as well as a natural writer?"

"Rosen put out his cigarette and lit another.

"She was a bloody fantastic lover," he said, quietly.

"Was she better than me?"

Rosen was startled and confused by the question.

"Oh, Christ, no, not anything like as good as you! We started seeing each other again after some years, until she died, but we didn't live together. We only slept together, on and off. By then, she'd written a number of provocative, brilliant books."

"I do feel, very strongly, that Ephraim should know the truth about the DNA," said Miranda.

"No! Don't you understand, he gets his warped, exhibitionist, quirky streak from his mother? No doubt, she encouraged him to be proud of some of Rendon's behaviour."

"I don't really see how necrophilia could be a practice, inspiring pride."

"How can you be so insensitive about child psychology?" said Rosen. "To Ephraim, it's something naughty and daring, not disgusting. I told you an important part of him would die within him, if he found out his natural father was not a necrophiliac. Imagine what a Gentile child feels like, when he finds out that Father Christmas doesn't exist."

"To make it easier for Ephraim to accept the truth, why can't you yourself become a necrophiliac? Of course, I'd always be prepared to die first, to make that possible," said Miranda.

Rosen crossed the room to get another packet of cigarettes and sat down.

310

He lit a cigarette, inhaled deeply and wheezed. He stuffed potato crisps into his mouth, something he always did when he felt edgy. He finished eating, before speaking.

"Was that supposed to be a joke?" he asked. "If it was, it was a bit sick, don't you think?"

"No."

He lost his temper. "What do you mean, 'No'? How can someone of your intelligence say a bloody, crass thing like that?"

Miranda had never heard Rosen shout at her before. She wiped the tears from her cheeks with the back of her hand.

Rosen went over and sat next to her.

"I've made you cry. I never wanted to do that."

"It's OK."

"Will you do me a favour?"

"OK, Ian. What do you want?"

"Get me some more whisky and put on my favourite song."

"Do you mean *Padam padam* by Edith Piaf, that song you play over and over again, sometimes even during the sex act?"

"That's the one. Go and put it on."

As Rosen listened to the song, he continued to chain-smoke. He stretched out his hands.

"What is it, Ian?"

"Let me touch your hair."

"All right, but don't get it in a mess. It's just been done."

"I can see that. I always notice these things." His tortured concern about his son, made his breathing heavy and laboured.

"Go down on me, Miranda. I think I'll go mad if you don't."

CHAPTER 61

The next few months of Ephraim's life were as happy as Juliet might have wished them to be, if not happier. His school work was good on a regular basis, and his sobering experiences in Marseilles had mellowed him a bit, causing him to desist from disruptive and attention-seeking behaviour during classes.

His many friends, except Pendary, who had left the school in disgrace, continued to flock to him in the playground and feed him with the audience he craved.

As before, he held his friends at a distance and only invited them to admire his shop window, provided they held no interest in the contents of the sealed, barbed-wired vault which lay behind it.

Little changed in his home. Rosen had been coughing a great deal, which Miranda assumed was due to his excessive cigarette smoking.

She became disquieted when he continued to cough after the passage of six months. He, Miranda and Ephraim, were sitting by the log fire in the drawing room. Rosen had just come to the end of a coughing fit.

"I'm very concerned about all this coughing," said Miranda. "I don't understand why it's gone on for so long."

"I'm not concerned about it, so why should you be? People are coughing the whole time. It's the fags."

"It's the way you're coughing. It goes on for so long. Can't you cut it down?"

"Cut what down? The coughing or the fags?"

"The smoking. You know what those things do. You're getting through four packs a day."

"You shouldn't nag him, Miranda," said Ephraim.

"Did you hear that? He's right. Come over here and sit by me, Ephi."

Ephraim did so. The boy put his arms round his neck. He could hear the loud, scattered crepitations in his chest, which sounded like the cracklings of an Autumn bonfire.

"I can hear it, Ian," he said.

"Hear what?"

"It's your chest. It sounds awful."

Rosen was becoming irritated by both his companions.

"What the hell is all this about? There's nothing wrong with me. It's true I had a chest infection a while ago. It hasn't quite cleared up yet. So what?"

"The cough's been going on for six months," said Miranda.

"What if it has? It will go away. These winter illnesses are self-limiting. It's true I've had this pain, all the time, but that will go away, as well."

"Pain? What pain?" asked Miranda.

"The pain in my chest. It's been brought on by the cough."

"I'm not going to feel at peace, until you go and see the man you refer to as 'Nick the Doctor'."

"Oh, Dr Jacobs. I haven't the slightest intention of seeing him. He's always banging on about me not believing in God. He made me have a chest X-ray, just before the terrible trouble in Marseilles. All the X-ray showed was that my lungs were inflamed. Apart from that, it was OK."

"*Please* go back to him, Ian," said Miranda.

"I won't. I can't stand doctors. I don't want them near me. I hate being examined by them. I can't even bear the sight of their instruments. Christ, Miranda, I thought you knew that!"

"Look at it another way," said Miranda. "When you cough in the night, it wakes me up."

"I'm so sorry. I do understand that. I'll get something from the chemist."

"That's not enough. I can get Nick to come here, to look at you. That way, you wouldn't need to visit him."

"I don't want Nick here!" shouted Rosen. "I don't want to be looked at. I don't want any bloody doctors. If I'm to stay in the room, you'll have to talk about something else. I'd like to talk to Ephi, for the time being. I hope you've stopped bringing classes to a standstill, by being naughty. What sort of a day have you had at school, eh?"

"I did well again in English Composition. I got an A minus."

"Well done. What had you written about?"

V

"I wrote about this boy who loves Edgar Allan Poe and is fascinated by people dying."

"I feel you think a little too much about that sort of thing," said Rosen. "What does the boy in your story do?"

"He meets a girl," he began, adding, "who is alive," in the cautious tone of a motorist telling a policeman he had not been drinking.

"I think it's fairly obvious she wouldn't be dead," said Rosen. "Go on."

"She talks him out of his fascination for death and she persuades him that there is more to be found in what is alive than in what is dead."

"That's better, Ephi. She sounds like a girl close to my heart. Have you got your work with you?"

"No, Ian. I left it at school. It's in my locker." Ephraim almost felt the end of the world had come. He had lied to the man he adored, because he was afraid of upsetting him. The boy in his story had not met the girl. Instead, he had broken into a hospital mortuary and pulled out the drawers containing the dead, in an attempt to find his father. He was afraid Rosen would be hurt by his continued preoccupation with a man he had never met. He also feared that Rosen was unaware of his besotted devotion towards him, because he was unsure how to express it.

314

CHAPTER 62

Rosen's cough worsened. This did not deter him from smoking, which made it even worse. It was only Miranda's continued nagging which caused him to agree to visit Dr Jacobs.

"I'm just doing this for a quiet life, Miranda. I'll go, only if you come with me."

"I'm coming with you, whether you want me to, or not."

Dr Jacobs was looking more tired and run down than on the last occasion he had seen Rosen.

"A cough for several months, and getting worse, you say?" said Jacobs.

"That's about it, Nick."

"Why didn't you come here, earlier?"

"You know I hate coming here."

"Any pain?"

"Yes. Well, it's brought on by the strain of coughing, I suppose."

"How bad is the pain?"

"It's not too good. Put it that way."

"You know this means you'll have to have a chest X-ray, don't you?"

"Christ, Nick, I don't think I can stand it!"

"Why not?"

"Because there are things in life I don't want to know."

"How much do want to live?" asked the doctor.

"I don't think you realize how much I love life. I didn't come here before, because I was afraid of being told it would be taken away from me."

Rosen ignored the pain and smoked while the X-rays were being taken. He flirted outrageously with the female radiographer who told him to put out the cigarette. As he and Miranda waited in Jacobs's room for the results of the X-rays, he shovelled two Valium into his mouth which he chewed and swallowed.

Jacobs was given the X-rays. He slapped them onto an illuminated sheet of glass, and studied them, his face expressionless.

"There's nothing wrong, is there?" asked Rosen, aggressively.

Jacobs leaned back in his chair and then leaned forward and clasped his hands over the blotter.

"You're not a child, any more, Ian, so I'm going to talk to you like an adult. Signs of lung cancer don't always manifest themselves on X-rays, but this is not the case here."

"I haven't got it! Tell me I haven't got it!"

"I'm so terribly sorry, Ian. I'm afraid these X-rays show that you are suffering from it."

"It's not advanced, though, is it? Surely, it isn't?"

Jacobs pointed to the illuminated films with a ruler, which he moved across them, from left to right, as he spoke.

"To use layman's terms, there is cancer all over your left lung, and the upper part of your right lung is also affected."

"Oh, Christ!"

"In lung cancer patients, the cough and the chest pain rarely manifest themselves until the tumours have developed. That's why lung cancer is so much more difficult to treat than other cancers. It's often too late to do anything once the cough starts."

"Can't I have an operation? Radiotherapy? Chemotherapy? I'm not prepared to accept this."

"I'm afraid it's too late for anything to be done. There's nothing whatever I can do to save your life. I suggest you live as happily as you can, while you can, until the time comes for you to go onto morphine."

"Just how long have I got until I need morphine?"

"It varies so much from patient to patient. I can't commit myself. I'm so very sorry."

Miranda was in tears.

"What do we say to Ephraim?" she asked.

"It's not a good idea to tell him, yet," said the doctor. "Leave it until as near to the end as you can. The shock won't hit him as hard as its anticipation."

Rosen leant forward and rested his hands on the edge of Jacobs's desk. He was breathing heavily and making swallowing movements.

"What's the matter?" asked the doctor, if inappropriately.

"Get me something to throw up into," said Rosen.

CHAPTER 63

While Ephraim feared that Rosen was unaware of the vastness of his child's love, Rosen was saddened and hurt by the pride the boy appeared to take in Rendon, and by his vow, brought on by his lack of self worth, that he would not tell his own son that he was his father.

He wondered whether the child would have been proud, on hearing the truth. He feared he would have been ashamed, were he to compare Rosen's slightly Welsh brogue, with Rendon's sophisticated Sloaney vowels.

He felt depressed and was desperately in need of sex, but he suspected that Miranda was feeling equally as exhausted and downhearted and would feel obliged to satisfy him, against her will.

He sat down a few inches away from her and picked up a copy of *The Financial Times*. He leant back and stared at its grubby pink margins, without looking at the print. He assumed Miranda was unwilling, due to their dismal circumstances. His physical need was so enormous that he thought of rushing to the bathroom, ostensibly to cough up blood, but in reality to indulge in maniacal onanism. He started to rise to his feet, still holding the depressing-looking, sand-coloured newspaper.

"Ian?" she said.

"Yes, Baby."

"Why are you reading *The Financial Times* upside down?"

He didn't answer.

"There are tears in your eyes," she said. "I'm sorry. Isn't this an awful time for us to be alive?"

"There's no need to worry about me. I brought it all on, myself." She kissed him on the mouth, pushing her tongue between his teeth. She remembered his words, expressing his wish that she take the initiative, sometimes, so that he would be prevented from pressurizing her.

"I want it on the floor, Ian, whether you want it or not," she said.

"What the hell do you think I want? I know you're very low.

317

I didn't want you to feel you had to give it to me. That's why I didn't ask."

"Why do you say that?"

"Because I don't think it would be a very kind thing for me to do."

"You sound as if you feel guilty," she said. "You've no right to. There hasn't been a single time when you've wanted it and I have not."

*   *   *

Rosen's cough got worse and worse. It was just after Christmas. A thick layer of untrodden snow covered the ground. Ephraim and Rosen were walking on Hampstead Heath.

Ephraim suddenly turned round and ran to the edge of a pond to see if there were any goldfish beneath the thin layer of ice.

"What are you doing, Ephi?" asked Rosen.

"I'm looking to see if there are any goldfish."

"I doubt if you'll find any there. Don't go too close to the edge. Matters wouldn't be made all that easy for me, if you fell in."

The boy moved backwards and stared at the pond's black water. As he did so, he felt something turn black within himself. He thought he was being warned that a terrible thing was about to happen to him.

"Oh, Christ, Ephi, do come on!" said Rosen, but the boy ignored him and continued to look at the pond, as if it held a message for him.

Rosen was seized by a violent coughing attack and spurted about half a gallon of blood onto the snow. He walked on as if nothing has happened. Ephraim caught up with him, raising his eyes to the oppressive grey sky. He then looked at the ground.

"Are you OK, Ian?" he asked.

"Yes. I'm OK. I'm fine. It's very cold. It's time we went back."

"Ian?"

"Christ, Ephi, what is it, now?"

318

"I've just seen blood in the snow."

"Blood?"

"Yes. Where do you think it came from?"

Rosen's spirits were so low that his voice was scarcely above a whisper.

"A dead bird, I suppose. There are a lot of poachers about."

The boy had no idea that Rosen had produced the blood. In his ignorance, he associated the coughing of blood with tuberculosis.

"That blood on the snow, Ian ..." he began.

"Christ, you're not still on about that, are you? What about it?"

"It looked wonderful, in a way."

"What are you talking about? In what way?"

"It's the rich, red colour on the clean, white snow. It reminds me of the film, *Doctor Zhivago*."

Rosen clutched his chest with both hands to ease his pain.

"Well I never!" was all he could think of saying.

The man and boy walked home. Ephraim knew Rosen was unwell but had no idea his days were numbered.

"Ian?"

"Speaking, my boy. Sorry I spoke a bit unkindly to you, before. What can I do for you?"

"The cough you've got, why won't it go away?"

"Because of the chest infections I keep getting. Maybe, the smoking as well. There's no need to worry about it."

"Are you sure that's all it is?"

"Christ, Ephi, is this some kind of quiz? If I was ill, I wouldn't be leading a normal life. I'd be in bed all day, wouldn't I?"

Ephraim seemed reassured. "Can we have *Voltava* tonight?" he asked.

"Perhaps not tonight."

"Then can we have it, tomorrow night?"

"I don't see why not."

Rosen did not go to bed until much later that night. He walked to the Royal Free Hospital and sat down on one of the damp seats outside. Many of these seats had been donated to the hospital by grateful patients who had been treated there.

Rosen broke into tormented mirthless laughter. "*Doctor Zhivago*!" he shouted, "bloody *Doctor Zhivago*!" He went on laughing like a madman and suddenly burst into tears of inconsolable grief.

* * *

There were days when Rosen tried to force himself not to believe he was dying. He mistrusted all doctors, even Dr Jacobs who had looked after his parents. He refused to accept that he had lung cancer, and even if he did have it, he reasoned, in a childlike way, that it would not, in any circumstances, be the cause of his death. He told himself that X-rays showed vague and unreliable pictures and that his cough was no more than a severe chest infection which he was unable to shake off.

He continued to smoke heavily each day and ignored the pain. His only desire was to get the excessive amount of sex that he needed and to witness Ephraim's eventual transition from boy to man. His ultimate wish was for his son to fall in love with a kind and reliable woman who would bear him healthy, happy children.

CHAPTER 64

Nearly a year went by. Rosen's health had deteriorated. He needed to rest every afternoon and most of the time, he was too tired to get up for dinner. At least, his illness had little effect on his looks. His weight had not reduced, in the way it nearly always does in the majority of lung cancer patients. He remained well-built, and his wild, facial features, forever irresistible to women, had become a little wilder, making him appear even more attractive to those unaware that he was dying.

He went to his offices in the mornings, and flirted with any female staff member who approached him. His despair made his sexual needs even greater. He did not want to exhaust Miranda, so he often invited pretty and willing secretaries into his office and made violent love to them, so tormented was he because his days were numbered. When Miranda made it clear that she wanted to make love, their sessions began to take their toll on her because he coughed loudly into her ear throughout the act and sometimes brought up blood which covered the pillow and bedclothes.

Ephraim knew what was happening without being told. He lost interest in his studies, truanted from his school and spent nearly all his time in his bedroom, crying.

One morning, Miranda went into the bathroom and found Rosen leaning over the basin, clutching his chest with his right hand, holding a cigarette in his left. His hacking cough, interspersed with desperate efforts to suck air into his diseased lungs, sounded like the death throes of a tortured animal. His blood had been coughed into the basin, onto the mirror facing it, the walls and the edge of the bath.

He banged the lavatory lid shut and sat down. He threw the cigarette into the basin and held his chest with both hands.

"Christ, Miranda, I think it's the end! Get Nick the Doctor out and ask him to give me some morphine. I don't want to go! I just don't want to go!"

She rang up Dr Jacobs who said he'd be coming within twenty minutes. She helped him into bed and lay down beside him, and relaxed him by rubbing his genitalia.

Jacobs was flustered and disorientated when he reached the house. He had just attended to a patient, who had had an epileptic fit in his consulting room, and kicked in the glass at the base of a grandfather clock, left to him by his mother.

As he looked in his bag for the syringe and ampoule of morphine, he tilted it on its side, spilling a pile of leaflets about the dangers of smoking. Miranda covered Rosen's eyes.

"There's a bed for your husband in the private wing of the Royal Free, Mrs Rosen," said Jacobs. "We'd better get him over there, now."

Rosen was cheered by the panoramic view of London from the room he would die in, although the sky was dark grey and the ground covered with muddy snow. Before getting into bed, he looked at the city he loved, in which he had been born and where he had enjoyed a mostly happy and hedonistic life.

Miranda helped him to undress. He looked over his shoulder and saw a reproduction of a *Landseer* on the wall, showing a Labrador lying on its master's coffin. He was about to get into bed.

"Get the fucking *Landseer* out!" he shouted.

"Easy, now, easy! I'll take it down. You won't have to see it, any more."

"I didn't mean to shout at you. It reminds me of what Ephraim's going to be put through, after I've gone. I don't know what's going to happen if he finds out Rendon was not his father and that it was only me."

"He can't possibly find out. I've told you all along how much happier he would have been, if you'd told him the day you found out."

"He would never have wanted it," said Rosen. "I'm sure he's got an image in his mind of a glamorous, white-coated doctor, serving mankind. Any boy would prefer someone like that as his father, to a man who's spent his life publishing books that he hasn't even written, himself. If I'm to rest in peace, Ephraim must remain in ignorance."

"He's outside, now," said Miranda. "Would you like

me to bring him in?"

"Yes. Do get him in. I want to spend a few minutes alone with him."

The sobbing boy staggered to Rosen's bedside and sat on the bed.

"I can't have you crying like this. Besides, it's very unmanly to cry. If you do it in front of your friends, they're going to think you're the most awful sissy," said Rosen.

The boy continued to weep, piteously.

"Can you see the pile of books on the table by the bed, Ephi?"

"Yes."

"Among them, is a book of Dylan Thomas's poems. Bring it here. There's something I want to show you."

Ephraim had difficulty in finding the book, as his wits were not about him.

"I don't think I can find it, Ian."

"Don't be silly. It's the only paperback book there. It's at the bottom of the pile."

Ephraim pulled the book out and dropped it. In doing so, he knocked the books on top of it, onto the floor. He handed it to Rosen.

"Why have you thrown those books on the floor, Ephi? I'm glad I'm not the poor, bloody author of any of them. I've found the poem I want you to read, and to show me you have courage, I'd like you to read it aloud to me."

Ephraim began to read, his voice laboured and shaky. *"And death shall have no dominion,"* he began.

"Go on, my boy. Don't be frightened."

"And death shall have no dominion," he repeated.

"Come on, now, prove to me you're a man. Read the rest of the poem, and when you've read it, I want you to show me you believe in it."

Ephraim read the whole poem. He just managed to cover his tears with the projection of his voice, if only to give pleasure to the man about to be snatched from him by the Reaper, to whom he referred privately as "the shitty old fart with the scythe".

"You read that very well," said Rosen. "Do you understand what it's trying to tell you?"

"Yes, I think I do."

"What is it trying to tell you?"

"I think the poet feels that nothing can die as long as life goes on and love reigns supreme."

"Well done. There is one line I want you to learn by heart. Repeat it to yourself in adversity. That way, you'll feel comforted."

"What line is it, Ian?"

"It is ...'Though lovers are lost, love shall not'."

"When someone dies, they leave love in the person they leave behind, and that person is you. Love cannot die, and no-one can take it from you.

"There's a piece of paper loose in there. Open it out."

"This is your writing, isn't it, Ian?"

The handwriting on the sheet of paper was generous and forward-slanting with a style of its own. Its only disadvantage was that it was hard to read.

"Yes, it's my writing. Can you read it?"

"Most of it."

"Good. Keep that with you at all times. It's a piece of me. It will lessen the grief."

"What exactly does

'The heads of the characters hammer through daisies'

mean?" asked Ephraim.

"It means love is stronger than death, so much so that it hammers through death, in this case, the daisies that may have been lain on someone's grave, not that daisies often are," said Rosen.

"Why do so many poets bring God into death, Ian?"

"Because they're bloody nutters! Talking about this sort of thing makes me feel pretty rough. Perhaps you should go, now, and let Miranda in. Just before you go, what is that line you're to remember?"

Ephraim sunk his teeth into his lower lip, to restrain the tears which would have disturbed Rosen so much.

"Though lovers are lost, love shall not."

"Are there any other lines you can remember?"
"Yes."
"What are they?"

"Though they go mad they shall be sane.
Though they sink through the sea they shall rise again."

"Good boy. That way, you'll always know that my love has become a part of you, which means I may go six foot under, but I'll still be with you. Don't lose the piece of paper. It will make you strong."

The boy left the room with his head lowered. He carried the book of poems and the paper in his hand.

Miranda took his place in the room. She was smiling.

"What's funny, Miranda?" asked Rosen.

"There's a priest up here. He asked me if you wanted to see him."

"Is that your idea of a joke?"

"No. Just lighthearted irony."

"What the hell does he want with a croaking non-believer? Tell him to piss off. Tell him to keep his God to himself."

"Its OK. I already have, but I used slightly more diplomatic language than that."

Rosen liked her dry humour and laughed.

"Will you do something for me?"

"You've got such attractive teeth. I remember, Juliet said that once." she said.

He ignored her.

"Ever at your command, sir. You ask. I obey."

"Put on *Padam padam*, there's a good girl."

She found the tape and fed it into the ghetto-blaster. The song's robust, life-giving strains filled Rosen's soul, the room and the entire corridor.

"Give us the fags, will you?"

"Are you mad?"

"No. The morphine's completely stopped the pain. Anyway, it's too late. It doesn't matter."

She handed him a cigarette and a lighter. When he inhaled, she was horrified by his gasping wheeze, as he sucked the smoke into his anaesthetized lungs.

"Lean over me. I want to touch your lovely hair."

"It hasn't been done for two weeks, Ian."

"As I see it, it looks as if you'd had it done only ten minutes ago. Can you do just one more thing for me?"

"You know I can. What do you think I'm here for?"

"Get up on the bed. That way, I can feel your hair better."

"It's very dirty."

"It's sexier."

She got onto the bed. Her nerves made her movements clumsy.

"Take my cock. When it's hard, try to get it inside you."

Rosen went on smoking, using his left hand and allowed his head to move from side to side, in ecstasy. He clutched Miranda's hair and twisted it round the fingers of his right hand.

"Oh, Christ, this is nectar! Get your head up, before I come down your throat and choke you."

Suddenly, his blood pressure rose dramatically and stopped his heart. The half-smoked cigarette fell from his fingers onto the floor.

Miranda continued to lie on the bed. Even in death, his liquid grey eyes shone straight at her, like stars. So extreme was her grief, that it denied her the luxury of tears.

CHAPTER 65

Rosen's headstone had just been erected at the head of his grave in Highgate Cemetery, quite a while after his death. Becket drove Ephraim to the cemetery and did what little there was in his power to cheer up the broken-hearted child, who sat, hugging a bouquet of white orchids to his chest.

Becket stopped and opened the door.

"Would you like me to come with you to the graveside?" he asked.

"No. I'd prefer to go alone."

"I don't know how long you'll be, but I advise you to stay in the shade. The sun's hotter than you think, and you could get sunstroke without a hat."

"It's OK. I've been here on other occasions in the past. The cemetery is very leafy."

Ephraim carried the orchids to Rosen's grave, his cheeks tear-stained, his innocent, angelic face set to break the hearts of even the hardest visitors, who were walking past him in droves.

Ephraim knelt down on the uncut grass by Rosen's grave. The headstone was curved in structure and was of white marble, engraved with simple upright black letters. The inscription gave his full name, date of birth and date of death. In smaller letters, slanting forwards, were the words, 'He had no enemies'.

Those were the words which drove the boy into a full-blown frenzy of weeping. He knelt on the grass and began to pull the orchids, one by one, from the tied-up bundle, to lay on the grave.

He stopped and took out Rosen's handwritten copy of *And Death Shall Have No Dominion*. He unfolded it and tried to read it aloud. His act of doing so, comforted him a little.

> *"Dead men naked they shall be one*
> *With the man in the wind and the west moon;*
> *When their bones..."*

He tried in vain to read other parts of Rosen's forward-slanting,

327

flamboyant scrawl. He lowered his eyes to the earth which covered his sacred love. He realized he was not alone. He turned and looked into the face of hate.

Kate Rendon was standing behind him, wearing a plain, dark purple dress.

She slapped him hard on the back. Her seemingly playful gesture, combined with her hatred of him, confused him. He lowered his eyes in an attempt to decipher Rosen's handwriting.

"Look at me, Ephraim," said Kate.

He did so. She threw back her head and made theatrical conducting movements in the air, and broke into loud, raucous song.

> *"The Rendon boy to the grave is gone,*
> *To find his natural father."*

"How do you like my singing, Ephraim?"

"I'm afraid I don't like it very much. I wanted to come here, alone. I didn't want to see you here."

"I'm sure you didn't. I knew I'd find you here, because it's June 14th, today. That's when his birthday was, wasn't it?"

"Yes."

"You never found out, did you? You didn't know, all along?"

"I knew perfectly well he was born on June 14th."

"That's not what I'm talking about, you little fool!" said Kate. "It's the other thing you didn't know, and you don't even know, now, do you?"

"Know what?"

"I was sent to prison because of you, but they let me out after a few months because of good behaviour, and the loop-hole caused by the notion that you were my nephew. After all, it's a bit less serious for an aunt to run away with her nephew, isn't it?"

"What do you mean by the word, 'notion'? Why did you say that?"

Kate broke into her witch-like song, once more, and roared

328

with mirthless laughter.

"So you want to know what I mean, do you? It's time you were told. You're not my nephew and you never were. You are not my brother's son."

"What are you talking about?"

"After I was put away, I had some investigations made, about your confinement with meningitis.

"I found out where you had been treated. In fact, I heard you nearly died, but unfortunately, you didn't. I got a medical secretarial job at the Royal Free Hospital. I heard that Dr Page, the man in charge of your case, was short of a secretary — maternity leave, something like that. I offered him my services, which meant I had complete access to your medical records.

"You don't know it, but your beloved Ian asked Dr Page to take blood from him and do a DNA on you."

"What's a DNA?" asked Ephraim, as he leant over the grave, laying down the orchids one by one, if only to have something to do with his hands, while the woman who haunted and terrified him, continued to torment him.

"You're an ignorant brat, aren't you? A 'DNA' is the name of a blood test, given to a child to determine who its father is. I saw the printed results of the blood test done on you, and to make sure I wasn't mistaken, I read the report over and over again."

"Could you get to the point and tell me what you're talking about?" said Ephraim.

"It's simple," said Kate. "Ian Rosen was your natural father, not William Rendon. That means you're not a Rendon, and never have been. It also means I get all the money my father and brother left to you."

"You can have any money you want, for all I care," said Ephraim. "I don't want money. All I want is to die and be buried by Ian's side. Anyway, I don't believe what you say about the blood test. If Ian had known, and he would have known, had he asked for the test, he would have told me, straight away. He understood the feelings of others, perfectly. He would have known how terribly happy I would have been, had I known

329

w

he was my real father."

"Well, he didn't tell you, did he?"

"If only I'd known in his lifetime! I loved him more than I can say in words. It wouldn't just have been an honour to be his natural son. It would have been something far more wonderful than that. Why didn't he tell me, Kate? Why did he hold it back?"

"Because he didn't want you to know, obviously."

"Why? Why?"

"Because he was ashamed. It all seems to be pointing to that, doesn't it?"

"Ashamed? What, of himself?"

"No, stupid, not himself! Of you. Can you imagine any normal father being proud of having begotten a son like you? What do you think he felt like, seeing his own child turning into a morbid, depraved, little monster, an odious little show-off at school, a braggart, someone whose favourite poet is Edgar Allan Poe?"

Ephraim continued to lay down the orchids. Their petals were soft and fluffy in his hands. He wondered whether Rosen had felt a similar sensation whenever he had touched a woman.

"Why do you hate me so much, Kate? What harm have I ever done to you? Why are you so determined to hurt me?"

"All I'm doing is telling you the truth. Ian Rosen held it back from you, because he was ashamed of bringing into the world, a creep and a freak who can't stop talking about necrophilia. It's a bloody revolting subject!"

"Did you read the whole way through my medical records?" asked Ephraim.

"Oh, yes. I know them by heart, now."

"Was there any mention in writing of Ian being too ashamed of me, to admit he was my father?"

Kate let out another depraved laugh.

"Perhaps, there was. Perhaps, there wasn't. That's what you'll have to live with for the rest of your life, not knowing whether there was or whether there wasn't."

"Ian was never ashamed of me," said Ephraim. "He loved

me with all his heart, and not even you can take that love from me."

"Oh, can't I? What's that letter I saw you reading, when I came up to you?"

Ephraim held up the piece of paper, as if brandishing a shield. His pride at that moment, broke through his grief. He held it in front of her face.

"That's a Dylan Thomas poem, isn't it?" she said. "Whose handwriting is that?"

"Ian's."

"Perhaps, he copied it out, to give you a message. That poem's theme is very anti-death and anti-morbidity, unlike you. Maybe, he gave it to you, to drag his pathetic son's face out of the filth." She snatched the piece of paper from him.

"You're cruel. You're nasty. You're wicked. Give it back to me!"

"Suppose I choose not to? What then?" said Kate.

"Then, I'll fight you for it. I may be in hell, but I'm still strong enough to know the difference between good and evil."

"Good and evil? Good and evil? You poor sap!" she said. "What about all that boasting you do at school, condoning a man who had sex with dead bodies? Perhaps, you think that's a right and proper thing to do."

The boy was in floods of tears, once more.

"Please give me my piece of paper back, Kate."

Kate tore the document up, in a sudden, abandoned state of viciousness. To make him even more wretched, she spat in his face. He was too proud to wipe off the spittle.

"So you delude yourself, that that bastard, Rosen's at rest, do you? I suppose you think your flowers from some flash, upmarket florist, will comfort him. I'm sure he's too ashamed of you to rest, too ashamed, I tell you. Why else did he hold the information back?

"He was too ashamed of you but didn't have the heart to tell you of his shame. He may have been godless but his heart was too kind to confess his mortification to you.

"He'd begotten a tawdry, rotten seed. Maybe, you're aware

331

of that. It might be what you were thinking of when you spoke about your alleged knowledge of the difference between good and evil."

Ephraim put the palms of his hands to his ears, in a vain attempt to prevent the malevolent stream of invective, being forced into his brain. He could still hear a bee, buzzing round one of the orchids on Rosen's grave.

Kate let out another laugh. She had become bored with her victim and the pain she had enjoyed inflicting on him. She was exhausted by her display of the sadism she had inherited from her father.

She backed out of his presence, her action theatrically obsequious, as if she were withdrawing from a Royal. She broke into song, again, her voice becoming fainter, as she faded into the distance, in the mysterious-looking, overgrown cemetery.

"*The Rendon boy to the grave is gone,*
To find his natural father."

Ephraim waited until she had left the cemetery. He tried to find the scattered pieces of the paper she had torn up. He found a few of them and could not arrange them as a whole, because so many had been dispersed by the mild Westerly breeze which had descended on the cemetery.

He lay down on the grave, crossing it at right angles, clutching the orchids, he had not managed to place on the ground, to his heart. He was disinhibited enough to cry out loud, and shout articulately through his tears.

"Why didn't you tell me, Ian? It would have made me so proud, so happy. I'm so very very sorry I was a disappointment to you. I loved you, even more than Miranda. You meant more to me than anyone in the world. I'm so terribly ashamed I let you down. If only you'd reprimanded me for being the kind of person I am, instead of staying silent. I don't want to live any more. All I want to do is die and be buried by your side. If only you had the power to stretch out your arms to me, as you did in life, and pull me into the grave and hold me for the rest of eternity."

He tried to comfort himself by remembering parts of the poem he had read with Rosen but his grief had drowned that section of his memory which could have given him strength.

He rolled onto his back and wailed, and onto his stomach, once more. He rubbed the orchids against his face and cried and cried and went on crying.

EPILOGUE

Good, without God —
Triumph over Evil.

Ephraim did not live long, after Rosen's death. Not even Miranda's selfless love could console him. He refused food and drink and locked himself in his room. He died of a broken heart.

It was a strange co-incidence that at exactly 7.00 o'clock that morning, Kate was woken by a violent, tingling sensation in her legs. When she tried to get out of bed, she could not move. She had become paralysed from the waist downwards.

She had hired an astute, streetwise lawyer, the day after she had spoken to Ephraim, and after a three-day hearing, a court had granted her access to Rowland Rendon's inheritance.

She had formed a liaison with her lawyer. He later agreed to accompany her to America, to find a medical expert, who might be able to restore the use of her legs.

She bought a luxurious house outside San Francisco and recruited eighteen servants. It was an attainment she had dreamed of since her father's death, but she had had no idea that this period of her life would be so unbearable. Her lover soon lost interest in his short-tempered, wheelchair-bound mistress.

Her second under-butler, for whom she had developed a *penchant*, escorted her from one top class surgeon in San Francisco, to another. X-rays were taken by each surgeon. None of them showed any abnormality in the bone structure of her hips and legs.

Physiotherapists, acupuncturists, faith healers and members of less salubrious "curing" professions, were consulted in droves, their accumulative expenses reaching to up to two million dollars. Not one of these charlatans could find any medical reason for her disability.

She frequented the rooms of a total of fifty-two surgeons in San Francisco. Though independently consulted, they were strongly in agreement about her diagnosis.

She asked her lover to accompany her to Washington, where the top surgeon in the country, Dr Dwight Sallinger, had twenty-seven sets of letters after his name, as well as the reputation for curing the incurable.

She was wheeled into his huge consulting room, whose walls were lined with his twenty-seven certificates in ostentatious silver frames. He surveyed her X-rays and scans at length, before giving her a detailed examination.

"Well, what can you do for me?" she asked.

"Lady, I'm afraid there is absolutely nothing anyone can do to rectify your condition. It transcends all boundaries of medical science. All I can say is, it is something no-one is capable of understanding. What has happened to you is called a 'jinx'."

"What do you mean by a 'jinx'? How can a man of your medical enormity, stoop to the use of the paranormal, to silly superstition?"

Dr Sallinger felt uncomfortable in the presence of a woman whose face reflected concentrated evil.

"You've come to me for medicine, Miss Rendon, but medicine's not the only thing in the world. There are dark forces, too, the supernatural, the inexplicable, things I wouldn't even dare to understand."

"What are you talking about? How could you have gained all these certificates by talking such rubbish."

"Rubbish, perhaps, but rubbish I don't understand. Do you mind if I ask you whether you've ever hurt someone, done them terrible wrong?"

"Why should you ask me that?"

"Because, sometimes, it transpires that, if one has committed an act of evil, some force, I know not what, can hit a person back, and punish them for what they did."

"What is the force? Do you mean God?"

"Not necessarily. It could be any force. It could even be a dead person's spirit. Have you committed murder?"

"Certainly not!"

"Have you committed an offence to a person who is now dead? Have you committed evil to an innocent party?"

Kate lowered her head, but her shame was insufficient to redden her cheeks. She remembered spitting at Ephraim and lying to him, by saying she had seen it on record that Rosen had been ashamed of being his father. She had no remorse for the torment she had inflicted on the bereaved boy.

"No," she said, after a pause, her head still lowered.

"I feel that 'No' is a 'Yes', Miss Rendon. I don't even want to hear what you did. That is what I meant by my use of the word 'jinx'."

"I'm not listening to this. I'm getting a second opinion."

"I think you mean a fifty-fourth opinion, Lady. And after you've seen *that* damned sucker, no doubt, you'll seek a good-for-nothin' fifty-fifth opinion, as well! Ask your companion to wheel you out of my rooms. I don't ever want to see you again."

Kate's lover wheeled her from the surgery to a tinted-windowed Cadillac. A strange-looking woman in rags, came up to Kate in the street, as she was about to be lifted into the Cadillac by a mechanical lift.

"I must speak to you. I must talk to you, now," said the stranger, in a thick Irish accent.

"Yes? What do you want?" said Kate.

"You have it in mind to walk again, one day," said the Irish woman. "I'm telling you, you'll never walk for the rest of your life. You can see every doctor in the world, and you'll still never walk, even though there's nothing medically wrong with you."

"How the hell do you know?"

"Because of your past. There was a man once. And a boy. Both are passed on. You were cruel and did serious wrong and you've been punished. The person behind your punishment bore the initials I.R."

A muscular American policeman, wearing a star, so fastidiously polished, that Kate could see every line in her face reflected on it, jostled the Irish woman and moved her away from the Cadillac.

Kate was in the vehicle and ready to be taken to her hotel suite. She turned to look at the Irish woman who had huddled herself in a doorway.

"What were you saying?" she shouted.

"You did serious wrong to a child who died of a broken heart. Another person, also dead, with the initials I.R., will continue to punish you, until you die."

336

"Who is this person?"

"It might be a man. It might be a woman. It's not going to let you go. If you meet me at 5.30 this afternoon in the lobby of the Hotel Jefferson Plaza, I might be able to tell you more. I can't, now. There's something in me which won't come out."

"Hell, Lady, wouldya move along, please. What ya doin' can land you with a vagrancy rap," said the vigilant policeman. He turned to Kate. "Say, is this dame bothering you?"

"Yes, she is. She's scaring me," said Kate.

"She won't bother you, no more. Say, are you from England?"

"Yes, that's right."

"Sure, England's one place I'd really like to take my wife to. You from London?"

"Yes."

"Say, do you know Leicester Square? Do you know Piccadilly Circus? Do you know Trafalgar Square?"

"Yes! Yes! Yes!"

"You, English sure have gotten yourselves quite a heritage, Robin Hood, the Krays, the Queen, Jack the Ripper."

"Don't you have any work to do, sir?" asked Kate. "Haven't you got anything better to do than stand in the street, talking a load of nonsense?"

"Hell, Lady, I was just trying to be friendly."

Kate travelled to her home outside San Francisco, later that day in her private jet. For the first time in her life, she felt a surge of guilt, emanating suddenly, from her calculated and accumulative cruelty towards an innocent boy.

She wheeled herself into her ground floor bedroom, and swallowed the remaining forty barbiturates from the bottle on her bedside table. She went into her multi-fountained garden, and headed towards the edge of the swimming pool.

She heard a strange, male voice coming from no-where. She turned round and saw she was alone. She assumed she was becoming senile. She heard abuse being shouted at her by someone with a trace of a Welsh accent, and felt an unseen hand pushing the wheelchair into the water.